Catfish

a novel

D1570901

ELLE CARLING

ISBN-978-1-7360736-0-5 (EPUB)
ISBN-978-1-7360736-1-2 (paperback)
ISBN-978-1-7360736-2-9 (hardcover)

Edited by Rosanna Chiofalo Aponte.
Cover design by Rebecacovers.
Author photo by Brandin Shaeffer.

Printed in the United States of America

First edition

For my daughters,

Avery and Carys

And my love, Jason ... *of course*

Acknowledgements

This novel was written before COVID-19 infiltrated our world—sweeping away the closeness and gatherings en masse at a music concert or a family dinner—normal living we'd seemingly taken for granted. Since February 2020, we have gingerly carved out new paths of dating in person and online, yet it's hard telling if F2F can be successful while practicing physical distancing. We are social animals.

Even prior to the barriers of wearing face masks and honoring the "six feet apart rule," it was difficult to meet someone of desirability and advance the relationship beyond the delicate three month mark. This said, I humbly acknowledge my friends who had listened to me lament about the ever fickle dating scene. You know who you are—and I love you for not running away from my persistent tales of woe.

My early readers, those who read the manuscript in bits and chunks and were always patient with my continuous edits—thank you! Above all, Cara Shapiro, Jason Liberman, Jeff Kantor, Sonja Reese, and Suzanne Cloutier. Daryl Evans, thank you for allowing Jewel to borrow your name.

I've always been a writer but never a novelist. In the words of Bruce Springsteen, "You can't start a fire without a spark." *Catfish* was ignited by a chance meeting with Spencer Miller and Abigail Shek—two extraordinary friends who suggested that I turn my lively stories into print. This transpired, of course, over a few margaritas.

Lastly, if you read about a person, place, or event in this novel that seems familiar to you—it's not. The printed words were indisputably crafted from my creative license to entertain and redirect you from the machinations of today's world.

Contents

1

Sliding Doors and Adam Sandler

Now

That must be him. Tallish, dark hair, and a dimple in one cheek. He is definitely my type, or Estelle's type. Estelle has long, silky red hair and the consummate striking green eyes reserved for the starlets of yesteryear, like Lucille Ball and Judy Garland. As an accomplished cellist and world traveler, Estelle owned a marketing company with clients such as BMW and American Express, which provided much financial freedom to her, so she was able to live the good life. She never had children or had found the time—or interest—to marry, but now she was looking for a LTR, a long-term relationship, on the dating app weConnect, when she'd come across Kyle's photos. Swiping Kyle's handsome mug to the right, indicating that he was a keeper, resulting in a *ding-ding!*—a connection. Kyle's profile was quasi professionally edited, which meant that one of his female friends had taken a stab at choosing the photos and writing his clever narrative. He enjoyed traveling—as did 95 percent of the population—a fine cabernet, skiing, hanging with great friends, and mountain biking. Beyond these standard interests, forty-four-year-old Kyle wanted to settle down with "the one." Since he'd broadcasted his intention, rather than asking for hook-ups or a casual fling, on a dating app, Estelle felt a glimmer of hope.

Kyle sat bellied up at the bar, a glass of red already half-way drunk, and seemed to be scanning the crowd for *her*. His fingers played with the squared, silver fob on the counter; he had not used valet parking for his Mercedes, a car that every third person drove in Santa Monica.

After a few glances at his phone, he appeared ready to leave. Estelle was more than thirty minutes late for their first date. If only Kyle had her phone number, then he could've sent a text for her arrival time but dating apps didn't work that way. Women rarely gave out their phone numbers to matches, that is if they hadn't deleted the connections first.

There was a seat available next to Kyle, which is what I had hoped for. After catching Kyle's roving eye, I nonchalantly meandered toward him, appearing without agenda.

"Can I have a reposado with a rock, please?"

The bartender by the name of Jim, as printed on his chest pocket, nodded and asked if I wanted a specific brand of tequila.

"Patron would be great. Thanks," I responded with feigned disinterest. An easy hop to the brown, leather bar stool, and I settled in beside Mr. Wonderful.

Kyle seemed nervous and apologetic, quickly telling me that he was expecting someone, so he would need my seat. "She will be here soon. She's just running late," he told me, although at this point, he and I both know that Estelle had bailed and would not be joining Kyle at the bar.

"Oh, yes, of course. I'll find another chair when your friend arrives."

"She's not really my friend. I haven't met her … yet," he admitted, looking somewhere between sheepish and embarrassed. "Online." That one word summed it up. He continued to stumble while trying to convince me and himself. "She's incredibly beautiful and smart. Worldly, educated, and speaks French. I think we'll really hit it off … when she shows up. LA traffic, you know."

Traffic wasn't even a consideration at 5:30 p.m. on a Saturday, especially in Santa Monica. But I had to let him give his excuses, because not only being stood up but being stood up by a vixen like Estelle was ego crushing.

"Yeah, rush hour in this city is brutal," I agreed with a surreptitious smirk.

Of course, Estelle was beautiful and smart. I had created her. I found her by searching for "gorgeous red-haired female" and after perusing the likes of Bryce Dallas Howard and Jessica Chastain, I eyed my Estelle, or Anne, which was her real name. She was a twenty-eight-year-old part-time model from Ireland, and not thirty-six as her online profile stated. Skillfully editing her screen-shot photos and ridding them of all evidence to her real identity, I established her Facebook account. This gave her a life, friends, and a prominent place on weConnect, because all the men swiped Estelle to the right. She was the prettiest, single gal on this app and had her pick of any of the eligible men in her age range, that was until she had to meet him in person or provide a mobile number. Therein lay the problem with follow-through. Estelle's many connections stayed within the confines of app texting, until one by one, they disappeared from attrition. It wasn't until I had seen Kyle's smoky-blue eyes and unkempt dark brown hair in a photo with a woman who turned out to be his mom, that I knew I had to meet him in person. The fact that I have blonde hair and I'm frequently mistaken for Claire Danes, am not five foot eight, but rather closer to five foot three, and can barely play chopsticks on the piano—let alone the cello—would be a big pill for Kyle to swallow.

His profile had the requisite six photos: on a chair lift in Mammoth, swinging the golf club on a course beside the ocean, a selfie using his bathroom mirror, in a group with three other guy friends while they each held a glass of wine, one of him kneeling beside an Australian shepherd, and the sweet photo with his mom. The combination of photos, narratives, and texts over a two-week period had given me the courage, or audacity, to meet with him in person.

"So, you come here often?" I wanted to put a fork in my eye for asking the most cliché of pickup lines ever spoken. Thank goodness he laughed and played off it.

"Yes, and what's your sign?"

After an inaudible sigh of relief, I sat up straighter and said with masked confidence, "Pisces."

"What?"

"I'm a Pisces. You asked about my sign."

Something between a snort and chuckle escaped Kyle's throat, making me feel invisible. Was he mocking me?

His rather large fingers combed through his messy hair with frustration. "Look, I was just being nice, but I'm really waiting for this girl to show. I don't want her to see me talking with you. It might make her feel insecure."

Whaaat? Estelle insecure? She was so out of every guy's league on weConnect that he should feel grateful that she, or I, had given him a chance. Now, *I* was starting to resent her for being so beautiful. And, tall. Estelle was statuesque and intoxicating. I had gone overboard with her.

"Yeah, I understand that," I said, with the slightest flip of my shoulder-length hair, and a defiant pout had started to form on my bottom lip. "Well, why don't you call her? Or send a text to find out her ETA."

The stupid guy hadn't asked Estelle for her number and had just assumed that she would show because she'd said she would. Hadn't he heard of ghosting? Everybody ghosted these days, even within the dating apps, although I couldn't imagine a real woman ghosting on Kyle.

"I'm sure she's going to walk through the door right away," he said pensively, probably wondering why he hadn't asked for her number. Forty-five minutes had passed since her expected arrival, so I decided to make my move. It was now or never.

"Well, if she doesn't, we can have a drink together," I said this more as a statement and less as an invitation, since I didn't want to give Kyle a chance to negate my offer. By comparison, and since I didn't have a modeling contract, I knew I had nothing on Estelle's beauty or mystique. "Are you originally from LA? Ah ... what line of work are you in?" I asked even though I already knew he'd grown up in Calabasas, had studied economics at USC, worked hard to play hard, was buying a house in Malibu, had a dog named Cesar, was allergic to pineapple, could say hello in twenty different languages, and had never hiked to the Hollywood sign.

"I'm Kyle, and I guess I've been stood up. Figures. She seemed too good to be true. Whatcha havin'?" he asked my drink preference, not bothering to notice that I was on my second tequila and had collapsed sideways into his chair. He gave me the once-over with slight curiosity, as though seeing me for the first time, and asked, "Are you here alone, or have you been stood up by your cyber date too?"

"I was meeting a girlfriend, but she had to cancel at the last minute, so I decided to come anyway. I needed a night out. Hey, don't be so bummed about it. These blind dates rarely work out. She is probably self-absorbed and has annoying habits that you can't get over, like leaving wet towels on the floor. Consider yourself lucky. You just saved a few months of your life finding ways to break dates or making excuses to go out with your buddies instead of dealing with her

4

craziness." I took another sip of my drink and looked around the room as though I sat next to cute guys every day in a hip bar. "Truth is, I saw her when I walked in. A tall, gorgeous red head, right? She was standing just outside by the valet, fighting with someone on her phone. Then she left." The lies just rolled off my tongue, which scared me a bit.

Kyle looked at me and then toward the small lobby. He let out a slow, labored exhale in response to my untimely news and sank a bit lower in his seat.

"It was easy to notice her because she was yelling and swearing like a truck driver. It sounded really nasty. Sorry to break it to ya." I couldn't stop myself. I had to throw Estelle under the bus.

"You're kidding me? Yeah, that must've been her. And I've been waiting for almost an hour. I'm through with this online dating. The women on there are crazy, just like you said."

Kyle looked angry, disappointed, confused, and defeated all in one moment. I felt a bit like a consolation prize, but considering that Estelle wasn't even real, I was the front runner.

He took the last pretzel from the complimentary bowl of snacks and popped it into his gorgeous mouth. His online photos didn't do him justice; the angular jaw structure and perfectly formed nose that made up his handsome face could be on any billboard for Tag Heuer or Porsche. It wasn't that I only swiped right on men of this caliber, because that would be pointless; guys who looked like Kyle were few and far between, especially those who were also on dating apps. It's just as gratifying to text with an average Joe who has a great personality.

Kyle stood up. "Look, I'm going to head out. It was nice meeting you. Sorry if I came across as an ass. I'm just tired of the games women play these days. What happened to just being honest?" He scanned the room again to make sure Estelle wasn't standing somewhere, also looking for him. Several women noticed Kyle for the first time, and they repositioned themselves to be seen. He turned back to me with gusto. "Have the balls to tell me to my face that you aren't interested. Isn't that what you women want from us? The BS goes both ways. I just wasted an evening and could've been out with friends or somethin'."

Well, what the hell was I going to do now? This night was going downhill fast. Should I come clean? This was what Kyle said he

5

wanted. Transparency. Hell no, and look as crazy as he believed women to be?

Perspiration started to pool in the small of my back, coalescing in a stream and cascading between my butt cheeks and coating my inner thighs. I felt a dotting of sweat in my nether regions, and my scent turned musky, almost primal. I smiled, hoping to distract him before he noticed that I was a complete mess.

"How'd you two meet? Which app?" I grasped at anything to make him stay. "I'm on weConnect. Have you heard of that one?"

Kyle rested a hip on the side of the bar stool, about to make his exit. "That's one of the apps I'm on. I haven't seen you on there," he said with certainty, but studied my face and body for signs of familiarity.

Yes, you have.

"You are probably out of my ten-mile preferred radius, which is why you didn't come up for me," he stated, more to apologize for not swiping me right, and less to show his disappointment that I wasn't tall, voluptuous, or ginger-haired. Entering certain criteria, such as height, age, and proximity with your resident zip code helped narrow down the probable matches on these dating apps and expedited the process of finding Mr. or Ms. Right.

He looked into my eyes for the first time this evening, and although I thought I'd feel something akin to fireworks or that heart-stopping moment when his gaze would linger and we would hold the stare for a beat too long while his fingers reflexively brushed a few strands of hair from my eyes … nothing. Nada. He didn't seem interested in me at all. He still had Estelle on his brain. I had made her too magnificent, too perfect.

Patrons occupied the rest of the available seats around the bar and the tables were almost at capacity as the happy hour crowd morphed into a dinner setting. A duo of pianist and singer began their medley of popular songs in the alcove, and the diners turned to hear the beautiful blonde's rendition of Alicia Keys' hit song, "If I Ain't Got You." The lights started to dim, and the mechanical blinds slowly climbed upward toward the ceiling, revealing the setting sun behind the recognizable Malibu coastline. The exuberant chatter around us seemed to close in, making it more obvious with every chuckle and clink of a wine glass that we were not a couple, and the chance date was about to expire just like Cinderella's evening at the ball.

6

"Cheers to us, darling. So happy we are out tonight …"

"I can't believe she'd say that … your mom is such a bitch …"

"If that waiter doesn't bring me another glass of bourbon in the next minute, I'm going to hit someone …"

The room was upbeat with familiarity and anticipation, something that was absent between us.

"Do you have a sense of humor, Kyle?" I asked with trepidation, mixed with a sprinkle of adrenaline. Positive that he could see my heart pulsating from beneath my blouse, or hear the loud boom of each abnormal heart rhythm, I adjusted myself on the stool, trying to divert his attention from my lack of composure.

He slowly slid off the chair and threw down two twenty-dollar bills toward the bartender. "Keep it," he said without waiting for his check. He didn't want to waste another moment.

Kyle turned back to me. "I like comedies. Jim Carrey, Adam Sandler … why?" This guy just wasn't getting it.

"Yeah, me, too, but how do you feel about two people who should have met, but situations and obstacles just get in the way, causing sliding doors?"

I had to reference the movie starring Gwyneth Paltrow when she missed her train, sending her on a completely different life path had she made the original departure time. Life's funny this way; taking the wrong direction at a fork in the road could cause a thirty-minute delay. Then the butterfly effect of that ensued, and you missed your work meeting and deadline and were subsequently fired from your job, and then you decided to go back to school and pursue a different career path … all because you didn't listen to Waze!

"Sliding doors? What are you talking about?" He scrutinized me, like I had a bit of cray cray. "What does this have to do with Adam Sandler?" Lord, help me.

"You know that movie, when Gwyneth's train doors close, and she has to take the next train and meets the wrong guy? Forget it. Maybe you came here looking for me and not the gal you intended. I know you weren't actually looking for me, but perhaps you were *supposed* to meet me. I showed up and she didn't." This is my Hail Mary, and I can't even throw a football.

Kyle tilted his head to one side, furrowing his dark brows, opening his mouth and closing it and then opening it again. "Are you a fatalist? Where do you come up with this stuff? I had an amazing conversation

7

with this sexy girl, online of course, and she dazzled me with her wit and knowledge of everything. Just because she didn't show doesn't mean that you and I are destined. Life doesn't work this way. We've barely spoken. You know nothing about me. Not. A. Thing."

Dude, I know that your dog is probably pissing on the carpet because you aren't home to take him out, you are about to close escrow on your seventeen hundred-square-foot bungalow on Pacific Coast Highway with its spectacular ocean view, your mom was upset because you cancelled lunch on her twice so you sent her an orchid, and your client yelled at you last week because you lost his subscription agreement for an important investment. I would say the opposite is true in that you, Kyle, know nothing about me. I am not five foot eight, and I've only been to three countries outside of the US because my passport expired five years ago and I was too lazy to renew it. I don't know much about marketing, except what Google can provide, and my nursing job at Santa Monica UCLA keeps me in scrubs and paper hairnets, which is hardly a place to meet an eligible man, as everyone is stressed out, yelling codes, and barking orders at me.

"Why don't we get to know one another, then?"

I tried that come-hither look and lowered my voice an octave to appear a bit sexy, hoping he wouldn't notice my attempt at seduction. From his six-foot vantage point, he looked down on my ample B-cup breasts, which showed welcoming cleavage and were nestled in a low-cut red blouse. The tight, dark-blue jeans clung to my curvy, but not chubby, hips, which I'd read that most guys liked rather than the rail-thin California type. My youthful, line-free face belied my true age of thirty-nine, having grown up in Seattle where the lack of sun staved off melasma and wrinkles that most home-grown California locals were now battling at their dermatologist.

Kyle grabbed his car keys and turned to me before saying, "You seem nice, but I think I'm going to head home. I'm actually quite tired. Good luck out there."

He started to walk away and then turned back, waving his index finger in the air as though it were a magic wand. "A word of advice … why don't you change your profile? Take some sexy pictures and tell the guys what you're looking for. It's really that simple. I haven't seen your photos, but I'm sure you'd get lots of connections if you write in such a way that hooks us. We want recent pictures, and if we have to struggle to find you in a group shot, we'll move on to the next girl."

Well, if it were that easy, we'd be ordering dessert by now, Kyle. I don't look like the girls on weConnect nor do I take sexy photos. Guys don't go for me because they are interested in girls who look like Estelle.

"What if I told you that I am super witty, adventurous, and would love to live in Malibu. I adore dogs, and kind of understand finance. I'll carry your golf clubs or drive the cart, ski down the easier blue runs but après ski is my specialty. I'll make sure you'd never eat pineapple, will hike with you to the Hollywood sign, and remind you of your lunch date with your mom before she gets mad."

He stopped for a moment, almost frozen in his tracks, and looked at me for an uncomfortable ten seconds.

"Enchanté. I'm Estelle."

2

Beginner's Guide to Fishing

Then

To "catfish" means to lure someone into a relationship by means of a fictional online persona, as in to create a fake profile on a dating app to catch the cheating boyfriend in action. Kyle ran for the hills, and rightfully so, but it wasn't before he told me that I was a lunatic and the reason these online matches never worked out. I beg to differ because I seemingly met the love of my life a few years ago on such an app. The reason it didn't work out with Jake had nothing to do with my craziness or the fact that we met by mutually swiping on each other but rather his desire to throw me back into the water and try his luck with another cast of his fishing rod. Of course, I didn't find this out until I became Chelsea.

My best friend, Cate, was tired of hearing me complain about being single and suggested I join weConnect. I was already familiar with the app because I was duped by it and my ex-husband, Robert. We were legally separated and in the middle of divorce negotiations. I'd overheard him on the phone, talking about the dating app, as though he were just throwing the idea around.

A search for thirty-eight-year-old men who were within one mile of zip code 90402 brought a long list of candidates seeking women, but after a few scrolls, I found him and his smug mug. Robert was calling all available single gals on this app to "host a barbecue on a Sunday afternoon." Apparently, I, his exiting wife, was not able to do this for him. My soon-to-be ex-husband was uncovered, looking exuberant in twelve photos, some taken by me in happier times and others that I'd never seen before. weConnect was just a ruse so that I'd let my guard down and not challenge his fidelity or financial settlement, as it appeared he'd left the marriage a while before and had started living a life without me. I conceded to his suggested offer because I believed it was for our mutual happiness to expedite the process and that money shouldn't be a factor in finding yourself again. A month after the divorce was final, he was already engaged to a woman I'd wondered about during our marriage.

Upon signing the decree, I chose to keep his surname of Evans rather than revert back to my maiden name and my roots. It was one more step into the abyss of anonymity, becoming comfortable at mutability and disappearing among the masses. My parents' last name yanked me back into my past, a life composed of childhood struggles and many unanswered questions. Reinvention had always been easy for me—change a hairstyle, move to a new neighborhood, or retain your ex-husband's last name and fade away.

A year after our split, I was ready to get back on the love horse and try to ride her again. I had licked my wounds and was determined to meet my guy, my love, my twin flame. This delusion I carried in my veins was from reading volumes of Harlequin romance novels as a young girl. My mom had a tall stack of them on the floor, by her bed. I hoped she would find love again after my dad had died. Instead, she could be found with her nose in these Book of the Month Club novels that arrived on the first day of every month, never to be seen gussied up and heading out for a date with an eligible bachelor. She had been reading these books well before I was born and named me Jewel for the heroine in book #471, "*Sparkling Jewel.*" There weren't apps in those days, but happenstance to meet a nice widower or divorcé while reaching for a melon in the produce section at the grocery store or at a social gathering. She never happened to meet anyone of value, mostly because she didn't try, so she bided her time reading about someone else's perfect life. I vowed this would never be me. I would find love if it killed me.

My first honest swipe to the right matched with Jake, a tall, sporty hedge fund manager with salt-and-pepper hair. His photos hooked me immediately because he smiled with that genuine kindness that said: "It's all going to be fine, and if it isn't, I'll be right by your side, holding your hand."

A ten-month love affair had developed. I rolled out the red carpet just to show what great wife material I could be. I was in it to win it!

You don't have time to take me for dinner? Then I'll just run to the grocery store, spend one-hundred dollars on steaks and wine, and make you a delicious meal. Just show up when you can and I'll be waiting. And waiting. You're too busy to see me this weekend because you're out with clients? No problem, love. I'll read or maybe binge watch a TV series. Do what you need to do, and we'll see each other when your schedule isn't so busy. You'd really like to shop and update your wardrobe, since you've been wearing that same blue T-shirt with the embroidered crocodile on it for twelve years, but just can't find the time? Don't give it a second thought because I can stop at the mall on my way home from work and buy a few shirts and pants for you.

Ever doting, ever patient, ever stupid.

On the first day of the tenth month, that carpet was pulled out from under me.

"Jewels, darling, you know I love you, but I don't have time right now for a girlfriend. My business is suffering, and I need every available moment to put into my work. I know you understand. You've been great, babe, but because of my time restrictions I can't be the kind of boyfriend it takes to make this work."

It was a load of crap, but I believed him at first—hook, line, and sinker. Yes, I was the gullible one. Take all the time you need, *babe*. I figured he'd come around after he missed me.

Five long weeks passed, yet Jake never circled back. They *always* circle back. Cate said to go back on weConnect and meet someone new. I refused at first because I was still in love and reeling from the breakup I refused to acknowledge. I thought Jake just had a momentary lapse in reason. We were the perfect couple and had a great run in the year together: never fought, always laughed, had great sex. I mean, who makes it to almost a year in Los Angeles? Hollywood marriages don't even last that long.

It was serendipitous that I happened to log on to weConnect and find Jake's supposedly deleted profile not only present but also polished with new photos and a fabulously written narrative that had the subject line: "Looking for LTR and hope to start a family." Whaaat? It was like a punch to the solar plexus. Vacillating between letting him find me on the dating app seeking someone new so I could stick it to him and deleting my profile because I was humiliated, had me at a crossroads. I actually valued our blossoming relationship, so it wasn't easy for me to forget the great times we'd shared and to begin with another guy as though the last ten months hadn't happened. So I deleted myself. Jewel, thirty-seven, nurse, loves the outdoors/beach/watching movies, was no longer a weConnect candidate looking for love. I was now looking for answers, and maybe satisfaction via revenge.

Since I was blonde, as was Jake's ex-wife, I figured that he was tired of the same flaxen-haired gals and would veer off the path and seek a brunette. The Internet was chock-full of beautiful, sexy, dark-haired mavens who would be perfect to reel in the jerk who screwed up my future, leaving me shattered.

A Megan Fox look-alike from Ontario, Canada, jumped out from the screen: dancer, model, with captivating bedroom eyes. Her real name, Doreen, just didn't do it for me, so I gave her a saucy, voluptuous identity of Chelsea. A girl in my junior year at UCLA, named Chelsea McGreggor, had every guy on campus lusting after her because she never gave it up. She'd entertain them for drinks at happy hour or let them think they had the pleasure of her company at a party, but I knew she was into girls. She played these guys like a fiddle because she was a tease and loved the power she had over them. I'd watch these hopefuls flatter her, believing they had a chance, but whenever we were together, she would hang on to me, pulling my body into hers while she audibly breathed in my scent and lightly brushed her lips across my neck. Chelsea had luxurious, silky chestnut hair that went on for days and a perfect body that made you feel really self-conscious about yours. I needed to be her, if online and in name only.

Chelsea found Jake again after thirty swipes to the left of many accountants, attorneys and guys who sold software. He looked happier than she remembered, which could've been the product of romanticizing him or he really was happier since they'd broken up. She had to believe the former, which was why she was on this expedition of truth. There had to be an explanation for this crazy turn of events, from being fulfilled and in love to broken and alone.

"Hi Jake. How are you?"

I didn't expect to receive any points for originality with my opener, or would I be graded on my efforts, so I let it slide.

13

Ten minutes later, he responded, "I'm doing well, Chelsea. Thanks. And, you?"

We were off to a very proper and respectful start. The nerve of him talking to other girls when he said he was too busy to date. "I haven't seen you on here before. You must be new." He acted as though he were the mayor of weConnect and knew every girl by name and age.

"Great. Thanks, Jake. Yeah, I'm new. You are the most handsome man on here by far."

I laid it on thick. I, beautiful model Chelsea, thought you, Jake, scumbag and breaker of hearts, is more of a catch than Trevor, forty-five-year-old heart surgeon, six foot two, who runs with his golden retriever and effortlessly spikes a volleyball with perfect form on a sandy beach. Not a chance! Trevor, if only I were Chelsea and could meet you in person as she, I would swipe you right.

"Chelsea, what do you like to do in your spare time?" Jake wrote with the flair of the finance guy he was, absent of thinking-outside-the-box. "You didn't write anything in your narrative." Well of course I didn't, Jake. This isn't about me and my fake life. This is about your lies and excuses.

Then he wrote, "Can you provide me with more photos?" What a rookie. Any super attractive model type on this app is bound to be a catfish, especially with one photo and nothing written about her life. It wasn't that I was an expert on my first attempt at false identities, but Psychology 101 teaches that if it appears too good to be true, the person is probably lying to you.

"Just signed up yesterday so I haven't had time to write anything. In my spare time, I pick up discarded plastic bags and bottles on the beach, read Hemingway and Joyce, work with handicapped children, and run a shelter for homeless teenagers." But I'm a tiger in bed. "I'm so glad we connected, Jake."

He was very self-righteous about his community service. He also touted being the most well-read of all his friends. After skimming the likes of Tolstoy or Rushdie, anyone within earshot would hear about *War and Peace* or *The Golden House*, and probably wonder from whose CliffsNotes he'd stolen the synopsis.

"Impressive. I happen to be an expert in both these authors, as well as Faulkner. Let's get together and discuss our thoughts. How noble of you to spend your time helping others. I place kindness above all character traits," Jake pontificated. Kind? Was it kind to just break up

14

with me, out of the blue, without contrition? Our dialogue was getting boring from my perspective, and I had to spice it up a bit.

"Why would someone as eligible and handsome as you be on here? You must have your pick of any woman everywhere you go." Yes, Jake, all the women must fawn over you. Your girlfriend fawned, but you felt it necessary to break her heart. "Have you had any luck on this site?"

Thirty minutes elapsed, and I wondered if he'd figured out that it was me on the other end, and not the sultry brunette. My paranoia was getting the better of me. Chelsea may be too sexpot for this site—either a catfish or just another gorgeous, has-been model from Los Angeles, the mecca for glamor. These women aren't easily asked out by men in the real world, since most assume they are already married to Jude Law.

A nurse, Miriam, from the hospital where I worked had met her husband on a dating app, and they'd married within six months. She hadn't wasted time texting men who didn't meet her criteria. She'd whittled them down like a second, third, and fourth job interview, until she'd found the perfect hire. "You have to be disciplined, Jewel. Don't be afraid to unmatch a guy and move on," she'd told me like a CEO who was addressing a boardroom full of fledgling trainees. "Men usually don't know what they want, so we have to be the choosers, not the other way around. Being attractive and accomplished can get you through the door, but it takes determination to close the deal. I'll help you find that one-in-a-million. Show me your dating profile 'cause I'm a master at choosing and fixing photos."

Great, but so am I.

He finally responded and I exhaled. This clandestine activity I was orchestrating had me holding my breath and feeling like a fraud. I was masquerading as a completely different person to find out why my boyfriend didn't want to date me any longer. Why couldn't I just ask him? Oh, that's right. I did, and he lied or didn't want to hurt my feelings with the truth. I wasn't wife material after all or the future mother of his kids. Don't men know after three months of dating if the woman is long term? My collection of relationship books had Dr. Pat Allen's at the top. She wrote that men usually know in the first few months if a woman is "the one." If they continue dating her without intention of commitment or marriage, they are just passing time until someone better comes along—someone who can host a mean barbecue with all the side dishes on a Sunday afternoon. Was this what had happened to me?

"If I had my pick of any woman I want, I wouldn't be on this site! But thanks for the compliment, Chelsea. I dated a woman I met on here for a while, but it fizzled." Jake wrote with conviction and a slight coldness that hurt my feelings. He was talking about me. My hands started to shake, and I felt like I was going to hurl my salad niçoise all over the pretty, checkered tablecloth at Cafe Delphinè, where I had sequestered myself and my MacBook for the inquisition. The cute French restaurant was sleepy and almost empty for the lunchtime crowd, save for a few ladies playing gin rummy at the corner table and an older couple at the most remote booth who appeared to be having an affair. The man and woman, who looked to be in their early fifties, were both wearing wedding rings and looked extremely happy, so they had to be cheating on their unsuspecting spouses. I was turning into a cynic.

"Oh really?" I wrote, tears filling my eyes. "What happened in your relationship?" There it was, and to the point because enquiring minds wanted to know. I didn't understand what fizzled meant. Was it like a sparkler you'd find on top of a birthday cake that when ignited, it lit up everyone and everything around with happiness and possibilities and then without notice or fanfare, it finished and the world went dark? Or was it a slow death of being bludgeoned with a stickpin until the ten-thousand cuts made you bleed out, hemorrhaging the relationship until you're both strangers to each other? Which one, Jake? Which kind of fizzle?

"She was really damaged. Deep-rooted emotional problems from her childhood and major trust issues that I just couldn't help her with. Drank too much, angry all the time. There wasn't anything I could do. Poor girl."

Who was he talking about? That's not *me*!

"That chapter of my life is over. I want to know more about you and when I can take you out. You're beautiful and just my type." He wrote like he was on a mission to ply her with alcohol and land her in bed. Chelsea wasn't his type; he was interested in cute, blonde, and safe. Chelsea was a knockout who would eat you alive just because she could.

"What kind of trust issues? What happened in her childhood?" I continued to berate him for answers. My fingers shook and could barely write at this point, as I strained to see the correct keys to tap through my glassy, watery eyes. He thought I was messed up.

Jake didn't communicate again until the next day, which was fine because my body needed to recover from the trauma of his projection. Usually, a person who places blame on another can't see himself in the story or his/her role in the demise of the relationship. He was acting as though he didn't have issues himself or that he had tried in earnest to make it work, but we were too broken, beyond repair.

I opened the app the next morning and found his words on the phone's screen.

"She never wanted to marry or have kids. Couldn't get over her dad's death and living alone with her alcoholic mother. I only knew about this stuff because she talked in her sleep. She had no friends or relatives. We had good times, but I knew it was short term from the beginning. She wasn't my kind of woman. Well, enough about that. So, Chelsea, when are we getting together? Free next Friday? How about dinner at the Getty and then we can watch the sunset together. Give me your number so we can chat live." Jake treated the forum like it was a therapy session. Once he unloaded his guilt, or excuses, for ending our relationship, he was ready to move on with gusto.

My sadness and tears were replaced with venom and chutzpah.

After three tequila shots, a box of See's Candies, and the requisite twenty-four-hour waiting period, I responded, "Look, Jake, you really aren't my type. I'm looking for someone of substance. I don't believe that you'd commit to a woman, as you seem self-important and not in touch with a woman's needs. That poor girl you dated should be lucky you set her free." Plus, your penis is probably small. Then I unmatched us. I didn't even wait for his reply. I didn't care. I should have written the penis part, but I didn't want him to figure out that it was me.

A few weeks later, I came across the weConnect app on my phone. It was a source of sadness and vindication rolled into one. Time heals all, and I felt much better. Jake wasn't worth my sorrow anymore. I did, however, wonder about any new men on the app. Since I was already registered as Chelsea, I could peruse the available singles under the radar to see if it was worth my time joining as a legitimate member. I'd rather be rejected as someone else than as myself. My ego was still in recovery mode.

There were a lot of the same characters online, with the same photos and same stupid narratives from the year prior when I matched with Jake. There were guys that stated their age as thirty-five years old but looked at least forty-five, and other men thought by using a celebrity shot from a chance meeting with Arnold Schwarzenegger or Cuba Gooding Jr. was going to earn them a swipe to the right.

And there he was. Adam. We had dated our senior year of high school, but he and my science lab partner, Sheila, had ended up sleeping together on Prom Night while I waited for him outside her parents' house. She threw one of the four parties that were going on that night, and my 25 percent chance of choosing her themed party of "Eyes Wide Shut" turned into dumb luck. Adam had told me the next day that because we'd worn the same gold-and-black masks, he mistook me for Sheila. An innocent mistake. They'd dated briefly, married, and divorced within that same year. I learned via Facebook that she'd cheated on him with his best friend.

Adam looked as handsome as I remembered, with a few wrinkles around his eyes and a slight receding hairline. Yet he did break my heart and stomp on the pieces with his Adidas.

Chelsea swiped Adam to the right.

3

Ghosts of Boyfriends Past

The quaint three-story walk-up in Santa Monica that I had moved into after my divorce had its share of singles and a few newly married couples. My financial settlement didn't bode well for the prospect of buying property, and neither did the salary from my nursing job, so I was relegated to living among the ubiquitous scent of barbecue from the shared common area in our complex, the constant barking of two Pekinese dogs from the floor above, and the pervasive sounds of Pink Floyd emanating from the windows of my next-door neighbor Sam.

Sam and I had met the first day I moved in, as my struggles to carry the boxes from the rented U-Haul yielded his chivalrous two hours of lifting, arranging and then rearranging, since I couldn't decide where I wanted the plants, coffee table, lamps, or side tables. We joked that he was my interior decorator, since my apartment was spacious and organized for optimal traffic flow, which wasn't easy to achieve with an eight-hundred-square-foot living space.

Sam watched Jake come and go during those ten months of relationship bliss but never commented on our status. Without fail, he offered to bring dinner. We enjoyed each other's company while discussing our week at work. Since Jake was busy with business dinners most Friday nights, I was happy to have Sam come over and commiserate about his technology company, or unload on him about the patients who had come in to the hospital from car accidents or advanced illness. I was working in the emergency room during the Jake days, which helped distract me from my thoughts of wanting to be with him and wondering why he wasn't making us a priority.

"Is Jake coming over tonight?" Sam would ask me on our regular Friday morning text check-ins. If it weren't for Sam, we wouldn't have seen each other as much as we did because as he would reach out like clockwork, making sure I wasn't alone every Friday night. "Should I bring over the usual, or do you want to mix it up with some quinoa or couscous?"

I was routine with my salad selection, always opting for a chopped spinach and kale with garbanzo beans, tomatoes, peppers, olives, and extra goat cheese. Sometimes I'd throw in grilled chicken or tuna, but usually I kept it meat free. Sam said he could set his watch with my consistency. That bugged me a bit because who wants to be a dependable Sally? Same old, same old. Little did he know that I had an entirely different identity as Chelsea, Goddess of Online Dating, Queen of weConnect. I had fifty matches at that time, regardless if I wanted to explore them. It felt good that I could command such interest, even if it was as a brunette beauty, and not myself. I was still the one typing, cleverly reeling them in with my coquettishness and abundant quips.

Women were never seen leaving Sam's place in the walk of shame hours, and he'd never come by late Saturday afternoons for my opinion on his shoes or belt. Sam had that strong and rugged look to him, like an older version of Liam Hemsworth with black hair, but he had maintained the gentle, reverent demeanor that could only be fostered through a loving female. Sam was very close to his sisters, and it showed in the way he wanted to take care of me in a very respectful way. Sometimes too respectful. I figured that he must be dating, on and off, even if the relationships were brief. Given that he never asked about my dating life or offered to share his, we kept our relations light and easy. He'd bring me takeout almost every Friday evening, and we'd sit in front of my massive TV and watch sitcoms or rom-com movies, without expectation or agenda.

I took whatever wasn't nailed down when I had moved from my marriage house, and that included Robert's expensive wall-mounted TV. He would spend hours watching cable news on that TV, shouting at anchors with whom he didn't agree. And when he wasn't yelling at an electronic, he was yelling at me for not being perfect. When I was eighteen years old, I thrived on concocting meals after shopping for ingredients at various specialty grocery stores. I tried my best to make dinners to Robert's liking, but his constant protests of subpar contradicted the months of cooking and perfecting recipes over the summer before nursing school, so I stopped entirely and let him order his own takeout.

It took Adam a few days to swipe Chelsea to the right, and after the connection was made, he wasted no time telling her about his Ferrari and the mountains he'd climbed. He'd done everything in the world there was to do—faster, better, and before everyone else. Adam always had a narcissistic personality and was more interested in bragging about his pursuits and accomplishments than having a real conversation. Even though we were only seventeen at the time we'd dated, the foundation had been lain, and his character was still the same so many years later: self-serving and boastful.

"I have a lot of connections on here and so many dates. I don't have enough time to go out with all these woman, so I'm being selective and cautious," he wrote, as though he were on *The Bachelor* and had twenty runway models vying to be the next Mrs. Adam Green, while they cried, backstabbed, and manipulated their way into his coveted heart. "Let's go for a drink this Friday night. What's your number? I'll call you later tonight if I'm not on a conference call or negotiating a business deal."

Of course you want to go out and be seen with Chelsea. She's stunning and prettier than your ex-wife and my ex-friend, Sheila, who broke your heart after you broke mine—that is after you screwed her while I waited for your ass in your Toyota MR2.

"I'm not available this Friday night," Chelsea responded. I actually was busy because of a standing date with Sam to fight over reruns of *The Big Bang Theory* and who could make a better margarita. I could because I refused to use the premix Sam preferred. The fresh lime juice combined perfectly with the liquid sugar that I made from scratch, simmered on the stove for ten minutes until it was a clear, syrupy sweetness. Adding a shot of Grand Marnier also helped, but he didn't know I did that. He thought I was a master mixologist. When margaritas weren't on our drink menu, a few shots of fine tequila, either neat or surrounding a big ice rock, was our go-to.

"Why are you single? What's your history?" I asked Adam, not being careful about my questions, as he would never know it was me but rather just a nosy, single candidate devoid of online social skills. "Have you ever been married?" And why did you cheat on your high school girlfriend when she was really awesome and just wanted to date a loyal, trustworthy guy her senior year of high school? Was it worth being such a jerk, Adam? You could be married to a fabulous nurse, have three kids—Emily, Ava, and Adam Jr.—live in Malibu with an ocean *and* mountain view!

While I waited for Adam to respond, I checked out some of the hundreds of available men on weConnect.

Rory, forty-two, owner of a winery in Napa Valley, loved dogs, chocolate desserts, hiking in the Santa Monica Mountains, and traveling only with a backpack. He had short, blond hair, a cleft chin, and listed his height as five foot nine, which really meant five foot eight.

William, forty-one, liked jumping out of airplanes, heli-skiing, and white water rafting down any challenging river he could find. He hadn't eaten out of his house for ten years because he doesn't trust what restaurants did to your food. Maybe this was his way of telling women that their first date was not going to be a fancy dinner at the latest, hip eatery. A few of the single nurses on my floor were using the hookup dating apps to eat; they'd lure the guy in with a few phone conversations and insist on meeting him out for a steak dinner and then they'd move on to the next single profile. William may be on to something, after all.

Chris, forty-five, liked bike riding and star gazing. He was looking for casual dating in a private setting and was married but thinking about divorce. This cute, dark-haired single guy probably went on this dating app to bridge the gap between married and dating. He was an over-lapper. Chris, why don't you tell your unsuspecting spouse that you no longer want to be married rather than broadcast it, because one of these single women might know your poor wife? He couldn't handle being alone and ending his marriage the difficult way, which meant just being forthright and honest. I had no business using misrepresentation as my gripe, since I was the pot calling the kettle black, but I could counsel him into doing the right thing. Chelsea swiped Chris to the right for safekeeping, like collecting flies in a jar.

It was Friday night, and I expected Sam to appear at the door any moment with a plastic bag of takeout. We planned to watch *The Hangover*, as I was on a Bradley Cooper movie crusade ever since we saw *A Star Is Born* together at the theater, and Sam had watched me sniffle my way to the car. Even though we weren't dating, or considered our friendship to be anything other than platonic, I counted on him when a sappy, romantic movie beckoned, and I didn't want to leave the theater alone with tear-filled eyes.

Sam seemed as affected as me when it came to unrequited love stories, or those with a happy ending. He had a soft heart, and although he didn't cry during those movies like I did, he never balked at my constant requests for romantic comedies. The moment he'd agreed to watch *Fifty Shades of Grey*, I knew that he was a great catch. I hoped he wouldn't meet such a woman until I was settled in a secure relationship of my own. I couldn't imagine the three of us sitting in my living room, discussing the plot of the latest film, while I watched Sam and his girl hold hands, or while I cuddled with my guy as Sam sat across from us on my tan chair.

"I'm here. Jewel? Where are you, babe? Ready to watch the tele?" Sam called out from the entryway, bearing a British accent.

"Is that you, darling?" I tried my best to imitate him, but my inner Emily Blunt just wasn't cutting it. "I'll be right out." I was busy swiping, flirting, and unmatching while I stood in the closet, looking for something to wear after my stint in the emergency room.

The day was mostly comprised of needles, compresses, stethoscopes, and bandages. An elderly man had been admitted right before I was supposed to clock out. He'd fallen and broke his femur while helping his wife make banana bread. He told me they were in the kitchen, and he was passing the eggs to her one at a time, when one dropped from his hand. He bent down to clean up the mess and just collapsed, breaking his thighbone on the hard tile floor. A CT scan told a different story. The man had a rare form of advanced osteosarcoma, which wasn't usually found in the elderly. The radiologist was reading the images when I left, and before the sad news was shared with the patient. Losing patients to disease and complications from accidents and then seeing their relatives deal from the anguish wore heavily on me. Alcohol helped numb things I didn't want to think about. My drinking was under control, but it always made me feel better after a long work week—as did Sam. He imbibed right along with me, week after week. I was ready for a margarita and the distraction of weConnect.

Adam had responded. "Wow. The Spanish Inquisition. Yes, I was married, but it didn't work out. I'm ready to settle down if I can find someone lucky enough to meet my qualifications. I'm from the Seattle area but have lived here almost ten years. You?" Adam wrote with lackluster, and his answers weren't the ones I wanted to read, although he reconfirmed how arrogant he still was. A leopard never changes its spots. Something like that.

"I'm coming, Sam. Hold on. Make me a marg, please." I dropped the British accent because I couldn't play that game and Adam's at the same time. I mean, I was talented, but this was above my pay grade.

"Why? Are you divorced? What happened with your wife? Did you ever find true love? What about when you were younger?" Why not just go for it? I had nothing to lose by asking such forward questions, plus, there was a margarita waiting. I shoved my twelve-hour scrubs in the hamper and pulled out some gently used sweatpants and an oversized sweatshirt. After a quick glance in the mirror, I was almost disgusted with myself. I really let myself go after the Jake days. If I was ever going to have a boyfriend again, I'd have to put myself together with more than a high ponytail and fresh deodorant, in lieu of a shower.

His backside faced me as he portioned out the salads on plates and arranged the food on a tray. He was singing a song to himself that sounded familiar, something about the sun and being older. He looked really good. Too good. Sam had shaved, and his hair was about a week too long, giving him that James Dean appearance in a white T-shirt and blue jeans, which hugged the legs that made up his six-foot frame. He had absolutely no idea how hot he was. Seeing Sam through new eyes gave me a tinge of nervousness, and I retreated to the bathroom before he noticed my presence. Returning a few minutes later with a yellow, cotton T-shirt, black leggings, combed hair, and a coat of lip gloss, I tried to appear nonchalant.

"Hey, Sam. How are things? How was the week?" I rattled off, pretending to look for the margarita that was beckoning me from the coffee table, but hoping he wouldn't sense my lack of control.

"The week was good, all good. Salad. Drink. I have your movie queued." He took his usual place at the end of the couch and pointed the remote at the TV.

I was looking forward to seeing Bradley Cooper, but I didn't have the strength to debate. Last week, I'd mentioned wanting to watch *Pretty Woman*, and somehow, he'd remembered. I wondered if Sam had learned those skills from his parents or just his dad, as the entire family sat in front of the TV, watching hours of *I Love Lucy*. That kind of family scene was foreign to me and had only appeared in the movies I watched or in the romance novels on my bookshelf. It was thirty minutes into the movie when I fell fast asleep.

White Lotus Esprits whizzed by, some of their drivers honking and catcalling while others hurried to their destinations. The air was crisp, making me shiver, or maybe it was because I was wearing a white tank shirt and blue skirt in the middle of November. The tall, black come-fuck-me boots hugged my knees, elongating my petite legs. I stood among other down-and-out women on Hollywood Boulevard, all trying to turn their next trick with an eager John. My short, blonde hair had transformed into a long, brunette mess of teased hair, a hairstyle I would have worn in my high school days.

I glimpsed a reflection in the window of a slow-moving sedan, which revealed a hooker who had run away from home and lived in a dingy rooming house, or maybe she was a sad girl running from herself. I watched the prostitute pull her sheer skirt down and over her butt, her movements mirroring mine. Suddenly realizing I was half-naked and exposed, I shrank deeper within my black boots. The car stopped, its reverse lights illuminating the dark street as it backed up and then rolled to a stop beside me.

"Hey," I said, bending to peer inside as the window rolled down. Robert, Jake, Adam, and Sam sat in the car, like a foursome on their way to see the latest film at a drive-in movie theater.

They looked as confused as I felt, but it was Robert who finally piped up.

"Not you. We're looking for Jewel."

"But … I'm Jewel." They belly-laughed and sped away, leaving me standing in the silence of the night. A lone car across the street opened its door and then closed it, startling, but not scaring, me. I crossed to see if it were someone I knew, but with each step forward, I couldn't reach the white Plymouth—our family vehicle when I was young—that sat idling. My feet seemed to sink into the asphalt with every labored stride. A young, female voice sang "You Are My Sunshine" from within the old boat-of-a-car, and a little hand pressed itself against the inside window, saying hello or waving goodbye.

I awoke to the click of my front door closing and Edward Lewis waving red roses through the stretch limo's open roof at his newly realized love, Vivian Ward. I crawled into bed and remembered being eighteen, getting ready for the prom and Adam. I'd worked for

25

months at the local grocery store to afford the baby-blue, satin dress and matching satin heels that were mesmerizing in their day. Little did I know at the time that Adam's lack of moral decency with an innocent, fledgling woman would interfere with the choices I would make for the next twenty years. It's not as though I had a perfect role model in a mother, who had believed that love could be found on a white steed that galloped to her door and whisked her into the sunset. She'd made that notion a construct in my psyche, along with the stacks of romance novels and hours of movie watching taking its toll on my reality and approach to relationships. Love required effort, and so did sifting through hundreds of available men on weConnect.

—~—

Saturday morning's pounding headache was mitigated with a hair of the dog, specifically a Bloody Maria. It should have felt odd, drinking tequila at 9:00 a.m., while the rest of the city was at a yoga class or taking their kids to soccer practice. I was perfectly happy sitting in bed, enjoying my spicy tomato concoction until I needed another.

I settled back in bed with my second cocktail and opened my app. Hmmm. What's going on with you, Adam? How's your social life? It doesn't seem to be too exciting, being that you messaged me twice since last night.

"You ask a lot of questions. We can discuss our pasts at some point," Adam wrote. And then a few hours later, he added, "Are you going to give me your number, or are you just toying with me? Do you think that just because you are beautiful that you can dick a guy around? I've seen plenty of girls like you on here, and I'm tired of this shit."

Whoa! Ballsy move. Like this was going to earn him points and make Chelsea give up her precious mobile number. Then another message popped up. "WHAT THE HELL, Chelsea???" How dare he scream at Chelsea in all caps.

With a few taps on my iPhone, I wrote, "Yes, I am beautiful. Much too beautiful to go out with a guy like you. I also know your type. You'd cheat on me like you've cheated on other girlfriends. Karma's a bitch. Cheers!" It was trite, but it felt good because it was true. I added that cheers bit to confuse him, because he couldn't see me raise my glass as I took my last sip. Then I unmatched us. Good riddance, Adam.

I dialed my best friend Cate's number and asked her to go out for a late lunch. I figured I'd be hungry in a few hours, after my liquid breakfast wore off. I also needed a *Pretty Woman* day, but instead of Rodeo Drive, I went to the mall.

4

Doctors Without Morals

The little girl looked to be around seven years old; she wore a Disney princess dress, a tiara, and uncomfortable looking glass-like slippers on her little feet. She stood eating a multi-colored ice-cream cone, wiping her blue-and-red sticky hands all over her dress. She stamped her left foot hard on the tiled floor, while her mother worked furtively to unpack and then repack miniature windup music boxes. They stood just inside the door of a little trinket shop at the outdoor shopping mall.

"That's not it! Find the right one! I want it now! I told you; it looks like a pink piano." The sassy girl punched her mother in the back. The mother was scattering the boxes, trying in vain to appease her daughter's demands.

"Charlotte, honey, I'm doing the best I can. I don't think they have it. The man said we'd have to look for ourselves, but I'm sure it's not here."

The girl walloped her mother again and then gave her an intense kick to the calf, making the woman wince and almost collapse from the pain of the glass shoe. "I'm Tiana. Why can't you remember my name?" She jumped up and down on her glass slippers, grinding them into the tile and threatening their structure. "Find it! Find it now!"

The scene made me stop and watch for a moment. The girl was a quintessential brat, and her mother was perpetuating the behavior. Had I pulled a display like that when I was seven, my mother would have slapped me across the face or dragged me by my hair from the store.

"I want that music box!" She punched her mother in the ribs and then kicked her again, but this time in her other leg. The woman let out a small squeal, similar to a baby pig's cry. She had to steady herself by holding on to the doorframe.

"What about this one, Tiana?" The mother inhaled with composure but appeared at her wit's end, as she bent down and presented a music box that was a black-and-white version of what the little brat wanted. The silver arm was cranked in small circles, emitting the song "What a Wonderful World," but her efforts were met with a generous yank of the mother's hair by sticky, blue fingers.

"I said PINK! Can't you get anything right?" With that response, the girl turned on her glass heel and started out the store.

As I passed behind the girl who was on a tear, her mother still inside trying to return the unwanted box to the pile, I put my foot out a wee bit too far in front of me, sending the little girl flying.

After I corrected the princess brat's behavior, I continued along the walkway where I'd be meeting Cate. There she was, standing alone in front of a mobile kiosk with her back toward me. She was stunning. Cate's long, curly blonde hair clung to her shoulders like ivy clings to an oak tree, giving her that siren look on the Starbucks logo. I stood behind a large pillar and watched her for a moment, while she perused the newest sunglasses on display at a pop-up sunglass store. She tried on an avant-garde pair of blue shades, the kind you'd see Yoko Ono wearing, and then whipped out her iPhone to take a selfie. Then she gingerly placed a look-alike pair of black *Breakfast at Tiffany's* sunglasses on her delicate face, looked around to locate the store owner, and then slyly stuffed them in her oversized athletic bag, which was slung over her shoulder.

"How much for these?" Cate asked the proprietor, who made his way over to her, looking at the blue Yoko Ono sunglasses she still held in her hand. "Can you take 10 percent off?" She waved them in the air like a noisemaker you'd find at a New Year's Eve party.

Smiling in that coy, alluring way, she captivated any man in her presence. But before the owner—who was wearing a name tag that read "Hi. I'm Oscar. How can I help?"—could respond, Cate handed the glasses to him. "It's okay. They really aren't my style." With a quick glance around, she spotted me against the pillar and rushed towards me.

"Jewel!"

We hugged and linked arms, while she ushered us in the direction of our favorite outdoor eatery. "What's going on? Tell me everything."

After settling in at the end of the bar on sleek high top stools, and amid the bevy of activity on an early Saturday afternoon, she pulled out her Audrey Hepburn sunglasses to avoid the southern California's sunny glare. "You like?" Cate asked, striking a pose similar to Holly Golightly's iconic countenance.

After taking the five seconds to steady my breathing so that I wouldn't lunge after her and strangle her pretty neck for shoplifting, I looked into her eyes and raised a groomed brow. "They look really nice on you. Did you buy them just now?"

"Yeah. The guy gave me a deal, so I couldn't resist."

She and I had that quiet Mexican standoff, as we gave each other a stare down, absent of guns and the ten-gallon hat. We both knew that she was full of shit, but neither one of us was willing to broach the subject of her kleptomania. For as long as I'd known Cate, she'd always had an impeccable wardrobe with every possible accessory and shoes to match. She worked as a physician's assistant and made a good salary, but she couldn't afford the Gucci and Yves Saint Laurent fashion she often wore. After many years of asking where she shopped and how she could afford such luxuries, but hearing her say they were fake or that she bought them on eBay, I gave up. Sooner or later, she would end up in jail, and I'd have to address Cate's inability to pay with her Visa like the rest of us.

I fell for Cate the moment we met ten years ago at a pharmaceutical conference in San Diego. The only available seat amongst a sea of hundreds of noisy interns, nurses, and PAs was beside me. She chewed gum and talked through the entire lecture on clinical immunology and their treatments, giving me the play by play of her life in Flagstaff, Arizona—the many stepdads she'd had and homes she'd lived in since birth. I empathized with her upbringing, not because I'd had a similar one, but rather, not having a father in the picture struck a chord. I once read that adult women seek a certain life path due to the absence of a fatherly figure in their lives, and Cate and I were proof of this reality. She sought reassurance and validation from me from the first thirty minutes we were knee to knee, while telling me about her various relationships and absentee father figures who had come and left. She listened to the one-minute spiel of my life, responding to the heartfelt moments that had coincided with hers. My dad had bought into the cool factor of holding a Marlboro cigarette between his lips every waking hour of his adult years, which eventually took his life and left my mom alone to raise me, although I kept those facts to myself. Upon meeting someone for the first time, divulging gut-wrenching stories of death and tragedy did not a happy time make.

Cate's friendship meant more to me than anything in my life. Though she had me at hello, I never fully let her in to my world, piecemealing the areas of my life on a need-to-know basis. There wasn't anyone I'd rather spend my time with, sharing and creating special life moments. Yet sometimes when you hold someone too closely, making them the center of your universe, fate intervenes and takes them away.

Forgetting about her five-finger discounted sunglasses, I ordered enough food to feed a family.

"Whoa! What gives with the fried food? Why not just order a charcuterie plate and martini like me? Is there something you need to tell me, Jewel?" Cate asked, genuinely concerned for my lack of healthy food selections, which in her experience meant that I was substituting french fries for a necessary come-to-Jesus moment. "What's going on with you? I'm all ears."

A heavy sigh and huge swig of my double Patron reposado begat a sharing of the Adam catfishing.

"So you see, I'm a huge online fraud. I don't put *myself* out there, so I can fuck and not be fucked. Does this make sense?" I turned to Cate, picked up two green olives and shoved them in my mouth. "Dating just isn't what it used to be. Gone are the days when we meet someone shopping for groceries or sitting with our laptop at a coffee shop. Guys just don't approach women anymore, and we are unapproachable anyway because we all have our faces in our phones, with our thumbs swiping away."

I looked down at my drink to see it was empty. "I'll have another." The bartender gave me a nod.

"I get it. If it weren't for Jason, I'd be competing with you on weConnect for a date. What about going on as yourself, and forget about trying to catfish?" Cate chewed on the plastic stick that held the two olives in her martini glass before I stole them. I never understood the dirty taste of olive juice mixed with vodka. It somehow seemed

31

wrong to me, which was why I stuck to the tangy flavors of lime margaritas and five-year aged tequila served neat.

"What are you going to do when you have to meet these guys in person? Don't you think they're going to ask questions when you don't look anything like your photo?" she asked me.

Sighing, I bit off the end of an egg roll, washing it down with a sip of replenished tequila. "Well, it hasn't come to that, but there are some handsome and interesting men on this app, so sooner or later I'll have to figure it out. Look—" I held my iPhone up to her face— "this is me, or rather, who is representing me."

I showed Cate the profile photo of my proxy, Chelsea, with her luscious brunette locks cascading down her shoulders and décolletage. "Quite something, aren't I?"

Cate nodded slowly and then self-consciously smoothed her own hair and reached for lip gloss from the handbag on her lap. Chelsea had this effect on me too. I never felt adequate by comparison, but that's because I did have about ten years on my fictitious online persona. Wrinkles were threatening to develop, and my breasts were starting to sag, something that Chelsea wouldn't experience for a while. In Los Angeles, specifically on the west side, being a single gal in her late twenties, as opposed to almost thirty-nine, was as close to being footloose and fancy-free than anything I'd ever experience again. Chelsea had it made.

She stared at my phone. "She is really pretty. Maybe too pretty. Are these guys for real that they think someone who looks like her would be single? Jesus, I'd like a date with her." Cate turned to me with a resolved look on her face and admitted, "I'm so glad Jason isn't on an app. I wouldn't stand a chance."

Cate and Jason met almost a year ago through mutual friends, and while they weren't serious or discussing their future, Cate had already walked down the aisle a few times in her mind and designed the wedding china. He really didn't know her, as far as I was concerned, and their easy-breezy relationship could be blown away as effortlessly as ten candles on a birthday cake. She constantly made excuses for his lack of sensitivity and inability to be the kind of boyfriend she deserved. Last week, Jason had told Cate that she should take cooking classes and learn to set the table properly, just like his mother. He also compared her to attractive women who walked by or those on the big screen. "Why can't you cut your hair like hers, or wear those kinds of clothes?" Cate believed that he was just trying to bring out the best in her, making her into the perfect Cate because he really cared and could see her potential. Those kind of backhanded compliments usually had a way of coming full circle to later slap you in the face.

Later that afternoon, I sat on the sofa with my phone, checking out the latest profiles. Chelsea had almost sixty connections, which was really egregious of her. She was being selfish, hogging not only the good ones but also the men whom most women wouldn't swipe right, let alone meet in person. She wasn't going to meet them face-to-face either but felt that the flirting and online banter were harmless. It was also good for her fragile ego, and mine. Chelsea and I were on the same page.

Ding-ding! My notification on weConnect yielded yet another message, holding me hostage to an app tied to a profile that was not me. Like it or not, it was my entertainment *de la nuit* and just as tantalizing as Netflix. Let's see who's also home and without a social life on a Saturday night. I scrolled through the list of connections I'd made over the past few weeks. An investment of an hour mindlessly responding to boilerplate questions from men I'd never meet left me tired, lonely, and in need of human contact. Leaving the confines of my apartment, I knocked on Sam's door. After a few moments of silence outside the door marked 211, I retreated and settled in for an early night of solitude.

Days morphed into a week, and I found myself once again sitting on the sofa with my phone, swiping men left and right, awaiting delivery of my Saturday night sushi order. Sam was out of town at a conference, so we missed our Friday movie and salad catch-up session.

"Well, who do we have here?" I asked aloud to an empty room. Dr. I'm-Too-Hot-and-Awesome-to-Ask-a-Lowly-Nurse-for-a-Drink's photo jumped out at me. The anesthesiologist who worked on my hospital rounds was known for his womanizing and cyber Rolodex of girlfriends. He could be heard bragging among colleagues that he'd taken this woman out, and screwed that one, and then had his way with another woman who was a mercy screw, which meant he sacrificed his maleness for the betterment of the female population. It was exhausting how many women would fall for his charms and antics, like he was the George Clooney of *ER*. Although we weren't on a first name basis, I learned that Andrew, forty-one, physician, hailed from Chicago but had studied medicine at Harvard, was an animal activist, loved Italian food, had been raised by a single mother so he knew how to treat a lady right, and believed chivalry was alive and well. Who was he kidding? Last week I'd heard him mocking his date's cheesy thighs to another doctor, like we all spend three hours a day on the treadmill. He also said there was no excuse for a woman who couldn't put out seven days a week, because aren't all women in the mood to have sex at the drop of a hat? Chelsea took advantage of this opportunity and swiped Andrew right. *Ding-ding!* Chelsea and Andrew had chemistry. It was an instant match because he had already viewed Chelsea's profile and liked what he saw. The guy wasn't a complete idiot.

"Hello, Andrew. Wow. A doctor. My mama always wanted me to marry a man in medicine," I typed but added the obligatory eye roll. He loved it when he didn't have to chase them, so he could get the womanizing underway without much effort. One would believe his ego was quite healthy in that he never uttered words of heartache or regret when it didn't work out with a perspective female. It was the offensive way he spoke of the opposite sex, keeping women a few arm's lengths away, that made me believe he genuinely disliked us, like he was only dating to prove he was heterosexual. It was difficult to surmise, but any self-respecting female should stay the heck away from Andrew, the anesthesiologist. That was why Chelsea had to engage him. Chelsea didn't have to look in the mirror every day and feel good about herself, or have her friends judge her actions.

"Why, hello, Chelsea. You are stunning. Let's just cut to the chase. How soon can you be at Olympic and Bundy? I'm a successful doctor and have rounds tomorrow, so I don't have time for drinks and chitchat. I'm sure you want the same thing. Did you see the photos of me playing beach volleyball? I'm just as impressive in person."

Andrew not only confirmed every suspicion I had of him but was worse than I thought. Not even a glass of wine and an appetizer? No foreplay? What makes him think he can command such attention? Maybe he was really amazing in the bedroom. That was when a brunette wig would come in handy.

"Excuse me. What do you mean?" Chelsea postured, but was really buying time for an appropriate response.

What should I do? Tell him I'm going and stand him up, or something worse?

"Is this how you treat all your connections? Why not try a true hookup app? Women enjoy getting dressed up and meeting their date out for a drink and fun time. You must be quite sure of yourself," I wrote, as breathing became difficult, and my line of sight veered off the screen. I focused on the spider that was making her way down my wall, millimeter by millimeter. It was impossible to make eye contact with Dr. Andrew at the hospital, let alone speak with him in person. Chelsea gave me confidence to find the words to interact with him, if only behind the guise of her name and likeness.

"I'm sure you've done this before, sweet thing. I can have a date over to my house within the hour, and I'd like her to be you. If this isn't something you're comfortable with, I'll take someone else. I don't want to waste your time."

Waste my time? I'm in my pajamas, between episodes of *Game of Thrones*. I have all the time in the world.

My sushi arrived, and I settled back on the couch to multitask between the irreverent doctor and a platter of nigiri and shrimp tempura. He hadn't written again at that point, which meant he was concentrating on another hopeful and probably sealing the deal.

Ding-ding! "So am I going to see you tonight or what?" he wrote. He apparently couldn't get another gal to take the bait. Andrew was really good looking, and his self-confidence made him appear even more handsome, but once you peeled away a few of his arrogant layers, what remained was just another cocky, smooth-talking, narcissistic, almost-middle-aged, single guy in Los Angeles. They were a dime a dozen in the city, but a lot of effort was needed to find a good one. Dating was like panning for gold during the California Gold Rush in the bitter winter with the threat of frostbite and fighting off bears and bobcats, only to later find one nugget the size of a green pea.

"As enticing as it sounds, because I've always wanted to sleep with a bona fide doctor, I have a better offer for the evening. Good luck." You really get what you pay for, and he didn't want to pay at all. Maybe he should, then he could save the time trolling on this site … just as I'd been doing.

I had to work the next afternoon, because I was picking up extra shifts to save money for a trip to Europe one day. As I entered the cafeteria on my break, I saw the industrious doctor at a table with a few other male physicians, laughing and carrying on like they were at Club Med.

"Chelsea left her clothes at my place. Lucky Uber driver!" Andrew's voice escalated to an obvious attempt at pleasing his audience. The guys surrounding him lapped it up and hung on every lie that came out of his mouth. "She's coming over again tonight. What a sexy brunette, that one. I don't even know what she does for a living. Probably a fitness model. Looks like Megan Fox."

I really wanted to let his cat out of the bag, but I thought if he had to fabricate tales to make himself a Don Juan, then it was his cross to bear. I already knew his deal, and it wasn't pretty. Dr. Andrew would probably be single and swiping when he was sixty.

Cate texted me earlier and asked if I wanted to grab a bite. Her boyfriend, Jason, was busy, so we met for Thai food near her place, and later, I was in my pajamas by 8:00 p.m. My life had been reduced to working, eating, and swiping. I needed to find some hobbies. I needed to find a boyfriend.

weConnect was a beehive of activity for Chelsea, with Toms and Georges and Bills leaving their messages and phone numbers in her message center. "Hey, lovely. Call me, and I'll take you out for a night you'll never forget." "You look like my first wife. BTW, I've never been married." "Hi. How are you? How was your weekend? What's your favorite movie?" Amassed, there were a lot of connections, but none that could take me away from Jon Snow.

A strikingly familiar photo of a light brown-haired guy named Greg appeared on Chelsea's feed of eligible men. I swiped up his profile to get a better look not because he was my type but his name of Greg and the photo didn't equate in my Sunday-night brain. He posted a few pictures, but since he was featured wearing sunglasses, was in a group with other people, and the last photo showed him in a bike helmet, it was difficult to place him. Why do you look so familiar, Greg? My phone alerted me to a message from Cate, thanking me for treating her to dinner. Holy shit.

Greg was Cate's boyfriend, Jason.

5

To Catch a Liar

The act of bamboozling has many layers. Either you are the one duping someone, and you carry guilt, remorse, or rationalization to justify your actions, or you are being duped and feel anger, hurt, or betrayal. But when your best friend was being bamboozled by a guy whom she believed to be the future father of her kids, the claws came out.

With the phone still in my hand, I froze, looking at Jason/Greg with disbelief and shock. What was I going to do? Moreover, what was Chelsea going to do? Chelsea did the only thing she could do. She swiped his cheating ass to the right.

"My pleasure. The food was really great. Hey, Cate, how are things with Jason? I didn't ask you about him tonight." I responded to her text about our Thai food, but really wanted to flesh out why the hell the guy she had been doting on for a year was online as Greg, and had stated his profession was "legal," whatever that meant. Jason was in medical sales, and he'd met Cate in the pharmacology clinic she had worked in before she'd changed jobs to work for a small surgical center. Legal, my ass. You sell adult diapers, bed pans, and catheter tubes.

"Good. Haven't seen each other much lately because he's been working on new accounts at MedSupply. Thinks he can make assistant manager by next year. Come by for dinner soon. We'll BBQ. Nighty night."

Cate signed off, but the off-gases from the last five minutes hung in the air like a helium balloon at the state fair. I was upset, but I couldn't blame Cate. She was in love with the schmuck and had been making excuses for him, explaining away his absences for months. Maybe the relationship was over, according to Jason, but the lack of decency to at least let his girlfriend know that he was moving on, rather than airing it in a public forum like weConnect, made my blood boil. What if she found out her boyfriend was trying to trade her in for another? Should I tell her? I needed to sleep on that one, and slept, I did.

I was ten again. My dad was vomiting all over the floor, completely missing the red bucket my mom had placed beside his hospital-issued bed. She had moved him out of their bedroom and into the living room because the frequent visits from health care nurses to our home required easier access to his IV bag. Plastic pill bottles had spilled out blue, white, and yellow capsules all over the counter, which were my dad's refuge from pain and coherence. He was dying. I overheard my mom tell her friend on the phone that it wouldn't be long before he walked through the pearly gates. Our dog, Buster, had died the year prior, and although he'd been hit by a car that had mangled his hind legs, somehow he'd managed to walk to those pearly gates.

Mom was passed out on the sofa. The sticky, half-filled glasses of rye and Coke littered the coffee table, as well as cigarette butts and empty cartons of Marlboros. Pizza boxes were strewn on the floor, completely hiding the filthy carpet beneath them. My mom's snoring was epic, caused by a combination of anti-anxiety pills and alcohol. Dad was calling out to her but she couldn't hear him over the cacophony of snorts and gurgles emanating from her throat and sinuses.

"Jeanie. Jeanie, I need you." He was scared. Then he started calling for me, "Baby-darling. Help me." He vomited again and knocked his IV to the floor. I walked slowly toward him, my dolly clinging tightly to my chest, just how a protective mother would treat her baby.

He stank of death. The odor stabbed my nostrils, and I could feel the bile rising from my stomach. My dad's eyes rolled back in his head for a moment as he braced himself for a sweeping stab of pain. That was it. He was a goner.

His hand shot out and grabbed me, pulling me toward him. I flinched, but he yanked me into him. His skin was wet and fleshy, in a bloated, medicinal way. I pushed against him and tried to steady myself, but my ten-year-old body was no match for his strength. "Hold still, dammit." My dad's hand tugged my pajama bottoms and slid them down to my knees.

It was then that I fell backward, out of his grasp, shimmying on my butt until I could stand up and escape from him and my mom.

—~—

My phone's alarm told me it was morning, but it felt like only a few minutes had passed since I'd closed my eyes. The air was heavy with my breath, causing a film to cover the insides of my bedroom window. My brain pounded against my skull from a lack of proper sleep. I was about to call in sick but then remembered it was a mandatory work day. A psyche evaluation that I'd rescheduled a few times was due—the final task to apply for the mental health department at the hospital. The irony was that I had to pass a psyche test in order to help others who needed help in the same area.

"Nurse Evans, your seat is ready for you. Sit beside Nurse Sawyer, please." The administrator looked like she'd stepped off the *Psycho* movie set. Her beehive hairdo and horn-rimmed glasses, which hung by a gold chain around her neck, added to the ambiance of the situation. She pointed her long, skinny index finger toward the only empty desk. The tips of her fingernails were painted blood red. "Just acknowledge your ID on the screen, and the software will automatically advance you to the next section. Don't spend too much time on each question, since you have fifty of them, and we don't want to be here all day."

The small conference room was outfitted with ten desks and ten iPads. Fellow nurses had already started their hour-long session either for continued education or to move into a new department, as I was trying to.

The last question on the evaluation was:

- Your patient suffers delusions, hallucinations, disorganized thinking and speech, and exhibits abnormal motor behavior. He claims that aliens have hijacked his mind. He could be diagnosed as having a) schizophrenia, b) bipolar 1 disorder, c) major depressive disorder, d) opioid withdrawal, e) stimulant withdrawal, or, f) alcohol withdrawal syndrome.

The patient was definitely suffering from alcohol withdrawal, as I experienced something akin to an alien last night, one who took me through the many scenes that played out in my dreams—scenes from someone's pathetic life. This alien with the puke-green body and large, oval eyes stood in the corner of the room, a director of my childhood movies, watching and judging while I moved in and out of takes, having to repeat them over and over as they made their reprise every night. I had watched my parents deteriorate into human shells hundreds of times, and no matter what I did between the hours of midnight and 6:00 a.m., they still died. Every time.

The small house from my youth never changed. The interior paint was permanently greyed, and the odor was never quite right, like a combination of life and death meets hope and regret. Levity didn't hang in the air because there wasn't room; yelling, crying, fighting, and bickering took up the space. Friends' parents preferred that I visit their homes—everyone at school knew or at least suspected what lingered among my four walls. A taste of normal—parents who had full-time jobs, manicured yards, clean clothes, and family dinners—was only experienced during after-school playdates. Even the city of Seattle gave up trying to force my parents to cut the grass or fix the broken, wooden fence that threatened the ankles of passersby, usually stopping to gawk at the dilapidated front yard. Old, rusted bicycles and a Radio Flyer wagon were semi-dismantled on the overgrown patch of weeds and grass, while the vines grew around them, pulling them down into the earth.

Homelife, after my dad's death, was like living with a ghost. Unable to deal with her grief, my mom existed in the house as if unseen by anyone. She didn't communicate on any level, and most times I didn't know if I'd come home from school and find her dead on the living room floor, surrounded by the many bottles of rye or vodka, which she had bought with our welfare checks. Her job as a stenographer ceased right after my father's funeral, and she had no intention of returning to the real world. She barely spoke with me during my teenage years and missed out on my milestones of having my first boyfriend and going to the prom.

My parents had tried to make me just like them—a cardboard cutout of who they were: angry, lazy, desperate, sick. I had refused my dad's hands when he'd reached for me, wanting me to make him feel better. When I fought to disappear into the chasm of grieving and self-isolation, just as my mom had, I knew I had a chance. I bided my time, waiting to graduate high school and become someone else— anyone other than Bruce and Jean's daughter.

The scent of bergamot filled my senses.

"Nurse Evans. Are you finished?" The administrator stood in front of me, peering at my progress above the rim of her readers. She held a cup with an Earl Grey tea tab that was attached to a flimsy string and dangled along the side of the ceramic mug. I could relate. I looked around at the empty room. Just the two of us remained.

"Ugh, yes, sorry. I'm done."

I checked a) schizophrenia and submitted my evaluation.

—~—

The Jason/Greg juxtaposition plagued my consciousness all day.

"Can you pop over tonight?" I sent a quick message to Cate on my way home from work.

Sam's front door was ajar, and there were sounds inside his apartment. I was about to call his name, but his voice told me he was close by.

"Looking forward to it. Yeah, can't wait. Okay, I'll see you then."

I pushed the door open wider.

"Can't wait for what?" I asked him, but something told me that I didn't want to know.

His apartment looked like a single man lived there save for a bouquet of fresh cut flowers which lay adorning his kitchen table. They were still in the plastic wrap from the store but stuck out like a sore thumb amid his newspapers, empty Coke cans, and takeout containers.

Sam stood in the living room, his black, wavy hair was still wet from his shower, and he wore baggy sweatpants, which hung low on his muscular hips. His signature woodsy bodywash wafted toward me like Aladdin's magic carpet and made me dizzy from the possibilities.

He held a towel in one hand and his phone in the other. Sam caught me staring and then smiled. "Oh, the phone call. It's nothing. A work thing." He rubbed his hair with the towel before asking, "So, what's goin' on?"

"I need your help. Cate's coming over and I think her boyfriend is cheating on her." The words spilled from my lips, while I collapsed on his couch. "She doesn't know. What do I do?" I really didn't make

41

sense but hoped Sam could help without my having to divulge my catfishing hijinks.

"You think or you know?" He sat down beside me, shirtless, which made me sit up straighter and suck in my stomach.

"I pretty much know. Cate has no idea that she's in love with a cheater. Should I tell her, or let her find out for herself? I should tell her, right?" I had already made up my mind that I was going to spill the beans on her lying-ass-so-called-boyfriend but wanted Sam's approval. "She deserves to know. You'd want to know, right, if your girlfriend was cheating on you?" I looked toward the flowers, their colorful spray making his dismal room appear almost cheerful.

He grimaced and nodded. "Yup. Definitely. Been there, done that. Was cheated on. Not the cheater." Sam stood up and threw on a T-shirt that had been waiting for him on the counter. "Let me know what happens. That really blows for her."

I also stood and made my way to the open door, since it looked like he was heading out. "Did someone give you flowers?" I asked with trepidation, because if he was the recipient of a bunch of peonies from a new girlfriend, I didn't want to know.

Sam's head cocked to the right where the flowers sat on his table and then responded slowly, "Ah, no. They aren't for me. Hey, good luck with tonight." Then he walked toward his bedroom.

Back in my apartment, I poured a triple neat tequila for myself and downed the sedative, resting for a quick moment before my door buzzed.

Cate breezed in like Farrah Fawcett in a scene from *Charlie's Angels*, with her smile bright and blonde hair flowing. She showed no signs of having a rough day. It really wasn't fair. If I didn't love her so much I would have been jealous.

"Hi, babe. Where's my drink?"

I placed a glass of cabernet in her outstretched hand.

"So, how's Jason?" It was the only segue I could think of at that moment.

"Fine … why?" She looked at me sideways and then added, "Okay. What do you know and when did you find out?" Intuition was definitely her strong trait.

"Last night. I saw him on weConnect. I'm so sorry."

If I knew anything about Cate, she was stoic, and a cheating boyfriend wasn't going to take her down. She took a deep breath, exhaled, and admitted, "I felt something was up. He was acting weird, always on his phone. He seemed to be in a constant texting conversation with someone. Even during the night. Damn. So … now what?" She downed her wine like water and reached for the bottle.

My pause was a beat too long. We locked eyes and said in unison, "Catfish him."

Three drinks in, we sat knee to knee while my laptop brought up his profile.

"You lying, cheating sack of shit!" Cate screamed at the screen, as if Jason's face would respond with a denial or admit that the jig was up. "How could you? I was so good to you, and so damn patient. What do you mean *legal*? Who ARE you? Jewel, what the hell is this?" She was hyperventilating at that point, and I had to calm her down.

"You need to breathe, Cate. I know this is hard, but let's get Chelsea in on this." Jason/Greg had already swiped Chelsea. He thought she was as much of a catch as I did.

"Hello, handsome. Are you a lawyer? So impressive." Chelsea worked her magic as Cate and I commiserated.

Jason had told Cate that he'd be working late, but it appeared instead that he was working on finding a new girlfriend.

"Hello yourself, Chelsea. You are stunning! I was hoping you'd swipe me. We are a perfect match."

Cate read his words aloud but then put her hands over her mouth and stifled a scream. "No, WE are a perfect match, Jason. You and me. Jason and Cate. I fucking hate you!" Cate pointed at his smiling photo that seemed to taunt us and curled her hand into a shaking fist. I thought she was going to punch my computer screen. "Write some more. Now … pleeeease. Is there an emoji for asshole?"

Chelsea typed. "Yes, we'd take beautiful pictures together. Was thinking the same. How can you possibly be single? You were waiting for me, weren't you?" Chelsea was being coy, but trying to hook him quickly because I only had one bottle of wine left.

"You and several others. LOL. I'm playing the field. Newly single so I'm being super selective. Let's meet for a drink."

Cate's fury turned to mockery. "Newly single? Screw you! You were lucky to have me. Oh, and just when did we break up, Jason? Did you forget to tell me or was it the amnesia? This is NOT a rerun of *Dynasty*!" she muttered to herself and dialed Jason's number, but it went to voice mail after three rings. She called twice more, but he still didn't pick up. He apparently was having more fun chatting with Chelsea than being admonished by said girlfriend. She didn't leave a message.

Deferring to Cate, I asked, "What do you want me to write now?" A tense pause followed, and I felt really bad for her.

"Tell him she'll meet him. You. We. You know what I mean." Cate was pacing, wearing away a path in my area rug but holding the wine bottle next to her chest like a life preserver. If she was going down, the wine bottle was going to save her.

Not asking questions, I did what she wanted and wrote back to Jason. "Tomorrow night. 8:00 p.m. The Standard in Hollywood. I'll be the brunette sitting alone at the bar, waiting for my handsome date."

"Nice! OK, great. See you then, gorgeous."

—~—

Cate picked me up at 6:30 the next night, giving us plenty of time to drive to Hollywood. We sat at the end of the bar, and as the sun went down, I looked at the single Angelenos sitting around the pool with drinks in hand and laughter in the air, wondering if they were truly happy. Fake profiles, fake laughs, fake lives. It was exhausting.

"Well, hello there. Can I buy you lovely ladies a drink?" A man around sixty stopped in front of Cate and me, surveying the action at the bar and deciding that we were his best bet.

Cate was fidgeting, bobbing her head as people entered the bar area, making sure to spot Jason before he saw us. I spoke for the two of us. "That's so kind of you, but we just ordered. Thanks anyway."

The older, slick man with nothing to lose, licked his lips and continued, "Can I have your number then? Or, both your numbers?"

Cate seethed. "She said no. Now beat it, gramps."

Right on cue, Jason walked in, looked around, and then ordered a drink from the pretty waitress near the bar. He looked better than I'd ever seen him, and I felt even worse for Cate. She really liked him, or who she thought he was. Jason took a swig of his sidecar and then smiled at a cute brunette sitting alone at the bar. He looked like he was going to approach her, making moves on any eligible woman with a pulse. That was all it took for Cate to slide off her chair and walk up to him.

She tapped him on the shoulder. "Greg?" He turned around with a hopeful, but confident, look on his face, excited to meet sexy Chelsea. The color drained from his cheeks as his mouth opened and closed repeatedly, like a ventriloquist's dummy. Cate stared at him, enjoying the moment and awaiting his reaction.

"Cate, honey. What a surprise! Who is Greg?" He acted confused with a dumb smile reserved for people who are caught with their hand in the cookie jar. Nervously, he combed his hair with his fingers and took a deep inhalation. "Seriously, what are you doing here?" Deep down, he knew his goose was cooked.

"Do *you* think I'm stupid? A year of my life has been wasted. Wasted! I expected so much more from you than this bullshit. Why couldn't you just break up with me, like normal people? Consider yourself blocked. We are so over." She turned to walk away but changed her mind and pulled a 1960s big screen moment, pouring her red wine down the front of his white, linen shirt.

—~—

A week flew by without a call or text from Cate. I was certain she was licking her wounds. She deserved so much better than the way Jason had chosen to end their relationship. I wondered if the dry cleaners could clean his button-down.

Summer was almost over; the days were shorter, and the nights, chillier, which justified being in bed at 7:00 p.m. on a quiet Sunday night and checking weConnect to see if any new guys had signed on. Caught off guard to see Jake's face cycle through on Chelsea's feed, I sat up and let the reality of the past year and our breakup take its stranglehold. He had new photos and had updated his narrative. He was still trolling, which meant he was single. It had been six months since I saw him or his photo.

"Jake. Forty-two. Six feet tall. Successful, well-traveled. Seeking smart, vivacious, sexy, and financially independent." And a pot of gold at the end of the rainbow. His pictures showed that he had vacationed somewhere in Europe over the summer. Probably Prague or Budapest. In one of the pictures, he was smiling and was among bar patrons, who wore Eastern European festival clothing. He was holding a beer stein, making a cheers gesture to the camera.

45

Closing the laptop was my weak attempt at trying to erase Jake from my head and heart. Ditching me as easily as he had and later revealing to Chelsea that I was messed up was beyond hurtful and cruel. He hadn't even met her. She was an online persona, yet he'd shared private stories and opinions with a stranger, using someone's sad story as relationship fodder. He thought he knew about me, about Jewel, but he had no idea who I was—and never would.

—~—

It wasn't the anger so much as the disappointment that made Chelsea become Raquel. The thought that a man could dump a woman so easily just because she'd had a rough go at life and then replace her with a shiny, unblemished penny made me want to cry. But I didn't.

Raquel looked like Jessica Alba but with blonder hair. I found her on Facebook and living in Berlin, with a German name of Mila and profession as a makeup artist. This fräulein had so many photos to copy to authenticate Raquel that I had the new profile on weConnect live within twenty minutes. Raquel became a thirty-eight-year-old high school teacher, who had lived in ten countries, was a gourmet chef, and was training for the Honolulu Marathon. Her narrative was extensive and impressive. Chelsea was envious. It took Raquel a few minutes to find Jake, based on specific search criteria, and then she gave him a hard swipe to the right.

Sadness over reverie of the past, slid me into unconsciousness, but the ding of my app awoke me to reality. The clock said 9:10 p.m., but it felt as though days had passed, and I had become a different person—one who could speak a foreign language. It took seconds for my vision to adjust and realize that Jake had connected with Raquel. Of course he had. Did he think this was the law of attraction, like *The Secret*—willing a beauty like Raquel to materialize into reality? He must believe that he is the cat's pajamas and that every woman who looks like Jessica Alba is vying for his time.

"A world traveler. Well-read. Super handsome and in finance. Guys like you don't exist on here," Raquel wrote. She wasn't wasting a moment on formalities. I knew his interests, and based on the bullet points in his profile, I had just enough to hook him. He also loved *Fantastic Four* and *Sin City*, so my work was halfway done.

"Hello, Raquel. You are stunning. I'm happy to see lots of photos. That means you are a real person, and not some fake. There is a lot of that on here."

And for good reason, perhaps. *If you'd just tried harder and loved me, we wouldn't have to do this, Jake.*

"Has anyone ever told you that you look like Jessica Alba?"

Raquel and I rolled our eyes. "No, never."

"Well, you do. She's a great actress if you've never seen her work. So where do you teach?"

Being from the Pacific Northwest, I couldn't name a local high school off the top of my head. "I won't say, for personal reasons. I'm sure you understand." *Should I divulge my home address and Apple ID password, too? Who asks such questions out of the gate?* "Are you single and actually looking or having fun and playing the field on this app?"

"Ha ha. I've met a lot of women on here but no one of substance. I don't have time for games or drama." *Well, you're in my game now.* "What about you? Been single long?"

"Here and there. How do I know you aren't married? You seem too good to be true." *Becoming pen pals wasn't of any interest, but I wanted him to feel flattered so that he'd let down his guard.*

"No, not married. Was engaged but we broke up."

How could Jake have met someone in the past few months, become engaged to be married, broke up, and now was healed enough to be out on the prowl again? I hadn't breathed in five minutes, and my chest was tight. It was the beginning of a panic attack. I reached for my Xanax.

"Oh, that's rough. This happen recently?" I wrote between tears.

"It's been a year now."

Not possible. He was with me a year ago.

6

Ex and the City

Betrayal is a trauma that is felt after someone whom you've relied on for survival and support, leaves you by the curb and discarded like yesterday's *LA Times*. Betrayal sits on your shoulder and whispers in your ear, "Don't trust him. He will disappoint you. He'll leave you. He's not telling the truth." Betrayal sits behind the wheel of the bus and steers it down roads, alleys, and places unknown, ever cautious and suspicious. Betrayal is not your friend or foe, but in dark times, it will hold your hand until the smoke clears.

I had been holding hands with Betrayal most of my life because my parents discarded me as did my husband and several boyfriends along the way. Being seen by those you love shouldn't be insurmountable; when you love and feel that love in return, anything should be possible. Romance novels were the foundation for love in my formative years, but they skewed my way of thinking. All you need is love, love will conquer all, someday my prince will come, blah … blah … blah. There were no ruby red slippers to send me home or a prince holding my glass slipper. It simply wasn't true.

Without sending a response to Jake's statement, I turned off the app and my computer. Engaged? Jake couldn't have been engaged. We met and then two months later, we dated exclusively for ten months but had been apart for the past six, so the math didn't compute that he'd been engaged a year ago. He must've been bullshitting, broadcasting to the female population that he not only was he a catch but was capable of proposing marriage. Women eat that stuff up and were perpetually suspicious that their man would never commit. My heart felt like it was being put through a meat grinder, and I was watching the sausage come out the other end. I passed out from the shock of it all.

Sleep slowly overtook my body and mind, rescuing me from my misery and distorting my reality. I wasn't miserable. In a way, I was given a chance to be free and unencumbered by my past; no more looking in the rearview mirror but only through the clear, expansive windshield in front of me that had infinite possibilities. Aunt Carol, my mom's sister, was the glass half full influence in my life. She used to tell me I should imagine a blank canvas with a handful of fabulous brushstrokes and an abundance of colorful paints. "Each day is an opportunity to create a new picture on a fresh canvas," she'd tell me. I hadn't seen Aunt Carol since I was seventeen years old, and after the move to Los Angeles at eighteen, we completely lost touch.

Carol was my mom's only living relative, but also mine, since my dad was an only child. She was married briefly to a car salesman, and when Bill stopped coming around, I overheard Mom and Carol talking about Bill driving off with his receptionist and how she hoped his tires wouldn't be the only flat thing. Mom and Aunt Carol laughed a lot at Uncle Bill's expense, but I knew that Carol was hurt over losing her husband to a woman named Floozy.

I awoke in a twisted knot of sheets, atop my king-size bed. Tossing and turning all night, between dreams of Jake and living alone with my mom during my teens, I had sweat through my Def Leppard T-shirt and boy shorts. Aunt Carol came to mind, since she must have been flitting around in my subconscious all night, poking at me with her manicured fingernails. I made a mental note to look her up via Facebook and reconnect. I never posted photos or comments on Facebook or Instagram but had an account on both to remain relevant in the social media world. The constant gnawing at my thoughts meant that I was supposed to reach out and find Aunt Carol. That was my Spidey-sense tingling and also my intended Sunday afternoon project.

My computer sat on the easy chair in the corner of my room. It was the conduit of many things. I could use it to find Aunt Carol somewhere in the contiguous fifty states, source a tasty chocolate cake recipe, check my bank account balance, or have Raquel tell Jake that he was a slithering snake in the grass.

A latte, created by someone who knew how to steam milk properly, motivated me to walk to my local coffee shop on Sunday morning. Couples sat dispersed throughout the popular Santa Monica cafe, drinking their caffeinated elixirs and reminiscing of their night out

49

dancing as a happy people somewhere in Hollywood or at a fantastic party in Malibu, probably at a beach house owned by a Clive or Rande. Just as social media presents, everyone appeared to be having the best life and looking their best while living it. Aunt Carol would be furious at my victim-like outlook. She'd sit me down, make me close my eyes, and have me imagine a blank canvas surrounded by acrylics and brushes. "This is your day, your world. Now paint it."

"Is this your coffee?" a tallish, dark-haired guy asked me. He leaned in and took a whiff of my steaming oat milk latte, then asked, "Are you going to drink this or use it as an exfoliator? I smell oats." He chuckled and stepped aside, waiting for my reply.

Dumbfounded and unable to speak, I looked at him and then my drink, before noticing the tetra pack of oat milk right beside my coffee. "You cheated." That word was so easily and aptly used these days. "I'm going to drink it. Are you jealous because you ordered a boring coffee?" I managed a giggle and tried to join in the harmless flirting, but knew that my messy hair and oversized T-shirt would soon be the focal point of his thoughts, once he realized that I must have rolled right out of bed and into the cafe.

"I suppose I am. Jealous, that is. Mine's just a regular dripped. Not too exciting for a Sunday morning." The cute stranger took his personal mug from the pick-up counter in his left hand and extended his right to me. "Grant. And you are?" He looked a bit like John Mayer, but not as scruffy. I wondered if he could carry a tune and play the guitar. He leaned backward and almost took a step away, probably because I must have waited too long to introduce myself.

"Jewel ... my name is Jewel. It's nice to meet you."

His hand was nice and large but on the softer side, which meant he either sat at a desk all day or was always on his phone. Self-consciously, I tucked my disheveled hair behind my ears and caught a glance into the stainless steel fridge that must be keeping the many oat, soy, and almond milks cold. It was confirmed that I was a disaster, and there wasn't any way John Mayer was going to continue this conversation, once he snapped out of the awkward discussion of our beverage choices.

I waited for the obvious follow up of, "Do you live around here?" But in its stead, he asked, "Are you busy tonight, or will you be with your husband or boyfriend?"

That I was not expecting and almost choked. He couldn't be serious. Is Cate around the corner, putting this guy up to asking me out, for pity's sake? "Why don't we go for a drink? A real one." He took the lead, since I was shaking my head with fervor.

"Ah, yeah. That would be fun. I'd love to."

After exchanging phone numbers and deciding to meet at a local lounge nearby at 7:00 p.m., I walked home in a fog. So that's how it's done. Just order a latte and look like someone who lives in a van, and voila, you'll be sipping a cosmopolitan by nightfall.

—~—

After spending two hours with the straightening iron and the world's most expensive collagen-producing face mask, I was ready to see my new boyfriend. We were to meet at the rooftop bar at Hotel Erwin in Venice, and even though it was starting to become chilly at night, I wore my favorite cobalt-blue sleeveless blouse and short black skirt. When my Pedro Garcia wedges were strapped on, I looked into the mirror and thought "perfect." It had been a long time since I felt that good. Since I arrived thirty minutes early due to sheer excitement, I ordered a drink and waited at the bar. Two double margaritas in, Grant walked toward me, moving with an easy athleticism that I'd somehow missed this morning. From the look on his face, he barely recognized me. Better … or worse? The former, I hoped.

"Jewel! So great to see you. I'm happy we could do this." He kissed me on the cheek and addressed the bartender. "Gin martini with a twist and another one for the lady." Grant gave me a cursory glance and sat down beside me. "So, how was your day? What kept you busy, young lady?"

We chatted for twenty minutes, and I was suddenly on my fourth margarita, which seemed to be getting stronger. In my nervousness, I neglected to eat dinner and couldn't recall what I had for lunch, if anything. He was either becoming more handsome or I was getting drunk.

"Will you sing "Your Body is a Wonderland" for me?" I prodded, but he just looked at me with curiosity and then laughed.

"I can't sing very well. Ah, excuse me, we'll have two more. Thanks." He looked up and nodded to the bartender, who seemed

51

bemused by our relationship. If we had been dating awhile, my boyfriend was being very tolerant of my drinking, but if we had just met, my date was being very tolerant of my drinking. Teetering on the precipice of coherence and obliteration was going nowhere fast.

A familiar chuckle caught my attention. It was dark, but the glow from the waning moon cast a spotlight on a figure I'd tried to forget. My ex-husband, Robert, and his wife, Anna—or "Anna Conda" as I liked to say—were two tables away. They were drinking wine and nibbling on what appeared to be flatbread. He'd heard something funny because he started to snort and wipe his eyes. Robert cried when he laughed, which I used to find endearing but now the snorts followed by the tears were like nails on a chalkboard. Scanning the room, as men do when there were gorgeous women aplenty, he caught sight of me and then leaned in to tell Anna the good news. They both turned and gawked at me, Robert moved toward Anna, wrapping his arm around her shoulder and pulling her close as if protecting her. Maybe she was chilly. Or maybe he was worried I'd lunge at them and try to pull the hair out of her head. A shake of my own head brought me back to the task at hand. Grant was telling a story that involved bungee jumping, Coors beer, and a guy named Pete. It was too late to piece it together, so I nodded politely, while keeping Robert and Anna within earshot.

"And then he offered me a cold one before he jumped off the bridge. Good ole Pete. I'll never forget that day." He laughed heartily and raised his glass for a cheers. I realized that it was the fifth or sixth time he'd clinked glasses with me in a toast of some sort. It had become annoying.

"I'm going to the restroom. Be right back." I really needed to pee after five skinny margaritas. A slight stumble off my barstool was quickly remedied by Grant's swift catch of my arm.

He waited a moment until I was steady and whispered into my ear, "We should probably take it easy now. I'll order some food for us."

Grant reached for the menu and scanned the available bar food while I made my way toward the restroom. An audible laugh from Robert's direction almost made me turn and scream with aggravation. It shouldn't have bothered me as it had. I knew it was partly the alcohol pulling my strings and the other part being Robert and Anna making a big "we are so happy together with our incredibly brilliant lives" display for my benefit.

What felt like an hour in the restroom was a welcome reprieve from the energy that had been emanating from the nearby table. Between laughs, Robert had been kissing Anna's neck, causing stares from other patrons. Neither had seemed to care that they'd become a spectacle. It was a painful reminder of the past; as long as Robert was taking care of Robert's needs, everything else could take a back seat. While I had eyed their PDAs, the reality of the situation stared me in the face, or more accurately, slapped me so hard I had a red welt across my cheekbone. In retrospect, why wasn't I happy that Anna had taken him off my hands? He hadn't been right for me, anyway. We were different people and never should have been married in the first place, let alone raise children together. He would have been an absentee father, and I would've been home by myself with the kids, while he was climbing a mountain or on a surfing trip. He wasn't a bad, mean, or callus person, but rather, he was self-absorbed and prioritized his needs and had little consideration for anyone around him including his significant other. Robert was always on a search for self-discovery and self-interest. He was a Leo, after all, and Leos are ruled by the Sun, while the other star signs are like the planets that revolve around him. He would walk into a room, expecting everyone to kowtow to his anecdotes while he commanded their attention. He'd made it clear to me during our marriage that I had little to offer and should be silent, giving him the stage. The question of why he wanted to marry me rang in my ears for years, until the sound became a dull din, like the twenty-four seven of traffic and sirens ignored by Manhattan residents. The long, forgotten exhale finally came, and I had to steady my intoxicated self as I made my way back to our table.

Grant rose to his feet as I approached. "Hey there. I was getting worried. Thought you dumped me already. I ordered some hummus and veggies. Also, some flatbread. The bartender said it was really good."

His mention of flatbread made me remember how Robert and Anna had been nibbling on their flatbread. Yeah, if licking your date's neck like you're cleaning your plate after a Southern barbecue and laughing so belligerently that everyone around you, including the ex-wife, takes notice, well then order that flatbread. Robert and Anna LOVE the flatbread.

Grant smiled down at me the way a pet owner flatters himself after he offers his puppy a treat. Here you go, little fella. Just something to tide you over. Now go fetch.

I collapsed in the chair, making it teeter for a moment.

"Feeling okay?" He moved in close until I could see the fillings in his teeth.

"Yes, I'm great. Happy to be here. Thanks for ordering."

We talked for a bit longer, but my divided attention between Grant's lips and what he was saying and the giggles and hoots coming from Robert's table, left me playing with the cutlery on the table. I had amassed a small pile of forks, spoons, and condiments in a haphazard teepee, like a makeshift Jenga that would topple over if the wrong layer was pulled out. I just wanted to leave, go home, and pull the blankets over my head. Maybe suffocate myself. For the sake of the evening, I zeroed in on my date and tried to put things in perspective. Grant was actually very good looking and had that boyish charm that you could get lost in, making you forget that he was probably around forty years old. He'd asked me out in public over a latte while I was in my pseudo pajamas and had taken a risk, hoping it would pay off. Was he expecting to get lucky? It was hard to get a read on him.

Then all the drinking I'd done hit me. The five margaritas had united in my bloodstream; they joined their little limey hands and made a circle, twirling me like I was on a merry-go-round.

"Can we have the check, please?" His request to our server was barely audible over the ringing in my ears. Had I just been roofied? This couldn't be *just* the tequila. Grant must have slipped something in my drink when I went to the restroom. A recent *Dateline NBC* episode told the story of a guy who stalked women in Santa Monica coffee shops and then lured them to fun and fancy Venice rooftop bars, where he plied his dates with margaritas, flatbread, and hummus. Before he covertly put Rohypnol into their beverages, he let them make fools of themselves in front of their exes and later murdered them in cold blood. My pulse quickened, sending me into fight-or-flight mode.

"Did you Uber here or drive your car?" Grant asked, but the actions of putting his wallet away and reaching for his jacket were all I could focus on, otherwise I was either going to vomit the flatbread on the blue tile floor or curl up on the nearby lobby chair until the room stopped spinning. "Jewel? Should I take you home? Jewel, are you okay?"

"What did you do to me? You put something in my drink!" The sound that came out of my mouth was in the vocal range of bass and reserved for Barry White. The accusation hitting Grant squarely in the face. I clutched my purse to my chest and tried to get up, searching for the exit.

Grant's body stiffened from my sudden change in personality. He reached for my shoulder, trying to steady me since I was heading to the floor, face first.

"Don't touch me. Let me go!" I fumed. My breathing increased so that I was now hyperventilating. I grabbed Grant's arm to regain my balance while my other hand hit his chest. I couldn't stop screaming at him, as he tried his best to dodge my free hand, worried I was going to punch him in the face. "You poisoned me!"

Even in my state of inebriation, I could feel *them* approach. Damn. Why me? Why now?

"What a shocker, Jewel. Always drunk. Always a disaster." Robert said as he and Anna now stood before us. They were looking down on me with distain and pity, shaking their bobbleheads in unison. "Good luck, my friend. I'd get out fast, if I were you." Robert nodded at Grant, chuckled and then made his grand exit with his shiny new wife.

As they walked away, Anna turned and stole a glance, but her cat eyes caught me in their crosshairs long enough to show pole position. Just like her smug and entitled self, she raised a middle finger but furtively used it to smooth a piece of hair that had fallen over her eye. My date watched the exchange of pleasantries and looked confused but then a sliver of clarity creeped into his eyes. A modicum of understanding wasn't enough to save this evening. I had blown it to epic proportions.

"There's an Uber coming. Two minutes away. Let's go downstairs."

Grant's words were distant and absent of feeling. He was clearly embarrassed and wanted the night to end as much as I did. The Audi A3 pulled up as we exited the lobby, with his Uber sign illuminating a bright purple from the dashboard saying "GRANT." Grant confirmed that it was for him, opened the car's door, and put me inside.

55

"Feel better."

And that was it. The date was over.

As I rode home in the backseat, "New York State of Mind" played on the radio. The song brought back memories of watching *Sex and the City* while in college. My night had been reminiscent of Jack Berger breaking up with Carrie Bradshaw on a Post-it note, and my defeat echoed her pain.

—~—

Daylight glared at me through the bedroom window. Even the sun was upset at my conduct. My phone alarm saturated the confines of the room, coercing me out of bed. Let's make this quick. Shower. Coffee. Work. Home. Bed.

—~—

Nighttime came sooner on those days because daylight savings time was over. It was a welcomed relief to be in early darkness, as it enveloped me in its void. Numbness took over my cocooned body on the sofa, while the events from the night before clawed their way into my psyche. Unwittingly, I had confirmed to Robert what he believed of me for years. Maybe I was a drunk. Maybe he was right. Robert and Anna had clearly enjoyed themselves while I provided their evening entertainment. Why is this city so small? Why can't my ex live in Texas, as in the song?

I looked down at my inner thighs. A hint of scarring from a razor blade brought back memories of painful teenaged years. Visible two-inch lines were forever etched into my skin, reminding me how easy it was to escape trauma. Redirect the hurt. Run from the pain. A few cuts into the flesh felt better than the sting of insults or being ignored by a parent. Blood would trickle down my thigh and pool on the bathroom floor, until more slices with the blade created a puddle made from superficial wounds. I clutched my glass of reposado, my new razor blade.

The laptop's chime told me it was ready for weConnect, and Raquel was ready for Jake. The screen illuminated the dating website and our text exchange. Jake's photo smiled at Raquel, as she and I read his additional words written after he'd last logged off.

"What happened? Where did you go? I said that I didn't get married. We were only engaged." And then, "Hello, Raquel." Also, "LMK when you can FaceTime or meet IRL. Let's get to know each other." And, "Raquel, let's chat." Finally, "How was your weekend, Raquel?"

The guy was very persistent to connect with a woman, just based on her photo. In the two days that the computer was off, he'd reached out repeatedly, hoping to generate momentum. If he had tried half as hard to make our relationship work, we'd have two-and-a-half kids by now.

All that Raquel could muster with labored strokes of the keys, given the recent events, was, "I wish you'd have married her."

Then I wouldn't have had to deal with his bullshit.

Did it even matter anymore? After waiting for the app's notification of "received," so he could read that she didn't give a damn, Raquel unmatched Jake.

7

You've Got Aunt Carol

"I think you just need a massage, not Swedish but a deep tissue, and then a soak in the hot tub. Maybe a big glass of wine too."

Sam was trying hard to make me feel better. He'd come over at dinnertime to say hi but found me in a crumpled heap on the sofa. Luckily for me, we had exchanged keys when I first moved in. After I had bellowed out loud that I was incapacitated, he let himself in. Sam's strong hands rubbed my tired feet while I remained horizontal with my eyes closed. "So, what's been going on since we saw each other last? How's Cate? Is she still single?"

"Yes. Yes. Yes. Yes. Nothing. Fine. Yes."

"What?" Sam stopped rubbing my feet and looked at me like I had gone off the rails.

"Yes, I need a deep tissue massage, a soak, wine, chocolates. I haven't been doing anything but work. Cate is fine and isn't dating anyone. I think she needs a break from men. You interested?" Banking on him saying he wasn't interested, I added, "What about you? You dating anyone?"

We'd never discussed his side of love before, as I always had the floor with Robert and Jake. He patiently listened to me lament over my failed marriage and then the Jake Diaries without any contribution of his own.

"Yeah, here and there. Nothing serious. You wanna grab some dinner? Have you eaten today?"

It had been a week since the coffee-turned-date-from-hell happened. There was no denying that I had single-handedly ruined my chances with Grant and left an indelible impression on my former husband. Just to ensure I wouldn't bump into John Mayer again, I switched my coffee shop of choice to one closer to the hospital. A chance encounter with Grant would just send a reminder to both of us that organic love doesn't happen in modern day. It isn't possible to meet someone over a latte, discover commonalities, become enamored, and then spend every available moment together until it resulted in a lifetime of happiness and adventure. That's why dating apps were invented.

The day slipped away from me; laziness begets laziness, and I finally made my way into the kitchen at noon. Spending my time searching through Facebook, Instagram, Pinterest, and LinkedIn yielded many Carols, but not my Aunt Carol with the smile and attitude reminiscent of Goldie Hawn's. She even looked like the blonde actress from the *Private Benjamin* movie, always positive and approachable.

"No, I haven't eaten much today. Only a handful of cashews and a coffee. Let's get out of here, or were you thinking of ordering in?"

Hoping he'd choose delivery of some pasta or a pizza from a local restaurant was trumped by an energetic "Let's check out that Mexican place on Ocean Avenue. I've heard it has excellent tacos and margaritas."

A glance at my casual attire of sweatpants and a ripped, vintage Iron Maiden T-shirt gave me pause. I changed into a pair of tight jeans and a cute, mint cashmere sweater. A heavy metal music phase in high school had kept me in clothing adorned with drawings of blood and skulls, which was a respite from Mom's music that consisted mostly of Barry Manilow. It wasn't that I didn't like the song "Copacabana," but when it was on repeat all day, because Barry wrote songs to make the whole world sing, a little metal balanced out the house's energy.

A high ponytail and a dab of pink lip gloss were the finishing touches as I exited the bedroom to hear a "wow" from Sam. He stood in the living room with his mouth agape and a look on his face that I'd never seen before.

"You look beautiful."

"So sweet. Thanks, Sam. I don't feel it, but as long as you think so, that's all that matters." I brushed off his compliment as though I received them all the time.

We ate fish tacos and drank mango margaritas until closing time. Sam shared stories of his life in Missouri with his younger twin sisters and supportive parents, Maxwell and Melinda. His childhood in

59

Kansas City sounded idyllic, complete with a loving mom and dad, and sisters who called or texted him every day. Ever since we first met, Sam hadn't acted very confident in terms of women and what he had to offer, which was surprising because he seemed to have it all: good looks, higher education, successful career, intelligence, a normal upbringing, wit, charm. Many guys in Los Angeles were still in dead-end jobs, trying to find themselves working as a barista or waiter, or worse, an actor. "The biz," as it was called in LA, really meant that they would be earning a minimal wage for maximum hours on set, but they'd have huge bragging rights when they could drop names at a dinner party, having worked with Denzel Washington or Bruce Willis that day. Of course, I had leaned in a few times to hear the privileged details of Denzel's catered food preferences or Bruce's methodology to memorizing lines. I wasn't above wanting to be privy to such juicy knowledge of the big screen's leading actors. I just didn't want to date a guy who worked as an extra on set and touted that it was his back we were looking at in a scene of crowded people.

I couldn't remember a time when I had laughed so earnestly with a man, especially one with whom I wasn't romantically involved. Sam put his arm around me as we made our way to the electric scooters outside the restaurant. I forgot my phone, so he used the app on his, and we shared a scooter the ten blocks home, while I held on tightly around his waist. He made me feel safe and protected—more than any man had my entire life.

After Sam gave me a shoulder squeeze and a quick kiss on the cheek, I returned to my apartment, ready to retire for the night. The date had made up for the one I'd had with Grant, but then I had to remind myself that the night out with Sam wasn't a date. It was just two hungry neighbors sharing a dining experience at the same table. He paid for the bill, but only because I forgot to bring my purse, which had my wallet and iPhone, so technically it could have been a date.

—~—

A *New York Times* article appeared on the front page of Sunday's edition, and the caption "Fake Online Dating Profiles" caught my eye. It was like a beacon trying to get my attention, but not as a lighthouse would because the rotating beam of light that circulates from a lighthouse is there to warn or guide vessels away from dangerous waters. This beacon felt intentionally conspicuous, like a small, smoldering fire in need of additional wood and ignitable material. The more combustible the logs added to the flames were, the more dangerous—but mysterious—they became, and the harder it was to move away from its warmth and energy. Like a moth to a flame.

A quick perusal of said article told the story of unsuspecting women who tried their best to meet an eligible man online, since it was impossible to strike up a conversation in a public arena or find commonalities with male counterparts within the New York City workplace. Gone were the days when an organic chitchat in a coffee shop resulted in an actual date. Wrong! They should have spoken with me. The women who were interviewed for the article were duped into believing their potential connection would create a dopamine reaction and lead them to live happily ever after. As long as an online match occurred, the rest would just fall into place, like a long trail of dominos. Instead, these hopefuls embarked on a blind date, if you will, because men and women don't FaceTime to legitimize their connection before they waste their precious date nights out, and later, they're disappointed, surprised, heartbroken, angry, or vengeful because the guy they were expecting to meet turned out to be the imposture's antithesis. He was older, or younger, than his profile stated. The guy shaved off ten years from his photos, or worse, six inches of height. The one thing that couldn't be described in a photo or narrative was the guy's personality, or a guarantee that there'd be mutual chemistry.

Feeling a bit ahead of the curve, I almost patted myself on the back. Although I was contributing to the demise of online dating, apparently, I was smarter than the average bear. I didn't need a degree from MIT to screenshot a hottie from the Internet and then give her a plausible identity. She was the fishing rod to a lake of hungry and willing fish. It's the person who doesn't realize or care to discern that a profile with only one beautiful photo and a scant bio is surely a fake and will never result in a real experience. Knowing I wasn't messing with these guys to be mean, but moreover, to glean valuable information from an ex or two, I mentally removed myself from the category of cheater/scammer/mountebank and took on the philosophy of "buyer beware."

We should know what we are getting into when we post multiple, real photos of ourselves on a dating app and then disclose our age, the city we live in, our job, and academic background. We may as well list our Social Security number and blood type. With all of this personal information in the hands of thousands on a free dating app, we are collectively at the mercy of anyone who is creative or dillydallying behind a fake photo. Caveat emptor, my friend.

—~—

I checked Monday morning's in-box. Just as in the AOL "You've Got Mail," I saw there was a "You've Got Aunt Carol" email, much to my pleasant surprise. Facebook had reached, informing me that I'd found my long-lost aunt. Facebook was truly ingenious. It had searched for every Carol in the United States and suggested Carol from Wilmington, Alabama, to Carol from Boise, Idaho. The sister of my late mother wanted to be my Facebook friend, to which I hurriedly accepted.

—~—

A frail, diabetic lady named Mabel from room 2203 coded within ten minutes of my shift, which set the tone for the rest of the day. Mabel's insulin levels had shot up, and she'd been admitted in the early hours of the night. Her loved ones were sobbing as they sat by her bedside, but when I returned to her room an hour later, they'd been replaced by an elderly man who was holding her hand. Tears slowly trickled down his cheeks, as he made no attempt to wipe them away. Little sniffles escaped his nostrils.

"She was the love of my life. I don't know what I'm going to do without her."

He spoke for my benefit, since I was the only person in the room, but he didn't turn to see my face or my response. He didn't care who I was, only that he was in the last moments in Mabel's presence before the orderlies took her body away. He was relishing the time he had to say his silent goodbye while he stroked her white hair. Respecting the awkward, but tender, moment, I quietly exited the room. Although I had a few protocols to complete before they removed Mabel's body, I gave him a few more minutes of closure.

It was easier to reconcile the grief of losing friends or relatives than to empathize with someone who had lost the love of their life. Given an opportunity in this world, I'd relish the heartbreak and anguish of my love's death because that would mean I'd found that once-in-a-lifetime connection. Saying goodbye to my parents should have been sad, but I didn't know what I was saying goodbye to: was it the tears, sleeplessness nights, rejection in days of solitude, or mere helplessness? After many years in healthcare, and watching people heal and others perish, the concept of closure was multilayered and subjective.

—~—

Aunt Carol was reincarnated within the confines of Facebook. She appeared to have stopped aging, and her cheerful, resurrected spirit shone through the many photos she'd provided to the social media platform. She had recently traveled to Morocco, as evidenced by a camel she sat upon and the expansive sand dunes in the background, and had also drunk from a coconut in Fiji, while her traveling buddy sipped from the second straw. Her companion, a grey-haired man who looked to be in his early seventies, appeared in most of the photos and was the constant in Aunt Carol's life. They had traveled the world together and now lived in Florida.

"Hi, Aunt Carol. I'm so happy we connected. How are you? I've missed you so much."

The short and sweet words on Facebook Messenger summed up everything I wanted to feel about a woman I didn't know but who was somehow part of my DNA. How was it possible that half of my life had elapsed, and the chance to be reunited with my only living relative was just a few keystrokes away? My parents left this earth before smartphones, social media, and instant access to every morsel of information ever digested by a human existed—a phenomenon that only a digital immigrant could truly understand. Had they been alive today, they could have witnessed the advent of instant messaging to any contact, using a small phone that was carried in your pocket, unlike in their day when they had to place a call on a rotary dial phone to a friend's landline, hoping the recipient would be home and pick up the receiver. If their call went unanswered, they'd wait until the next day and try their luck again. Dad passed away before the answering machine made an appearance, and Mom had never learned to use a computer but had relied on our typewriter to write important letters. Her job as a stenographer, which used a stenotype machine, had kept her reliant on chorded keyboards and detached from the digital world.

"Jewel! I'm so happy to hear from you too. I didn't know you were on FB. You have a different last name. Why don't you have a profile photo, or any photos at all? Please send some pics my way. It's been over twenty years since we've seen each other. How are you, sweetheart? When can we talk?"

We exchanged phone numbers and spoke until 9:00 p.m., which was midnight on her East Coast time. Aunt Carol was lively and had the same positive personality I'd remembered. She had married a wonderful man named Malcolm over fifteen years ago, and they'd been inseparable ever since. My tales of college, relocating to Los Angeles after my parents died, marriage and divorce, and a nursing career, kept our conversation moving along until the present time of living the single life in a Santa Monica apartment. Even though the details were succinct and matter of fact, Aunt Carol could detect the sadness and longing for a love connection in my voice, something that she had been able to find years ago. How had she done it? How had she found love again?

Carol and Malcolm had met on a singles cruise through the Caribbean Islands, somewhere between Martinique and Saint Lucia. The band that was playing her favorite song, "Could You Be Loved" by Bob Marley, was positioned on the lido deck next to the ship's heart-shaped pool, lending to the romantic atmosphere when Malcolm asked her to dance. She was smitten immediately, and they spent the next five days together, exploring Barbados and Saint Vincent and The Grenadines, unaware that there were three thousand other people who were island-hopping.

Malcolm's older boys became Aunt Carol's stepsons, as their mother had passed away from breast cancer when they were very young. She said they turned out to be wonderful young men, thanks to Malcolm's doting fatherly ways, and that she couldn't wait for me to meet them. We planned to reunite in the summer of next year. They had the next six months already mapped out with an African safari, the Inca Trail trek to Machu Picchu, and later, an extended excursion to the Galápagos Islands. She promised to post photos on Facebook and send messages through Messenger whenever she would have the opportunity and a good Wi-Fi connection.

—~—

My head rested easier on the pillow and my heart was lighter that night, knowing I still had family who cared about my well-being. Dad didn't have siblings, and Aunt Carol didn't have biological kids, so she and her new ménage were all I had left of my lineage—that is, until I had children of my own. Thoughts from the past few hours were swirling around in my brain, and it didn't seem like I was going to fall asleep anytime soon, so I turned to weConnect while remaining cozy under the duvet.

What's been going on since we last saw each other, oh dear app? Marc, forty-one, firefighter, surfer, and a single dad, appeared first on the screen. He was mesmerizing in a Rick Fox sort of way but lived in Manhattan Beach, which was too far to drive in Los Angeles traffic.

Bruce, forty, finance, never married, 50 percent custody of a ten-year-old daughter, and political activist, was a profile that struck a chord of familiarity. He frequented my new coffee shop and always ordered an Americano with double cups and chatted with anyone nearby about the current state of our White House administration. Typically, when someone engaged in a political discussion, regardless of the slant or affiliation, I steered clear and moved to safer ground.

Jason's photo appeared after the swipe of Bruce's profile to the left, and his name now displayed as Jason, rather than the pseudonym of Greg he used when Cate and I catfished him. He'd decided to come out in the open, fishing off the same pier as the rest of us. It wasn't that I thought he and Cate were a great couple and would miss out on an opportunity of happily ever after, but how he had ended their relationship in a sneaky, cowardly way left me disappointed. He had a few new photos posted, for a total of six. He seemed very motivated to meet someone, and perhaps he might.

What made one man try to make it work with the current woman in his life, yet throw the baby out with the bath water with another, hoping the next attempt had greener grass? It was the grass is greener syndrome that plagued most men these days. A new relationship was just an exchange of one set of problems for another. Unless the woman was a total nightmare, he's still going to run into the same set of issues: being admonished for not taking out the trash or clogging the shower drain with long strands of hair, not having enough sex, arguing over finances, realizing she's a regular human with flaws. Perfection doesn't exist.

Drifting off to sleep, I was atop a cruise ship, off the coast of Montego Bay, with a rum cocktail in one hand and the other on the arm of a tall, handsome stranger, while we swayed to the music of The Beach Boys. The sun was setting over the warm Caribbean Sea, and any care I had in the world evaporated with every touch of the steel drum.

8

Christmas Stalking

"To me, you are perfect."

Andrew Lincoln's character in *Love Actually* stood outside his unrequited love's house while her new husband waited inside, and unaware that his bride and best friend—the guy who was outside holding signs that declared his true feelings—shared one of the most celebrated love scenes of the decade. Every time I watched it, which was right before Christmas, all I wanted to do was run Mark over with a truck and slap Juliet across the face. Hard. How perfect was she, allowing her husband's best friend to have an emotional affair with her? And Mark wasn't brave or valiant for walking away. He was vanilla: a common, take it-or-leave-it flavor that you'd find anywhere.

December was already half over, and the new year was just around the corner. It used to matter that I'd have someone special to kiss as the clock struck midnight, but it wasn't worth pretending the men in my circles were more than what they were, just to share a kiss. The lack of substance must've been overwhelming, otherwise there wouldn't be so many guys still out looking, month after month. weConnect also had the same men on a loop, because Barry, Joe, Ethan, Noel, and Parker appeared every forty swipes to the left. Perhaps there weren't many new prospects because of the holidays, and once the new year began, there'd be more available men. At least this was what I kept telling myself. Knowing that I wanted to join weConnect again and as a legitimate single: Jewel, thirty-eight, nurse, only drank premium tequila, enjoyed Friday night takeout with cute neighbor, and industrious with Photoshop, had to be worth the effort.

Cate rang my apartment buzzer early. Sam was out of town at a conference, so we positioned ourselves on the couch with some Mexican food and the remote control. It was Friday night, and routinely, it would have been Sam seated beside me. For good measure, I fired a few texts his way so he'd know that he was duly missed.

"What's it gonna be tonight, Jewel? Sitcom reruns or a Hallmark special? Hey! Let's watch *Love Actually*. It's such a feel-good movie." She had that puppy dog look about her, the face of a cocker spaniel that's expecting a treat or pat on the head. Her hands were practically under her chin, and her breath was a labored pant. "Andrew Lincoln is just dreamy."

"Yes, he really is, but I'll punch something if I have to watch that movie right now. I'm not in the right frame of mind to pretend that all men don't suck." I reached for my margarita and took a long sip.

"Well, not all men, otherwise you wouldn't be on weConnect."

"Whatever you want to watch is fine, just make it realistic."

He's Just Not That Into You was queued.

"Ha! That's the story of my life. We don't need to see it on my fifty-inch TV 'cause I can just give you the play-by-play."

We watched the first few intertwining of relationships, which seemed confusing but would reconcile later in the movie had I not drifted off to sleep.

Jake stood over me, his caricatured, stretched face was spewing words as he spoke, "Not interested. Nope. Would rather have someone else." Robert slowly pushed him out of the way to be center stage while displaying a cocky sneer. "A waste of time. Not worth the effort." Then he was Sam. I reached for him. Surely, *he'd* save me, telling me that he cared and that he wouldn't leave like everyone before him. His handsome face morphed into a clown, similar to Pennywise from the horror film *It*. He scared me. His words were Svengali-soothing but had a menacing, textured quality. "I will never choose you, Jewel. You are sweet ... but so, so crazy. You kill people."

I am not crazy! I try, dammit. I am kind. People tell me that I'm kind. I'm a nurse, for God's sake! I reached forward to pull off his mask. I needed to see Sam's face. His hair got caught in my fingers as I pulled on the latex. His voice screamed at me but it sounded more like a girl's.

"Stop it, Jewel. What the fuck? Wake the hell up!"

Cate hovered over me, both of her hands on mine while trying to dislodge my fingers from her long, blonde ponytail. "Let go of my hair!" She looked at me with fear in her eyes until she was free of my hold. Backing up a few feet, and with a wild expression, she asked, "What's going on? Was that for real, or did you have a crazy nightmare?"

Why does everyone keep saying that? "I am NOT CRAZY!" I screamed back at her.

She recoiled in shock from my accusation. Looking at my best friend, I suddenly realized what I'd done. "I'm so sorry, Cate. I don't know what came over me. Yes, I had a bizarre nightmare. It felt so real. Must have been from the takeout. Too much spice in the enchiladas."

She was standing at my wall mirror, examining her cheek. "Jewel, you scratched my face." Cate's look of disappointment told me so much. She didn't understand or trust me at that moment. I wanted to crawl into the tiniest hole.

I walked over to her, confirming that I'd really made three-inch-long scratches on her cheek. "Cate, I don't know what to say, except I'm truly sorry. I don't even know what I was dreaming about. Sometimes my dreams are so vivid that I can't separate imagination from reality. I'd never hurt you intentionally." I put my arms around her and pulled her close, holding my breath. I slowly exhaled. "You are my best friend."

We talked a bit longer before she left, but it only took moments for her to forgive me. "We're watching a rom-com, not *Poltergeist*. Next time you decide to dream about a murderer, do it alone in your bedroom." She thought that was a funny statement but didn't know how true her words were. "And lock this door behind me."

The last scenes of the movie resurrected the silent room. I curled up on the couch, watching Justin Long's character, Alex, arrive at the apartment of Ginnifer Goodwin's character, Gigi. Alex declared his love for Gigi, which was after he'd convinced her throughout the movie that she was the rule but then after passionately kissing her, told her she was the exception. The movie was not a spoiler alert for life, as we live and breathe men's love rules, which are in effect one moment and then change to accommodate the new situation, relationship, or the next moment.

All women wanted to be Gigi and the exception, as the rule was purgatory. It came down to boundaries; mine were undefined but inching their way along. Knowing that I wouldn't find organic love in a coffee shop while waiting for an oak milk latte, I also knew I wouldn't find it online, masquerading as a hot brunette. My boundaries needed to be clearly drawn, so any eligible man knew when, or if, to approach, or to continue walking. Darwin said, "A man who dares to waste one hour of time has not discovered the value of life." Having wasted hours and hours of time online, being married to the wrong man, dating the wrong men, and watching endless Hallmark movies, screamed to me that I had not discovered the value of my life.

—~—

Cate called me the next morning, the previous night already a distant past.

Feeling awful at how I reacted to my dream, I needed to show her a good time. "We need to do something fun. Our world's becoming very small. Let's put on some hot clothes and go out tonight. There's a new bar that just opened nearby, like a westside extension of Hollywood, and I'm dying to go. Wear that black jumpsuit I've only seen you in once and the cute booties that are still in the box. What do ya think?" Rolling off the bed and into my slippers, I added, "Let's get our nails done and a blow-out. My treat."

I met up with Cate at the salon. Her long, blonde tresses were blown straight, making her former curls became sleek and shiny as they rivaled any model's hair from a Breck commercial. I reflexively touched mine, playing with the ends that sat on my shoulders. My once long hair had been cut to the shorter version I'd had right before college, a transformation and attempt at a new life, a new Jewel.

Sitting beside one another with our nails in the dryer, Cate asked me if I'd seen or heard from Jason since the night out in Hollywood. The fact that he was on weConnect with gusto, using his real name with an updated profile, sent her over the edge.

"What a scumbag. He's soap scum. He's that greenish-white frothy scum that sits atop stinky, hot lakes in Louisiana, with mosquitos and flies buzzing and cows shitting nearby." She snorted and we broke out into uncontrollable laughter, causing heads to turn. She wiped her happy tears and added, "How do his photos look? What did he say in his narrative? Oh, Jewel, why do I care?"

"I don't know but you really shouldn't."

Trying to be diplomatic, I wanted Cate to forget about her ex and enjoy the night ahead. There were single men aplenty, and all of whom weren't like Jason, or Jake, for that matter. There were honest and loving relationships out there, or we wouldn't be hearing wedding bells ringing on Saturday afternoons. People were getting married; there were still great guys roaming around, and they just needed to be found. I conjured an image of mindless zombies from *The Walking Dead* and figured I couldn't be too far off.

We reconvened at my place. Cate exited the bathroom in a fabulous beige dress and black heels. She stood statuesque with a glass of sauvignon blanc in her hand, giving the model Bar Rafaeli a run for her millions.

"Cate, you have a tag." She turned around to retrieve the Bergdorf Goodman price tag that was sticking out of the back of her dress. The whopping amount of $1,800 made my eyes bleed. "What the hell? You didn't spend ..." Of course she didn't. She lifted it.

Cate grabbed the tag from my hand and shrugged. "No, it was from the twice-yearly sale, and they practically gave it to me. Do you have any more of this white? It's delicious. Is it from the Napa trip we went on last year?"

"There's another bottle chilling in the fridge. Hey, Cate. Did you really buy that dress? I mean, that's a lot of money, even at a discount."

Cate shot me a look that said, "Mind your own damn business and bring that wine already."

How could I argue? I wasn't present among the thrifty buyers at the Bergdorf Goodman fire sale, and it wasn't my ass that was going to end up in jail, unless catfishing was a criminal offense. I'd have to look that one up, just to be on the safe side. It's crazy to pay $1,800 for a dress at the rack price, and even with a 50 percent discount it would be exorbitant. Nobody would appreciate such fine fabric and design in this singles scene. Most of the women we knew were in lower level paying jobs like nursing or pharmaceutical sales and weren't comfortable shopping the likes of Nordstrom's.

It isn't that Cate couldn't afford to dress in fabulous clothing, as her only expenses were her rent and car payment. Before I suspected Cate of shoplifting, she had an addiction to buying Beanie Babies from eBay. Her collection was in the hundreds, and the debt involved was at least in the thousands. Before that, she was obsessed with yoga, shoes, and key chains. If she wasn't collecting, she was working out incessantly, learning everything there was to know about yoga, going on retreats, and aligning herself with every instructor and yogi. Years ago, I spoke with a psychologist from the hospital about Cate's continued addictions. He told me that she may be eliciting a sense of euphoria from her current obsessions, and once the adrenaline rush subsides, the darker side of the compulsion manifests itself. I'd never seen Cate's darker side, if she had one.

—~—

The new nightspot turned out to be a sister hotel of Hollywood's finest, and one whose rooms were sold out months in advance. Moreover, it appeared that the entire Hollywood clientele had, in mass exodus, driven to zip code 90403 and were congregating around the rooftop pool. We hadn't seen so many Manolo Blahniks and sequin skirts since our barhopping adventure last summer on the Sunset Strip. Edging our way between two groups of single millennials, as evidenced by their homogeneous ensemble, Cate waved her newly manicured hand at the bartender, who was trying to appease fifty thirsty patrons at once. He nodded and winked at her and then made his way over.

"What 'ya havin', darling?" His smooth southern drawl was captivating, and I immediately wanted to pack and move to Georgia.

Cate giggled, which surprised me because she appeared off her game. She was the master at flirting and holding her own with handsome men. "Two Hendrick's and—"

"No, no, I'll have a reposado. Neat. No salt. Thanks," I interrupted. What in the world has come over Cate? She knew I was not a gin drinker.

"Cate, are you okay?" What I thought were nerves was something different. She ignored the blunder and scanned the expansive rooftop, looking at the people, but mostly the men. "Who are you expecting?"

Cate's shoulders sunk and she looked ready to cry.

"I'm just not feeling it. I'm sad, and mad, about Jason. Do you think he's here? Could he be here on a date with one of these beauties?" She was almost finished with her gin and tapped the rim of her glass for the bartender to begin round two. He looked my way, and I nodded my head in agreement. Why not? We had planned to have dinner, but I supposed the chicken pot pie I'd heard so much about was not going to happen.

"I can't imagine he is out at a place like this. He's probably at his home with a date."

She tucked her drink between her purse and her waist and then grabbed my arm. "Let's go."

"Where the heck are we going? I haven't ordered dinner and I'm starving. And what's that?" I asked, referencing the gin in the fancy highball glass.

"My roadie. Where's yours?" Cate scoffed.

We made our way out of the hotel and toward her car. Jason lived nearby in Brentwood, the residential area made famous by O. J. Simpson, in a small condo nestled within a cul-de-sac. We parked on a neighboring street and cut the engine. Cate was already tucking her hair under a black ball cap she'd found in the back seat, as though we were seasoned cat burglars and about to commit the heist of the century.

"You ready?"

"Ready for what? What are we doing here, Cate?"

She zipped my dark grey fleece over her dress and gave me an exasperated look.

"What do you think? We are Christmas stalking Jason. We need to see what he is up to. Who he's with. Come on."

We didn't need to see anything. *We* couldn't care less who he was with or what he was doing on a Saturday night, especially when there were fun, eligible men back at the bar.

Having no choice but to follow her down the dark street, I exchanged my sexy heels for Crocs that I kept in the trunk. I always had an overnight bag in the car for emergencies, just not of this nature. I was thinking more like tsunamis or a zombie apocalypse. Many of the houses were dark, but a few of them were alight from TVs. Jason's condo appeared quiet and soulless. As we walked up, my back against the stucco, I put my hand over my mouth to stifle a giggle. The entire thing was absurd.

"Shhhhh." Cate was exasperated. She tucked herself against the house. Jason's bedroom window appeared innocent, but she pressed her face against it and peered into his room. Her hand batted my leg excitedly because she detected movement. "He's home. He's in there." She switched places with me so I could also peek through the glass. Any moment a security guard was going to shine his massively bright flashlight at us, and we'd be in the clink. I could just feel it.

73

Jason was in his bedroom, there was no denying it. He and another body were in bed, half covered by blankets. A naked woman slowly stood up, the sheet falling to the floor in slow motion cinematography, then she repositioned herself on top of him and they resumed whatever they were doing.

Cate was trying to shove me out of the way to regain her orchestra pit vantage point.

"You shouldn't see this. Hell, *I* shouldn't see this. We should go," I whispered, uncertain as to the thickness of the walls.

"Move aside." A quiet gasp escaped her lips as she looked inside. Turning to me, Cate tripped over a rock and sent us both to the dirty, wet ground. She fell beside me and then started to cry.

"Be-e-e quiet. Oh my God, he'll hear us." Grabbing her hand to help her up, I took it in mine and didn't let go until we reached the car. "Are you okay? I know. I know. It sucks. He is such an asshole. I hate when they move on so quickly. And usually just for sex."

We sat in my car while Cate lamented over her past relationship with Jason. She knew it hadn't been all she'd cracked it up to be, and it had been mostly ego whenever she'd talked it up. Cate wanted to be married, have a family, and a secure future. Jason wasn't the right candidate, and she'd known that from the beginning. Trying to shove a square peg in a round hole only delayed the universe's plan. Letting life simmer to work itself out seemed to be more prudent than forcing the wrong agenda.

"Was it worth it?" I asked.

Cate nodded, then shook her head and then nodded again. "Yeah, I guess. It's closure, you know. I don't care anymore. He's with someone else, or maybe many people. Who knows?" She smoothed the muddied dress over her scratched legs and pulled a thorn from the material. "Maybe he'll end up with a nasty disease." She snorted.

Closure was difficult but necessary to obtain. Either you didn't care anymore because you'd successfully moved on and to another relationship or because the scumbag told you why he broke up with you. Other times, it was because you'd caught him in bed with a beautiful, leggy woman. All of these scenarios contributed to the jilted party being able to close the door on the "whys" of the broken relationship and not turn back.

I looked at Cate with her streaked mascara tears making black tracks down her cheeks. I reflected on the resolve I could see in her eyes and then said, "I need closure too."

We drove to West Los Angeles and parked the car a block from Jake's house. He'd lived in a cute one story for years, having inherited it from his father. His parents were real estate investors and had bought many single family homes in the '80s before the prices had skyrocketed, which had led to most people not being able to afford them. His house was in desperate need of updating, and I'd joked with him about the oak kitchen and wall-to-wall shag carpet. He had told me he'd been waiting for that woman's touch in his place, because he was a Restoration Hardware type of guy.

"I can't tell if he's home. Let's get a closer look."

Donning the ball caps and Crocs, we embarked on round two. The tequila had worn off by then and I was starving. Atypical of most Saturday nights, we had reached a new level of camaraderie. Our friendship would never be the same.

Music played from the living room as three couples sat around the dining room table, drinking wine and eating dinner. Glasses clinked, and the laughter among them was so palpable that it was apparent these couples had known each other a long time. Aromas of yeasty bread, roasted chicken, and maybe garlic slipped through the window cracks and right into my sinuses. My stomach growled loudly. Cate's sideways scowl would have made me laugh if it weren't for the sobering scene ahead.

It was dim. The only light in the dining room was from lighted candles, but I could make out Jake sitting next to a brunette, her back to me. She whispered something in his ear and then he leaned toward her, kissing her gently on the cheek. Seeing him with another woman made my heart sink. He was already happy and maybe in love. There was a small decorated Christmas tree in the corner, next to the sofa, that shrouded a few wrapped presents. Was one of these gifts for the brunette? Were they at the gift-giving stage already?

Cate and I stood shielded behind a huge, overgrown bush next to the living room window, making it impossible to be seen by neighbors or passersby. The curtains were drawn, save for a ten-inch gap in the middle, which gave the dinner party more intimacy. Cate had her arm linked through mine, and her breath was hot next to my face. I knew she felt sad for me, just as I had for her when we stood outside Jason's window. They had moved on, because that's what men did. They detached their feelings and found interest in someone else.

—~—

After dropping Cate off at her apartment, I drove to the beach and parked the car. It was late and there were a few people milling about in the dark. They looked harmless, so I put my Crocs on once again and walked. The moon was a soft crescent of orangey yellow, which barely illuminated the bike path that dissected the sandy beach. It was quiet, just the way I wanted it. Life seemed different now. It was crystal clear that Jake and I were over. He was never coming back. It wasn't that I thought he would just snap out of it and come for me, or that I wanted him to, but the clarity made my heart heavy.

With sand in my shoes and a rumble in my stomach, I went to McDonald's. A Big Mac and small fries later, I sat among the late-night owls, who also hadn't gotten their chicken pot pie, and wondered how on earth I ended up there—the "life part" of the situation. Life was what happened to you when you were busy making other plans, as some wise person who was too smart for his own good had once said.

"Closing up. Last call!" the only worker left on the late-night shift bellowed.

An elderly man sat quietly outside in the dark, his back leaning against the glass window, and covering up the weekly special—"2 for 1" something. His trousers were stained and torn, and he was wearing only one shoe. He looked at me as I exited the fast food restaurant, wonderment in his teary eyes as I handed him a bag full of hot burgers.

The only signs of life in my neighborhood were the twinkling of colorful Christmas lights adorning balconies and outlining the windows, while I made the short drive home. The $1,800 price tag that was ripped from Cate's dress lay on the kitchen table next to the half-drunk bottle of tequila, a glaring reminder of how an outrageously expensive garment can go from a designer rack at a boutique to being rubbed in the soil outside a lover's window.

The bottle of caramel-vanilla flavored añejo slid down my throat and warmed its way throughout my body until I felt it in my extremities, making it harder to carry myself to bed. "It's just you and me tonight." The quiet bedroom didn't answer, permitting me a retreat to my adolescent years.

"Mom, we don't have any food. I'm hungry." The cupboard doors were open, showing scant supplies of expired cereal and stale soda crackers. A loaf of bread sat on the counter, but the visible green-and-grey hues of mold shining through the clear plastic bag made me want to gag. The putrid odor of rotting meat still hung in the air. Our electricity was turned off again by the city. "Third notice" was stamped in red ink on the correspondence from Seattle Power. I closed the refrigerator door to stop the permeating stench of raw hamburger, which didn't get cooked before we lost our lights and heat, its slow oozing of blood making a red pool on the glass shelf.

"My daughter, a bourgeois!" The whiskey bottle in my mom's hand sailed across the room, smashing against the flowered wallpaper. The once colorful irises and daisies were instantly covered in brownish liquid, the oaky alcohol descending in long streaks toward the floor along with the glass shards. "Well, go buy some! Why is everything up to me?"

She sank lower in the couch, an already deep divot in her upholstered square that was perfectly aligned with the TV. She still wore her nightclothes, not having taken them off for weeks since Dad's funeral. Mom's acrid body odor challenged the kitchen's pungent malodor.

The cookie jar's lid was already on the counter. Our rainy day money was hidden in it. Sometimes the funds were used for cab fare or to pay the babysitter, but they were now reduced to a few one-dollar bills and a hand-full of coins. $3.83. A receipt for five bottles of vodka and a carton of cigarettes was also in the jar—the essentials.

"Name something you take with you before leaving the house," Richard Dawson posed the question to his contestants on *Family Feud*—his voice booming from our TV as Mom leaned in, trying to play along and give answers.

"Car keys … jacket … hat … umbrella … gloves."

Wallet was the number one answer.

Mom's wallet was empty, but I suspected as much. There were three quarters and a dime at the bottom of her purse. I put on my big jacket with deep pockets and slipped out the back door, walking the three blocks to the corner grocery.

Mr. Wilson, who was in his early '80s, had owned the little convenience store as long as we'd lived nearby. His hearing was as poor as his vision. He was talking with a customer at the back of the store, when I shoved three boxes of mac and cheese, a can of tuna, a few apples, and a package of Twinkies in my pockets, exiting the store as quietly as I had entered.

9

New York State of Mind

The flight to New York's JFK airport boarded on time. I sat in my respective seat, 9B, and hoped the window seat beside me would remain empty.

"Is that one available?" An older woman stopped in the aisle, pointing at the vacant spot to my left.

"Of course not," I almost barked at her. "My husband's going to sit here." Well, it could happen. I patted the dark blue upholstery with my hand, indicating where my imaginary spouse would be sitting for the five-hour flight. The woman continued walking toward the back of the plane. It seemed everyone was either paired up or part of a family as they made their way to the Big Apple, a constant reminder that I'd be a solo tourist for the next three days.

A new protocol was being implemented at the hospital, so I needed to attend a medical conference in nearby New Jersey. Hydration IVs were making a big play in the medical field, and the palliative care wing on the floor that I was working on was going to begin with new procedures. The innovative hydration program, with vitamins and minerals, was different from the traditional bag and saline solution that everyone used. The perks were few and far between in the nursing world, and I took them whenever they were available.

Two nights weren't long enough to explore the city that never sleeps, but they sufficed when the blinding snow blanketed every outside surface and freezing temperatures created icicles on my eyelashes. It felt like the deep freezer we had when I was little; we used it to store veggies from our garden and bargain cuts of meat, but when the lid was open, it was so cold that it took my breath away. Manhattan didn't seem to notice and carried on, business as usual. Even though the visibility was eclipsed due to the blizzard-like conditions, the colorful lights and holiday adornments could be seen and felt in the vibrant city.

My mom said I'd traveled to New York City when I was five years old, and in the days before Dad was ill. Remembering the feeling of being a happy family, but not being able to recall actual memories of walking in Times Square or visiting the Statue of Liberty, I took in the sights and sounds like a returning tourist. Believing we'd ridden in a carriage around Central Park and experienced the energy of Rockefeller Center during Christmastime, I felt a bit closer to my deceased parents and my long-lost childhood.

I spent the day walking around the city and needing a drink, but not before visiting the 9/11 Memorial. Because of the cold weather, there were only a few people walking outside amid the memorial and museum commemorating the 2,996 victims who perished that tragic day in 2001. Snow overlaid the inscriptions of their names in the granite.

Later that afternoon, I found a quaint neighborhood-looking pub in Tribeca's newer condo development, which was recently gentrified and had become the new hip area.

"I'd like the angel hair pasta with red sauce and a side Caesar salad, please. What do you have for tequila?" I asked the waitress.

It was a jackpot find, since the little pub turned out to be a tequila bar with every kind of agave-based alcohol. Everyone was happy, eating their dinner with a shot or a margarita. A woman of similar age sat across from me at the communal table. She gripped her fork in one hand, while the other held her phone as she smiled and swiped with her thumb.

"Any good ones on there?" I figured that she was on a dating app.

She held her smartphone high in the air, like it was a conduit transporting her to another world. "Oh yeah. Plenty. That doesn't mean they're decent guys in real life. There's probably a service that edits their photos and writes something clever to hook us single gals. I've dated a lot of guys from here, and they aren't the same in person, trust me. Most times, I'd rather have a relationship on the app than meet face-to-face." I knew exactly what she meant. She was really pretty with short auburn hair and looked like a younger version of *Sex and the City*'s Miranda. "Some of them need to be taught a lesson." My red-haired table partner speared a bite-sized piece of artichoke from her salad and continued eating her dinner.

"I hear ya. I'm from Los Angeles and haven't had any luck with dating apps because of the same situation. Most times, guys never look like their photo. What's the point of that?" I was embellishing and just trying to carry the conversation, but what was I going to tell her? I'm on an app but as a beautiful schoolteacher named Raquel who resembles Jessica Alba, and not yours truly. Trying to explain my reasoning to her was as futile as my self-awareness for doing it. Raquel wasn't hurting anyone, nor was I by hiding behind her fabricated image and likeness.

The woman smiled at me. If I lived here, we'd be friends. She had good energy, and we seemed to be in the same boat of life, or the same lifeboat. It was hard to tell. Then she picked up her glass of chardonnay and we clinked glasses.

She continued, "I think men are the same in every city and in every country. It's in their DNA, and they can't escape who they were meant to be. I'm not trying to be mean or feel sorry for myself, but I really believe they seek a certain woman at a certain time in their lives to procreate and spread their seed, because that's what evolution has created. Dating apps just help us all get there sooner."

She spoke as though she'd just finished a social sciences class at NYU. I liked her rationale, even though I couldn't be as altruistic about Jake and those who'd come before, partly because I had an insider's view through Raquel's beautiful eyes. Raquel not only made me privy to how quickly and easily men could discard their mate and their rationale for doing so, but also to their pursuit of a woman solely based on a photo and a few words. Timing was important in dating, committing, and starting a family, but the stuff in between was exhausting. Relationships needed a daily check-in, to make sure both parties were on the same page and heading in the same direction. It was when one of the two people veered off the path that it blew up.

"Where it began, I can't begin to knowing." Neil Diamond's "Sweet Caroline" started to playing through the speakers, and the entire bar started singing. The "bum, bum, bum" part was loud and cheerful, creating a solidarity among all patrons, which led to more drinking. Men clinked their mugs of beer and air toasted to those around them, while the group of girls at the next table put their arms around each other and swayed to the song, singing at the top of their lungs.

81

The woman said goodbye and wished me good luck. I didn't need it because I had Raquel and weConnect/New York. I fired up the app while sipping on my fourth margarita. From the proximity algorithm, it indicated that there were three men in the bar who were using the service at that exact moment. Mike, Daryl, and Logan. The place was packed, and it was hard to match the men with their profiles and without looking obvious. There were two men at a nearby table, and one of them was practically in the other's lap as they both looked at the guy's phone and then scanned the room. Logan.

He was an architect, thirty-nine years old, originally from Maryland, divorced, no kids, didn't own a car, and his claim to fame was traveling to eighty-one countries thus far. Logan had sandy-blond hair, liquid-blue eyes, and a beard of about five day's growth. He stood up and looked around the room in search of someone. "She's got to be in here. Maybe the restroom?" he asked more to the crowd than to his friend.

Who's he looking for? Logan's photos were abundant. He'd been in Cairo, Beijing, Moscow, London, Perth, and Lima, according to his selfies. Apparently, he traveled alone too. We had something in common. He'd enjoy hearing about my travel plans. I'd start with Paris, of course, and work my way through Europe and down to Africa. Maybe we'd be traveling buddies, getting to know each other's hopes and dreams and then fall in love in Casablanca.

He imperceptibly eyed the smartphone in my hand, my right thumb swiping and scrolling, but continued to look among the many beautiful women who crowed his immediate area. I moved my drink down the long communal table and toward Logan and his friend until I was three feet away.

"Cheers!" I raised my glass to the two men who looked up and acknowledged my presence with a nod. "So, how are you guys? Having a good time?"

The friend spoke for Logan, who didn't seem to want to engage. "Yeah. Great. You?" He answered without concern for my response, looking through me as he got up and walked to the bar. Before I knew what I was doing, I was sitting across from Logan and clinking my glass against his, which was on the table. He was visibly startled by my directness.

"Looking for someone?" I asked as though we were old friends from high school. He made another attempt at scanning the room. I tried again. "You look like you lost somebody."

Logan was appalled that I'd take his friend's seat and answered me as though I were forcing him to decide between eating snails or grasshoppers. "Ah ... yeah. I am. A woman. She's in here, but I can't find her. Her name's Raquel."

I choked on an ice cube and corrected my posture. What were the chances!

"Really? I was just sitting with a Raquel. Kind of blonde, looks like Jessica Alba?"

Logan's eyes widened, and he leaned toward me, ready to pounce like a tiger who sees its prey. "Where is she? Is she still here?" He looked around again, wondering if he missed her after all. His friend returned with two drinks and placed them down, his face contorting in annoyance that I was sitting in his chair.

"Nah, she left. She a friend of yours? No offense, but she was a real bitch. And she stuck me with her bill. Said she was unemployed and on the prowl to meet a rich dude so she wouldn't have to find a job." I got up, expecting them to invite me to stay, but they let me walk back to my table, alone.

Just as "Miranda," my earlier companion at the bar, had said. Men deserved to meet in real life someone like Raquel who could chew them up and spit them out.

—~—

My flight back to Los Angeles was scheduled for early the next morning. All in all, the quick trip to New York was a success. The medical conference was informative and would lead to more opportunities at the hospital, while the Broadway show *Ain't Too Proud—The Life and Times of the Temptations* was reminiscent of the music that played from the radio when I was a child. My mom used to sing the song "My Girl" and twirl me around the linoleum kitchen floor, but that was before she had become a shell of herself and no longer noticed that I was alive.

I sat between two elderly women, who were also at the theatre alone. They were both widows, and neither of them had any desire to meet men or discuss them. They seemed happy to take care of

83

themselves, since they'd had enough of "catering to the opposite sex," as they put it.

The small hotel room off Fifth Avenue felt like a cave, while I sat in my pajamas in an oversized chair, watching the snow fall in cotton ball clumps. New York was as lonely of a city as Los Angeles, but since the dating apps had thousands of members who were looking for that special someone, it was hard to understand that we could all be single and alone.

Travis, forty-two, accountant, collected baseball cards (especially the Yankees), was a single father to a young son, and spent half the time at his cottage in Southampton. His tight, blond curls, green eyes, and big, bright smile made me want to swipe him right, but then, what would be the point of that? It would only make him feel worthy and in demand by hotties like Raquel. He probably didn't need the attention and had plenty of dates. What are these guys holding out for? Why can't two people who find each other attractive start down a road together, enjoying this short time we have on earth? The holding out for a better situation was what kept us all in a holding pattern, to be forever on a dating app until these single men realized they were sixty years old and then they'd take the first woman who would have them. There should be an algorithm embedded within these apps that displayed the amount of days, months, or years someone's date has been active; similar to an expiration date on a carton of milk. We'd think twice swiping right on a man whose profile had been active for three years, just as we'd discern buying the milk that had been expired for weeks. The stuff stunk and would eventually make you throw up.

Closing down weConnect/NY, I curled up under the giant duvet as Manhattan was transformed into a winter wonderland.

—~—

The Los Angeles grind didn't seem as taxing as it had before I experienced the bustle of New York. The weather was warmer, and the people seemed more laid back and not as interested in waking at 5:00 a.m. to begin the workday.

It was Christmas Eve; fake Santa Clauses who shook their bells for donations to a charity, and the people who milled about with shopping bags of last minute purchases to put under the tree all lent to the holiday experience. We didn't have the snow or winter parkas to complete the Thomas Kinkade Studio painting, but there was definitely something in the air that spoke of holiday and that a new year was about to begin.

Many businesses closed for the holidays, but of course the hospital was open twenty-four seven, all year round. Being a single gal, it was nice to have somewhere to go and people who needed me—or expected to see me because they were paying for me to be there. Although it was nice to hang at home with the remote control in one hand and a margarita in the other, it was rewarding to know that I could be of help to patients spending the holidays in the hospital, away from their loved ones.

A lovely thirty-year-old woman named Evelyn was admitted in the morning for an ongoing, pervasive migraine and after many tests and a CT head scan, the on-call neurologist had to inform her that she had a malignant brain tumor, a glioblastoma multiforme. She had moved from France ten years ago and lived alone in the city, having recently broken up with her boyfriend of five years. She planned to move back to Paris the following year, but the attending oncologist told her that she most likely didn't have more than a few months without radical treatment. Rather than sit in the coffee room for my break, I sat with Evelyn and listened to her story of life and love. Her beautiful French accent mixed with a resemblance of Kristin Scott Thomas was captivating. She spoke as though she were narrating a book about a romantic war drama set in the Sahara.

"Would you like me to call Gerald? Maybe the news would be better coming from medical personnel." Thinking that the ex-boyfriend would want to know about Evelyn's illness and be there to comfort her, I suggested that I reach out to him to explain her diagnosis and soften the blow. Gerald was the closest person to a relative that Evelyn had in the country, and she needed the emotional support to get through the next stretch of time.

"Everything's happening so fast." She put her hands over her face, covering her eyes and taking slow, deep breaths. "I wasn't thinking clearly, and now I know why. Nurse Evans, it was all my fault. I drove him away. We broke up three weeks ago, and I haven't heard from him since. I imagine he's moved on, and news like this will make him come back only out of obligation, and that's not how it should be. I am not a, how do you call … a charity case. It's best left alone, madame." She closed her eyes and slowly turned away, her body resigned and defeated, disappearing within the hospital issued blanket. "I'm completely broken. *C'est terrible.*"

Evelyn was discharged later in the day. She was expected to be under the care of a cancer treatment center, but I'd heard from another nurse that Gerald had come for Evelyn. Their tears and cries had visibly shaken all the medical staff. A modern-day love story, without apps or technology.

—~—

Days later, I still had Evelyn on my mind. I wondered if she was going to find a miraculous treatment to rid or reduce the tumor, and if Gerald would stay with her, giving the support she needed. These thoughts weighed heavily on my mind. Sam was a repository to all things "what if," since that's all I seemed to want to discuss.

I goaded him. "If you were in love and she was suddenly cancer-laden, would you leave her because it was too much to deal with, watching the love of your life deteriorate and die? Or would you stay with her just because she was sick and help her through the illness, just waiting for her to expire so you could move on and find love again, or what? What would you do, Sam? Which one of these?"

We spent four concurrent evenings together because his company had closed for the holidays. Sam listened to me ramble about love lost, love requited, and love abandoned. The requisite romantic comedies accompanied the thought pattern that gave me an inside look into Sam.

"Nah, I don't think that way, in hypotheticals. Guys don't do that. That's Mars and Venus stuff, and clearly you've been reading too many relationship books."

I splashed more reposado into his glass.

Sam paused *500 Days of Summer*, turned to me, and shook his head while pointing to the TV screen. He made the claim that a guy in his twenties wouldn't obsess over a woman after she broke up with him but would just move on and meet one of the other seven billion people on the planet and try his luck again. He wouldn't let the movie resume and begged me to start another one, with a more realistic version of life and love.

"Well, what about us, Sam? We aren't in our twenties, but if we were dating and in love and then broke up, would you obsess or just move on?"

"*Us* ... dating?" Sam got up, allowing a low, cynical chuckle to escape his throat. "Are you sick with cancer and dying, or did we break up because you couldn't stop obsessing about relationships? I gotta go. Early morning tomorrow."

He left but I sat there dumbfounded. It wasn't a completely ridiculous idea. Why couldn't we be boyfriend-girlfriend? Although I didn't know what his type was, I knew that we got along better than most friends and couples, but maybe it was because we didn't have to share a bed or bank account.

After fifteen minutes of tossing and turning, wondering about Sam's comment, I opened weConnect.

An interesting guy caught my eye. Max, forty, sales (but of what, he didn't specify), and lover of movies. His brunette, cropped hair and caramel-brown eyes definitely spoke to me. He didn't write anything at all in his narrative; it was completely blank, which was intriguing and disappointing. He either figured that his one photo would suffice or perhaps his life was so boring he had nothing to contribute. Or maybe he was just on to check things out, as was I. Cute Max was swiped to the right for safekeeping. He and Raquel would make a stunning couple with beautiful babies.

The next evening, I checked weConnect, and Max had connected with Raquel. She was beaming.

"Well, hello. How was your holiday, Max?"

He was live on the other end because he responded immediately. "All good. You're very pretty."

Yeah, I'm all that and a bag of chips. "You didn't write anything. Tell me about yourself."

We texted through the app for an hour. It was hard to maintain an honest dialogue without going overboard with who I made Raquel out to be and trying to get to know this guy as Jewel. He was smart and witty but didn't give me much about his personal life. We talked about life in Los Angeles—restaurants, the beach, traffic, hiking trails, people—and about movies we'd seen and enjoyed. Max and I had watched a lot of the same movies that Sam and I had watched together. As impersonal as it was getting to know one another via texting, I didn't know what else to do to move this forward. I couldn't give him my phone number, with me being Raquel and all, nor could I suggest meeting in person. In all the time I'd spent communicating with guys on weConnect, the connection with Max was the strongest and most interesting of any guy. If he was this great from an hour online, I could just imagine how intimate we could become in a relationship. It was worth exposing myself to meet him.

"Can you post more photos of yourself? I need to see more of you and meet up ASAP." I was hoping this would help clarify my interest in him so that I could hatch a plan to meet as Jewel. But then Max disappeared. Poof! He was gone and had unmatched Raquel. This told me that he didn't like our conversation, yet we were texting nonstop. It didn't make sense. Just because I asked for photos, he unmatched us, or maybe he'd just met someone more suitable. I must have been too aggressive, and he wasn't comfortable with me leading the direction. Or did my asking him to meet up ASAP make me sound super desperate, clinging to him like Saran Wrap? Wasn't this an equal opportunity app giving women the confidence to ask for what they wanted? It was hard to know, but as it stood, he was gone. I didn't even get a chance to screenshot him for a memento.

Lying awake that night, I tossed and turned over the events with Max. I supposed I could create a new profile as Jewel and try and find him again, but he probably wouldn't be interested in someone who looked like me. After an hour-long text session with a babe as gorgeous as Raquel and then being discarded like yesterday's newspaper, the chances of him liking or even swiping on *me* would be slim to none.

—~—

Tracey, a medical billing manager for the UCLA hospital group and who was about to give birth to twins, was honored the next week at a local beach hotel to celebrate the impending arrival of her little ones. The baby shower was a combination of pink and blue, and the intended names of Olivia and Oscar were inscribed on the balloons, napkins, and special lunch menu. A small group of doctors and nurses from my hospital was present, enjoying the delicious spread of seafood and sandwiches, as well as a lot of women I'd never seen before. Tracey and I had met ten years prior at a medical conference, but we bumped into each other every few months when she'd visit my ER's billing department. We always kept our conversation on the professional side but knew that if we were in a social setting, we'd be close friends. The gathering of ladies from the Westside and the valley showed me a whole different version of her. She was laughing and taking pictures with longtime associates and friends from college. Not bothering to look at her registry for baby items she'd requested, I enclosed a gift card to a local baby store in a fun greeting card and set it on the table with the other presents.

"Jewel, so glad you could make it." Her stomach was enormous. Since she'd taken her maternity leave three months ago, due to possible complications, I hadn't witnessed her expanding waistline. I tried to hug her but couldn't get closer than a soft peck on her cheek.

"Have you met my husband, Jake?"

Jake, the lying snake, turned around with a crab claw in one hand and a handful of crackers in the other. The color drained from his face. "Uh … hi," was all that was audible from his lips. With disbelief, I stood there, looking from Tracey to my ex-boyfriend and trying to come to terms with what she'd just said. Husband? Tracey had moved on to another guest, letting the woman feel her burgeoning belly. She was oblivious to her husband's discomfort and my unexpected whammy.

Jake stood before me, once tall and arrogant but now suddenly two feet tall and miniscule. That's what being a liar and a cheat will do to you.

"Don't say anything. Follow me," I uttered, but I really wanted to kick him in the groin and leave him writhing on the floor.

Jake had that pleading look on his face, and I suddenly felt sorry for him. He was terrified I'd expose him in front of his wife and her friends for the creep he really was. It now hit me. Tracey was the brunette I had seen sitting next to Jake at the dinner table the night Cate and I had been looking through his window. She was going to have his babies. She was probably also the one he was referring to when he'd told Raquel he was engaged. It just goes to show that you never really know anyone, not the ones you date and certainly not the ones you sleep with. We all have our stories—our lies and half-truths. The only good outcome was that he finally seemed to be committed to someone. He would have to step it up and be a father to twins, and by the look of Tracey, any day now. I knew more than he could ever imagine, thanks to Chelsea and Raquel, which didn't make it easier. But knowledge was power. I also had the power to walk away without another word. Tracey had no idea that while she was in her early trimester, Jake was online trying to meet or hook up with someone who was not her, the mother of his offspring. That really sucked for her, but thankfully, it didn't suck for me. I had dodged that one.

We stopped in the hallway, out of earshot of the party room. Jake stood wringing his hands and looked like he was going to vomit all over the pretty beige carpet runner. He opened his mouth to speak, or probably to try and lie his way out.

I held up my palm in front of his face. "Save it. Just keep your mouth shut 'cause I really don't want to hear any more of your lies. Those babies need a good father, and Tracey needs a great husband. Oh, and stay off the dating apps, or I'll tell her." He didn't have a chance to say anything but just looked at me with a stupid expression. Turning on my heels, I walked back into the baby shower, grabbed two sandwiches and a sushi hand roll and made my way to the valet. Tracey wouldn't notice my absence, as there were so many people who were occupying her time. To stay one more moment would surely cause me to say something I'd regret, and I didn't want to ruin her special day. Jake wasn't worth it.

—~—

Although TV wasn't cutting it for me, it was too early to turn in. But Raquel had earned her keep and was ready to retire. She had helped me in ways she'd never know. Thank you Mila from Berlin. You've been fantastic. A real friend.

Next up, Josie from Australia. Midlength strawberry-blonde hair, thirty-five, optometrist, and avid runner. They'd never miss her from the other side of the world.

I'll call her Amanda.

Sexy Amanda, meet weConnect.

90

10

Mad Max

Although it didn't snow in the Southern California cities, the winter temperatures dipped into the cold sixties, which brought out jackets and scarves that had been forgotten about after they'd been crammed into guest room closets during the warmer months. I put on my red cashmere coat with the faux fur accent and met Cate for an early dinner. Walking towards her table, I caught three very handsome men from the bar, eyeing her with interest. Cate had that effect on men. Although it was easy for her to meet a guy, she didn't seem to have luck finding the right ones or keeping the good ones.

"What do you think about going online?" I asked her.

We shared a burrata and heirloom tomato plate and split a bottle of merlot. Cate was back to her old self again, so I thought she should try her luck anew and cast her net into the sea of single Angelenos. The abundance of good-looking and successful men on weConnect proved that it would require little effort to match her with such a man. She was as fabulous as Chelsea and Raquel, but being a real person, Cate could share her phone number and meet in person. Then she could ghost or block them if she so desired.

"Like weConnect?" It was a weak attempt at pretending that there was a better dating app. Everyone preferred to use weConnect. The competing apps were exclusively for one-night stands and hookups, or used scientific methods and were contingent on questionnaires to match two people. Others were proudly faith, or religious, based or weren't well established. weConnect had the majority of members and was quickly becoming a generic name for dating apps, similar to how Kleenex had become the ubiquitous name for a tissue and a proprietary eponym. Since my mom hailed from a British background, she would ask me to Hoover the carpet, while I used our

Electrolux to pick up dust and debris that collected in corners and crevices.

"No, I'm asking if you feel like checking out Amazon. Of course I'm talking about weConnect. It's time that you get back out there. Stop licking your wounds. They've healed. Be brave, Cate, I know you can do it."

Sometimes she made me feel exasperated, like I had to drag her kicking and screaming into the real world. Why wouldn't she be looking for her life's love, since the wrong one had been removed from her path, leaving room for someone who would treat her with love and respect? Love was the easier of the two; you could love a dog, love your child, and love your partner because you said, "I do" and meant it. Respect was the wild card. Respect was earned over a period of time and was the outcome of challenges and situations after you did the right thing for yourself and those around you. There was a reciprocity element to respect, as one has to give respect to receive it. It's a shared action and feeling that was missing in many relationships. Clearly, Jason hadn't respected Cate, or he would have been honest that she wasn't the one for him.

We fought over the last piece of yellow tomato and then asked the waitress for another order. Cate rationalized her excuse to eat more by saying they were just vegetables and protein. She made a good argument for tasty eating.

Giving her hand a quick squeeze, I said, "I'm going to help you. Let's put you on tomorrow. Come over after work, and I'll have you live and up online for grabs before your second margarita."

"Just because I'm saying yes, does not mean I'm going to date any of them." She took a sip of her wine and almost choked before swallowing. "Hey, isn't that your neighbor?"

Cate motioned with her head toward the lounge that was full of couples who were dining and drinking. A handsome man standing against the large bay window and chatting with a tall dark blonde in red stilettos caught my attention. They were deeply engrossed in conversation, and he was brushing the hair away from her temples in a loving and familiar way.

"No, that's not him, but they sure look good together, like Gisele and Tom Brady."

"Not him … *him!*" Cate physically took my chin and moved it about forty degrees to the left so I could see Sam and a cute brunette sitting at a table together. Their heads were about six inches apart and were laughing over something they were watching on an iPhone. He looked happy. Really happy. I felt sick. What was he doing? Was he on a date?

"Wow. Yeah, that's Sam. I didn't know he was with someone. When did this start?" It was more rhetorical than wanting Cate to respond.

"Why don't you ask him?"

I launched into why that was not going to happen, explaining that Sam and I kept our private lives "private," so I didn't want to hear details. But my words only caused Cate to begin her interrogation. After ten minutes of talking in circles, I finally admitted that I found Sam interesting, handsome, and a great catch. Suffice it to say, I wouldn't act on my lusty feelings, because it was apparent that he didn't, or wouldn't, feel the same way about me. Sam and I had been friends and neighbors for a few years, and if there was a snowball's chance in hell of ending up with Sam, he would have made a move a long time ago. That ship hadn't sailed, because it never made it into the harbor.

Cate segued into an anecdote of her workday, and I half-listened because I was focused on Sam and his date, while letting my mind wander about possibilities of a mutual relationship. Nodding every minute in acknowledgement so that I didn't hurt Cate's feelings, I imagined life with Sam. Our two children would have dark hair, since he probably carried a dominant allele for his black, wavy hair, but I hoped his deep blue eyes would carry through to our little ones. He'd make a wonderful father and husband, ever doting and present.

"He's leaving! I can't let him see me!" I panicked. Cate quickly moved her chair in front of mine, shielding me from his view while I sunk lower in my seat. "How do they look? Together like a couple or first date-ish?"

Cate took out her mirrored compact, like any clever wife would when following her unsuspecting husband, and watched through her 3" x 3" view as Sam and his date rose from their chairs and walked out of the lounge. They walked side by side, neither touching nor speaking. They could be cousins or business colleagues, for all she knew.

Glancing at me with omniscient eyes, Cate then turned to the passing waiter while clinking her empty glass with her fork. "More wine." She applied more lipstick, looking into her mirror. "It was hard to tell, but easier for me to figure you out. What gives? If you like him, tell him. It's really that simple," she nodded sagely. "By the way, what's the big deal if he sees you? It's a free country, isn't it?"

Obviously, I liked Sam. What wasn't to like? The mere fact that we had remained platonic friends over the many dinners, drinks, movies, and sleepovers on the sofa was all the proof I needed to know that the delineated line was to remain intact and should not be crossed. Not to mention that if we'd date, it would most likely result in a breakup and then we'd have to live uncomfortably next door to each other until one of us moved.

—~—

Amanda hadn't made her debut but was almost ready to take center stage. Her real identity of Josie yielded many photos of holding koalas, petting a wallaby, and standing in the city of Sydney with the Opera House in the background, all of which I'd have to crop. Narrowing it down to five images that could place her in Ohio just as it could in Australia, I uploaded the pics to weConnect and wrote a few sentences, giving her a benign profile.

Amanda, thirty-six, entrepreneur, enjoyed skiing, comedies, and outdoor concerts. Cooking, not baking. Coffee, not tea. Wine, not vodka. Candles, not electricity. Walking, not driving. Moonlight, not sunshine.

It was a fun experiment to see which guys would be attracted to Amanda, if only for her crafty narrative. She was also very striking— that is, if you liked that beautiful Amy Adams look.

Kevin, forty-four, self-employed, six foot three, short blond hair, from the UK, loved every brand of beer and karaoke. He looked like lots of fun, with twinkling eyes and a broad smile that spelled mischief.

I swiped right and then … *ding-ding!* We matched. That was fast.

"Hello, Kevin. What do you like to sing?"

"Anything and everything, but fancy Elton John and Oasis. And I have to be completely pissed to do it. Do you karaoke?"

"No, never have. "Me and Bobby McGee," is one of my faves but I wouldn't get on stage. I prefer to watch and cheer the singers on."

"Well, now's your chance. Heading to a pub in Santa Monica with friends. They do karaoke there. You should join. I'll buy you a warm beer."

It didn't take me long to change my clothes and apply new makeup, and within an hour later I was walking into Ye Olde King's Head in Santa Monica which was packed with diners and drinkers. I regretfully ordered a house special margarita and sat on the stool in the corner.

"Is this all you have for tequila? It looks like it was made in my uncle's back yard. Are you sure this is from Mexico?" I asked the bartender but he just nodded and placed my drink on the counter. I could feel a headache snaking its way into tomorrow morning. The overhead lights were reminiscent of an authentic British pub, and if I closed my eyes to the chatter among the patrons, I could swear I was sitting in one of London's historic public houses.

Two thirty-something women were on stage, sharing a microphone and singing horribly to "I Will Survive." Two guys dressed in jeans and matching blue button downs were cheering uncontrollably and then started to dance around their betrothed.

"Those two couples just got engaged—they all met here one year ago today. Great story, isn't it?" a pretty woman with long, dark hair volunteered the ditty. She stood beside me with a beer mug in her hand. The scent of roses wafted toward me when the woman flipped her hair in the air but it was her pretty foreign accent that had my attention. "We're celebrating that they didn't meet online like the rest of the population." She whistled shrilly toward the stage.

"Really? I'm so happy for them. So they met here, at this bar, hanging out?" I asked the woman, patting my hand on the smooth, mahogany counter.

"Heck no! The gals, Avery and Joy, were on a girls' night out, on stage, and singing this exact song. Men eat this up, you know—like an aphrodisiac. What's your go-to song? You single?"

"Yeah, I'm here alone, but I'm just watching. I hope someone sings "Me and Bobby McGee." I love that song. I'm Jewel by the way."

The woman smiled warmly but had a mischievous twinkle in her eyes that I didn't understand until later. "My name is Carys. I'm on holiday from Windsor and the karaoke DJ is a friend of mine." She winked and then walked away. I leaned against the old bar and watched the newly engaged couples' encore.

95

I turned to the bartender, who had just finished pouring a large pitcher of beer from the tap. He tipped the pitcher to the side and let the white froth fall into the sink. "Another house margarita, please. Can you put some tequila in it this time? Thanks," I yelled over the music. He shook his head like he'd never heard that one before.

"Up next, we have Jewel singing "Me and Bobby McGee," the young man who controlled the music announced, while his helper, who turned out to be Carys from Windsor, handed me the microphone.

"You've got this!" Carys squealed, her excitement was so palpable that I almost believed I could do it.

"What? No way! I am *not* a singer ... well, not in public anyway."

The crowd was cheering and clapping, waiting for me to start singing. "Jewel! Jewel! Jewel!" they all yelled in unison.

That familiar sound of guitar strumming at the beginning of the song, made famous by Janis Joplin, filled the British-style pub, and Carys pulled me off my chair and led me toward the stage. I felt like the beef cow that was being prodded to walk to the slaughterhouse.

Before I knew it, I was at the chorus and at the famous line of "Freedom's just another word for nothin' left to lose." The four minutes went by in a flash, and when I was finished belting out the lyrics with reckless abandon, I had forgotten that I had come to meet Kevin, the Brit who enjoyed karaoke.

"Excuse me, but that wasn't bad. I'm Kevin," the very tall, blond man smiled at me while he looked down my blouse and was probably trying to figure out which shade of pink my bra was and how it would look on the floor of his bedroom. "I came here hoping to meet my new wife but you'll do. I usually date supermodels, but after a few pints of beer, don't all the women look more attractive?" Kevin slapped his thigh and guffawed to his own joke. Kevin's face then took on an intense, almost paranoid, appearance while he aggressively combed his fingers through his hair. "Seriously though, did someone put you up to singing that song, like a gorgeous red head?"

Kevin had a pungent odor, which emanated from his armpits and his breath when he spoke, and the worst teeth I'd even seen. He was extremely drunk and kept putting his forearm on my shoulder to rest as though I was a hitching post.

I downed the last gulp of my margarita and looked not-so-charming Kevin in the eyes. "If this is your way of trying to meet a woman, you need some serious help."

Kevin looked stunned. He didn't understand why I'd come across so hostile. "Lady, I'm not trying to meet ya. Maybe just a shag or two. Plus, I have myself a real hottie at home."

"It figures. You're a cheater." And then I added, "You really need to do something about your teeth. Did I just say that? That was my inside voice, wasn't it?"

"Huh?"

I didn't waste another moment and left the pub, deleting Kevin from Amanda's connections midstride on my way to the car. I think we both needed help in the dating department but my ego was feeling quite robust from my four minutes of spotlight while I channeled the great Janis.

Later that night, swiping a few more guys left and right, Amanda came across Raquel's Max. She swiped right, but with hesitation. Why did you disappear, Max? It was getting late and I had an early morning at the hospital. It was time to close the app down when the bells and whistles went off for Max and Amanda. He liked her. Smart guy!

"Candles, wine, coffee, and the moonlight," Max wrote. "Cooking AND baking. Electric scooters."

It was like he already knew how to get to me. Witty banter via text went on for an hour and then I signed off to get some shut-eye. He said he'd reach out again the next night. Thanks to Amanda, I had a second chance with Max.

Sleep overcame me, and I dreamed of meeting Max, the real man behind the keystrokes, who'd take me dancing and dining. We'd travel the world as a doting couple and have brilliant children. He became alive amid the stages of neuronal activity that enveloped my consciousness. As a couple, we were happy and fulfilled, but somehow I had light auburn hair and an Australian accent.

—～—

Cate sent a text early in the day, reminding me that she'd come over later so I could set up her dating profile. It was the easiest upload, since she had lots of recent photos to establish her place on

97

weConnect. She wasn't my competition, because Amanda wasn't going to meet any of these single men over a drink and chicken masala. If I was going to hide behind a fake online persona, then Cate should have her choice of any man in the city.

"I met someone." There, I came clean. Cate wanted details, but all I had to provide was the grit of my texting with Max.

"I thought you actually *met* someone. Like in person. What are you going to do with a texting relationship? What do you get out of that?"

She was right. It wouldn't go anywhere, but it felt good for the duration. If only in my daydreams, I was smitten about someone. Years ago, my college friend, Julia, had a "boyfriend" whom she spoke with on the phone. They had a phone relationship for eight years but never met or exchanged photos. Julia moved to Cincinnati after she graduated, and he, supposedly, lived in Miami. Whenever they were going to meet, he was unexpectedly was whisked away by the CIA to attend a private meeting with the President of the United States or at a Summit with important dignitaries from Iraq or Saudi Arabia. Every secret meeting was shared with her, but this was after it was televised on CNN, absent the mention of his name since he was CIA. We all knew that this guy was probably married and had four kids, or was calling from prison, since they never met. Julia was in love with the idea of being in love, and the fact that this guy was lying to her, learning about the international news like everyone else who watched cable TV, and passed it on to her as his inside scoop, made zero difference to her. Lord help me if my online relationship turned out to be a sixty-year-old man in San Quentin, serving time for armed robbery or murder.

Cate sprawled on the couch, with her feet on the arm rest and her head dangling off the side. "Jewel? So now what?"

It was a rhetorical question, as far as I was concerned, so I ignored her. With my face in my phone, I clicked and clicked, and voila! She was live.

Cate, thirty-eight, pharmacology, lover of animals, fine food, and creative cocktails, world traveler, *parle français*. She had six photos posted that didn't do her justice, because she was very pretty and energetic in real life and that didn't transmit through to digital. She was going to be a hit on weConnect.

"Now you are online and will have hundreds of awesome guys vying for your attention. Pick of the crop." I stood up and stretched. "You're welcome. Now pour me a drink."

Cate rolled sideways and then practically fell on to the floor, making her way into my kitchen. She picked up the colorful bottle of Dos Artes and poured us each a lofty amount.

"Here you are. Straight from Jalisco." She handed me a little glass of the amber liquid. "Cheers to me. Cate from Santa Monica. May she meet an amazing man, ready to date and procreate." She threw her head back and I winced. She treated my expensive tequila like it was dime-store quality.

I walked Cate outside to her awaiting Uber.

"Hey, I really want to thank you for doing this. Jason kind of did a number on me, but maybe I'll meet a great guy from this, who'll sweep me off my feet." She stood before me, looking wistful.

"Yeah, there're lots of guys online but don't get too excited that you'll meet the perfect man for you, right out of the gate. These things take time, like a lot of damn time, so just have fun with it. It could take months to weed out a few good ones. That's what I'm doing, or what Amanda's doing."

"Amanda? What about Chelsea? I thought your name was Chelsea."

I chuckled. "Good night, Cate."

As excited as I was for Cate to have her time on a dating app, I was also envious because she could meet up with any guy whom she fancied or give out her phone number and talk until dawn. I wouldn't be meeting Max out for a drink or chatting on the phone any time soon without coming clean about who I really was and wasn't.

Walking back to my unit, I heard soft music playing from Sam's apartment. There weren't any lights on that I could see or noises coming from within. We also hadn't spoken since I saw him out with his dinner date. Our regular Friday night movie/dinner was on for the next day, so I'd have to wait until then to find out what was new in Sam's life.

Hoping that my cyberdate, Max, would be live on weConnect, I logged on. He hadn't messaged yet.

Dave, forty, single (well, that should be a given, but, okay), extreme animal lover and dog rescuer, extreme sports, and extreme personality. He was extremely good-looking, which presented a

99

conundrum. Amanda wanted to swipe right, just to find out what was really going on with Dave, who looked like a better version of Brad Pitt, if that were even possible, but he was a can of worms waiting to be opened or worse—Pandora's Box. Some things were better left to the imagination, and mine was running rampant. What if I met Dave out at a sports bar, although I didn't watch any kind of athletic movement on TV, and we hit it off, only to find out that he'd make me climb Mount Everest or freebase jump in a wingsuit? I could barely run around the block without hyperventilating and didn't know the difference between the LA Lakers and the LA Kings. The vetting process should be a checklist of twenty questions, provided to men and women, that would help both sexes determine if they should continue with a second or third date. When a couple progresses to the tenth or thirtieth date, only to find the other has a neurosis that can't be tolerated or overcome, it becomes a sunk cost fallacy, and thus, a huge waste of time.

"Hi Amanda. Are you up?" Max reached out. A butterfly was fluttering its wings in my stomach. Keeping things in perspective, as he was interested in Amanda, and not me, I quickly responded.

"Hey. How are things, Max?" Amanda was not a wordsmith.

"Super. Excellent day and now even better that I'm talking with you." We weren't talking, nor would we unless Max had a sense of adventure.

We texted for almost an hour, but again, didn't touch upon anything of personal nature, of which I found odd. It was idle chitchat but interesting, light-hearted, and something to pass the time. Max was really easy to like and enjoy. He didn't ask me anything about my childhood, my faux job as an entrepreneur, or details that could link Amanda to me. I followed suit and kept it easy-breezy. Even if our little text affair didn't escalate beyond keystrokes, Max was starting to feel familiar because of the time we had both invested. It felt like we were in an awkward dance of tentative movements before taking another step forward. Max wrote that he was busy the next night, which was fine because I was going to be with Sam, so we put Saturday night on the books.

I lay awake, thinking about Sam. Seeing him with another woman had made me feel jealous. Texting with Max made me feel desired and hopeful about men in general. But being Amanda made me feel empty and transparent.

100

A daydream drifted into my head of a figurative tug-of-war between Sam and Max. Sam had easy access to see me whenever he wanted, but he never took the time to foster a romantic relationship, allowing us to become something real. We'd known one another for a few years and enjoyed most of the same things, yet he had never made a move. He clearly didn't find me attractive, or he would have at least tried to sleep with me. Salads, margaritas, and movies were all we'd ever be.

Max was new and a bit of a thrill. He was the unknown, the wildcard, and came without the uncomfortable energy of living next to me for years. Max was careful with his approach and didn't take our connection for granted. Just because we were a match on a dating app didn't mean that he had the right to dive into my life, my world of memories and secrets. He was taking his time, allowing me to catch up to where he was. Maybe I was standing beside Sam, both of us holding the rope in the tug-of-war, pulling just enough so Max would come our way.

My hand moved reflexively to my inner thighs. Fingertips felt the deep grooves I'd made over twenty years ago, scars that told my story, like a blind person reading braille. I closed my eyes and gingerly trailed the ridges. Every healed cut was a tear of sadness or hurt from being struck by my mom; the words from her lips had stung as much as her hand. Some of them were carved into my skin to ease the pain of not being liked by a Jeff or a Mike, wondering why they'd ask other girls out on a date and not me.

I retrieved a new razor blade from the bathroom cabinet and sat on the floor. Twirling it between my fingers, the blade picked up the light from the overhead bulb and shined brightly, showing me how powerful it was. I compared its length to the scars on my thighs, and it was a perfect match. Twenty-three cuts, all of them one-inch long, had almost disappeared in my fleshy legs, but not the memories of why they were made. Like a recovering alcoholic and in the AA Program who says, "I'll drink tomorrow," which affords another continued day of sobriety, I thought, "I'll cut tomorrow," and put the razor blade away.

Just before I turned off the bedside light, a text message from Cate came through.

101

"So excited! Connected with this gorgeous guy who loves animals, like me. Omg! Looks like Brad Pitt. Chatted on the phone! He wants to take me skydiving this weekend. Should I go?"

Therein lies the rub. What would Hamlet do?

11

Down the Rabbit Hole

The cafeteria at the hospital was abuzz with activity when I arrived early for work. Moving closer to see what was going on, Dr. Andrew, the anesthesiologist who bragged about Chelsea to his cohorts, was heavily engaged with several of the other doctors and nurses.

"How do you do it, man? You are the stud of the century!" another doctor gushed.

Dr. Andrew was being slapped on the back by Ian, a recently married male nurse, who looked at him like a phoenix rising from the ashes. My interest was piqued, so I laboriously mixed powdered milk and sugar into my coffee while eavesdropping.

Our industrious doctor was at it again. Through snorts and guffaws, he recanted his near castration by the husband of the woman he had relations with the previous night. Andrew had met Elizabeth online, of course, and after several drinks at a nearby bar, they returned to her place in Beverly Hills. Her husband was supposed to be out of town, but at 1:00 a.m., the front door opened, and Andrew made his way out the window, from the second story of their home. The husband had called the police because Elizabeth claimed someone was trying to break in through the window at that exact moment when he'd arrived early from a trip to San Francisco. The husband had believed her malarkey, and Andrew watched the entire scene unfold from his hiding spot across the street. They had Ubered, so he didn't have his car and had to wait until the boys in blue departed.

"What are the chances? Unbelievable." Ian thought Andrew was a god because he'd managed to have sex with a married woman and not get killed by a San Francisco 49er football player—and he had another date lined up with her for the following week.

Elizabeth must be stupid or a figment of Andrew's imagination. He'd lied about being with Chelsea, so it was hard to believe this story was true. He also didn't seem to be walking with a limp, having jumped from a two-story window.

"I came the moment the door slammed downstairs. It was powerful."

The crowd cheered.

The fact that newlywed Ian was in awe of Andrew's participation in Elizabeth's affair made me sad for his wife. How was this impressive or something to admire?

Another nurse on my rounds, Beverly, stood beside me and was as amused as I was to hear the Andrew Chronicles. She gave me a sideways glance and asked, "Do you believe that drivel? Sounds like bullshit to me. Who does he think he is, McDreamy?" Then she slapped her hand over her mouth and doubled over with hysterics. "Oh, wait! I almost forgot! My friend dated him a year ago and she told me he couldn't get it up. A complete limp dick. He expects us to believe he could successfully ejaculate when a two-hundred-pound football player is about to snap off his cock?"

We walked to the fourth floor together and laughed so hard that tears streamed down my face. Because of my watery eyes, it was almost impossible to read Mrs. Donovan's chart in Room 402 or to give Mr. Spencer pain meds through his IV.

"Dear, if you aren't going to give me my morphine drip, at least fill me in on what has you so joyful. I need a good laugh too." The elderly man in the bed grimaced as he tried to reposition himself for comfort.

Irwin Spencer was practically a resident, since he'd been admitted over a month ago. In his late seventies, he had women at least ten years his junior coming and going.

Adjusting his pillows and tucking the grey-and-red blanket around his frail torso, I smiled down at him and sighed. "Just silly hospital antics." His eyes fluttered as he tried to keep them open, anticipating a small dose of morphine to ward off the throbbing pain in his left leg. "My sweet Irwin, tell me your secret. You have lovelies here every day, and the parade just doesn't stop. How did y'all meet?"

He began to cough and his body shook in response. I handed him a miniature container of apple juice and removed the bowl of green Jell-O from his tray, waiting until he was calm once again.

I then added, "Your lady friends are very pretty. It's great you have so much company, 'cause it's not easy being in here day after day."

I noticed the get well cards, balloons, and flowers that covered his table by the window.

"It must be my reputation that precedes me, as they say. I had quite the social life before the cancer decided to take hold of my hip. The ladies called me seven nights a week. I've had more sex in my seventies than my entire life. Thank God for Viagra. I figured if taking those little pills didn't kill me, that something else would, like sickness or a heart attack. Either way, I won, I suppose." He grinned weakly and gave me a wink.

We discussed his love and sex life. I felt like Dr. Ruth in a therapy session. Irwin had met these women on a dating site for seniors. I was happy for him and hoped he'd have a speedy recovery, making it back to life as he knew it, although based on his charts, his cancer was aggressive. A fetching brunette entered his room as I left to continue my rounds.

—~—

Like clockwork, Sam arrived at 6:30 p.m. with a plastic bag of sushi takeout and a small box of dessert from a local bakery.

"Cake too! What did I do to deserve such attention?" I slid my finger over the chocolate icing and put it in my mouth, tasting the butter and sugar. "Yum … this is orgasmic. It really is."

I looked up to find Sam watching me, his eyes fixated on my mouth. He blinked and cleared his throat. "Uh, yeah, I was driving by the bakery and thought I'd take a look inside. It's really nothing special. A friendly gesture." He divided the rolls on plates and set them on the coffee table. Sam must have been ruminating because then he said, "Just a neighborly thing to do."

"I think you're setting the bar, and kinda high, because it's my turn next week, and I'll have to find something to top this neighborly slice of heaven."

Rather than watch a movie, as we had done almost every Friday night for years, we sat and talked while *First Blood* remained on pause in the opening scene. Sam said he was having issues at work and needed my ear to vent. I didn't believe him because he was acting twitchy—talking too fast, not making eye contact, and sitting on the edge of his chair. After ten minutes, he circled around to dating, lightly dusting the topic in that he was interested in someone but didn't give any details. This was the real reason he'd come over. He wanted either my approval or a counteroffer: *Yes, you should definitely move forward with this one, Sam.* Or ... *Why don't you date me instead?* My heart sank deeper into the couch's overstuffed cushions and furry blanket until I was unrecognizable, even to myself as I groveled with my thoughts. *Yeah, Sam, why don't you want to be my boyfriend?*

"How did you meet her? Who is she?" I asked with aplomb, looking him squarely in the eyes and daring him to look away. My confidence betrayed me as a trickle of perspiration slide down my temple.

Sam moved closer to me, our faces within inches from one another. "Jewel, you're sweating. Like a lot. You feeling okay?" Sam had taken a napkin from the coffee table and had attempted to wipe my forehead.

I took the napkin from his hands. "Not really. I think I need to lie down if you don't mind."

After Sam left, I lit a candle and took a hot bubble bath. So much for Friday night fun. Although we weren't a couple, I felt a bit slighted—always the bridesmaid and never the bride. He didn't owe me anything and could date whomever he wanted, so why was I so bothered? Eddie Fremont. That's why.

Eddie had been the captain of my high school's lacrosse team in my junior year. He was impossibly single with curly jet-black hair, cobalt eyes, and a smile that always rendered me speechless. I jumped through hoops to get him to notice me. I joined the cheerleading team, campaigned for school treasurer even though I couldn't even balance a checkbook, and agreed to edit the yearbook, which disappointed the entire grade because I mixed up many classmates' photos and their names. Molly Jensen's headshot appeared with the name Bruce Gold, and Brian Dorsey's photo was paired with the moniker of Annabelle Wade, and all because I wanted to date Eddie. He was tall and charismatic; a Good Samaritan who participated in community service and brought his grandmother to school events as his date. After chasing down the "least-likely-to-do-everything" Brandi Sherwin, a wallflower who was forever in the library and wore heavy brown eyeglasses, Eddie brought her to the junior prom. It wasn't until my first year in college that I found out Eddie was gay.

106

That knowledge should have made me feel better, especially since my persistent advances couldn't have changed his sexual preference. Twenty years later, it was "see me, choose me" time, all over again.

The manifestation of Max was more alluring than the man who lived thirty feet away, so I logged on to weConnect with anticipation. Last week, there were almost sixty connections in my arsenal, but after some time, they'd been whittled down to twenty-two good ones. It wasn't worth my or their time to say "Hi" or "Hey, how was your day?" or "Wow. Thank you for the compliment. That's so sweet of you." Amanda's good looks and impressive profile garnered an outpouring of messages that would take a full-time assistant to answer all the fan mail. I wished that I could trade Amanda's problems for my nursing workload and the anxiety about my uncertain future. It wasn't that I needed to be married or have children, because the single gals in my area who appeared to be happy were evidence that it wasn't a requirement to have a family to feel whole. It was the feeling of something missing in my life that kept me searching for my "twin flame," as my mom had romantically termed it so many years ago.

Max did not disappoint. He'd left a message in my in-box twenty minutes prior, meaning that he'd likely been out on a hot date and had just come home.

"Amanda, how was your day?"

Was it me, or was the vocabulary and lack of effort to write something that was out of the box too complicated for these men? Maybe that was why they were single; everyone stopped trying to impress and lure with thoughtful questions and comments. There were so many available women and men on those dating apps that minimal effort was required to have a conversation. If it wasn't up to snuff for either party, just throw the fish back in for the neighbor to catch.

"Hey, Max. The day was great, thx. Yours?" And then, "So, what kind of sales are you in?"

Crickets.

Ten minutes later, he countered. "Computer stuff. So, what did you do today?" He was fishing, as was I, but I was better at it than he was.

"Really? What do you sell?" The clock was ticking. I needed to know this guy on a deeper level before I invested too much of my time, if only on an app. "What kind of computer stuff?" Hardware, software, laptops, desktops, routers? If he gave me a chance, I could relate to his business. I wasn't completely out of touch with the world of technology.

"Software and things like that."

Things like what? "That's great. Max, which company do you work for?" That was a valid question, and by now, legitimate or not, I had a right to know if he actually had a job. Going Dutch on dates was okay—or even taking turns paying for meals—but out of the gate, a man should pay for the first three outings. Yet if employment was lacking or non-existent, I'd like to know sooner rather than later.

"I'd rather not say. So, have you watched any good movies lately?"

Was his last name Gates or Jobs? Why so secretive?

"Max, please tell me you're employed. Do you have an actual job?"

Poof! He was gone. Disappeared—again. Max must have unmatched Amanda for asking a normal question, and one that would be asked if they were on an official first date. It was a good thing she didn't ask him about his yearly income or to see his retirement portfolio.

—~—

The weekend was fraught with missed calls, one-line texts, and excuses from both Cate and Sam as to why they were busy and couldn't get together. A reprise of The Adam and Sheila show—when my high school boyfriend went behind my back and dated my lab partner Sheila—invaded my Sunday night thoughts. It was senior prom all over again, but this time it was with my best friend and neighbor. The malformed figures of the only two people I depended on floated before my eyes—a pathetic display of deception meant to knock me off-kilter and put me in my place by showing me that things aren't as they seem. Hadn't Sam and Cate always fancied each other, the way they'd sneak glances when they didn't think I was looking, or spontaneously show up at my place when the other was over? They were probably curled up on her couch now, watching a film and sharing a piece of strawberry cheesecake. Sam was softly kissing her head to which she responded with a giggle and then spoon-fed the sweet dessert into his open mouth, like a barn swallow feeds her baby. Then Sam would rub Cate's tired feet while she groaned and slid down to make room for him beside her, anticipating his excited body next to hers. As if on cue, the lights dimmed, the soft piano music started to play, and the intoxicating scent of honeysuckle wafted toward the happy couple, granting a love scene that would rival any Hollywood movie.

I reached for my iPhone. "Cate? Hello? What's going on?" As usual Cate left my recent messages unread.

The bottle of Patron emptied itself into my glass until the meniscus line reached the rim.

—~—

After another week had passed, I messaged Sam since he hadn't checked in or responded to my many queries. He and Cate fell into the abyss, just as Alice had fallen down the rabbit hole. They were on track to meet the Caterpillar, The Queen of Hearts, and The Mad Hatter, while they battled their way out of the fantasy underworld of anthropomorphic creatures. The bottomless glass of tequila prompted me to hallucinate twins and a very smiley, purple cat. I really needed to pass out.

Ding-ding! Cate's one-week late response was halfway between truth and fiction. "Jewel, so sorry. I've been busy with this guy I met online. Catch up this week? Miss you."

"Are you fucking kidding me right now?" I wrote but didn't hit send.

How did this happen so fast? I singlehandedly got rid of my favorite person by putting her on a dating app, and now she was probably shacked up with some guy who was trying to persuade her to move to Nebraska and raise chickens. Single people didn't successfully connect on the first day they signed up on a dating app and then start spending all their time together. This was real life. Who was this Sir Galahad, anyway?

Sniffling from the onset of a cold, I slowly made my way into the bedroom, dragging my feet from the combination of Sudafed, aspirin, and a hidden bottle of extra añejo I'd been saving for a special occasion. Discarded white tissues left a trail on the floor and surrounded the garbage bin, keeping in time with the past almost forty years of my life. "Pick up this mess." "Why are your dirty clothes on the floor and not in the hamper?" "For pity's sake, you live like a pig."

109

The words from years gone by reverberated in my brain like a pickaxe that chips away at the side of an icy mountain, just as mom had chipped away at my youth and soul. My carefully chosen steps over the minefield of trash on our floors, the hills of dirty clothes and towels, and food-encrusted dishes left on the carpet and stairs eventually gave way to my walking through them without regard. My mother's hoarding practices guaranteed that we never had friends visit our tiny house, yet she always chided me for the condition of our home. Somehow I was responsible for all her problems—like I had influenced her to hoard empty Mac and Cheese boxes, Coke cans, magazines, and bags of forgotten clothing. She couldn't afford a housekeeper, but I could.

The room spun so fast that I had to steady myself against the doorjamb, lest I passed out six feet from a comfortable bed. Each labored step I took felt like I was running a marathon. Hurrying through a labyrinth of distorted, mirrored hallways and funhouse decor, I tripped over a fat, white rabbit in a top hat. He was leaning against a bright red toadstool. The rabbit shook his head, pointed his furry finger at me, and admonished, "Clean your apartment, Melissa." The stupid rabbit had me confused with someone else. I ran hard and fast, but every time I turned around, there he was at my side and hopping without effort. My legs were aching from trying to outpace him, and I couldn't catch my breath. I had to stop and rest; I made it to the bed and gave in to sleep, succumbing to everything and everyone around me. The rabbit lay snoring, his head on the other pillow.

The morning sun pierced my brain. "I'm sick and can't come in today. Thanks, I'll try," I said into the phone before I pressed end.

I've always hated rabbits, especially during Easter. The chocolate bunnies my parents bought didn't last very long before I bit off their ears, turning them into brown mice.

—~—

weConnect, I've missed you. Never thinking I'd hear myself say that, I logged on, anticipating new men, new photos, and new opportunities.

Same old, same old.

110

Curtis, forty-four, auto sales, enjoyed walking, traveling, and good food. He stood beside two vintage Ford cars in a parking lot. Locks of curly, black hair showed hints of greying by the temples, and his wireless rim glasses completed the picture of someone who looked more like a librarian than a car salesman. He was a dead ringer for Will Smith in his younger days. Another photo showed him holding an avocado toast with a soft-boiled egg on top. He smiled earnestly as though he were introducing a new invention rather than the latest food craze.

Liam, forty, real estate, technology enthusiast, ocean swimmer. He was cute, almost borderline hot. Liam listed his height at six feet, but weren't they all? The height factor made me laugh out loud. Women appreciated knowing how tall their date would be, on the off chance we'd tower over them in flip-flops, but stature was something to share on the phone or via text, not within the first twenty words allotted in a dating profile. Women who were dead set on being with a man who meets their minimum height requirement could miss out on their perfect match who is just an inch or two shorter than desired. Liam's dark blond hair was slightly wavy, competing with his piercing hazel eyes for my attention. The incentive to swipe right had me at a disadvantage. "Love margaritas and classic movies." Was this guy created by the gods, dropped down from the heavens and into this dating app? Liam must have been new. As Amanda hadn't swiped for over a week, we would have seen his handsome face before today.

—~—

The morning air was damp but fresh with a slight floral fragrance. Spring was trying to make an appearance, although it was technically still winter. The cafe near the hospital was abuzz with coffee drinkers and others picking up a breakfast burrito or croissant. I sat outside with my latte watching people come and go before my shift was to begin. Two guys around my age loitered near the next table, trying to decide to sit or walk with their coffees. The taller one of the two kept looking at me, hardly paying attention to what his friend was saying. I wondered if he thought I was attractive and was going ask me for my number, that was until I noticed they both wore matching black-and-gold wedding bands on their left hands.

"Eddie, what do you think? Should we go? Eddie?" The smaller guy held a takeaway cup with the name Alan written in black marker. Alan stood patiently, trying to divert his husband's interest back to the conversation. He placed his hand on the other man's sleeve and pulled a bit of the light blue fabric toward him.

Eddie couldn't take his eyes off me. I watched him look me up and down, scrutinizing my face and movements. Ignoring his partner, he slowly made his way toward me as though he were an android on his first test run. "Ugh … hi. Sorry to bother you, but you look really familiar." He towered over me, sinking to one knee with an attempt at achieving eye level. Eddie Fremont from high school and reincarnated in Southern California stood before me—a few years too late by my watch.

"Really? Well, you don't. Excuse me," I responded and then picked up my bag, laid the cup on the pile of overstuffed garbage in the nearby bin, and began the three-block walk to work.

Through the din of chatter, I heard Alan say, "No, I don't think so. It says her name's Jewel." Before leaving the cafe's courtyard, I looked over my shoulder. Eddie stood where I left him and watched me make my quick exit while his husband handed him my discarded paper cup that he'd retrieved from the trash. He looked from me to the cup, and then back at me again. His mouth was slightly open as though he were going to say something else to no one in particular, but his eyes said everything. They were penetrating and accusatory. His oblivious husband stood behind him, tapping him on the shoulder.

I didn't have time to play in a twenty-year-old game and was almost late for work. Putting the event into perspective, I looked like every fifth person in the area: blonde, perky, somewhat Californian.

—~—

Tequila-loving Liam didn't lose any time and connected with Amanda, a fan of skiing and comedies. He had no idea how amazing she really was, accomplished and perfect in every regard. Her level of communication skills and knowledge of most subjects was a bonus that any man could only dream of having in a mate.

"Hi."

"Well hi, yourself, Amanda. So, so glad we connected!!"

One thing I'd say about Liam, he was definitely enthusiastic.

"So am I, Liam. How long have you been on this app?"

We texted on and off for over an hour about current events, the city and local happenings, and movies. He was always a step ahead when discussing favorite movie lines, actors, and restaurants in the Westside. If we hadn't met on weConnect, we'd eventually bump into one another at a local hangout or the beach because we frequented the same restaurants, lounges, and cafes. Would he find me as enticing as he did Amanda? He had a great personality and sense of humor. We were about to say goodnight when Liam wrote, "Amanda, what about family? Sisters? Brothers? Parents? What's your deal?"

My deal? Divulging details of my family and childhood wasn't something to just throw out to a complete stranger, exposing my life because someone wanted to know. Should I tell him about my parents' death, lonely childhood, or exodus from my hometown after high school spat me out? Did he want to hear how my mom stopped living eight years before she died, or how my dad left us without a penny in the bank? Would he be interested to know that my mom barely called me by my name, except to scream at me and tell me how awful and disappointing as a child I was to her?

"My parents are alive and well, living the good life on a yacht in the Bahamas, helicopters and all. I have a brother who's killing it on Wall Street, and my sister is a heart surgeon in London. What about you, Liam?"

I was Amanda, after all.

12

Viva Las Vegas

Cate finally surfaced two weeks later. Optimistic that she could take herself off the singles market because she had found "the one," Cate shared her dating stories and future plans with her new man, an NBC Sports commentator. He was into adventure, living large at any cost, and had three yellow Labrador retrievers in his impressive home in the Hollywood Hills. Cate showed me a photo they'd just taken together, paddleboarding in Newport Beach over the weekend. He looked vaguely familiar.

"Wait. What did you say his name is?" I asked, but somehow I already knew.

"Dave!" We spoke in unison, but her eyes grew large and suspicious when she realized that she never told me his name.

She breathed in noisily and appeared visibly worried that I'd say something to dissuade her from the new beau, and her eyes squinted which caused a massive set of deep grooves in her non-Botoxed forehead. "Jewel, how do you know him? Please don't tell me something bad. I really like him."

Amanda had seen Dave a few weeks prior on weConnect. I couldn't tell her that I had steered clear of him because of his extremisms. Cate seemed settled with him, even just three weeks out of the gate, so who was I to be a spoilsport?

"We've spent all our free time together. He really gets me, which is more than I can say for anyone who came before him."

It just went to show that you couldn't judge the proverbial book by the cover, but I'd hold off throwing an engagement party for Cate until the honeymoon period was over.

"I'm looking forward to double dating—that is until I find someone to date."

Not divulging too much of my weConnect goings-on, I explained that the sea of fish was a bit scant, and I was lying low these days. Actually, I was playing it ultracool with Liam. We'd been texting almost every day, but the messages were short and sweet—hopefully not like Liam. That is, the short part. I was in a rush to ride off into the sunset but didn't want to scare off every guy off by being too inquisitive, even though Liam hadn't shared his life story yet. Giving this micro-relationship an expiration date, I settled on two months.

Sam seemed occupied most days but made time for our Friday night movie. He'd come over the previous evening and brought my favorite pasta and turkey meatballs.

"Whatcha havin?" I nodded toward my bar.

"Geez, Jewel. I was hoping you'd have something good here to drink," Sam joked. He'd used that line one too many times. "Turn around for a sec. I want to see if you know your tequilas." He had me face away while he filled five shot glasses with different tequila brands, but they were all within the amber spectrum of reposados and anejos so they were difficult to judge by appearance alone.

"Don Julio añejo … Patron reposado … Clase Azul repo … Ocho añejo … and 1942. How did I do?"

Sam smiled and leaned in to smooth the hair from my eyes. My heart skipped a beat, and we both froze for a nanosecond. He swallowed a bit too loudly and then turned away.

"Ah … wow … if nursing doesn't work out, you can always be a quality control tester for Patron," he mused. He was trying to be nonchalant, but I could tell he was slightly rattled by touching my face. It was flattering. Maybe he liked me, or he was just unnerved by the close proximity. He smelled woodsy, which was either his deodorant or aftershave. Sam had let his hair grow a bit longer, and coupled with the week's growth of facial hair, he had that rustic, countryman appearance.

"You know I love nursing almost as much as tequila. Oh, Sam, I forgot to tell you. I won't be here next weekend. It's my birthday, and I'm going to Vegas with Cate."

"No kidding? I'll be there on Saturday night. There's a trade show during the day, and my company has a booth. Let's meet up. We can celebrate." Sam seemed excited and scared at the same time. I was the one who had just drunk five shots of tequila and should be out of sorts, not Mr. Stoic, but it was fun to watch him squirm. "Where are you staying?"

———~———

The week seemed like the movie *Groundhog Day*, as Monday's hospital traumas spilled over to Tuesday and then to Wednesday. Mr. Choy in Room 419 had multiple surgeries for three faulty heart valves, and by Friday morning, his family had been called in to say their goodbyes. He'd moved to Los Angeles from China the previous year with his family of beautiful twin daughters and a wife who looked like an older version of Fan Bingbing. I'd learned that age wasn't always the definitive marker with heart disease, and even someone as young as Mr. Choy, who was fifty-four, could succumb to cardiovascular degeneration.

Mrs. Choy and her girls were asked to wait outside while the attending physician performed a few tests. They'd been at the hospital throughout the night.

"Can I bring you girls something to drink? There's a little fridge in our kitchen. I'd be happy to get some Cokes or juice." The fifteen-year-old twins shook their heads, their eyes cast toward the floor, but the mother looked at me with strength and knowledge.

"Thank you, but we'll be fine." She simpered but more to herself than to me.

"Yes, of course … Mrs. Choy, my condolences to your family and what you're going through. Please let me know if there's anything you need. Especially for your daughters. We are all here for you."

I picked up my clipboard and was about to leave when she continued, "And you'll be fine too."

"Me?" I whispered, pausing for a moment, not certain if I'd heard her correctly. "What do you mean?"

Her voice changed to a slow delivery of specific words, as if in a trance. "You'll enjoy your travels and the people you meet. Don't look back. No calls, no messages. Those days are over. Take what life offers, with no regrets. Adventure awaits." The message was spoken as though read from a fortune cookie. Before Mrs. Choy and her daughters reentered the hospital room, she turned back to me and said, "Really cool hair. Love the pink and orange."

—~—

"Who's knocking? Cate, did you forget to put the Do Not Disturb sign out?" I asked. Our Las Vegas hotel room overlooked the busy boulevard of visitors walking by at all hours of the day and night.

"Delivery. Delivery for Room 1539. Hello?" someone said from the other side of the door as the knocking continued.

Cate opened the door to a stocky man with abundant tattoos that snaked their way up from his arms and chest to his neck and head. *Mi vida Mi manera* was the message in cursive that was creatively penned in dark blue ink in the man's skin. At 11:00 a.m., Cate still wore pajamas and her hair looked like freshly spun cotton candy but she offered no apologies to the deliveryman who was holding an impressive bouquet of flowers. Peach, pink, red, and white roses, as well as exotic flowers and greens filled a massive vase.

Reentering our room with the arrangement, Cate displayed a quizzical expression. "It's because you rocked on the slots last night. It must be you because I lost all my money. Look at these stargazers! And the peach roses are so pretty. Nice job, hon. Now, let's go for breakfast." Cate set the glass vase on the table in the center of the room and then took off her top, ready to shower. The aroma of the fresh cut flowers had already wafted toward me.

"What? I made a lousy thirty-five dollars in three hours of plugging quarters. No ... no. The card says, 'Happy birthday Jewel. Looking forward to seeing you later. Hugs, Sam.' Cate, these are from my neighbor. Wow. What do I do with this gesture?" Dumbfounded, I doted over the many flower varieties, moving the colorful sprays to accommodate the widemouthed vase. "Well, what do you think?"

"Besides you being an excellent floral arranger, I think that Sam wants to be lucky at the poker table and with you. These things usually start with an unexpected flower delivery in Vegas by an Adam Levine wannabe and go from there."

Then she retrieved a small box from her suitcase and handed it to me. "Since we're giving gifts ... this is from me. I know you're going to love it!" she squealed. "Open it!"

I was overwhelmed. So far, it was the best birthday I'd ever had. As I lifted the lid on the little brown box, Cate's face was just an inch from mine. A gold necklace looped through a colorful butterfly pendant sat inside the little box. I caught my breath for a moment.

117

"Remember when we were at that jewelry store last month and you saw it in the window? I went back for it. Of course I paid for it." Cate laughed as though the joke were only meant for her.

"It's ... it's beautiful. I can't believe you got this for me. It's really too much, Cate. I wish you wouldn't have." I truly meant that as I leaned over and gave her a hug so that she wouldn't notice that not only did I hate the necklace but I also wouldn't ever wear it.

We ate breakfast at the Aria Cafe, amid the many late Saturday morning hotel guests. My egg white croissant and Cate's scrambled eggs on English muffin helped fill the acidic holes in our stomachs that had been left behind from our night of drinking. We studied the Build Your Own Bloody Mary drink cards provided on the table, which looked like general election ballots.

"Double shot of Herradura. Check. Extra Tabasco, medium spices. Check. Citrus salt rim and three dill spears. Check." We handed our cards to the waiter for the specially concocted Mexican Bloody Marys. One more drink card later, and we were ready for the Nevada sun.

Lying poolside with a snoring Cate on my left and an oversized, pasty-white man from Germany on my right, I logged on to weConnect to see the variety of men offered in Las Vegas on a Saturday afternoon. Before my prospects populated, the paperback of *Der Report der Magd* fell off the barrel-chested man and on to the wet cement between our chairs.

"Oh, *The Handmaid's Tale*. I love the series."

The man grunted, grabbed the book from my hand, and rolled over to continued baking in the sun.

weConnect works on a proximity algorithm, in that it searches the members online at that time and within the desired radius and then cross-references them against age, education, etc., and the interests you are looking for in your new mate. Then, voila, you have a list of possibilities within your new location. It was like using Google search to find a date with +hot, +tall, +kind, +positive, +funny, +intelligent, and +adventurous.

Manfred, forty-six, international exporter of precious gems, enjoyed snowshoeing and telemarking. What in the world was that? I wondered if he'd misspelled the word and meant to say that he likes *telemarketing*, as in when those annoying phone calls come during dinner, and the person on the other end is trying to sell you solar panels for your Seattle apartment.

Juan, thirty-eight, movie director, lived in Spain, loved to gamble and drink fine whiskey. In Vegas for a week. Meet for drinks, dinner, dancing. DM me.

A dark blond hottie with bright, hazel eyes smiled from my smartphone's screen. What? It can't be. "Cate. Wake up. Cate!"

"Oh my gawd, what is it?" She turned over to reveal a checkerboard of chaise lounge impressions on her hot, sweaty face. "Please tell me that you just saw Zac Efron in a Speedo."

"No, but that would be a great birthday present. Cate, that guy, Liam, who I've been chatting with online is here in Vegas. On weConnect. Look!" His location was within ten miles. "Should I text him or just wait?"

"I'd wait. What if you and Sam are supposed to hit it off? Liam will still be around when you get home."

"Yeah, I guess you're right. Cate, do you believe in clairvoyance? Or psychics?" I shared the story of Mrs. Choy and her cryptic words. "And she said I have cool hair. Mine's just an average hairstyle. There's nothing cool about it. Just regular blonde. She said it was pink and orange. What do you think she meant?"

"It sounds kind of creepy and doesn't make any sense. She was probably losing it because she had to say goodbye to her husband. I wouldn't pay any attention to it." Cate sat up and adjusted herself and then took two more drinks from the pool waiter. She fit right in amongst the other pool side beauties—her amazing hair that was long and thick was easily swept up and piled high in a haphazard bun. Shimmery gold strands had escaped the elastic band and framed her face that was pink from the desert heat. "Oh Jewel! I can't wait to see you wearing the necklace tonight. It's perfect for you."

I smiled; a tight, horizontal line formed across my forehead, which screamed into my ears and wanted to slap Cate into the next day. Please stop talking about that damn necklace.

"Can we have our bill please?" I asked our pool waiter before he walked away.

The cute server stopped and put his hand on my leg. "Ladies, I don't have a tab for you. I thought you were with the chubby fellow beside you, so I put your drinks on his tab. He already paid, so I guess you're good to go!" He winked and then walked away.

I clinked glasses with Cate. "This day is full of surprises! My birthday just gets better and better."

—~—

The Unknown Bar in the lobby of the Palms Casino Resort was a scene out of a commercial for Las Vegas tourism. The constant ding, ding, ding of slot machines and shouts of victory from the tables overtook the chatter from the glamorized visitors at the casino bar. Patrons occupied almost every seat or stood in small groups with pretty cocktails, positioning themselves for passersby to admire their sparkly evening attire. Before Sam's scheduled arrival, the couple next to us gave us the spiel about the dissected shark by artist Damien Hirst.

"It's a thirteen-foot tiger shark from Australia," the woman who was part of the couple informed us. The massive fish was sectioned among three boxes of formaldehyde, adding to the decor and inspiring conversation. "Kind of New Age art."

We sipped our ginger and elderberry infused margaritas, while we were mesmerized by the shark art and the couple's evening attire. The aging wife wore a hot-pink, sequined tube top, which competed with her snakeskin pants for attention. The husband, who looked curiously like Wayne Newton, wore all white and was dripping in diamonds and gold. He looked as though he were a bride-to-be at the Graceland Wedding Chapel on Las Vegas Boulevard.

Cate snickered as she watched the couple and then whispered in my ear, "What a woman won't do for a Chanel bag."

"Jewel!" Sam and a colleague walked toward us with drinks in their hands. "Jewel, happy early birthday. Cate, so nice to see you again. Ladies, this is Troy, my vice president of marketing."

Formalities were exchanged in the posh hotel bar. "Jewel, you look so pretty in that dress. I've never seen it before."

Well of course you haven't. You've only seen me in sweatpants and the occasional pair of jeans. My sparkly blue dress with its white, drapey collar fit right in among the other flashy outfits worn in Las Vegas. Cate wore black leather pants and a glamorous sequin blouse, making her look like a *Vogue* cover model.

Sam tapped his friend on the arm and spoke in a tone that sounded possessive, as though laying claim to some newfound treasure. "Jewel and I have been neighbors for a few years. We're very close." He bent down and gave me a kiss on the cheek and then asked me, "Whatcha havin'? I'm buying. Another round for the ladies." Sam was drunk.

—~—

After a few cocktails later at the Bound Bar, we arrived at Chandelier and were lucky to find a table for four. It was nearly midnight and Cate was spent. She almost fell asleep at the table, so Troy offered to Uber her back to her hotel.

"The sun at the pool did me in." It couldn't have been the eight margaritas along the way.

"Text me when she is safe at the hotel. Thanks, mate," Sam said to Troy as he and Cate made their way out of the lounge. Then Sam turned to me. "I guess it's just you and me."

We went to Caesars Palace and commandeered the cheapest blackjack table we could find.

"Fifteen dollars a hand. Not bad for this place."

Sam seemed to have the lay of the land and knew that fifteen dollars, or about the price of three lattes at Starbucks, was a good deal.

The dealer explained that since it was after midnight and we were in the crappy section, or the less popular area for tourists, it was more affordable. The little stacks of chips materialized and disappeared as rapidly as taxi cabs in Times Square. But after an hour, we each had turned a profit.

"How much is this?"

After Sam did a quick count, he said, "Would you believe around $300 each? It almost beats going to work!"

I offered my chips to Sam. "You should take these. I didn't thank you for the amazing flowers and they must have cost a fortune." My outstretched hand showed a few red and blue casino chips.

"I wouldn't hear of it. Happy birthday to my girl. You deserve it. Now let's cash these in."

After exchanging our plastic for paper at the cashier, we decided another round of drinks was needed to celebrate. "Sam, do you mind watching the bartender make our drinks to make sure he actually adds tequila this time?" I asked him. Who do they think they're fooling?

It was past 2:00 a.m., but neither one of us was tired. Sam rationalized that it was because of the oxygen that casinos pumped in. An urban legend, I responded.

"Let's walk back to the hotel. It can't be far."

It was far. We walked The Strip together; Sam's arm was around my shoulders, making us look like a real couple. His body was strong and protective, and his sweet breath touched the top of my hair with every exhale. I could feel his heart beating through his jacket, or maybe it was my heart that was pounding—palpitating and freaking out over new territory with my platonic neighbor.

"Ahhh!" I stumbled and pitched forward. Sam caught me before I fell on my face.

"Where do you think you're going? I can't let you out of my sight."

I felt something between embarrassment and pride at having a tall, handsome man at my side, protecting me from being Vegas roadkill.

We arrived back at the hotel, where Sam saw me safely to my door. "Where's your key?" he questioned.

I fumbled in my purse for the piece of plastic. Exhausted and tipsy, I collapsed on the carpeted hallway while the contents from my clutch spilled out, displacing lip glosses, credit cards, and my phone.

"Oh, look—" Sam pointed—"a twenty-dollar chip we didn't cash in. It's mine for safekeeping." He flipped it high, watching it twirl, and tried to grab it in midair but then tumbled on top of me.

He was surprisingly heavy. It had been awhile since I'd felt the weight of a man's body. Sam took me by the waist and helped me up, but before we steadied ourselves, the Earth swallowed us for a moment as he held my gaze.

"You have … beautiful eyes … and a sexy mouth." Before I could make sense of what I'd just blurted, the space between us disappeared.

Soft lips brushed mine, while one of his hands held the back of my head and the other rested on the small of my back. My arms encircled his waist, as I held him tight, not wanting the moment to end.

"Hey guys, come to my room for another drink. I've got plenty!" A group of late-night stragglers infiltrated our scene, romping toward us and chatting amongst themselves, unaware of our intimate moment.

Startled, Sam backed away and bent down to pick up the rest of my things. He glanced at me sheepishly while he picked up what appeared to be an obscure looking credit card. "Here's your key. Now you don't have to sleep in the hallway."

Sam placed the card in the slot, but the door opened only a crack. Cate had engaged the metal security feature from the inside, so unless she removed it, I *would* be sleeping in the hallway. She was in a deep slumber as our calls of "Cate, Cate wake up. Cate!" through the inch space didn't elicit a response.

After a few moments, Cate's face appeared in the crack of the door. She uttered a loud and annoyed "ugh."

She closed the door and then reopened it wide, giving us access to the room. "It's after three. I hope you partied for me too." With that, she turned and reentered the semi-private sleeping area, almost diving back into her bed. "Oh, happy birthday, hon!" she bellowed from under the duvet.

We stood, unyielding to one another. The silent, dark room made it obvious that the night was over. Seconds ticked by and I wondered who was going to speak first.

"I have an early flight, so … um, happy birthday." Sam gave me a quick peck on the cheek and left, not turning to look back.

Seriously? We almost made it to the finish line—me with the handsome neighbor in Sin City and he with the ever supportive and wistful friend. We could have continued our romantic interlude from the evening into the wee hours of the morning and then we'd further discover our feelings for each other when arrived back in Santa Monica. I'd show him which of my dresser drawers that he could keep his socks and underwear and find out exactly how he likes to have his eggs cooked. I touched my fingers to my lips. They were still quivering from our moment in the hallway. Happy birthday to my girl, indeed.

The city lights were radiant at 3:14 a.m., accentuating the many pedestrians walking the boulevard, and even from the fifteenth floor, they appeared to have an agenda and a fun destination. The night was still young as far as I was concerned—and so was I. I grabbed my handbag and room key, as Cate's purrs escalated into snores that rivaled most men's sleep noises.

The casino at the Aria hotel was bustling. Tables were at capacity, and the slot machines were vocal with dings, rings, and shrieks from winners and losers. I was feeling lucky. After thirty minutes, my stack of chips at the roulette wheel had doubled in size.

"Well look at you! Lady Luck, be mine." A dark-haired man wearing a beige cowboy hat sat next to me and piggybacked two black chips on top of mine, which had claimed number five. He winked at me and extended his hand. "Wayne."

He had a tan face and arms peppered with freckles but it was his distinct Texan accent that overtook the atmosphere, commanding attention. He looked as though he was used to being heard. I'd always had a thing for strong men with accents.

"Hello, Wayne. Nice to meet you." I slid my hand into his, which he squeezed ever so slightly, exuding body language of which only those awake and alert in the middle of the night could relate.

"Number five, red!" The dealer interrupted our exchange and placed a small, silver weight on top of our chips. He pushed a stack of gold chips in Wayne's direction and a sandcastle of black chips toward me.

"Oh my gosh, you just made like $7,000 dollars!" I gushed.

"Yeah, and you didn't do so badly yourself, pretty lady. What'd that be? Almost a grand? It's what we call a win-win. And what's the significance of five?"

I shrugged and looked at Wayne, batting my eyelashes. "Oh, it's just my favorite number. That's all. You were quite sure of yourself to risk losing $200."

Wayne looked down at my cleavage and then into my eyes. "Nah, I'm just sure of you." He placed his right hand on my inner thigh and then slowly caressed it. He was good-looking, in a younger Alec Baldwin sort of way. He leaned toward me and kissed my neck—his lips were soft and demanding. Wayne smelled of something familiar, like frankincense and sage. His scent not only captured my senses, reminding me of Sam, but the combination of a windfall at the casino and a handsome, secure man at my feet sent me into a sexual frenzy. My ovaries cried a little.

"I'll cash out please." I surrendered my chips toward the dealer while he exchanged them for a pretty gold disk.

"Be right back."

Wayne's silence spoke volumes. I could sense him watching my butt as I walked toward the cashier. Our eyes locked as I returned to our table, his gaze as steady as a marksman before taking his shot. I felt a bit like prey but I didn't care. It was my birthday.

124

I cleared my throat and smiled awkwardly. "I'm rich!" My open palm showed my winnings for the night. I really wanted to throw the bills in the air and let them rain down on me like confetti, alerting gamblers around me that I had beat Las Vegas. My losses were not going to help build another casino.

"No, sunshine ... I'm rich. Mega-rich. I'm in the oil business. I'd like to see you on my yacht in the Caribbean, drinking the finest of champagnes while we sail south. I'll take you shopping ... buy you whatever you want. I have a G4 waiting at the private strip, all gassed up and ready to go. You in?" His left hand reached for his drink. The overhead lights caught the gold in his wedding ring.

I laughed but more out of incredulity. "And your wife? What would she think? Will she be joining us?" I was about to move to another table when he took my arm.

Wayne had pulled me so close that I could feel his erection. He reeked of all-you-can-eat salad bar and cheap cigarettes. His dress shirt showed many rings of sweat stains coming from his armpits, indicating that he'd worn it throughout several meetings in the day. When I looked at his eyes, I was moved by that longing that many men had who'd suffered from heartache possessed. I'd seen it hundreds of times at the hospital. He let me go and took a step back so that we had distance again.

"Uh ... yeah ... the ring. She died last year. Em ... Emily. I ... I ... shouldn't wear it anymore. It's just hard to take it off." Wayne focused on the wedding band on his left hand, turning it reflexively with his fingers. "Breast cancer."

"Oh. I'm sorry. That's so sad." I had just mocked his late wife's memory. Smoothing my clothes that had crumpled against Wayne's body gave me a moment for composure. "Do you want to have a drink? It's on me." I pointed to the nearby barstools and then flagged the bartender.

"Hi there. Can we have two ... what are you having, Wayne?" He'd made his way toward me and sat on the next stool.

"A bottle of Cristal. And a charcuterie." He placed his hand on mine and lowered his voice. "This is my treat ... luck be a lady. What's your name, by the way?" He repositioned himself on the stool so that my knee was inside of his thighs. "Let me guess. Jennifer? Amy? Sara?"

"Close. My name's Vicki. After Vicki Stubing of Love Boat. My mom loved that show." She really did.

Wayne met my champagne flute with his and a small "ting" was shared between us. "Cheers to you, Vicki Stubing. I'll be your captain for the night. All aboard!"

The hour passed, and the sun was threatening to make its appearance—at least, according to my watch, since there never seemed to be windows in casinos. "This has been lovely, but I should go and catch a bit of shut-eye before checking out. And I have a morning flight to O'Hare. Thanks for the nightcap, Wayne."

"What time does your flight leave for Chicago? Maybe we could have breakfast together." Wayne was pulling from his bag of tricks, anything to make me stay. "I want to see you again."

He followed me through the casino and down the hallway, toward the elevators. Once in, he pressed thirty-one for the penthouse floor while his other hand moved mine away from the button marked fifteen.

"Fancy." I turned to him and tried to tame my disheveled hair, feeling a bit nervous, knowing I was going up to a stranger's room. I was going to have birthday sex.

"Only the best, baby, only the best."

The ping of the elevator told us we'd reached the top, and I slowly peeled his hand off my ass. "Easy, tiger."

Wayne's pores emitted a pheromone, an animalistic scent that screamed to me "we are going to have a fucking awesome time in the next thirty minutes." I'm sure I had my own scent to share at that point. I thought back to my afternoon selection of a bra and panties, wondering if I'd worn the black lacey bra and matching underwear or a mismatched set. He probably wouldn't even notice.

Wayne's penthouse suite was straight out of a movie. I half expected to see Zsa Zsa Gabor walk out of the bedroom. He draped his jacket on the red leather couch, which was about twenty-feet long. It snaked its way along the massive floor to ceiling windows that looked out over the city. The sun was rising, just as I had suspected.

"Glass of wine? Beer?"

"No thanks, Wayne. I think I've had enough. Really great suite you have here." I placed my palms on the perfectly clean windows, as though I were going to be body searched by a policeman. Frisked, handcuffed, and booked for indecent conduct.

Wayne moved his hands down the length of my body and then lifted the back of my dress and pulled down my panties. I braced myself against the glass and let him have me. It wasn't because he was hot or that I was severely sex deprived, which I was, but rather I was trying to make up for what was missing in my life: raw, deep feelings. Not the emotional kind as when you are rejected by a love interest or your dog runs away, but that feeling of being stabbed in the heart with a dagger, while you're left standing with your soul spilling out on the pavement and then beg for more because it had been a long time since you felt something. Kind of like that.

Wayne's hands cupped my breasts and pulled me close, his breath hot and heavy in my hair while he had his way with me. Despite barely knowing this man for an hour, it wasn't a horrible experience. There wasn't any kissing, caressing, or foreplay. No promises of tomorrow or even a compliment on how fit my body was at almost forty years old. "What happens in Vegas, stays in Vegas" rang in my head like music at a rave. I barely noticed that he was finished. All of two minutes. I mentally checked "one night stand in Las Vegas" off my list.

"You made me really excited," he explained, but not as an apology but a mere fact. Wayne wasn't the type of man to make amends for his sexual shortcomings. His hands moved to my waist, and his lips grazed the back of my neck.

"Mind if I take a quick shower?" I escaped his grasp and was already unzipping my dress and walking toward his bathroom.

The rinse felt good because I needed to rid myself of his odor. After I showered, I stood naked in the apartment-sized bathroom and listened to Wayne talking to someone on the phone from a distant room. Something made him laugh, and his roars pierced my eardrums. He was a bit of a pig—wet towels, tighty whities, and socks were strewn on the bathroom floor. I took the opportunity to rifle through his toiletry bag. A plastic bottle of blue, diamond-shaped pills mocked me from behind the Crest toothpaste, almost a parody. Yeah, yeah, touché. If it weren't for the Viagra, I'd be sitting in a bathtub, alone. Or was that a commercial for Cialis?

As I was putting my dress back on, Wayne came into the bathroom and handed me a glass of orange juice. "You'll leave your number for me, won't ya, Vicki?" He placed an old-fashioned pen and paper in front of me. He'd changed into sweatpants and a T-shirt. The bravado he'd presented at the roulette wheel was nowhere to be found on this Wayne. He looked as lonely as I usually felt, and his forty-some years had been replaced by a boyish version of himself, a young, hopeful lad.

I wrote down my number and finished the juice. "You take good care, Wayne." I set the paper down on the bathroom counter and without another word, I walked out of the suite.

Riding down the elevator to my floor, I knew he was holding my discarded butterfly necklace his hand and looking at my phone number: (555) 555-5555.

13

Twenty-one Flavors

The winters in Seattle had always been wet and dreary. I'd wear my makeshift snowsuit while playing in the backyard, hoping for snow to fall. It rarely did, but my dreams of making angels on the white, powdered ground kept me staring at the sky, waiting. I was nine years old. School had been closed for two weeks over Christmas break. It was time to go back but then a blizzard blew in, and since the city wasn't prepared with snow removal machines, school was closed once again. My friends took turns gathering at each other's houses, except mine, to construct snowmen, which didn't last for more than a day or two before the temperature rose and they melted like the Wicked Witch of the West.

Finding love was like making a snowman. Start with a hand-sized ball of tightly squeezed snow and then roll it forward, collecting more snow from the ground until the ball becomes the size of a beanbag. If the snowball breaks during the rolling process, try and put the pieces back together to repair it, or just start over with another ball of snow. After three of these rather large, snowy masses, you might be in love. Liam was my little snowball.

We exchanged weConnect messages every night. The text was proper and informative, just like people who hadn't met or seen one another, even by video, would write. Nothing of a personal nature was discussed, such as careers, childhoods, or background details, but just knowing that Liam would respond to my texts made up for the exodus of Sam. Three weeks had passed with no sign of my neighbor, and it was like he fell off the face of the earth. He replied to my one and only text about our Friday night dinners with "Can't. Busy. Sorry." How quickly they forget.

After I pulled the letters from my box marked 209, a peek through the clear plexiglass for 211 showed that Sam's mailbox was full. He'd usually give me a heads-up so that I could retrieve his bills or important packages before he went out of town. Apparently, what happened in Vegas had followed us to Los Angeles.

—~—

"Dave and I are still in Banff. Home tomorrow night. Call soon. Love you!"

Cate's Saturday night text from her heli-skiing trip in Canada almost sent me over the edge. Now they were traipsing around the world, like a new couple does before they settle down to marry and raise a family. The next thing I'd hear was that he had proposed to her while trekking through Kathmandu. That wasn't what I'd had in mind when I registered Cate on weConnect. She wasn't supposed to meet a great guy right out of the gate and then leave me alone on Saturday nights. Maybe it was time to have a pet. I'll be that cat lady, single and alone at sixty, with little tins of Fancy Feast scattered on the floor.

Grabbing my jacket off the wall hook, I slipped on my shoes and headed out for ice cream. The local small batch creamery boasted quality over quantity and had introduced flavors like lavender honey and chai toffee. There was always a line out the door, but every minute spent waiting was worth it.

Life was either understood as a series of coincidences or one that was fated to bump into her ex-husband and his pregnant wife. Lessons learned came in uniquely wrapped packages, which wouldn't divulge their contents until the bow had been pulled off, the paper had been peeled away, and the lid had been removed. Should I slink away before detected and miss out on the blood orange and mint gelato, or stand my ground, showing the burgeoning family that their presence was of no consequence? No longer would I feel small and insignificant, affected by the ex and his choice to start anew. Looking around at the couples and families enjoying their frozen concoctions, while Robert and Anna stood within throwing distance, her belly protruding in front of her like she'd crammed a watermelon down her shirt, I realized something.

Everything had its time and place. Before any of these people had become a part of something more, they'd all been singles; the express lane at the grocery store, sleeping single in a double bed, and a table for one. Perhaps I was feeling nostalgic or optimistic, but it hadn't been Robert's and my time and place to be together. What we'd had was fine for the duration, but that was all it was ever supposed to be. He was Anna's.

Standing my ground and remaining in line, I moved up the queue to the front, ordered my gelato, as planned, and walked away with my head held high.

"Jewel? Is that you?" Turning and expecting to see Robert with his mouth agape, ready to apologize and make amends for our failed marriage, instead it was Sam with a slightly older woman who held two empty ice cream bowls in her hand.

"Sam."

Not knowing what more to say, since I hadn't heard from him in weeks, I waited for him to lead the conversation. His friend looked at me and spoke first.

"Hi, I'm Essie, Sam's mom." She was tall and slender with light brown hair that fell in soft curls around her shoulders. Her eyes were dark brown, not the deep blue color of Sam's, and her complexion wasn't the same as his olive tone but instead was very light and fair. They looked nothing alike. Plus, I remembered that Sam's mom had passed away so this scene did not make sense.

"Stepmom," Sam corrected, sounding slightly annoyed. "Essie, Jewel and I are neighbors." Essie checked me out, from head to toe, as females who are of similar age frequently do. Sam's dad had a thing for younger women, or so it seemed.

Sam kicked the ground with his shoes—his hands pressed deep in his jeans pockets. "Jewel, my dad passed away three weeks ago. It was a routine back surgery but there were complications from the anesthesia." He looked at me. Pain showed in his eyes but he spoke with a stoicism uncharacteristic of the man I'd known for a few years.

I knew Sam and his dad had become close after his mom had died about five years ago. He must've been devastated. No wonder he hadn't been around or called.

"I am so sad to hear this news Sam. I didn't know. I should have been there for you." I gave him a hug but it was met by his stiff arms. "Wish you'd have told me." I backed away and gave him some space.

Essie swiftly moved between us, sensing Sam's discomfort and almost trying to protect him from me. "Nice to meet you, Jewel. Are you originally from Los Angeles, or a transplant like everyone else?"

An unintentional laugh escaped my throat. "Something like that. I call this city my home now."

After regaining his composure, Sam responded for me. "You're from Texas, aren't you?"

Just then Robert and Anna passed by, pausing for a moment to gawk—no doubt wondering what my connection to Sam was. Robert placed his arm around Anna's shoulder while the other found its way to her belly, which he rubbed, obviously, all for my pleasure. They moved as one, a massive iceberg that destroys everything and everyone in its path while it leaves devastation in its wake.

Sam noticed the distraction. "Ex?"

"Yeah."

We walked away from the ice-cream shop but Sam and Essie seemed to be on their own mission. They headed toward Sam's car, and he neglected to ask if I needed a ride, even though we were neighbors and my commute from his apartment would be all of thirteen seconds.

"See ya," I said aloud to no one in particular as they drove away.

Electric scooters—which were once a commodity but then turned copious after many transportation and ridesharing companies had vied for their share of the pie—littered the sidewalk outside the ice-cream shop. Using my Lyft app, I activated a healthy looking scooter and rode toward home, but before I reached the apartment, a few laps were necessary around a fun roundabout in a residential neighborhood. Around and around the median I went, like I was ten years old with my hair flowing in the wind, and the stars and moon overhead to light my way. Sam and I used to scooter off the busy sidewalks, away from the tourists of Santa Monica and among the streets with the large houses and nine thousand-foot lots. It made me feel a little bit closer to him, although at this point I knew that he was drifting away.

—~—

"Liam, I think we should meet."

132

He had sent a message earlier in the day, but it was the standard, "Hello and how are you?" text. Starting to become exasperated at the process, I pushed the envelope a bit. At this point, my investment wasn't earning dividends, nor was it losing, so it was a wash at best.

"Meet? In person?"

No, by proxy. I'll send my friend Cate to meet your friend, Bob, and they'll report back.

"Yes, I think we should meet for tea. What about next weekend?" It was already Saturday night, and he might have made plans for Sunday, so giving him a week's notice was very proactive of me.

And then just like that, Liam was gone. He didn't unmatch us, as Max had, but he immediately signed off. Why are these men on the dating apps so weird? It was beyond exhausting, like they were delicate flowers that needed a precise combination of water, sun, and nutrients, and had to be placed on the windowsill facing southwest, and with an exact ambient temperature, or they'd shrivel and die at a moment's notice.

The night's dreams were a mixture of Sam, Max, and Liam, but oddly they were the same person. One of them was always present while I went from one abstract scene into the next, although they shared one common face, like a hybrid of the three. A moment before the alarm rang at 6:00 a.m., I was resting in Sam's arms, and Max and Liam were nowhere to be found.

—~—

A message in WhatsApp arrived from Aunt Carol, detailing her trip in Peru. She and her husband had spent a week hiking the Camino de Inca from Cusco to the Belmond Sanctuary Lodge, outside the entrance to Machu Picchu. The photos were stunning, her bright smile and laughing eyes brought tears to mine. With my parents' having passed away many years ago, I barely knew what it was like to have family. Although Aunt Carol and I hadn't seen one another in person since I was seventeen years old, she'd taken time out of her trip to reach out, just as family should.

I replied, "So happy for you! All is well here. Hope to see you soon, Auntie. Love you!"

I wondered what it would be like walking hand in hand with my life partner along the Inca Trail. After coming to the end of the majestic Sun Gate, we'd witness the citadel of ancient ruins and steep cliffs that had been built as a refuge for the Inca aristocracy. The adjectives that came to mind were mystical and life changing. Believing that I would experience that one day gave me the courage to move forward and take all necessary chances to make it happen.

I sat in my car, which was parked in the underground structure of my apartment building and reread Aunt Carol's message. Since it had been so long, she didn't look as familiar to me. Time that has elapsed will erase the memories of years gone by, muddying their existence and challenging our minds as to specific details. Sometimes I couldn't remember what my parents looked like—was my mom's hair more blonde than gray, or the other way around, when she died? Were my dad's eyes hazel, like mine, or a darker, brown color? Sounds echoed in my parking structure, breaking my reverie and reminding me that I should bring in the groceries. The enclosed stairwell to my floor exposed familiar voices that danced around the dark and cold spaces, bouncing off the steel and concrete.

"Why wouldn't you? She's fantastic. You'd be so lucky."

"We're just friends. I wouldn't go there."

"You should ask her."

"I'm not ready for anything with anybody."

"Well then, don't you think you should say something? This really isn't fair."

"What would I say? Let's just leave it the way it is."

"Which is what?"

Backing away from the open door and retreating into the shadows, I became one with the pillar that held up the first floor of apartments. Was that Sam? Who was he talking with ... Cate? It sounded like Cate. What was going on? They were meeting behind my back and discussing me, like whether or not to pull the plug on my life support system.

Waiting for the voices to subside and the silence to return, I stood on the stairs that led to the parking structure. I attempted to return to my apartment but not until I stopped in front of Sam's door. So he wouldn't go there because we're just friends! The friend zone was like wearing cement blocks as shoes while wading through quicksand. I wanted to throw my body against his door, battering it ram style. Sam's music was suddenly turned up a few decibels so I went home.

Later that night, I once again entertained myself by going on weConnect, which seemed to be the only constant in my life and something that wouldn't negotiate my fate.

Carson, forty-two, from Scotland and on a work-exchange program, sought a fun time/not a long time with dancer/model/actress, preferably blonde. He didn't look like anything to write home about, as his average looks and unkempt hair jumped out from the photo he'd chosen to use as his main profile picture. He leaned against a hot-pink Ferrari and was wearing a huge Rolex on his wrist and a shiny black shirt unbuttoned to his navel. He stood under the establishment's sign of "Gentlemen's Playground." Was this an ad, ripped out of a magazine, for Ferrari, Rolex, or the stripper-joint? Amanda swiped him right, solely for amusement.

Ding-ding! A message from Liam was waiting. "Hey, Amanda. What's going on?"

"Not much. Liam, I'm thinking that we should get together next weekend." I braced myself for his profile to disappear just as the last time I suggested we meet.

"Yeah. I guess we could do this. Where and when?" Well don't get too excited, Liam—I just might be the love of your life and the mother of your future kids, so my apologies if I'm interrupting your crossword puzzle.

Our plan to meet for a drink occupied the recesses of my mind every day leading to Saturday. The few mistakes I made while on rounds at the hospital were met with disdain by my attending supervisor.

"Jewel, did you order 400 milligrams of Cipro in Mr. Paxton's IV? I don't see it here in his chart."

"Nurse Evans, Mrs. Yuh has been waiting for her discharge paperwork since 2:00 p.m. What's the holdup?"

"Whose signature is this? Jewel, is this yours or Stephan's? We need to see clear writing and sign-offs."

Having one's head in the clouds because of romantic daydreams was not a legitimate excuse for bandaging the incorrect hand or discharging the wrong patient.

—~—

135

A flattering, crimson blouse with intricate black stitching had been hanging in my closet for months, just waiting for an opportunity to be worn. Coupled with my beige skinny jeans and low profile boots, my ensemble looked perfect to meet Liam. Arriving twenty minutes early at a restaurant overlooking the Santa Monica beach, I located the best vantage point to watch people come and go, but especially to observe Liam as he made his way into the bar area, looking for Amanda. Of course, Amanda wouldn't show because she was flaky and undependable. After a few drinks and laughs with me, Liam would forget about meeting sexy, fake Amanda, and focus his attention on lovely Jewel.

Two guys who looked like brothers made their way to the whitewashed bar. They stood next to the high stools and ordered drinks, while the blonder man scanned the crowd. He caught my eyes for a moment and then a smile broke out on his face. A wave in my direction almost made me respond, but the "hey!" and "darling!" in high-pitched female shrieks from behind, stopped me in my tracks. The two couples took their drinks and moved to a nearby table.

Another man, handsome, but considerably older than my preferred forty years, took the seat next to me and ordered a beer. "Do you have Modelo Negra?"

He focused on my breasts before looking at my left hand. "You single?" His more salt than pepper hair fell in soft waves around his tanned face, giving him an older George Clooney look. He had a slight accent, which sounded French, and while he seemed to be propositioning me, his eyes darted around the crowd, making me feel invisible. There wasn't any point engaging in conversation as Liam could walk in any moment, so I quickly put an end to his inquiry.

"No."

Without a comment, he picked up his beer and saddled up next to the dark-haired woman who sat alone at the end of the reclaimed wood counter. She looked as disinterested by his presence as I had been a moment earlier. It was fascinating how the adult male appeared unfettered by rejection and would move on to the next opportunity until successful.

Where was Liam? Had he come in, looked around, and left—unnoticed by me? In the past thirty minutes, there weren't any single men who could have been the six foot tall, blond real estate hottie. Surely he would order a drink at the bar, holding his vodka and tonic while searching for the beautifully designed, strawberry-blonde beauty who would never materialize.

I motioned to the bartender. "I'll have another. Stronger this time, if you don't mind."

"Jewel?"

Sam stood before me, brawny and beautiful. His inquisitive eyes demanded answers, which I wasn't going to divulge. He wore an off-white button down collared shirt and dark tan pants, appearing taller than his six feet. His lips turned up into a slight smirk, beckoning attention.

"What a pleasant surprise. What are you doing here? Following me?" Without waiting a beat, he picked up my freshly made margarita and downed half of it, sans apology.

"I could say the same thing about you. Do you have a hot date or something?" Please don't be on a date. Please don't let her be skinny and have just walked off the cover of Victoria's Secret catalogue and be best friends with Gigi Hadid. Standing my ground and acting nonchalant, I smiled. "I can order a cocktail for you … or you can just drink mine."

"No … I mean, no I'm not on a date, and no, I can order my own drink. It was kismet that I walked in and craved a margarita, and here it was in front of me, like old times." He winked at me and then paused a moment before asking the bartender for two more. "What about you? Am I interrupting something?"

"Me? No. Thought I'd meet Cate for a drink, but she couldn't make it at the last minute, so I came anyway. It's been a long week. How are you doing, Sam? I know the past month has been really tough on you."

We talked about the sudden death of his dad and his stepmom's inability to cope. She started taking heavy prescription drugs, rented a beach house in Malibu, and invited a thirty-year-old surfer to move in with her. She told Sam that she hadn't had good sex in over three years and had to make up for lost time. He also didn't apologize for the disappearing trick after Las Vegas, but I let it slide since he'd just lost his father. Death affects people in unexpected ways. I would know, more than anyone. My mother was the prime example of going sideways after losing a loved one.

After two more margaritas and flatbread disguised as a pizza, I realized that Liam had flaked, or perhaps I had flaked on Liam. Sam and I spent some much-needed time together, but at the expense of not meeting the hazel-eyed ocean swimmer and movie line repeater. We'd sent texts to one another for weeks, anticipating the moments when we'd see each other's messages. Or at least I had. Although I shouldn't speak for Liam, I was sure he was as interested in me, or Amanda, as I was in him. Granted, he was motivated by a beautiful photo, but it was our daily banter that kept him reaching out. A person could look like a supermodel but have the intellect and communication of a rock. Had he come in when I was with Sam, he would have been on the lookout for light auburn-haired Amanda, my Amy Adams look-alike. As far as he was concerned, Amanda had stood him up.

"Let's scooter home. You can share mine."

I stood behind Sam on the electric scooter and held him tightly around the waist as we rode twenty blocks. He was finally circling back as the old Sam I knew and adored but walking up the stairs to our second floor, he suddenly grew cold and distant.

"So glad we bumped into each other, Jewel. Hey, I'll see you soon. G'night." Without another word, he closed the door to 211.

What the hell? My body ached from whiplash—the Sam on one side of me being receptive and interested, and the Sam who was on the other side, acting like a stranger. Was he scared that I'd pounce, forcing my lips on his, or worse, that I'd demand we become boyfriend-girlfriend? Oh, it would be so awful for everyone involved! The pain and the suffering—how would we cope?

My barely worn clothes fell in a heap on the bathroom floor. It was the elephant in the room, reminding me that it was a "good college try." The hot bubble bath welcomed my tired mind and body. My mom loved to take baths, and during her healthy years, would draw a warm bath for me while she sat on the edge, playing with me and the many Barbie dolls and plastic toys that made up my young world. After I was finished and my pajamas were on, she'd add more water for herself and then relax with a glass of wine until the tub turned cold.

As I flashed back, I was suddenly fourteen years old again. Mom had been passed out on the couch for hours, and the empty vodka bottle she cradled like a doll threatened to roll from her grasp and on to the floor. Virginia Slims cartons and empty Coke cans took up their usual place on the dusty coffee table.

I laid in the hot bathtub and concentrated on the drip, drip, drip from the faucet rather than her lumberjack snoring. Most nights, I'd sleep with one pillow under my head and another on top of my exposed ear to drown out the noise. I lowered my head until my ears were submerged; the bathwater formed a protective shield, calming and comforting my mind and body, and muffling any sounds.

I'd looked up in time to see the empty vodka bottle whiz through the air and smash against the wall above me. She loved throwing things at me, although never intending to actually hit me but more to show her power and authority. The clear shards of glass fell into my bathwater, making it impossible to move lest I'd be cut to shreds.

"Well! Look. At. You. You're a woman, already. And when did this happen?" She cackled and then started to cough, spitting all over the bathroom floor. Then her voice became mean; her face twisted to ugly as though she were going to pitch forward and drown me. "You think you're fancy because you can lounge in the bathtub? This isn't the Four Seasons! What about the laundry? And the dishes? There's work to do. Get it done NOW! … OUT!" She waved her index finger from me to the bathtub as though witnessing a crime.

"Mom, please … I … just give me a moment to dry off, okay?"

She turned to leave but slipped on something wet—probably my fault when I ran the bathtub. She lost her footing and came down hard, her head hitting the linoleum with a thud.

I tried to lift myself out, but a large piece of glass wedged itself in my foot while another cut my thigh, instantly clouding the bathwater a bright red. Losing my grip on the tub, I fell back into the water and on to more glass. The pain was more tolerable than the preceding years of living alone with my mother while she mourned the loss of my dad, blaming it on me.

Mom stood up, but instead of admonishing me again, she just walked out of the room, leaving me in a pool of bloody water.

"Ahhh!" The gasp escaped my lungs. I quickly rose to the surface of the cold bathwater, fighting for air. I must have fallen asleep. I looked at the water to make sure it was still clear and that my body wasn't cut and bleeding. That was many years ago—another lifetime. I wasn't that girl anymore. Now I was the one in control.

Liam's excuse for not making our date was flashing at me from the weConnect app. "Sorry I couldn't make it. Got caught up with work. Another time."

Another time? I don't think so. If Sam hadn't shown up, I'd have been sitting alone at a bar, drowning myself in skinny margaritas and eating a dinner of cashews and pretzels.

"Do you want to unmatch Liam?" the app asked, to which I hit "confirm." Being stood up with a lame excuse seemed to be the norm with men. Who's working on a Saturday night?

Hasta la vista, Liam. Next time, find some better excuses.

14

With This Ring

The passport office had a line out the door, spilling applicants on to the sidewalk of Ventura Boulevard. The sign by the entrance read "First come, first served. Last interview at 3:00 p.m."

"Excuse me, is this the line for scheduled appointments?" I asked an older, Hispanic woman, who stared at me blankly. "*Por favor, línea? Apointamente? Donde?*" That was the extent of my Spanish.

A similar looking woman, who could have been her sister, appeared and asked me in English what I needed.

"I have an appointment at 11:00 a.m. Do I have to wait in this queue?"

The second woman redirected me inside the building and told me to sit near a small table and listen for my name.

It was time to travel. Spain, Japan, Australia, India. It didn't matter.

"Evans. Jewel."

Within twenty minutes, I had signed the paperwork and paid the fee that would give me international freedom. I'd see the Great Wall of China, eat sushi in Japan, walk across the Thames, buy spices in Istanbul, and take a boat ride around the Galapagos Islands. The human resources manager at the hospital informed me that my unused vacation days from the past three years were going to expire, since I could only accumulate a certain amount before they dropped off.

Cate and I met later for Friday afternoon happy hour on Melrose Avenue in Beverly Hills. She breezed in, wearing what looked like a kimono over a tight T-shirt and skinny jeans. Her face was alight with happiness, a glow that could only mean one thing.

"Oh my God! You're in love."

"No, I'm engaged! Look." Cate shoved her left hand in my face, revealing a shimmering, oval diamond ring. "I mean, yes, I'm in love. And engaged. He asked me last night."

"You mean Dave, right?" The month and a half of dating, resulting in an engagement, was like running a marathon in a minute. How could she be getting married, and I can't get a guy to meet me for a drink?

"Jewel, be happy for me. Let's toast this magnificent event. We need tequila." We always need tequila. Within a few minutes, two margaritas materialized in front of us.

Of course I was happy for her. It was just a nugget of information that I hadn't expected.

Cate proclaimed, "I want the wedding to be somewhere exotic, like Fiji or Bora Bora. Coconuts, rum, sunsets, tropical weather. Sky's the limit." That was where my passport was going to come in handy. "Except we aren't going to be nude."

Years earlier, Cate had attended a wedding on the beach in Tahiti, where all the guests, with the exception of a small group, had gone commando. It was a movement at the time called naked marriage, and she said she couldn't look at her friends the same way again after the event was over. "You should have seen my cousin's penis. No, I'm glad you didn't. You can't unsee something like that. It was bent to the left, like he'd had an erection at one time and had walked into the dresser, snapping it out of alignment. Poor guy."

Cate signaled the bartender for two more drinks, and a few minutes later, they were brought to our table by a man so handsome he would rival any GQ model.

"Just because I'm getting married does not mean I can't look or flirt with the hotties. Should I get his number for you?"

Why would Mr. GQ want my number when beautiful women were a dime a dozen on Melrose Avenue? Looking around the room, I saw numerous blondes and brunettes who, if they were on weConnect, would be Amanda's direct competition. Maybe they were.

"Jewel, he's checking you out." My pulse quickened for a moment, but it turned out Cate was not referencing the bartender. A slightly balding man with light brown hair sat alone at a nearby table. He had a martini in one hand and was spearing the olive from the glass with the other, using a plastic stick. He nodded and smiled brightly; the olive's pimento was stuck between his front teeth. "Why don't you go and say hi?"

Since Cate could meet someone and be engaged in under fifty days did not mean that I had to proposition any guy who looked my way, showing even a sliver of interest in me.

"Any luck on weConnect lately, or are you still a brunette?"

Grabbing a handful of my blonde locks and shaking it toward Cate, I let out a loud sigh. "I'm a redhead. There are plenty of guys on there. I'm just not ready to take the plunge yet. If I see a few really good ones, I'll go on as myself. For now, I love being under the radar, like a voyeur."

It wasn't as rewarding as I let on, insomuch as I'd prefer to be sitting at happy hour, telling my friends about my impending marriage. Masquerading as someone else on a dating app was as lonely as it sounded.

"When you stop having so much fun as someone else, let me know. Dave has lots of single friends, and they are all like him—daring thrill seekers. We'd have a blast together."

Oh fabulous. I passed on Dave the first time, so this must be my lucky, second chance. I hoped I wouldn't blow it.

"You know, Jewel, the way Dave sees it, and I agree, is that a couple who has been dating for years could marry and then have it end in disaster. The amount of dating time doesn't always equal longevity. We have as much of a chance as other couples out there. Look how quickly I found a boyfriend, and as myself, not someone I've stolen online. It's getting kind of weird, Jewel."

"Weird, or maybe just safe. Why can't I feel safe?"

Cate wasn't going to let the topic of my dating life subside until she had fleshed out what was really going on. "Okay. Be safe. Lock yourself in the house. Hide behind a screen. So, anything new with your neighbor?"

"No, I've hardly heard from him. We met out the other night, by accident, but that's all. Why?"

"I meant to tell you but it's been such a whirlwind since Vegas. I came over to see you a while ago but bumped into Sam instead. I tried to find out what was in his head but he wouldn't give it up. I'm sorry Jewel but he's just not that into you—you know, like that movie we love so much—or anybody right now," Cate divulged in a matter of fact way. "The timing's probably off for him. But I think you two would be great together."

I really loved leopard prints and polka dots, but that didn't mean that I should wear them at the same time.

—~—

Cate had a point: arranged marriages, when the bride and groom first met at the altar or just a week prior, were still going on today, and some of the couples were even happy. Since I didn't have anyone to arrange a marriage for me, weConnect was my best bet. I looked at Amanda's photo and profile—she'd lost a bit of pizzazz, and maybe the men had noticed it too. The prospects had dwindled, and I'd been on a swipe-all-men-to-the-left extravaganza, and a cramp was forming in my thumb. It was time to switch her out for a new version—a new catfish. Somewhere, someone said "third time's a charm," but I'm pretty sure they meant "fourth time's a charm." I thanked Amanda for the great times and sent her on her way back to cyberland. Her Facebook account was closed, and her photos and profile were deleted from the dating app.

There were only a few women on weConnect who had ginger hair, according to the men who'd messaged me, so I took it as an opportunity to stand out. I found Anne on an Irish website for part-time hair models. Her real age was twenty-eight, but she could easily be thirty-six in Los Angeles, the land of Botox, fillers, and facials. Her captivating, green eyes reminded me of my childhood cat named Felix, but it was her luscious, berry-colored hair that would set her apart from the rest.

Anne needed a Facebook account, but before she'd have a presence on social media, she'd have to change her name. Estelle was my best friend in ninth grade. We'd only known each other for a year before her parents had divorced and her mom had moved with Estelle to New Orleans. She'd hated her childhood and was embarrassed by her upbringing, believing she'd been slighted by having parents who fought and cheated on each other. That was until she heard about mine. Goodbye Amanda, hello Estelle.

Kyle, forty-four, investment analyst, six feet tall, loved cabernet, traveling, and dogs. His six photos told visual stories of golfing on a cliffside, sitting on a chairlift with snow skis and a helmet, drinking red wine with friends, holding a frisbee while kneeling beside a pretty Australian Shepherd, and standing beside an older woman who shared his angular jaw and strong nose. He was model handsome with dark brown hair and sapphire-blue eyes.

Mr. Investment Analyst, you could rock my world. He didn't seem as demure and safe as Liam, but since Cate had mocked my approach to men, Kyle was swiped right. And hopefully, right into my bed. I needed to get back on the horse, or bicycle—or whatever mode of transportation would bring me in the game.

"Jewel, are you home?" Sam's voice followed a few knocks from behind my front door.

"Yeah, hold on." A quick glance in the mirror stopped me in my tracks. My appearance of a high-top ponytail and a wrinkled pink hoodie could easily be mistaken for someone's teenaged sister. So I quickly dimmed the lights.

Sam stood outside my door, looking disheveled himself, and sloshed.

"It's Friday night. Where's my pizza?" He stumbled past me and plopped down on the sofa, confiscating my tequila midstride.

"Sam, what's going on? Are you okay? Are you drunk?"

"I've had a few. And what are you up to, pretty lady, neighbor gal of mine?" He picked up my laptop and was about to look at the screen of weConnect and Estelle, when I grabbed it out of his hands.

"Just work stuff. Have you eaten? I have leftover Chinese but it's gross which is why it's leftover. I mean, I didn't like it but you might. Here." I shoved a new glass of Patron into his hand, knowing he had all of thirty feet to stumble home. After fumbling in the fridge, a plate of egg rolls, some chow mein, and a fortune cookie was presented. "It's not Martha Stewart, but it'll help the hangover you'll have tomorrow."

Sam's laugh turned into a snort. "You're right. This is awful. At least I won't be marrying you for your culinary skills."

Marrying me? When did he start talking like that?

"What are you doing alone on a Friday night? No hot dates?" Sam asked as he pulled the small paper from the inside of the fortune cookie.

"No … no hot dates. I've been saving my Friday nights for you. Where were you tonight?" Although I didn't want to hear that he'd been out with a woman, the fact that he was on my doorstep at 10:00 p.m. on a Friday night said something.

"Just shooting pool with guys from college. Beer, chicken wings—you know the drill." It sounded like fun, and I wish I had been invited, but our relationship as neighbors and our private lives did not intertwine.

I smelled something almost unpleasant and it wasn't the chow mein. "Hang on. I'll be right back." A quick makeup check, a swipe of deodorant, and cursory brushing of my teeth in the bedroom took all of three minutes, but when I returned Sam was fast asleep on the couch. He still held the glass of tequila firmly in his hand, which was impressive. Carefully dislodging the glass from his clutches, I positioned his head on the throw cushion and lifted his feet so that he was completely horizontal.

"Sleep well, handsome neighbor of mine," I whispered into the air as I covered his limber body with a blanket. Before I turned off the lights, I looked at Sam's paper fortune that lay on the coffee table. It read "Love stares you in the face."

—~—

The Saturday morning sun shone brightly on my face. May in Los Angeles meant summer was in full swing. It was almost 7:00 a.m., and Sam's movements awoke me from my slumber. Before my feet hit the floor, the front door closed and Sam was gone. It was a perpetual game of Where's Waldo?

I jumped back into bed and grabbed my computer. *Ding-ding!* A message from Kyle. Who, besides me, was on a dating app on an early Saturday morning?

"Hello, Estelle. So glad you swiped me. You are beautiful."

Of course Estelle was beautiful, but could she carry on a conversation?

"Hi, Kyle. When I read your profile and learned of your travel exploits and saw your photos with friends and family, I was reminded of Helen Keller's inspirational quote: 'Life is either a daring adventure, or nothing.' Stevenson's compositions also resonated for me with your journeys of camaraderie: 'We are all travelers in the wilderness of this world, and the best we can find in our travels is an honest friend.' " There. She laid it on thick.

146

He responded immediately. "Yeah, I like to travel. Skiing's my thing." He may not be a Pulitzer Prize contender, but he sure was hot. "Mammoth's dope. Have you been there?"

"No, I haven't. Sounds lovely."

We texted over the app for an hour. Although the communication had begun slowly out of the gate, Kyle had a great sense of humor and came across very genuine.

—~—

A late afternoon yoga class was preempted by a call from the hospital.

"Nurse Evans, would you be able to come in for a bit? Ms. O'Reilly in Room 301 is asking for you. She is being kept comfortable with a morphine drip. We don't expect her to make it another day or so. She wants to see her favorite nurse."

Ms. O'Reilly had been in and out of the hospital for the past six months, treating it like a hotel. We had bonded over the chessboard, and she'd always let me win, since I was more of a checkers girl. She'd just had her eighty-ninth birthday, and the entire floor of staff had squeezed into her room to watch her blow out her faux candles, which was quite mean of us because it took a lot of lung strength to extinguish candles that weren't even lit. Her sheet cake was filled with vanilla and strawberry creme, and the greeting "Happy Birthday, Agnes. We love you!" was displayed in red icing. She was a special woman who had never married or been blessed with children. An only child, she had made the hospital staff the family she'd never had. Over the years, she had been suffering from coronary thrombosis, and the blockage of blood flowing to her heart had weakened her physical body, but not her spirit.

"Agnes, my beautiful friend. I'm so glad you had them call. I'd never forgive myself if something happened to you, and we'd never speak again." Her pillows needed fluffing, and she was listing to the right.

"Happened to me?" She chuckled in her true Agnes way, but the sound was throaty and labored. "It's been happening a long time, deary. This is it. Probably my last day. Quite frankly, I've had enough. It's time to go," she slowly uttered her words and then closed her eyes.

"Are you comfortable, honey? How's your pain level? Can I bring you something?"

"I'm all right … just happy to have seen my Jewel. You *are* a jewel. Don't ever forget it. You know, I never thought this would be how I'd leave. Have some babies so when it's your time, you'll have family around. Jewel, thank you for being my family." Tears escaped her closed eyes and rolled down her pale cheeks.

I touched a tissue to her aged skin, absorbing the moisture. "Oh, Agnes, I'll never forget you. You are my family too." I held her warm, frail hand in mine, hoping she'd feel my energy and know I was still beside her.

She had drifted off to sleep. Her words were the last ones spoken until her heart gave up. Sitting with her for another hour and watching the electrocardiogram display her waning vital signs, I thought about my mom and her final days. It was incredibly sad to be alone during the last moments of life. No one should cross over to the next life without someone watching over us.

Agnes began Cheyne-Stokes breathing, signaling the end, and within ten minutes, she had passed. The hospital monitor showed Agnes's heart rate had reached zero, and its flat line initiated an alarm, which also reached the nurses' station. Her do-not-resuscitate order, part of her medical directive, was evident to everyone who had cared for Agnes for many months.

"Godspeed, Agnes. Godspeed."

Even though I'd known and cared for so many patients who were admitted but then passed away in the hospital, Agnes had held a special place in my heart. She had reminded me of my Granny Mitchell, who'd died of breast cancer when I was eight years old. Hospital management and psychotherapists warned nurses to remain at arm's lengths and not to become emotionally involved with the patients. I tried to put Agnes out of my mind and treat her like any patient whose time had come up. I was a nurse, after all, and I had a job to do.

Dr. Judy Bernstein entered the room just as I laid Agnes's lifeless hand by her side. "Is she gone? She couldn't have passed already. Her vitals indicated that she'd be with us for at least another twelve hours or more." The doctor picked up Agnes's wrist and felt for her nonexistent pulse. "What's going on here? Why weren't we informed?" Dr. Bernstein stamped her foot like a child.

148

"Um … yes. I was just about to tell the physician in charge. Didn't the alarm go off in the hub? It happened very quickly."

Dr. Bernstein looked down at her chart and then again at me as I sat beside Agnes looking more like her close relative than one of her many nurses. "So, she died. Just like that?" The doctor snapped her fingers in front of her face, making a grand gesture of authority. "Right before your eyes. And so quickly. Hmm. Why are you here, anyway? Isn't it your day off?" She looked at me dubiously, as though I preferred to spend a glorious Saturday afternoon watching a person die than be on the beach with warm sand in my toes and a drink in my hand.

I picked up my purse and made my way to the door, turning midstride to respond. "Someone from scheduling called me to come. Agnes asked for me." A rogue tear threatened to leave my watery eyes and expose my vulnerability.

The doctor let out an exasperated breath. "Oh, it's Agnes now, is it? Well, *Ms. O'Reilly* hasn't spoken for the past few days, so I highly doubt that. And who is this "someone"? I'll need a name. In the future, Nurse Evans, I suggest you keep a distance between your work at this hospital and the patients you treat. Understand?"

—~—

The glass of tequila I had to pour after my interaction at the hospital seemed to calm my nerves. weConnect whispered to me, and I responded because I was such a damn good friend. The rest of the night was uneventful, having channel surfed for two hours without remaining on a show for more than ten minutes. Watching TV wasn't the same without Sam. His constant comments on the dialogue and plot would keep us amused. I'd sent him a quick text reading "Hey. You okay? LMK if you need anything." But it went unanswered, apropos of his strange behavior.

Kyle still loved me, or at least he loved Estelle. "How was your day? Let's chat on the phone later if you have time. I'll be up late." He provided his phone number.

"It was great, thx. Texting is best for me now, Kyle, if you don't mind. "

My day was crap. A wonderful patient died. This morning, my handsome neighbor rolled off my sofa and out the door, right after I'd

149

planned a delicious breakfast and fabulous life. I missed my yoga class. Somehow I've gained five pounds, and my favorite jeans are snug. I'm spending all of my free time texting a photo, hoping it will manifest into something meaningful.

We wrote to each other for a while, but of course with me as Estelle: cellist, marketer, world traveler, yoga aficionado, oil painter, marathon runner, nutritional chef. If only I were Estelle, we could meet for a nightcap, and I would learn to like brandy. How bad could it be? Kyle was very industrious, as it turned out. He was an economics major at USC, born and raised in Calabasas, took care of his mom financially, and had a loyal dog named Cesar. He indicated that he was on weConnect to meet a woman who shared his life philosophy and would settle down with him to raise a family. He would definitely be the perfect mate.

"You have my number. Call me if you get bored." Kyle signed off for the night.

Bored? I've spent half my life being bored, but that didn't mean I could finagle a successful phone conversation without divulging that I'm a complete fraud. Kyle wouldn't be very forgiving with a short, blonde gal who was masquerading as a tall, luscious Judy Garland wannabe.

Almost two weeks passed without many a word from Sam. He sent a few texts here and there, but mostly one-liners: "Hey, how are things?" or "Just checking in. Hope you're well." How did I go from Friday night fun gal to a "checking in" text?

Kyle and Estelle were communicating every night. Although he was in the process of closing escrow on a house while juggling clients and their investments at a private equity firm, he carved out more time than Sam, who was still missing in action. Kyle wanted to learn everything about Estelle, and she didn't hold back with her globe-trotting and humanitarianism acts. Like any alter ego, Estelle was everything I'd want to be in another lifetime, right down to her volunteer work with Habitat for Humanity in Zimbabwe. Realistically, before traveling to Africa to help build a shelter, I'd opt for a week in Maui, mai tais, and a luau.

"What's your day like tomorrow?" Kyle asked Estelle, but I already knew it was a setup.

"Not much. Saturdays are always chill. Why?" My chest was tight, and my throat was closing in on what felt like my last breath.

"Meet IRL. Tomorrow. 5:30 happy hour at Mastro's Ocean Club. I'll see you then." He signed off, and I opened a new bottle of Clase Azul. My Friday night was fraught with uncertainty and deserved a $130 bottle of reposado.

—~—

"In real life" was a scary place to reside, given "real" wasn't in Estelle's vocabulary. Oh, what the hell? It was time to jump off the deep end, so I picked out a sexy, low-cut, red blouse and skinny-ish jeans and laid them on the foot of the bed. If Kyle couldn't find Estelle, he'd have to settle for me.

15

The Elf on the Shelf

Now

"You are batshit crazy! No wonder online dating doesn't work. It's because of lunatics like you."

Kyle continued to walk out of the restaurant, not that I expected him to have a change of heart and take interest in me, as in: "Let's just forget about that Estelle person. So, Jewel, tell me about yourself. What types of movies do you like to watch? What do you do for a living? What's your favorite color? Red, right? Just like that pretty top and the sexy way you fill it out." Only in my dreams would a catfished date respond with forgiveness and indifference. Kyle was a really great catch, but his preferences seemed to lie with worldly, sophisticated, powerful, and gorgeous, otherwise he wouldn't have invested in Estelle every night.

"Wait! Please don't go. Kyle, wait for me!" I pleaded and ran after him like a youngster chasing after the ice cream truck. He continued to ignore me as he reached the parking lot.

Kyle's Mercedes responded to the click of his key fob, but before he opened the car door, he turned around and seethed, "Now you're a stalker too? Online *and* in person. I could get a restraining order for this." He looked rather ugly at this moment. Estelle and I decided that we didn't like him anymore.

I stood my ground and crossed my arms in defiance. "And what's so wrong with me? Do I have to be a supermodel for you to take notice? That's the problem with guys like you, Kyle. You're looking for perfection, when the normal, average woman is right under your nose."

Kyle looked exasperated. "Normal? You call this normal? Jewel, Estelle—whoever you are—take my advice and go online as yourself. I'm looking for the real deal and not some phony."

"But you didn't even try to know the real me. Kyle, you need to trust me!" I knew it was pointless to continue, but I was on a runaway train and couldn't jump off.

"I don't trust crazy. Goodbye." I barely heard his reply as he sat down in the driver's seat. Somehow my hand grabbed his car door and tried to stop him from closing it and leaving.

"Please, Kyle. Just hear me out. I am Estelle—I just look different from the photo. It was me writing to you and sharing my thoughts. How many nights did we spend texting? Doesn't that count for anything?"

Kyle put his foot on the door and was about to give it a good shove, which would have sent me flying. "Security! Security, I need help here!" Kyle yelled to the valet attendant, who subsequently laughed, thinking we were having a lover's quarrel. It was my cue to back down and admit defeat. The Mercedes sped away, leaving a large swirl of dust between me and Kyle from Malibu.

I entered my apartment, empty-handed, but it didn't require a psychic to tell me that Kyle had already unmatched Estelle, as I logged back on to weConnect. I would have done the same. If a guy, who I thought was a bona fide match on a dating site, showed up for drinks and turned out to be a fake, I'd be upset too. Except that I *am* the real deal. I just didn't know how to make a guy see that. Kyle and I wouldn't have worked out if we had met organically or on a blind date, anyway, so I'd chalk this evening up to a reconnaissance mission.

It comes down to beauty and background. I don't make heads turn. I look average—plain Jane, and the complete opposite of my catfish personas. I don't have a fancy pedigree—our family was poor and dysfunctional—certainly not the kind of childhood that any man could be proud of at a dinner party. "My wife? She had parents, but when they weren't ignoring her, they abused her. Doesn't have any relatives either. Jewel is as basic as they come." And that's why I don't go on weConnect as myself.

Many years before meeting Robert, and before the advent of dating apps, a friend from college set me up with her neighbor. We spoke on the phone a few times and then decided to meet for a drink at a popular bar in Hollywood. Eligible and interested, he seemed perfect and had all the boxes checked, or the boxes a twenty-five-year-old gal needs checking. When the big date came, I eagerly awaited his arrival at the bar, wearing my new dress and high heels. "Jewel?" he asked, or some guy who appeared before me at five-feet-tall and with the tiniest ears I'd seen other than on an elf. That sliver of time, wavering between honesty and bullshit, choked me, like a farmer with his hand around the neck of a plump hen before he twists and separates the head from the body. Something like that. "Uh ... no ... I'm Mary." The little elf walked away, scanning the room for another single gal who was also awaiting her blind date. Back then, I was just like Kyle—maybe the elf could have been my life's love and I missed out on a happily ever after because I assessed him by a mere glance, just as Kyle had done to me. History just loves to repeat itself.

Rodney, thirty-eight, automotive dealer, born and raised in Toronto, enjoys Canadian football, music by Blue Rodeo and Michael Bublé, and seeks a wife for green card status. He has chestnut-brown hair and jade green eyes, with soft wrinkles that form around them when he smiles. If I were on as Jewel, I might swipe right on him, since what's the difference between marrying to stay in the country, which could possibly result in happily ever after, and using a dating app to find real love? Chemistry is such that it doesn't matter how you meet someone—grocery store, Starbucks, friend connection, dating app, arranged marriage, an ad to marry for citizenship, but as long as you meet. Sometimes two people just jell and then fall in love, and as Cate says every moment she gets, "It isn't the vehicle but the passengers inside."

My phone dinged with a text message.

"Thinking about you. How are things? Let's get together." True to form, and typical of most men, Sam didn't acknowledge the few weeks he'd been out of touch. How are things, you ask? Well, let me tell you, Sam: What could have been a memorable night with the 3 Ds—dinner, drinks, and dancing, has turned into a lonely evening of the 2 Ps—pj's and pizza.

These women, Chelsea, Raquel, Amanda, and Estelle, are fabulous in every regard, because I made them so, but if I took them out of the mix, what would be Jewel's fighting chance? weConnect allows for simultaneous profiles, which must be an algorithm error but also leaves the door wide open for trouble. Perusing the photos on my phone, I find a few good ones of myself: at the beach on a hot-pink blanket, waving to Cate on the bike path while she took a candid shot, a slightly filtered selfie after a really great blowout.

Jewel, thirty-nine, ER nurse, beach volleyball, exotic destinations, sunsets and margaritas. My narrative reads: Looking for LTR, or just someone with whom to jet set while we enjoy each other's company and experience what this beautiful world has to offer. Just as Kyle suggested, I indicated that I was looking for a long-term relationship and a traveling partner.

Now live on weConnect, I felt my heart pound out of my chest and the undigested pizza I'd eaten moments ago start to rise. Rejection was debilitating, and having been rejected many times, I was familiar with that feeling of inadequacy, like the runt in a litter of nine puppies that no one chose to adopt.

Blonds, brunettes, tall, short, heavy, slender. Some profiles have one or two photos, and others are using the site as a photo album. A familiar dark-haired man appeared within the screen of my smartphone. Max. It'd been a while. He still had only one photo displayed, but had altered his narrative a bit to include cooking, hiking, and trustworthy people. Here you are, Max. This is me—Jewel—being trustworthy. I swiped Max to the right.

George, forty, ocean photographer, PhD in marine biology, sought casual and hookups. His two photos showed him in a wet suit while holding an octopus, and the other at the helm of what looked to be a fishing boat. The photos were taken at a distance, so it was hard to see his facial features and hair. A strategy used by a lot of men on dating sites was to swipe every woman to the right or a thumb's up or heart them, whatever the mode was for yes, and if by chance, one of the desired candidates liked them, a connection would be made. Swoosh—George was swiped to the right.

Minutes passed, and a *ding-ding!* finally sounded. George sent a message which read, "Hi, Jewel. So glad we connected. It's weird, but you look like a girl I once knew. Are you from the Pacific Northwest? They say everyone has a twin."

He swiped on me because he thought I looked like someone else? It felt like a backhanded compliment so I unmatched us.

After scrolling through what seemed like thousands of men, and many of whom Estelle had already seen and swiped away, a quiver of

155

a panic attack stirred in my stomach. A glance in my bedroom mirror showed lonely eyes and thin lips, which said more than any narrative on a dating profile. A once stylish hairdo sat on my shoulders in a haphazard fashion, begging for a flat iron. Although there were trace amounts of makeup from hours earlier, if any guy wanted to video chat, it would be his first and only time. I was not Estelle, nor was I a contender for any man's attention.

Squeezing the warm, sudsy water from the facecloth, I cleaned off the remnants of Maybelline that clung to my eyes and cheeks from the morning's application. The makeup bag with newly purchased cosmetics sat on the bathroom counter. Tinted moisturizer, lipsticks, rose colored blush, jet-black mascara, an array of earth tone eyeshadows, and waterproof eyeliners filled the pink cloth bag, which had the scripted words "You Are Beautiful" detailed on the front—a reminder to the owner that she didn't need to conceal her natural beauty, but only enhance it.

My mom's face stared back at me in the bathroom mirror.

"Makeup! Where did you get money to buy makeup? Did you steal this stuff?" My mom's accusations filled my head. "It'll take more than rouge to make *you* beautiful." Her cackle turned into a throaty, dry cough, and her next words came out as a stutter, "W-w-wipe that shi-shi-shit off your f-f-face."

"But, Mom, all of the girls my age are wearing makeup."

"You l-l-look ridiculous! Like a whore."

Tears fell down my cheeks as I wiped the mascara that had migrated under my eyes.

I tapped my smartphone. weConnect responds: Do you want to delete "Jewel" and your account?

Yes.

Are you sure?

Yes.

I disappear from every man's feed.

—~—

The Sunday morning sun shimmered through the blackout curtains, like a toddler playing a game of peekaboo. The vibrant rays touched my grey walls with intention, creating a deliberate contrast between the dawn of the new day and the dismal reminder of the one before.

I rolled around in the bedding, twisting it into a knot. It's going to be a lazy, easy day.

The doorknob jiggled fervently from the outside door, and Sam's voice reverberated through the wood.

"Jewel. You up?"

Ugh. "Hang on!"

Sam stood before me in black Adidas sweatpants and a grey hoodie. His hair was a messy heap, just begging for my fingers to make their way through his tousled locks.

We sat on the sofa and discussed the past few weeks. Sam was on several work trips and had spent some time with his stepmom's son from a previous marriage. I had little to offer, other than my date with Kyle that had blown up in my face and the Liam's disappearing, so I said nothing.

"You must miss your dad a lot. You two were really close."

A look of sadness and regret plagued Sam's face. "Hey, if I'm going to talk about my dad, we'll have to switch to tequila."

"It's ten in the morning!"

"Let's pretend we're in Paris, so that puts us at about 7:00 p.m. Right? Have you ever been to Paris, Jewel?"

We sat on the sofa, under a blanket with our bodies touching. Sam took my feet and started to rub my arches. His soft hands were surprisingly strong.

"Mmm, that feels good. No, never been, but it's on my list."

"You want to travel, right? That's something you'd like to do? See the world?"

It was as if he'd read my weConnect profile and was responding in kind. I'd only been on for an hour before I signed off, and I would have remembered seeing Sam on a dating app. It was either kismet or he was reading my mind.

"My passport should be here any day so yes, international travel is on the horizon."

After an hour of drinking, catching up, and more drinking, Sam suggested that we go for lunch.

A street food festival on the Venice Beach Boardwalk was in full swing. Hundreds of people milled about with paper plates of sampled nibbles, from Korean BBQ to Thai chicken skewers. Chatter and

157

laughter was almost drowned out by the music. A local DJ from Malibu created an impromptu dance crowd as he sang karaoke along to The Rolling Stones "Satisfaction" in true Mick Jagger style. The crowd surrounded him while they danced and joined in with his "I can't get no … Oh no, no, no … hey, hey, hey, that's what I say."

Sam and I danced along with the crowd, as he took my hand and tried to twirl me, just like my mom used to do when I was eight. I looked up at Sam. Although he'd always been hard to read, the light in his eyes returned.

My phone's notification told me that multiple messages awaited. Cate had called three times and had sent four texts.

"Sam, hang on. I need to reach Cate. I think something's wrong."

She answered on the first ring. "Are you okay?" I asked, but she talked over me.

"I've been arrested. I'm at the police station. You need to come. Now!" I knew it. Which store did they catch her stealing from— Macy's or Saks Fifth Avenue?

I left Sam at the festival and took the short scooter ride to the police station. Cate was easy to find. I spotted her through the large, glass windows in a little room on the second floor. She was crying and softly shaking. Her makeup had streaked down her face, but it was the only semblance of disorder. The yellow sundress and tan wedges made her look like her usual, put-together self. Seeing me, Cate stood up. The administrator looked my way, waving me in.

"Would you mind filling this out, please?" the police representative asked. It really wasn't a question, because if I hadn't signed the form, Cate wouldn't be leaving with me. The woman towered over me. Her arms were crossed, and there was pity in her eyes. She'd witnessed this scene hundreds of times. Westside affluent women who shoplifted for the thrill of it, while they added another Gucci handbag to their burgeoning collection.

After twenty minutes of formalities of signing paperwork and the process of being fingerprinted, Cate left with me. She'd been shopping at a local boutique earlier in the day, when a camera captured her putting a $150 bracelet in her purse. I put my arm around her and pulled her toward me after she relayed what had happened.

"Oh, Cate. If you really wanted that bracelet, I would've been happy to buy it for you. I don't understand." Although I already knew the answers, I had to ask, just to hear her say the words.

"I have the money, and I really didn't want or need the bracelet. I don't know why I did it. Maybe because I could. Please don't tell Dave. I need to get through this without him knowing." She fixed her dress and put on her *Breakfast at Tiffany's* sunglasses to hide her puffy eyes as we walked down the Santa Monica Police Department's stairs to the awaiting Uber.

"He won't hear anything from me. Don't worry. I just want you to figure things out."

—~—

Sam rummaged through my fridge, moving eggs and cheese around like he'd been searching for something he's convinced I had bought. "Where's the … what about having … Jewel, why did she do something like that?" He stood upright and turned around, his hand holding an orange pepper. "I mean, she has a good job. I don't get it." He lay the pepper on the counter and then proceeded to practically empty the contents of the refrigerator.

"It's not about money. It's a *thing*. Like compensating for something missing in her life. She obsesses, and it's her way of controlling the situation. I'm not condoning it, believe me, but sometimes people have to take things that don't belong to them. Like if they're starving and there isn't food in the house." Or other peoples' identities.

Sam shook his head. "Which tear-jerking drama is this from? Jewel, I completely disagree. Stealing for any reason is wrong. Starving or otherwise."

"It's not from a movie. Sam, if you were a little boy, and your mom spent all the grocery money on booze and smokes, and you had nothing to eat, you'd steal too." I turned on the TV and took my place on the sofa.

Sam shrugged it off. "That'd never happen to either of us, so what does it matter? Besides, we've always had enough money for anything we've wanted to buy, especially expensive tequila." He picked up the bottle of Tears of Llorona, read the label, and took another sip. "Wow. That's good stuff. So what did this cost? At least $300, I imagine."

The staff at my hospital had a lottery last year. Everyone had put in ten dollars to win one of eight bottles of wine or liquor, and the proceeds were donated to a local charity. I won a bottle of 1989

159

cabernet, and another nurse on the floor was lucky enough to win the Tears of Llorona. She wanted the wine so we swapped.

"Yeah, at least $300. Cost me a day's wage, but it's worth every catheter and temperature reading. Cheers!"

We clinked glasses. I drank mine way too quickly for the retail price of the bottle, and then refilled it. Sam didn't notice because he was busy trying to resurrect a meal from my paltry refrigerator. I watched him move in the kitchen; the way he took over, looking through cupboards and drawers, taking out plates and cutlery, like we are a real couple, struck a chord.

This was how it should feel. Organic. The swiping and texting, unmatching and connecting, now felt contrived and arduous, when all it took were baby steps with your willing neighbor.

"Let's get delivery." I admitted defeat on his behalf and picked up my phone. "Chinese. My treat."

Sam resigned himself and came over to the couch. We flipped through channels until the food arrived. He suddenly noticed me for the first time tonight and moved closer so that our knees were touching. "Where have you been hiding?" He tenderly smoothed my hair from my face.

I have been right here, under your nose. "Sam, it's you who has been hiding—ever since Las Vegas."

He laughed, but I could tell I'd made him uncomfortable. The buzzer rang, and he let in the delivery person. I refilled my eight-ounce glass with the expensive amber liquid and drank out of nervousness.

"Whoa, take it easy. Why don't you have some rice. It's filling." Sam passed the plate of dumplings and Chinese fried rice toward me, atonement for his disappearing act.

"I'm really not hungry," I said as I placed my empty glass on the coffee table.

Moments later, I sank into the couch, letting it swallow me whole, first taking my back and shoulders and then my butt and legs, until I disappeared into the fibers—my lucidity dissipating as the buzz from the tequila took over. Sam was above me, talking with his hands. His face moved toward me, within an inch of mine, and his lips mouthed words that didn't make sense. He placed the back of his hand on my forehead and moved it over my temple, as if to feel my temperature.

He furrowed his eyebrows, taking the bottle of tequila and returning it beside the other pretty Mexican glass.

A blanket covered my body and was tucked around my torso, but I moved through the fabric as though it were gauze. Sam was on the other side, waiting. He smiled contently. I wrapped my arms around his waist while he lowered himself on top of me. His lips found mine while his hands took my shoulders, pulling me toward him. Romantic music played as the film's credits flashed through the TV screen. The austere simplicity of the violin's melody filled the space around us, adding to the moment. Sam's mouth tasted like tequila, and his familiar masculine scent captivated my senses, making me instantly high. Sam's tongue searched for mine, and his kiss deepened until I surrendered. I groaned and wrapped my legs around his. We pressed our bodies against each other's, as though finally reunited after a four-year war. His soft kisses became more aggressive, but in a longing, hungry way.

"Oh, Jewel. You are so incredibly beautiful." Sam took my face in his hands and stared into my eyes and then kissed my cheek, nose, lips, and down my neck, toward my breasts. "Beautiful … mmmm … you are stunning." His hand caressed my stomach and made its way upward, under my shirt. He was gentle but assertive, showing me in his touch how much he wanted me. My fingers moved through his thick, dark hair, while I pulled him even closer to me.

"Sam … Sam … Sam … plee-ee-ase."

"Can we get off this couch?" he asked, but didn't wait for an answer as he took my hand and led me to my bedroom. He slowed down a fraction and whispered in my ear, "I want you now. It's always been you, Jewel."

Still kissing and holding on to each other, we fumbled toward the bedroom, like a bad tango. The surfaces were alight with hundreds of small votive candles, and red rose petals in the shape of a giant heart lay on the bed, reproducing a hotel's honeymoon suite. Soft spa music played from somewhere beyond the four corners of the room and the scent of lilacs wafted toward us. Clothes flew and blankets were pushed aside as we collapsed on the mattress and into each other's arms.

"I love you, Jewel."

You love a ghost.

—~—

The putrid stench of vomit that filled the air awoke me from my drunken sleep. I lay prone on the living room floor, with my wet hair plastered to the side of my head, and undigested food chunks covered the hardwood floor. The early morning sun shone a spotlight on the mess I'd created around me. I'd thrown up only a small amount food from the day before, but lots of liquid. My good tequila. From where I lay, between the coffee table and the couch, I saw the blanket Sam had used to cover me, fallen halfway on the floor.

Open containers of Chinese food littered the coffee table, which added to the room's pungent aroma. The apartment was quiet, other than dull thumps and bangs from the family who lived next door. The digital readout on the microwave read 6:16. It's Memorial Day.

A cursory swipe of the sticky floor with some wet paper towels was all I could muster. I gathered the takeout containers of teriyaki chicken and dumplings and shoved them in the garbage can so that they wouldn't be anywhere near the vicinity of my senses. After a few minutes in the hot shower, I slipped under the blankets of my bed, still made from the night before.

16

Bob & Carol & Ted & Alice

My dad's hand gripped my arm, gently shaking me. The twin mattress beneath me shrieked from its old, rusty springs that conformed to my nine-year-old body. The floral nightgown that was too small for my sprouting frame and the flannel bedsheets that should have been changed out for cotton months ago, were completely drenched. I'd sweated through every piece of fabric near me. Not daring to reach for Daisy, my soft cloth doll, since I'd make her damp, too, I remained still. My father shook me again, and I resisted the urge to open my eyes.

"Leave me alone, Daddy." I reflexively pulled on my nightgown to cover my underwear.

His large hand closed around my bicep, but the voice was somehow different, younger.

"Jewel. It's Sam. Wake up."

"Daddy … no … please … "

"Jewel. Jewel. It's me."

Me? Fighting through the many layers of heavy darkness, I clawed my way to the surface, grasping for that elusive gulp of air.

"Arghhhhh." My eyes opened to find Sam sitting beside me on the edge of my large, king-sized bed, a worried look on his face, like he was observing someone he'd never seen before.

"God, Jewel, you're sweating." He retracted his hand as though bitten. "I … I tried to wake you. Uh … why did you want your dad to leave you alone? Did he hurt you, Jewel?"

"What … Sam? What are you talking about? What are you doing here?" I blinked and everything came back to me in slow motion. Tequila. Electric scooters. Cate. Police station. Chinese food. More tequila. Sex. Vomit. I sat up and looked at my neighbor who'd returned after a long night and morning, while I remained alone in my acrid apartment.

He squeezed my thigh and then smoothed my hair with his hands. "I just came by to check on you. I used your key. Hope you don't mind. I'm glad to see that you made it into bed. How 'ya feeling now?"

"Better. Much better. Sam, did we … ?" I hid my face in the pillow for a moment, waiting for his response. Was it good? Did he like it? Did I please him?

"No, you pretty much passed out on the couch as soon as the movie started so we'll have to watch it another night. I know it's one of your favorites." Sam paused for a moment while he looked toward the living room. "It smells funny in here. Hmm … were you sick?"

"God no. It's the crappy Chinese food from that dive restaurant out on Pico. Big mistake. We won't order from there again." I inhaled deeply through my nostrils as the funk punctured my delicate sinus membranes. "It really does stink. I'll clean it up in a bit."

I wanted to put some sweatpants on, but Sam was still sitting on the bed's edge.

"Well, gotta run. This is the catch-up day I've been waiting for. Let me know if you need me for anything."

"You're going? But I thought … since you … it's Memorial Day. It's a Monday … working in the office, nobody will be there." I paraphrased and left sentences with dangling participles, or whatever they were. My seventh grade English teacher, Miss Wells, had tried to drill certain aspects of pervasive grammar mistakes into my head, but I had emerged barely unscathed with a 65 percent grade in her class. I was thirteen years old and more concerned with boys, social groups, and if my eyeshadow was supposed to match my T-shirt or hair scrunchie. My mother didn't seem to care that my final mark in the class was a C-, so neither did I. After I went through puberty and realized that the opposite sex and social status were irrelevant in the scheme of things, I pulled up my socks to achieve an A- at the end of eighth grade. "Sam, aren't you the boss?"

"Yeah, but I'm swamped. Piles of paperwork and spreadsheets trump suntan lotion and a volleyball net." He made his way to the door and turned back to me. "What about that coffee you always have percolating?"

I suddenly couldn't be bothered, and then grimaced. "Not today, sorry."

—~—

The rest of the day was spent organizing my closet and bathroom. By late afternoon, I had five trash bags filled with aged clothing and shoes to donate to the Salvation Army. There was barely anything left in my closet, except the essentials. The majority of Los Angeles residents were sharing the California coast with tourists who had come in from other cities and states to experience the beaches, nightlife, and all that SoCal had to offer, as the approaching summer overtook the spring months and turned it into magic. My Memorial Day consisted of four walls, but that was mostly due to the lack of energy it would require to be social.

I pulled out the Tory Burch shoebox that was concealed among other unassuming shoeboxes. The small receptacle of printed photos and trinkets from the past forty years consumed my thoughts as I rummaged through the nostalgia. Clutching the multicolored butterfly necklace tightly in my palm, I turned it over to see the inscribed J ♥ M, etched so many years ago. Its presence took my breath away, just as it did the first moment I'd seen it.

A picture of me as a toddler, after just finishing a lunch of raviolis, slid off the top of the pile. My chubby cheeks were full of pasta, and one of the ravioli squares was flapping out the corner of my one-year-old mouth. My mom stood beside me, holding my hand as I took what could be a first step. Another photo showed the same blonde toddler wearing a "1st Birthday" hat. I sat on Dad's lap, his hair still black, and his face belied his age of forty-five years. He was beaming. He always seemed to be happy and positive, but that was before his lungs had succumbed to cancer, and he wanted to die more than live. It wasn't until I began a nursing career that I realized how painful advanced lung cancer must have been for him. The delirium had caused a great divide in our father-daughter relationship, and I had become scared of him. Sometimes he'd call me by the wrong name. One night at the dinner table, he asked me if I was lost and needed help finding my house. Mom didn't intervene and correct him, so I sat awkwardly, eating my potatoes and carrots wondering if he'd follow through and start knocking on neighbors' doors. And when his invitations became demands to see me naked, I'd take my nine-year-old, barely pubescent body and hide in the closet. His grips weren't a

165

match for my skinny arms that easily slid through his grasp. Dad's attempts to be alone with me after my baths became less frequent when his lungs turned as black as coal; cancer had taken his body along with his mind.

I gathered the contents of the box to restore them to safekeeping. My phone rang, and I exhaled, hoping it was Sam calling to ask me for dinner or a fun night out.

The number was from a 323 area code. "Hello. This is Jewel."

"Jewel Evans? I'm Garth Shanahan. I'm an estate planning attorney and represent the late Agnes O'Reilly. Sorry to call you on Memorial Day. Is this a good time to speak?"

Mr. Shanahan went on to tell me that Agnes, an unmarried, only child without dependents or close friends, had mentioned me in her will. Agnes was a collector of post-impressionist paintings and modern artworks that had yielded her millions. Upon her death, she donated the money she'd received for the artwork to a local Los Angeles foundation that funds education curriculum for orphanages in Malawi, Africa. Agnes was very philanthropic and had the most generous heart. Last year, one of the nurses, Gabrielle, had lost her husband to a tragic car accident, which had left her a single mother with three children under the age of ten, and without life insurance. Gabrielle was gifted college funding for her kids and enough money to tide her over for years while she put her life back together. It was an anonymous donation, but the whispers on the long-term care unit all agreed that the generosity had come from Agnes O'Reilly, although we never knew for sure.

"Ms. O'Reilly was quite fond of you, Miss Evans. She wanted to make sure that you'd see the world and left you some money to ensure time and travel. When can you come into my office?"

He didn't disclose how much money, nor did I ask. It was an uncomfortable question. Even when my mom had passed, the funeral expenses, her medical bills, and personal debt ate up what little amount had been stashed away. A check in the amount of $400 arrived in our Seattle mailbox a month after her death, which seemed like such a paltry amount to have defined a life. I cashed it only because I needed to pay the landlord to fix up our small house before I moved to Los Angeles.

Rather than revel in the realization of a windfall, I would wait until the Friday meeting with Mr. Shanahan. It could be a $1,000 or

$5,000, but the amount wouldn't significantly change my life. I had enough funds in my bank account for a ticket to Europe and two weeks' stay in a decent hotel, as well as money for excursions and general spending.

It was almost dinnertime, so I ordered a BBQ pizza and chopped salad. I'd worked up an appetite but wasn't quite ready to consume alcohol; the slight odor of last night's vomit fest still lingered in the living room.

My phone rang with Cate on the other end. "Happy Memorial Day!" Cate's speech was light and easy. She went on to tell me about her day of beachgoing, party hopping, and wardrobe changing. "I wore that red, silky dress from Barneys to Jessica's lunch, and I sweated so much that it was ruined by dessert. You should have seen the decorations. She went all out. Catered by Nora's Bites, and she also used that company, Drowning in Decor, for the tables and flowers. Sprays of blue-and-yellow flowers. Just gorgeous! I have so many ideas that I want to be married five times. That doesn't sound very good, does it?" Cate was already planning her engagement party and the wedding preparations were underway. So much for waiting and enjoying just being engaged for a while. "What's new with you?"

I was going to tell her about Agnes O'Reilly and the call from her lawyer but instead asked her when we could get together.

"It's been a while, Cate. I miss seeing you."

"Same. I've been so wrapped up with the wedding plans. Speaking of, what's new with your love life? How is Evelyn?"

"Estelle. She's fine. Lying low these days."

"I really think you should go on as yourself. 'Jewel, nurse extraordinaire. Makes a mean margarita.' What do you think? I'll help you with your photos and narrative. You'll meet someone fabulous. Just as I did."

"Yeah, maybe. I gotta run. Pizza's here. Let's talk tomorrow."

A middle-aged man with a ball cap that read "Can't Adult Today" handed me a bag and a pizza box. He stood on my welcome mat, looking around my apartment and then scrutinized my left hand. "You married?"

"What does that have to do with anything?" I took a step back and away from the innocuous-turned-Ted Bundy character who was standing in my doorway.

"I figure a gal ordering dinner for one could use a night with a great guy. How about I take you out on the town?" As if on cue, he scratched his crotch.

"And how about I throw your ass out of here?" Sam appeared behind the man, towering above the guy, who looked scared enough to pee his pants. He turned and mumbled what sounded like "sorry" and almost mowed Sam over while trying to escape.

"What the hell was that about? Why are you letting men come into your place?" He looked ready to hit something, with his hands in fists by his sides and a stance reserved for a warrior.

"I was just trying to get something to eat. What's it to you, anyway? It's not like you're my boyfriend." I walked toward the kitchen and opened the pizza box. "I almost had a real date, too, but you ruined it." It was poking a bear with a stick, but at least Sam was communicating. He nostrils flared as he took a deep breath.

Folding a slice of pizza, he looked around, focusing on the trash bags that were accumulated by the door. "Cleaning or moving?"

"Just organizing. What were you up to all day?" My tone was sightly accusatory. "It was Memorial Day, after all. Eating, drinking, laughing, you know, fun times on the best day of the year."

Sam wasn't good with nuances. "Why does that question sound like an interrogation? I'm really busy, Jewel, and don't have time for this. Thanks for dinner." Without a word, Sam crammed the last bit into his mouth, grabbed another slice, and then left my apartment.

What should have been a day filled with bike riding, barhopping, and good times with good friends, turned out to be miserable. At 8:30 p.m., I heard people on the sidewalk, chatting as the day dissipated into intimacy. A hot bath with eucalyptus salts wasn't enough to quiet my mind or calm my nerves, but maybe weConnect was.

Wake up, Estelle.

Her profile photos were breathtaking. I looked in the mirror and saw my honey-blonde hair in a high, tight bun, a few wrinkles starting to form around the nasolabial folds, and my hazel eyes sparked a hint of sadness, teetering on tears. My dear Agnes, I'm not exactly the shining light you made me out to be. I'd sorely disappoint you if you could see me now.

There's Bill again, oh, and Craig, Jeff, Brent, Gerald, Scott with two t's and Scot with one t. Oscar. Bradley. Three different Michaels. Joe. Ethan. Either these guys are super picky, and the women on the other side are subpar, or the women have already vetted them and are waiting for improved prospects. After many months of being Chelsea, Raquel, Amanda, and now Estelle, and seeing the same men cycle through, we, as a society of singles, either prefer to play the dating game or our bars are set too high. Granted, I'm guilty of all of the above, but does that mean we are all doing the same thing? What is the point of dating apps if after a year the same men are on them, forever in search of "the one"?

Ryan, forty, real estate attorney, had two rescue dogs, enjoyed gardening, building birdhouses, and dabbled in brewing his own beer. His sandy-brown hair and blue eyes made him look like a young Harrison Ford. Estelle swiped right.

Ding-ding! An instant match. Hello-o-o-o, Ryan!

"Smart. Earthy. Handy. You are my kind of man." It was easy to be flirty and forthright when hiding behind a computer screen and an identity of my choosing. In real life, I'd never be this aggressive, but now it's all about the lure of the catfish.

Another few swipes to the right resulted in more connections, which became exhausting and fruitless. Estelle was the hit of the party. Every man she swiped right had already swiped right on her. I'd never have such luck. If Sam could admit to himself—and me—that he liked me, I wouldn't have to be a red-headed cellist from Ireland.

I was about to put weConnect to bed for the night when I heard a notification. Ryan had sent Estelle a message. "You are sweet. Thanks. I was being honest in my profile. That's a rare quality on here. I've heard that some men and women make up false profiles and lie about their jobs and education. Why bother? Like it won't come out in the wash. Anyway, tell me about yourself, Estelle."

Barely out of the gate, and I wanted to cry.

Where should I begin … with my philanthropy, collections of Picassos, triathlons, IQ of 132, or the time I've spent volunteering at animal shelters? Some men are fickle and need prodding, similar to an iron poker to move a fat heifer. If it weren't for Estelle, I'd have succumbed to a diet of peppermint chip ice cream, Netflix, and a membership to Weight Watchers. She was my ticket to navigate out of this world—witnessing for myself that there were viable men to date, understanding their wants and desires, how to write to them before meeting at a bar. This was what I told myself, anyway.

"I'm in marketing, enjoy yoga, travel, and whiskey." I actually couldn't stand the taste of whiskey, but it fit Estelle's sophisticated persona. She ordered Pappy Van Winkle bourbon whiskey at high-end bars, and every man nearby wanted to treat her to a two-finger pour, hoping to take her home afterward. She never gave out her phone number, nor left with a man she had just met because she was classy and certainly wasn't desperate. Estelle was the chooser and didn't wait to be chosen.

"Whiskey ... nice! Maybe you can try my beer one day. Great stuff! So, where do you like to travel?"

Did I really want to do this? "Spain, Israel, Italy, Portugal. The usual places." I left the conversation open-ended since I had an early morning at the hospital. "Let's chat tomorrow. Good night, Ryan." Without waiting for his response, I closed the app.

—~—

The four-day week vacillated between trying to remember which patient needed me and for what, and wondering what Sam was doing. He hadn't called or sent a text, and his apartment appeared quiet. Maybe he went out of town. We didn't know each other well enough to communicate on a romantic level, so the pitfalls were due to misunderstandings until we could work out our issues. John Gray would be proud of my rationale, and even though Sam had retreated to his cave, I needed to let him ruminate for a while. If I followed him in there, it would negate the rubber band effect. To be happy together, Sam needed to slingshot back to me, as per *Men Are from Mars, Women Are from Venus*.

The drive to Garth Shanahan's office took longer than anticipated. His firm was close by in Culver City, but Friday's afternoon traffic in Los Angeles sometimes doubled the commuting time. An hour in stop-and-go driving, and I arrived at Levi, Levi, Levi & Shanahan, LLP. Many of the employees had left to start an early weekend.

"Would you like a glass of water? Tea?"

I declined the offer made by the receptionist. Agnes's estate planning attorney appeared from a conference room and greeted me with a warm, rather long embrace. "That's from Ms. O'Reilly. She asked me to give you a hug, since she wouldn't be able to. She will be missed." He stood in front of me with his hands still outstretched, as

170

though he wanted to go in for round number two. I sidestepped him and took the nearest chair. Was this the new way of meeting single women?

"Yes, please sit. So, Ms. Evans, let me get right to the point. Agnes O'Reilly was extremely fond of you. Although she left the bulk of her estate to charitable organizations, she reserved a small nest egg for you to "get out there and see what the world has to offer"—as she put it. An amount has been placed in a bank account with your name on it. Just sign this paperwork, and you can be on your way. Jessica, our notary, will be in momentarily."

He placed a stack of documents in front of me and held the red Mont Blanc in the air, as though it were the holy grail. I took it and began to sign. Jewel Evans. Jewel Evans. Jewel Evans. Twenty signatures later, and Jessica walked in. She was incredibly busty.

"Do you have your driver's license, honey?" Jessica had a southern drawl, and based on her high, teased platinum blonde hair, long eyelash extensions, and super tight dress, she must have just moved here and hadn't assimilated into the conservative and professional appearance most law firms expected from their notary publics. Her four-inch heels click-clacked toward me as she bent down to witness my signature. "Were you born and raised in California?"

Taken aback, I tried to hide my recoil. "Is that relevant? I went to school here. Why does it matter?"

My attorney looked up, aware of my evasiveness, and countered, "It isn't. She's just making small talk." His smile turned into a thin line across his face. Then after one more flip through the papers, he handed me an envelope. "Well, that's it. Thank you for coming in, and please call if you have any questions. Oh, and you'll need to bring your birth certificate and two additional pieces of ID when you go to the bank."

"Mr. Shanahan, thank you. We all loved Agnes at the hospital. The nurses and doctors adored her. It just isn't the same without her laughter, stories, and lovely energy. I actually looked forward to work because of her. Although I'm glad she doesn't have to endure the hospital anymore, I'm sad that she passed. And I wish she'd have known how much this gift means to me." I put out my hand to shake his, since the hugging thing didn't feel acceptable after only meeting him for a moment. For the first time, I noticed the family photos strewn about his office.

"You have a large family. Four children?"

"Five. I'm truly blessed. Jessica is a saint."

"Jessica … the notary?" I turned to see the woman through the glass partition. She had her purse in one hand and was flipping lights off with the other. An epiphany struck me like a lightning bolt you'd encounter in an open field at dusk, right before the thunder split the sky open and rain drenched you. It went beyond the idiom "don't judge a book by its cover," and took on the entire premise of dating apps. To swipe right meant, "I like this photo, and based only on an image, I'll focus my time on the person behind the profile, bypassing other profiles with photos that don't catch my attention." A swipe to the left indicated, "I cannot see myself dating this person because of the hairstyle, nose, or smile. Next." I was feeding into the entire narrative of what everyone believed dating apps to be: shallow, impersonal, judgmental. As Estelle, I was the epitome of why the system didn't work for the majority. Her photo and profile were in the top 3 percent, I assumed, and made the remaining 97 percent look average, when they really weren't, because it was comparison game.

"Yes, my wife of eighteen years. The love of my life. I trust that you'll find yours. Agnes shared a few stories with me, and I apologize that I didn't disclose this early. Both Jessica and I were very fond of her too."

As I rose to leave, it dawned on me that I never found out the sum that Agnes had left. "Pardon me, but, Mr. Shanahan, what is the amount that Ms. O'Reilly gave me?"

"One hundred thousand dollars."

17

Can You Make This Mai Tai with Tequila?

Arriving home in a dream-like state, and after almost hitting a parked car and grazing a pedestrian on the crosswalk, I checked my mailbox. Apropos of everything, my passport had arrived. Property of The United States of America, yes sir! This little booklet would grant me entry into foreign countries never imagined. Belarus. Bhutan. Kazakhstan. Well, maybe not Kazakhstan. The hospital was still a priority and expected me to work outside of my vacation days. A quick email to the HR department regarding my banked time and request to access the days in question took all of one minute and then the pouring of the tequila commenced.

"Cheers to you, Agnes. May your spirit be light and happy, and your memory never fade. Without you, I wouldn't have the "gumption," and thanks for letting me borrow this word from your ever abundant vocabulary so that I can embark on a journey of foreign languages, border crossings, passport stamps, and ethnic foods." My glass of tequila was raised high in the air as I toasted Agnes.

An message popped up in my email in-box.

"Dear, Ms. Evans. Next week, there are five days of vacation time that will drop off from your allotted amount. If you wish to use them, I can allocate these days toward your Monday to Friday workdays for next week, and you will resume your designated shift schedule the following Monday. Please advise."

Where should I go? First, I was going to hit the nearest happy hour bar.

"Meet me at Morgan's Pub for a drink in twenty. Need to celebrate. Will explain later." A text flew through cyberspace and into Cate's iPhone.

She responded immediately, "On my way!"

—~—

The Irish pub was unusually busy, but two seats at the bar practically had our names on them. I had already drunk four shots of tequila before Cate sent me a text. "Be there in five."

I fired up weConnect to pass the time. Ryan and I had texted all week for at least an hour every night. He explained ad nauseam the new kegging system he had at his house and the different flavors of beer being created. Typically, I would zone out and make an excuse to redirect the conversation to something I could relate to, but Ryan's enthusiasm went beyond normal chitchat. His impressive dossier earned him a swipe to the right, but after spending many hours texting about fermentation, hydroponic gardening, and the secret to building a birdhouse, I became fond of him. It's the investment of looking beyond the photos to find out what made Ryan tick. He was an average looking man but had a zest for life and knowledge, which rubbed off on me.

I sent him a quick message. "Hi, Ryan. Just checking in. Are you up for a chat later? I'm out with a friend for happy hour."

As with all "texting relationships," they either dissipated or graduated to phone calls and then meeting in person. I knew it would be a matter of time before Estelle disappeared or a burner phone was purchased.

Ding-ding! "Estelle, where are you?"

"I'm at Morgan's Pub on Wilshire. Why?" I shook the imaginary dice in my hand and tossed them on the bar's counter.

A familiar floral scent filled my senses and feminine hands covered my eyes. "Jewel! Guess who?"

Cate hugged me from behind and then shared the events from her past two weeks with me. The lawyer she'd hired for her shoplifting arrest negotiated an outcome that had worked for both parties. Cate had paid a fine and had agreed to work one hundred hours of community service, to be completed within the next year.

"I also have to do twenty hours of therapy with their appointed psychologist. I suppose it's a good idea." Cate took my hand and said, "Enough about me. What's up with you and Sam, and is this why we're celebrating?"

"Gosh no. Sam's been really strange these days and is barely in the picture anymore. Guess what? I'm so excited. My passport came today!"

"We're celebrating over a little paper book? Well okay. Bartender, two more." Cate held up her glass and winked at the woman behind the bar. "So, where do you want to fly first?"

We opened a travel app on my phone, and within minutes, we booked a trip to Maui for the next morning.

"I really wanted to use my new passport. Hawaii's considered domestic. Baby steps, I suppose."

"Not a bad place to start." Then, Cate reminded me, "You know I can only go for two nights, so I hope you'll be okay for the remaining four."

A man behind me was chatting up the female bartender. "She said she'd be here. Red hair. Gorgeous. This is her." I turned and watched the man show his phone to the curious bartender before I realized that he was Ryan. "Her name's Estelle."

The sip of margarita made its way out of my mouth and all over Cate's blue dress.

"Jewel! Geez! What the …?" Cate grabbed a napkin and began blotting the splatters of lime juice and agave. "I'm going to the restroom to clean up."

Never dreaming that my catfished man would actually show, I had also forgotten that I'd texted my location. I swiveled my chair to meet Ryan head on and blurted, "I forgot. I mean I forgot how great it is to be single. Hi. I'm Jewel." I extended my hand to Ryan. He laughed and shook it but scanned the room, perhaps looking for a hidden camera for a new TV series on ambushing single men in Los Angeles. Or maybe he was searching for Estelle.

He was better looking in real life. And tall. Ryan had a guileless charm to him—an energy that didn't transmit through to his photos on weConnect.

Before letting him speak, I continued, "Ryan, can I call you Han Solo? You know, because you look like Harrison Ford."

Ryan still held my hand in his, but the confused look that crept across his face made him pull away ever so slowly, like that moment the babysitter realizes that the phone call is coming from inside the house. "Have we met? How do you know my name?"

Cate had returned and took her respective seat, giving Ryan the once-over. "Hey," she said, acknowledging our guest.

"Cate, Ryan here makes his own beer. And not the crappy stuff. Like real Budweiser quality. Oh and get him talking about his birdhouses. We'll be here all night. Isn't that right, my friend?" I smiled a bit too brightly, impressed with myself that I could rattle off details that only the two of us at Morgan's would know. I started to giggle and couldn't stop until I was almost choking, teetering on hysteria.

Ryan took a step back. "I don't know who you are, but this shit's too weird." He didn't waste a moment and wandered out of the pub, yet still scanned the room, looking for Estelle.

Cate shook my arm. "Jewel, what just happened? Who was that man?" She seemed genuinely unimpressed with the exchange and reached for the bowl of free pretzels.

I shrugged, feeling queasy from consuming too much tequila on an empty stomach. "Just some guy I used to know."

—~—

Sabotage—to deliberately damage or destroy any chance of establishing a relationship with a stable, normal man in a city where meeting one is like finding a unicorn. Somewhere between confidence and insecurity lies the truth with the many months of catfishing. The thought of Ryan was just that—a construct—just as the *idea* of Estelle was to Ryan. My mirrored refection made me catch my breath.

My shoulder-length blonde hair and heart-shaped face couldn't look any more different from Estelle's presentation and stature. Estelle had provided great odds, like betting on a pure-blooded thoroughbred on race day and knowing any waged amount would generate a win, place, or show. Ryan should have known that someone as perfect as Estelle would not be into him, so why did he even bother? Why did I even bother? That feeling of standing in a hole and trying to climb out of it, but the shovel in my hands kept digging a deeper hole, came to mind.

—~—

176

Cate stood waiting on the sidewalk as the Uber driver pulled up to her condo early the next morning. She wore a colorful straw hat and held a beach bag in her hand. "Aloha!"

"Good thing it's Saturday. We should have fewer commuters," Barry, our driver, explained as he weaved in and out of freeway lanes. His three iPhones were lined up in brackets that were attached to the car's dash, with easy access to navigation apps, but included weConnect as well. Estelle's photo smiled from the middle phone, her green eyes seeking mine, conspiratorially.

"Wow. She's pretty. I didn't know there are women like that on dating apps." Cate was busy on her phone, chatting with Dave, so she didn't see what I was seeing. "Are you going to swipe right on her?"

"Nah. It's just fun to look. She wouldn't go out with me, anyway. This Estelle is the hottest single on weConnect. Plus, my wife would be really pissed."

"You are married but on a dating app? I don't get it. What's the point?" Nothing surprised me anymore.

"That's the thing—there is no point. It's just something to pass the time in between fares. It's also good to see what's out there, you know, on the other side of the fence."

"On the other side of the fence is a quagmire, Barry. If I were you, I wouldn't look over there because you'll never like what you find. Stick with your wife."

"Huh?"

Cate finished her call with kisses into the phone. "Love you. Of course I'll call. Love you, love you, babe. No, I love you more." She turned to me, "Dave said hi and that you need to keep an eye on me. If he only knew what you do for me." She gave me a hug. "You and I are partners in crime. Ahh … you know what I mean. Bad joke."

I chuckled at the foot in her mouth. "Let's look forward, okay? Speaking of, we are almost at LAX." I whipped out my phone and send a quick message to Sam, who had been MIA since Monday.

"Sorry about last week. I'm going out of town for a few days. If any packages come for me, please bring them in. Thx. Hope you're well."

—~—

The flight to the Kahului airport on the island of Maui was bumpy, but the view outside the window made up for it. The Hawaiian

177

archipelago featured eight main islands, but the numerous atolls, islets and seamounts, which surrounded the more popular destinations, added to the beauty and mystique of its geography and history. The regional airport looked different from what I had expected. There weren't women dressed in traditional Polynesian dresses, holding leis in their hands for passengers who exited the plane, walked down the stairs, and on to the tarmac, as Elvis's *Blue Hawaii* had made famous. Cate and I deplaned the Boeing 767 and walked into a Starbucks kiosk.

"Order an oat milk latte for me. Thanks."

Cate waited in line for our beverages, and I checked my phone. Sam had sent a text. "Be safe. I'll check on things, no worries."

Well at least we were still communicating. I couldn't even remember what the argument had been about.

Our hotel sat amid a string of equally fabulous hotels on Kaanapali's beachfront. Scantily clad guests were milling about the lobby, holding on to pretty drinks of blue or purple, adorned with a little umbrella and pineapple garnish. A quick change of clothes, and we were poolside, ordering our first cocktail.

"This doesn't suck. Look at this place … just like paradise."

Palm trees swayed in the island breeze and stand up paddle boarders were making their way across the ocean in front of us. A group of young kids had built a sandcastle city on the beach nearby, covering at least twenty feet of space. Coconut scented sunscreen and a hint of plumeria flowers caught my senses unaware. Paradise, just as Cate said.

A childhood memory of a trip to Hawaii with my parents flashed in my mind. I couldn't remember which island we'd gone to or how old I'd been, but I could almost see my mom walking beside my dad, both wearing leis and sipping mai tais. They were happy and in love. Life held promise back then. Thirty-five years later, I had returned to the islands as an orphan of sorts, trying to forge my own way in the world.

"Make mine a double. Actually, can you make this mai tai with tequila?"

The twenty-something bartender, a little reminiscent of Tom Cruise in *Cocktail*, if just in my imagination, looked my way and chuckled. "Yes, I can, but it wouldn't taste right. This is Hawaii, the land of rum and pineapple. Try this." He passed me a tall, peach-and-red colored drink. "It's my specialty. Rum, fresh guava juice, sweet dark rum, and grenadine. I call it Island Beauty. Just like you."

Is he hitting on me? I could be his mother. Or young aunt.

"Wow! Perfect."

Cate and I sipped the day away until the music of a luau began at the nearby property. Couples, hand in hand, hurried past us in island attire to partake in the hula demonstration. A dozen traditional Polynesian dancers swayed their hips and arms in a luna dance, while other male dancers sat in a circle around them, softly chanting and shaking their red-feathered gourd rattles. The Hawaiian sun was arcing downward and behind a neighboring island. Cate argued that it was Molokai, and I finally let her win.

"How would I know? I've only been here once when I was very little, so I don't remember much."

Cate looked at me sideways. "Really? I thought your parents were avid world travelers and took you here many times. That's what you told me when we first met. Remember, you stayed in that suite in Waikiki and had the top floor all to yourself? You ordered so much room service that your parents had to request a reduction in the bill because the hotel shouldn't have been delivering food for a minor. What a gal won't say to get a date!"

The sweet rum concoctions were giving me a headache and making my vision is a bit blurry. There were two Cates, and they were moving around, making me seasick. "Can you stand still for a minute?"

Cate was swaying along with the hula dancers, trying to mimic their undulating gestures. "We should probably eat something. Let's rest in the room for a bit and then go for dinner, okay?" Cate asked me, but her attention was still on the muscular male dancers.

After an hour nap and a shower, we recharged to power through the rest of the night. My long, mint skirt and white, ruffled blouse made it look like I had planned the vacation all along, but the haphazard packing job and lack of summer clothes told a different story. We passed the gift store that doubled as a clothing boutique. Fuchsia, teal, sunflower yellow, and poppy-orange dresses and sarongs served as beacons, hanging in the storefront windows and beckoning travelers who had forgotten essential festive attire. Sun hats of every size and material hung on the metal racks, reminding those who planned to bask in the sun that they should protect their faces.

"Let's pop in there tomorrow morning, k? I didn't bring a hat or SPF." Cate was already out of earshot, so I had to run to catch up. "What's the hurry?"

"I'm starving. I can almost taste the mahi mahi with capers and lemon butter."

We sat at a small, intimate table that was almost on the sand. After finishing our fresh, local fish entrees, an older Hawaiian man played the ukulele as he walked among the tables, stopping occasionally by couples who appeared to be romantically involved.

I placed my hand in a loving way on Cate's and teased her. "Oh, sweetheart, the love of my life, do you think we look like a happy couple?"

She wasn't looking at me, but rather, across the room. "Yes ... ahh ... I mean no ... but they must think we are." Cate cocked her head toward a table, about twenty feet away, where a man and woman were staring at us. The man's face looked curious, but the woman's eyes were wide and unyielding. Her mouth was slightly agape, as though she'd seen a ghost. She obsessively tapped her date's forearm and then leaned in, speaking quietly in his ear. He turned to look at me, scrutinizing my face and hair. The color instantly drained from my face, and the sweat started to roll down my back. *Oh no. It couldn't be.*

"Cate, I'm not feeling well. Too much rum today. I'm heading back. Do you mind picking up the check, and I'll get dinner tomorrow?" Without waiting for her response, I left the table and walked out, but not before hiding behind the planter to watch the couple, who was now watching Cate. They remained seated, and as the dark-haired woman leaned closer to the man opposite her, she whispered a story to him. They didn't notice Cate rise and also leave the restaurant.

I ran to catch up with her, as she beelined back to our hotel on the sandy sidewalk that coalesced with the beach. It was pitch-black, but the half-moon offered a slight illumination of Cate's sun-kissed skin. She looked radiant with a red hibiscus flower tucked behind her ear. The sprinkling of room lights that hugged the path ahead offered little indication as to how far we had to walk, yet the warm wind and distant Hawaiian music told me that it didn't matter.

"Cate, wait up. I must have gone the wrong way."

Cate spun around, surprised to see me behind her. "Jewel ... are you okay? I told you we should have stayed with tequila. Rum and sun don't mix. Everyone knows this." We continued walking along the pathway. "Hey, it looked like that couple wasn't happy to see two women together." She put her pinkie and thumb up to her ear, as if mimicking a telephone. "1960 called, and they want their phobia back. That woman looked crazy."

We entered the lounge area at our hotel and sat on a sofa by the piano. The floor was made of marble squares that curved like lines of a yacht. Two young kids shared the bench and played their rendition of chopsticks on the keys. Their blonde curls bobbed up and down to the beat of the melody as they giggled.

Cate gazed at them. "They could be ours. If it doesn't work out with Dave, we'll have those kids we've always wanted. Speaking of, I'm going to give him a call. I'll meet you back at the room." She walked away for privacy.

—~—

"She's cute." He looks my way but can't see me because I'm transparent, like cellophane.

"Well, she's practically homeless. No father, mother on her deathbed. Sad. Probably won't make much of herself. I wouldn't bother." Her dark hair is held high and tight, with a blue scrunchie. Exasperated, the brunette turns to him, "I'm more your type. Forget her. Everyone has."

They start making out in front of me. One hand goes up the front of her blouse, and the other unzips her jeans. He is no longer my high school crush, but Robert. Then Robert morphs into Jake as he gets on top of her, entering her as he looks up at me with pity. Thrusting, he begins to laugh, mocking me. He gets off my high school nemesis, as she lies on my childhood bed, naked and satisfied, but also smirking. The poster of Duran Duran hangs on the wall next to Rob Lowe, a page carefully ripped from a *Teen Beat* magazine and held up by Scotch Tape. Sam is now standing in my bedroom. The small, white dresser, with its paint peeling and missing handles, showcases my treasures and prized possessions. He picks up my Michael Jackson action figure, a garage sale item I had rescued for fifty cents, and then

181

breaks it in two pieces with a chuckle. Sam pulls up his acid-wash denims, zips them, and walks right through me and out of my room.

"Noooooooooo! Stop! Don't! Don't!"

"Jewel, for God's sake, wake up." Cate stands over me, shaking my shoulder. "What the hell? Is this something we need to talk about? I'm seeing a theme here, like you're being taken over by aliens or worse. Are you on something I don't know about?"

The bedsheets and pillows were strewn all over the floor, making it look like some adolescents had had a pajama party gone wild. My T-shirt was soaked from sweating out my nightmare; an amalgamation of past childhood players and last night's restaurant surprise sent me back to the imprisonment I had left behind years ago.

"I ... I had a bad dream; that's all. It happens sometimes when I drink on an empty stomach. Let's get coffee." A cursory look in the decorative mirror between the two queen beds showed medusa-like hair and deep, hollow eyes. My cheeks had dried tear paths from the silent crying I'd been accustomed to now for almost forty years. "Gonna take a quick shower."

The morning sun shone through our expansive windows. We hadn't closed the curtains before retiring for bed, and now the bright light was challenging us to rise and join the other hotel guests who had already commandeered lounge chairs by the pool.

"Yeah, yeah, we're coming Maui. Hold your horses," Cate said as she opened the window, letting in the fresh air. "Jewel, I'm heading down. Meet you there." She donned her red-and-gold bikini, threw a cover-up over it, and grabbed her straw bag. "Latte? Extra shot?"

Still trying to piece together the events of the previous night, I shouted from the bathroom, "Please! And a toasted bagel!"

The ghosts of not only past lovers but also past friendships seemed to be following me, haunting everything I did, saw, and felt. The old adage of "you can run, but you can't hide" came to mind. My legs were so tired.

Thirty minutes later, I reunited with Cate on the chaise *longues*. She was chatting with the couple next to her who were on their honeymoon.

She turned to me and whispered, "If Dave dares to bring me to a place like this for our honeymoon, I'll divorce him."

—~—

Hours later, and $200 poorer after visiting the gift shop to buy sun protection related items, I awakened from an hour-long nap under the small palapa to an impossibly familiar voice. Cate, still in an island slumber, was oblivious to anything more than two feet around her.

"I know it can't be her, but it's weird, you know. Like we all have a double, a person on this earth who looks just like us ... a ... what do you call them?"

"Doppelgänger."

"Right. One of those. If I had to bet, I'd say it was her, but she's been gone for twenty years."

The voices drifted away; two people sharing a storyline from a distant life walked past the pool and out of earshot. I pulled the straw sun hat over my face and remained still. What started out as a relaxing vacation had turned into a game of cat and mouse, if only in my vexed mind.

My lounge partner stirred beside me. "I can't believe I have to leave tomorrow. Wish I could stay longer with you. What was I thinking, coming to paradise for only two nights?"

"Well, there is the matter of a fiancé. Hey Kate, I've been thinking too. I'm gonna check out tomorrow and try the other side of the island."

—~—

Alone in the small hotel room in Hana, I sat next to the oceanfront window and watched the beachgoers splashing in the water and trying their luck at boogie boarding. Someone was passing out hula hoops, and the boys who had made a sandcastle, which was as large as a sectional sofa, started yelling at the kids who were walking into the moat and drawbridge, destroying their creation with the twirling, plastic hoops.

"Aloha." I reached out to Sam by text. He hadn't uttered a peep since I'd told him I was going out of town, nor had he asked me where I'd be. Little did he know, I could be eating crickets in Bangkok or at a caribou chili cook-off in Alaska instead of drinking mai tais under the Hawaiian sun.

Cate was already safely back in Los Angeles. "Landed. Miss you already." She always texted me when she traveled, like a sister would.

183

Sometimes it felt as though Cate were my sister, yet the memories of sharing a childhood with a sibling were nowhere to be found. If I had grown up with Cate, I know she would have protected me through the harsh reality of sick and dying parents. I never had anyone in my life to help me cope or just to say that everything was going to be all right. Suddenly, I felt more alone than ever.

The setting Hawaiian sun offered no advice or comment. It disappeared, just as Cate, Sam, Jake, Robert, my parents, Aunt Carol, and every significant person in between had. Poof! Insta-alone. While I looked out at the shoreline—or what was visible at dusk—an image entered my psyche. I was walking passively into the warm Pacific Ocean, unnoticed by anyone, until the sea enveloped my body and my head sank into the abyss of the evening tide, as my lungs filled with salt water.

I could see her—walking with intention but without regret or a certain future. When she turned around, she had no face, just a body that was adrift and heading toward a safer place. A place where she could exist among others and among those who'd never known her for anything other than now.

18

Amarillo By Morning

"Where are you? Hawaii?"

Well, if I were in Italy, I wouldn't say aloha, I'd say ciao, so this is a silly question.

"What gave me away?"

A glance around the room showed an open suitcase, awaiting disheveled beach attire, hats, sunscreen, and flip-flops. I was in denial that I'd be leaving for the airport in two hours, which made it easy to hit the pool bar for that last drink. The empty bottle of tequila, bought from the only liquor store within ten miles, poked its head from the trash bin.

"You wrote aloha, so I assumed you are in Hawaii. When are you home?"

He wouldn't get a job in the CIA, that's for sure. Sam had his special qualities and was the only male I wanted to spend time with, but sometimes he's a bit clueless. "Leaving today. How are things?"

I received quite a bit of mail and packages, but other than that, he wouldn't have known I was gone. That's comforting.

The pool bar was littered with a few patrons watching a college football game, but at 9:00 a.m., it's surprising to see everyone imbibe. Fancy island cocktails adorned the countertops, and two newly seated girls, around thirty years old, sat nearby on high tops with their phones in their hands, laughing at what they saw on their screens.

"Who is dumb enough to believe this profile is real? World traveler, owns a winery, PhD, and looks like Matt Damon. And he's probably staying in a shithole like this hotel 'cause his location is within one mile. Come. On!! He'd have a nine-bedroom house with a full staff and driver." The cute blonde and her brunette friend sat opposite me, still intoxicated from the previous night, or they'd started drinking at 7:00 a.m.

"Swipe right on him, Sloane, just to see if he responds."

"Oh! Look at this one. Five photos, all selfies and without a shirt. This guy is not thirty. Looks more like fifty. So gross. Who wants to go out with a guy who shaves twenty years off his age? I hate when they do this. Total liar."

"No, no, I win. Listen to this one ... Leo, enjoys knitting, has three bearded dragons, has seen all *The Real Housewives of Beverly Hills* episodes, and can yodel. Looks like my Aunt Edna. See!"

I picked up my margarita and walked over. "Hi, ladies. I couldn't help but overhear. So, the online dating scene is pretty bad here, too, hey? I'm Jewel."

"Hi, Jewel," they said in unison.

"Yeah ... here, there, everywhere. I'm Sloane; she's Emily," the brunette responded as she turned her iPhone toward me. A selfie of a dark-haired man and only the left half of his beard shaved stared back. "This guy thinks that posting a photo like this is going to get him points. Clueless. So, are you single, Jewel?"

"I am ... and going through the same thing as you two. Sometimes I think it's better to take my chances in the real world, but it's really the same everywhere you go. It doesn't matter how you connect anymore. Dating apps just supply more available fish."

I ordered a round for the three of us while we commiserated about being single and the dating world. They were from Lubbock, Texas and celebrating Emily's thirty-third birthday.

"Ever been to Lubbock, Jewel?"

"Ugh ... no, but I've spent a lot of time in Texas. I ... ah ... lived there for a little while, when I was young."

Did I? I grew up in Seattle, but I also remember that we lived Texas. Our large seven-bedroom house was surrounded by a few hectares of ranch land. The farm animals were scarce, save for a few chickens for eggs, four horses, and a dog and cat. We must have moved to Washington when I was nine or so, but I remember our house in Texas. I'd run from room to room in the two-story colonial, playing hide and seek with our housekeeper, Ima, while Mom made cookies in the kitchen and Dad was instructing the farrier how to adjust our horses' shoes or to trim their hooves. Dad was an expert rider and taught me from an early age to ride on a saddle. He'd talk with me while brushing the horses after a long trail ride, showing me how to change their straw beds, water, and which food they preferred to eat. Before we'd go in for supper, he'd put me on the most gentle horse, Baby, and lead me around the corral, making sure I felt a part of the experience. Those days, before he'd succumbed to cancer, held the most precious memories I'd had with my parents. I wished we'd never left Texas.

"Cheers to you, Jewel. May you find a wonderful man. Heck, may we all live happily ever after ... we frickin' deserve it!"

We clinked our glasses and toasted to marriage and children.

—~—

Sam's apartment showed no sign of life. His blinds were drawn, and no music or sound of any kind seeped out from under the door. We had exchanged keys within the first month of meeting in case we couldn't reach the building manager if we locked ourselves out. Hmmm ... what are you up to, Sam?

I deposited my suitcase in my entry and listened for movement. Sam and I shared a common wall, but he's always been quieter than the woman and her teenage son on my other side. Beth and her fourteen-year-old, Bryson, seemed to be awake every moment of the day and night. If Beth wasn't crying, laughing, or yelling, Bryson was watching some kind of sports on TV or playing his hip-hop music. I had banged on my bedroom wall many times to prompt him to turn down the music or hockey game. "He scores!" reverberated through the aging building and right into my apartment. He was watching a Saturday night game with his buddies. Although it was a nuisance to hear the play-by-play of a hat-trick once my tan feet hit my welcome mat, Beth was a single mom and her son needed a break from her as much as she needed from him. When I was fifteen, our TV would break intermittently, and my mom rarely had the money to fix it, so I understood how important the outside world was for a teenager. Plus, it was only seven o'clock.

The key I'd never had to use for emergencies started to pulsate with electricity from within the little drawer by the fridge. I could feel it poking at me; its sharp edges hitting my pressure points and making long striations on my arms. The little piece of silver metal, with "SAM" in label maker tape looped through the top hole, sat in a little bowl that was tucked away beside my spare car key and a few paper clips. I knew it was there, because I could hear it calling my name. "Jewel, why don't you see if he's home? Maybe he's hurt, lying in a pool of arterial blood from a carved cantaloupe gone wrong."

Yeah, that could explain why he hadn't called, texted, or waited in my apartment with dinner and a margarita. Maybe it's a sign: The Universe was telling me to check on him. What if a quick, innocent entry led to saving his life?

The key fit easily in the door marked 211 and turned like butter to the right, giving me legal access to Sam's place. I walked in and locked the door behind me. A small lamp by the sofa had been left on, illuminating the identical floor plan I occupied, except our furniture couldn't be more different in style and function. No wonder he liked to lounge at my place; his brown leather sectional felt as stiff as it looked. I sat down and ran my hands on the large rectangles of cowhide. Maybe it's faux, like pleather. Had Sam had sex on this sofa? It would've had to be a quickie. The tech magazines that were squarely lined up on the coffee table disturbed me, like nails running down a chalkboard, so I gave them a swift push with my back hand, sending them askew.

The dishes in the sink showed he was probably in town but out for the night. A saucepan with remnants of mac and cheese sat among the dirty plates and glasses. I turned on the tap and let the water fill the pot, knowing how difficult it would be to scrub it clean once it solidified.

Sam's bed was made as well as a bachelor could make one; the four pillows stood at attention, ready to be used as back support while watching the TV that overtook his eight-drawer oak dresser. A few condoms were arranged innocently on the bedside table. Three little, square packages stating that Trojan's "Stimulate Her Where it Counts" instantly made my blood boil. Her? Just who was Sam stimulating? The bang of my hand slamming down on his nightstand stirred me into action.

His MacBook poked out from under a *Los Angeles Times* newspaper on the desk, concealed from prying eyes. As the techie he was, Sam had it password protected. Eight characters were required to gain entry to Sam's secrets. His last name, Dreyfuss, was eight but didn't work. I tried silly words that were eight letters and letter/number combinations. He'd spoken many times of his beloved dog named

Brittany, which shockingly was a Brittany, with her brown ears and white body depicting the classic spaniel. b-r-i-t-t-a-n-y ... bingo! I was in.

The computer opened to a page he'd been on recently. The shopping cart on Amazon contained multiple items: toilet paper, hair gel, socks, iPhone charging cable, queen-size bed sheets in bright white, pepper grinder. At the bottom of his screen was the row of icons depicting the applications Sam had on his MacBook. The purple and black logo of weConnect sat nestled between "Photos" and "Numbers," bobbing up and down from an earlier attempt at opening the app. I hovered the cursor over the "weC" to see who Sam was liking when a conversation nearby startled me. A key jiggled in the lock.

Sam and his date enter the apartment, giggling over a private joke and then tripping over the shoes he'd left in the entry. "Babe, these can't be yours? They're soooo '80s. Just how old are you?"

"They're vintage Doc Martins. What, you don't remember the '80s?"

The joyful couple stumbled to the bedroom, knocking over a plant, followed by expletives.

"Shit! That fucking hurts. I just jammed my shoulder in the wall. Goddammit, there's dirt all over the floor."

"Sam, darling, take it easy. We've got all night."

They hovered nearby, cooing and cajoling.

"Heather ... YOU are a Goddess."

"Babe ... mmm ... so hot ... the way your jeans cling to your fabulous ass ... And you own your own company? Jackpot ... so powerful ... damn, your body ... take these off now and finish what you started ... oh, God!! ... so fucking hot!!"

The bathroom door poked me in the thigh. I sat on the floor in the dark, hidden within two feet of space. My knees touched my chin while my arms hugged the legs that shook from fear of being caught. They were a breath away, their sex spilling out as they reached Sam's bed. Pillows and blankets cascaded over the side, falling on the floor and making a mockery of the perfectly organized bedroom. A metal belt buckle hit the wooden floor without apology, while a woman's heels thudded against the arctic white walls. The bed creaked from bodies disrupting its silence.

"Oh, oh, oh ... harder, harder ..."

The dark hall protected me as I crept to the living room, feeling the interlocked pieces of wood dig into my knees while Sam and Heather had their way with each other. Even the pleather sofa agreed that Sam was choosing a one-night stand over a lifetime of happiness with a fabulous gal.

I quietly exited his apartment and stepped out into the night air before entering my place. Once inside, I grabbed the nearest bottle of tequila like a life raft. Casamigos reposado was all I had in inventory, but George Clooney couldn't be wrong at a time like this. No need for a glass as I tipped the bottle, determined to finish it.

Robert, Jake, and Sam hovered above me, their faces morphing from men I'd loved before to scoundrels in movies. Sam's dark curls were smoothed against his head while his eyes were knowing and accusatory. Jake's salt and pepper hair challenged his normally bright smile that turned to a suspicious sneer. Robert's lips pursed as they formed words. "Liar." "Fake." "We know who you are." "Fraud."

"Leave me alone!"

The empty tequila bottle was chucked through the air and then hit the coffee table, smashing into pieces and disturbing the room's order. Shards skated across the hardwood floor and found their way under the sofa and crevices, which had yet to be cleaned in years. A large piece of glass lay on the *Glamour* magazine, pointing to an article about online dating. "28 Days to Love: How to meet him and keep him with a swipe of your thumb."

"That's bullshit! Complete crap!" I picked up the magazine and started tearing it into shreds. Discarded paper encircled my feet, a reminder that time was wasted on dating apps and on magazines that talked about them. "28 days … what a farce."

A knock at the door broke my reverie. Then it became a bang followed by, "Jewel. Jewel? Are you back in town? What was that noise?" Sam waited outside my door. "Hey, Jewel." Another bang on my door.

I stood perfectly still. The only brightness in the apartment came from a recessed, overhead fixture above the entry. It's a light I always left on when I was going out for the night or on vacation, which was enough to illuminate portions of the living room, but not adequate for reading a book. A minute elapsed and then footsteps outside the window carried Sam back to his home.

He's the last person I wanted to see, especially after his encounter with Heather. It's like he's living a double life. One night he's in my apartment, and the next, he didn't know my name. Who's the fraud now?

—∼—

The digital clock radio showed 2:07 a.m., which was really 11:07 p.m., Hawaii time. The neon green numbers shone through the darkness, reminding me that if I were still in Maui I'd be at the local pool bar, enjoying my last margarita. Dammit.

The pill bottle on my nightstand had been refilled before I'd left for Maui. Alprazolam, 90 ct, 1 mg, 1 refill remaining. I popped two Xanax and followed them with a swallow of tequila. Curling my legs around the king-sized pillows, which doubled as a willing bed partner, I lay on my side and watched the waxing moon as it shone through the mini blinds. Somewhere out there was my soulmate, among the city's chatter and daily grind. He's the one who wouldn't abandon me for an easy lay, while I crawled from his apartment like the cowardly lion. With one hand, I launched weConnect.

Scrolling through the messages sent to Estelle by unsuspecting hopefuls, no one in particular stood out. If it weren't for this dating app, I wouldn't know where to hang out to meet someone, considering I had few interests these days. I didn't care to fight for floor space amid the legging-wearing millennials at a yoga class. I barely shopped for groceries. I wasn't interested in doctors and left the hospital as soon as I punched the time clock, so the only logical place was a bar. My future soulmate was an alcoholic.

The antianxiety pills start to worked their magic as the room faded to black. I'm a little girl riding a horse named Baby on the Texas plains. Her chocolate brown body and black mane were groomed because of the hours I spent combing her coarse hair. I'd climb up on the wooden crate to reach above her round belly, stroking her expansive body with brushstrokes to make her shine like her mother, a prized mare named Wilhelmina's Joy.

Calls for supper are heard in the direction of the large ranch house, so I wave my hand in acknowledgment of my mother, the tall, elegant woman with blonde hair. She stands atop the wraparound veranda of our white colonial, a blue apron over her light pink dress keeps it clean

191

from the duck or roast she is cooking. A smile brightens her countenance—the by-product of an effervescent personality of someone who cooks from pleasure, rather than necessity. Our many staff work in the kitchen as well, but it's through the hands of love and nurture that my mother chops the vegetables, prepares the meat, and sets the dinner table for her family.

I hand Baby's reigns to the farmhand, Walter, and run toward our Norman Rockwell house. The foyer is laden with the aromas of yams and broiled meat. Bread was baked today, as the sweet, yeasty essence still lingers from the morning. Chatter is heard from the dining room. Aunt Carol came for a visit; two sisters bonding over their idyllic lifestyle and family.

An image stops me in my tracks. The hallway's full-length oval mirror captures the likeness of a pretty blonde girl, but it's not my face that stares back. She is happy and content with her life; her loving, supportive parents always present to dote on her every whim. The sorrow and anxiety that follow me everywhere jars me awake.

The clock read 4:41 a.m. My sweaty hair was plastered to my cheeks, making a veil across my eyes. Somehow I was a mess in the daytime and throughout the night as well. I threw on a new top, grabbed a blanket, and headed for the couch.

"I'm back. Just wanted to let you know."

I'd forgotten to message Cate, informing her I have returned to the mainland. She was the only one at this point who cared if I lived or died. I could have drowned while out on the Hobie Cat or stumbled into the fire pit at the luau, and no one would have been the wiser.

"Why r u up? Isn't it like 4:30 in the morning for you?" Cate's response came a moment later.

"For us, yes."

"No, for you. It's 1:30 p.m. for me. In Paris with Dave. 3 nights. He has a conference, so I went with him. R u ok?"

"Wow. Paris. I'd love to be there. I'm a-ok. Hey, have fun. Say hi."

I sign off first, because with Cate so far away I feel more alone than ever. Why didn't she tell me she'd been whisked away to France? The idea of visiting quaint brasseries and pâtisseries in Paris's *Le Marais* neighborhood was so overpowering that tears started to slide down my cheeks. One of my mom's favorite Harlequin romance novels was set amid the moonlit nights in Paris. She'd devoured the book and then read it again, savoring every dog-eared page until the book looked like twenty people had read it. The first year after my dad died had been the hardest. I'd hear my mom sniffling in her room, her door closed and the small bedroom lamp alight just enough to read the text on the pages. She'd always wanted to go beyond the contiguous United States, but specifically Paris. Right before her death, I had silently vowed that I'd see the city of love in her honor, tasting the pastries and eating the escargots because she never would. The fact that Cate was so cavalier about being in Paris when it had been my lifelong goal sent me spiraling.

It was like she knew.

I had told her that I'd always wanted to walk the thoroughfare of Avenue des Champs-Élysée, with its majestic monuments and fancy shopping. She was goading me—rubbing it in my face that she had a boyfriend, no, a fiancé, who had taken her to Europe, while I'd spent the last few days in Hawaii alone. Like a loser. A spinster. She's probably stuffing a croissant in her mouth right now, and not appreciating its buttery goodness. And those petite coffees. *Cafés crèmes*. They're the perfect complement to a morning croissant. Cate was certainly downing them like Americanos or ordering them in the afternoon, like a foreigner. Faux pas.

—~—

Chatter outside the kitchen window pulled me out of my slumber; the overhead sun shone brightly in the sky, warming the neighborhood as people walked home from brunch at a nearby cafe. My phone's screen showed 12:37 p.m. I'd slept in a ball on the sofa for almost eight hours. If the noise coming from the sidewalk hadn't woken me, my stomach's growls would have.

As usual, my favorite haunt for all-day breakfast had a line out the door. I scribbled my name on the waiting list and wandered into the little boutique next door. Abbot Kinney Boulevard, populated by shops and restaurants, was a destination for tourists visiting Venice, and locals who relied on everything they needed to be within a mile walking distance.

Even for a secondhand store, the prices were steep. Gently used jeans, $180. Refurbished dresser, $1465. Tarnished picture frame, $92.

"If you like it, I'll give you a deal."

193

A tall guy stood before me, his eyes curiously watching me handle the gold-and-silver specked 5" x 7" frame. Did he think I was going to steal it? It couldn't be worth more than five dollars.

"Ah … yeah, it's nice. I do like it. Seems a bit expensive for a used frame."

The corners of his lips produced a faint smile, making his eyes soften.

"Everything in here has been donated by Oscar winners, Grammy nominees, and people in the industry. The prices are suggestions, and 100 percent of the profits is donated to charities that promote youth literacy. How much would you like to pay?"

How could I haggle when somewhere there's a child who can't read or write, and all because I was cheap? I did, however, have $100,000 sitting in a bank account with my name on it.

"Do you take cash?"

Agnes O'Reilly generously paid one hundred dollars for a picture frame that once adorned the set of *Gone with the Wind*. It was carefully wrapped in recycled news print and placed in a generic brown bag.

—~—

A note taped to my door read "Checking on you. LMK if you need anything. Sam."

The crumpled stickie fell beside the garbage, which had been full for weeks. Dishes sat neglected in the sink, and a pile of laundry on the floor blocked the entrance to my bedroom. I couldn't remember the last time clean sheets were put on the bed. Five empty water glasses occupied the small space on the bedside table, and a crusty burrito wrapper took up residence on the dresser. Sam, it looks like I need a housekeeper.

Scrolling through photos on my phone of Cate and me in Maui gave me pause. We looked just as best friends should: laughing, hugging, smiling. One of my favorites was taken by our surfing instructor, Z, while we stood side by side on matching orange boards that were still on the shore. Cate's long blonde hair was braided around her head like a crown and adorned with flowers. I was wearing a blue-and-white bikini, and a purple lei that we'd found discarded on a nearby table. We couldn't have been happier at that moment.

The fact that she'd abandoned me so easily and quickly for a man that she hardly knew said so much. Who was Dave anyway? Had he been there for her, holding her hand and wiping her tears when Jason had cheated on her? Everyone cheats. Everyone lies. Everyone leaves.

Estelle could vouch for this. Every man wanted her, but they'd never be loyal. She had over thirty messages from different guys on weConnect, but none of these guys could be trusted beyond their photos, if those were even real. Eventually, they'd lie about their history, who they were, and what they owned. Nowhere was safe. The men online were just as deceitful as the ones in real life.

All of my walls felt like they were closing in on me.

Benji, forty-two, TV executive, hazel eyes and light brown hair. Loved classic rock, old movies, and riding his bike on the beach. Volunteered at food banks and shelters, rivaled most bartenders in cleverly crafted cocktails, and traveled to places unknown by most. He had one photo posted. Benji's intended selfie looked like it had been cropped from a larger photo, where there were many people surrounding him. Shoes could be seen in the bottom of the picture, and someone's arm was shown on his shoulder. Swipe right …

Ding-ding! Like that's a surprise. "Hi, Benji. How was your weekend?" I wrote with lackluster enthusiasm. It's late on Sunday night, and even though I have to work in the morning, I'm still on Maui time.

"Hello, gorgeous. I've seen your pic on here for a while. Why hasn't someone snatched you up?"

"I'm picky."

"You also aren't real, Estelle. You are fake. A phony. A catfish."

19

Ramen

The catfish, an abundant freshwater fish found typically in the southern United States, gets its name from facial whiskers that are synonymous to a cat's well-honed sensory tools, helping it maneuver by unforeseen obstacles. Cover is important to the catfish, as it hides from anglers and waits for an opportunity to feed, unnoticed by its enemy. To extract a catfish from the black, slimy crevices of an underwater cave, a noodler is required. Standing in deep waters, the noodler blindly reaches his bare hands into the dark space where he believes a catfish is lurking, and braces himself for the sharp teeth that might penetrate his skin and leave him wounded. The catfish latches on in protest lest it is captured.

The noodler doesn't anticipate the cleverness of the catfish and how much her livelihood depends on the games she plays or the extent to which she'll let the noodler know her identity. Just as noodling is considered a sport, catfishing is survival.

—~—

Fake? Benji went right for the jugular but had nothing to back up his claim other than suspicion. Granted, Estelle was as perfect as anyone could be on a dating app; she was gorgeous, accomplished, talented, independent, yet had only provided one photo. After many months of trolling the single male profiles, she was still without relationship, which, according to those who had viewed her, could indicate there's a lack of viable men or Estelle was gamefish. Benji was bold and tenacious to oust Estelle, yet those who pointed fingers to expose were in fact one and the same.

"What do you mean? I'm as real as you are, Benji."

Benji's single photo of a clean-cut Matthew McConaughey type complemented his narrative in that not only was he well-traveled and philanthropic, but he had a relevant career in the industry. Looking closer at his profile picture, I could see a slight smudge in the bottom right corner, which meant Photoshop had been used. It was bleeding obvious that Benji was also a catfish.

"Nice try. Someone who looks like you wouldn't be on this app. She'd be on TV or the cover of *Vogue*. Why don't you let us average men have a fair shot?"

"Average? You look like a guy I saw on *Grey's Anatomy* last night. Let's see a few more photos of you, my friend. If I'm a catfish, so are you."

Benji left the conversation but didn't unmatch Estelle. Did he think I was born yesterday?

A trending *Huffington Post* exposé featuring the many layers of online dating struck a chord with me. There were bona fide seekers of love who had created honest profiles and narratives to meet someone in kind, others who had tweaked their photos with filters and stretched the truth in their personal information, and the rest who had joined a dating app for the sheer excitement of knowing they'd intentionally reinvented themselves within a fake persona and never had to leave the confines of their living room or speak on the phone to their unsuspecting love match. There was a fat, bald sixty-year-old man who pretended to be a tall, dark, and handsome thirty-five-year-old man who had to turn down women because he didn't have enough time to date them all. Conversely, a woman who was never asked out on a date and had to steal photos of beautiful women on the Internet, while making her new life in print seem shiny and perfect. She couldn't go beyond the imaginary space of the app, beguiling the single male who thought he had a shot. The term "noodler" was defined in the article as someone who called out the connection as being fake, a fraud, a sham—or, going a step further, tried to expose the charlatan's true identity.

—~—

The workweek went by in a flash. Pills were administered, bandages were bound, blood pressures were taken, and tears were cried. A trauma patient named Liliana came in with multiple stab wounds on her head and upper torso. The thirty-three-year-old woman was found in an alley in Hollywood, bloody, bruised, and beaten by a man she'd met while on their first date. She lay on the gurney, crying and asking for her parents who lived in Chicago. She couldn't remember their phone number, and her cellphone hadn't been recovered by the police or paramedics. After two hours, the internal bleeding, which had gone undetected by the ER doctors, sent her into cardiac arrest and ended her short life.

"I'll have another, please."

My third margarita went down way too quickly, and with my fourth on the way, the Friday afternoon happy hour crowd started to swim before my eyes like a koi pond of fish feeding on their daily toss of dried peas. A blondish man of about forty sat down beside me and ordered a Stella.

"Is this on happy hour?"

The bartender shook his head and placed the Belgian beer bottle in front of him, along with a tall, frosted glass. The stranger eyed my pathetic display of drunkenness and pushed the peanuts toward me.

"Why so glum? Your goldfish die?"

"No, one of my patients a few hours ago. Her date stabbed and beat the shit out of her. She'd met him online."

"Oh … I'm sorry. That's really awful. See, that's why meeting in real life is so much better. And safer. I'm Nate." He extended his hand and with the other, picked up his beer and took a long swig. "You a doctor?"

"Nurse."

Nate told me that he was a recent implant from Miami and had moved to Los Angeles to work with a mortgage lender. Our banter turned into his sliding his hand up my skirt and trying to pull my panties aside. I let him.

An hour later, as Nate helped me put the key into my apartment door's lock, Sam appeared behind us.

"Jewel."

I turned around. Sam looked dumbfounded. His work backpack was slung over his shoulder, and he held a plastic takeout bag, which was from our favorite Chinese restaurant.

"Orange chicken? Pot stickers? Egg rolls?"

Sam looked down at the bag and then nodded his head in response. "When did ya get back?"

When did I return? Somewhere between Heather, the goddess of one-night stands, and hot and sour soup.

"A bit ago. Enjoy your night, Sam."

Without fanfare, Nate and I made our way into my messy, smelly apartment. He lingered at my sparse photo collection on the fireplace mantel and then looked around my abode. "Who's this girl? She's cute. Is she single?" Nate held a framed photo of Cate and me at a weekend getaway in Palm Springs last year. Cate wore a black jumpsuit, and her hair was swept high in a ponytail, giving her that don't-fuck-with-me red carpet look. I had just exited the pool and thrown on a cover-up. Though my wet hair was plastered to my head and I was catching my breath, I still had a semblance of equanimity next to Cate. She won the trophy for beauty, although I didn't know there was a competition. Our pool waiter had taken the picture, and until now, I was proud of our moment in time. Looking back, Cate always looked better in photos, always had composure, and always got the guy.

"No. She's almost married. Do you mind putting that down?" Nate was nonplussed and quickly replaced the photo on the mantel of my faux fireplace. "Please don't touch my stuff. You don't have the right to look through my things. And I didn't bring you here to introduce you to my life."

He looked at me like I had just slapped him in the face. "I'm … I'm sorry. I was just … my apologies. I didn't mean … do you want me to leave? I think I should leave." Nate moved toward the door and started to turn the knob but stalled, like he and I were playing hard to get and this cat-and-mouse game would generate a crazy night of unbridled passion.

Although it had been a while since I'd had sex, or even kissed a guy, the idea of a meaningless night with Nate was just enough to try and make him stay. "Why'd you bother fingering me and then come over if you are just going to leave?" Clearly, I needed to take a class in the art of persuasive negotiation, or at least be nicer to the man. He had paid for my drinks and the Uber back to my apartment and was expecting a bit of compensation.

Nate hesitated at the open door and a nasty sneer appeared on one side of his lips. "You are sloshed, and I don't want to take advantage of the situation. You're lucky 'cause most guys would. Plus, it doesn't smell very good in here. You should get a maid."

"You know what? Fuck you!" I physically pushed him out of my apartment and slammed the door behind him. It was unfortunate, since he seemed really nice and sweet. But who was *he* to tell me to hire a maid? I was perfectly capable. I'd never had someone clean my kitchen or change the bedsheets in my entire life. Since I was born, my mom had always cleaned our house, and I'd continue to do the same. She used to fold our laundry and place it in piles on the kitchen table while I sat on the living room couch, either coloring or dressing my dolls. I'd practice my math and count the stacks by twos and threes, or I'd pretend they were little houses in a neighborhood that my Barbie would walk around to find her other Barbie friends.

I polished off the bottle of añejo that I was saving for a special occasion. I managed to diss Sam, ignored Cate's messages all week, and almost had sex. This qualified as a special occasion.

The offensive odor coming from my bedroom was at an all-time high. I'd left some takeout boxes on the floor next to the closet with remnants of Thai or Mexican food from the past week. The fitted sheet was no longer fitted on my mattress, so I fought with the four corners of the bed, trying to smooth out the new beige sheets I had bought on Amazon. Having been too lazy to wash the existing sheets, I threw them in the garbage and ordered new ones.

Maybe I should hire someone to clean. I'd always wanted to have a housekeeper. I lay captive in the sheet that almost fits my deep, firm mattress, and covered myself with a thick blanket. June Gloom, as it's known in the Southern California area, was mixture of low clouds and fog that made the month of June chilly, rather than hot and sunny as tourists would expect. Any day now, as July approached, the air conditioner would be on, circumventing the pervasive city heat. I popped two Xanax and hoped for the best.

—~—

Just as the morning sun broke through the marine layer, children's laughter from outside danced through the air and mixed with the popular singing game, "Ring-Around-the-Rosy." Becky and Annabelle were dressed in their usual play dresses that were crisp yellow linen with a pattern of small, white flowers. "Pockets full of posies, ashes, ashes, we all fall down." We collapsed on the ground

200

and rolled around like we're supposed to, the nursery rhyme from generations before us still impacting our innocent playtime.

"Jewel, your dress is dirty! You have mud all over your backside." Annabelle was aghast that I'd fallen into a mud pile. "We can't play anymore until you are clean, or it just won't work. The Black Death will find us!" Our mothers always bought two identical dresses for each of us from the shop in town.

"Ima! Ima! Please come quickly!" I yell for our housekeeper, one of the many staff who keeps us organized, clean, and with everything at our fingertips. A dark-skinned woman makes her way toward us from the big colonial house, her smile bright and her face ready to please. She's loved me since I was a baby and doesn't mind that I've soiled my dress.

"Child, what have you done? Let me help you." Ima pulled off my dirty dress and promptly replaced it with a replica. My mother knew to buy more than one. Eight-year-olds always found their way into the dirt or tore the fabric of their favorite playwear. As Ima was fixing the collar on my dress, her fingers moved to touch the skin on my chest. "What in the world? What happened to your scar? It's completely gone ..."

"Hey, stop that! Give it back. Jerry, that's *my* ball. Mom! Mom! Jerry took my ball. Mommmmm!"

I awoke to sounds of kids fighting in the background and a few of the neighbors talking outside my window on a Saturday morning. The clock read 9:39 a.m. My tequila/Xanax hangover was creating a throbbing sensation that could only be remedied by either more tequila or a few bottles of water and an aspirin. I reached for the Patron.

—~—

Bing, ding-a-ling! A Facebook Messenger notification woke me from my coma; the third notification in the past week, that I'd been too lazy to read, poked me in my already tortured brain. The setting sun cast a warm, orange glow on the brown kitchen cabinets reminding me that I'd slept the day away. Messenger told me that Aunt Carol and her husband, Malcom, were finished their trip around the world and had returned to Florida a week prior. A few photos of them in the Galapagos Islands showed a happy twosome.

"Jewel, let's plan to meet. I'd love to connect after all these years. Heading to Southern California. Let's discuss. Love, Aunt Carol."

Now that the reunion was finally near, the reality of seeing my aunt seemed daunting. It's always just been me. I've taken care of myself for over twenty years without anyone bothering to care. The idea of a relative I hardly knew interfering in my life left me feeling anxious. She'd interrupt my flow, judge my life, and tell me what to do. Aunt Carol would be so disappointed in the things I've done since we last saw one another. Relatives loved to meddle in their family's business. I didn't respond. Instead, I tied my hair back in a loose ponytail and went for a walk in search of dinner.

—~—

The line at the People's Bank of California was only a few people deep. I clutched to my chest the envelope that Mr. Shanahan had given, along with my birth certificate and newly acquired passport. Typed in a serif font in dark blue ink were the words: Jewel Carol Ann Parker. Born in Dallas, Texas, on March 8, 1981, to mother, Diana Elizabeth Parker, and father, Thomas Edward Parker. The state seal of Texas was prominently displayed at the top of the 8" x 10" legal document. It was a duplicate copy, stamped and dated on November 14, 1999, when I was eighteen years old. Apparently, the original had been misplaced, and I'd had to obtain a new one in the first year of nursing school.

"How can I enhance your day?" An older Asian man peered at me from atop his frameless glasses. He was uncomfortably tall and spindly, with his question leaving his mouth half open, already anticipating giving me a response to my reply.

"I'd like to speak with someone regarding an account in the name of Jewel Evans. Ah … that's me, Jewel Evans. It was set up by Levi, Levi, Levi & Shanahan a few weeks ago."

The banker picked up his phone and spoke in low tones to the person on the other end. "Won't you have a seat over there?" He pointed his long arm toward a cubicle with a name marker that bore the name of "Bart Abernathy." A pretty honey blonde-haired woman about my age sat behind the desk, banging away at her keyboard.

I walked over, sitting in the chair opposite the woman. She spoke without looking up. "You're a client of Mr. Shanahan." A statement rather than a question.

Not certain if I should call her Bart or Ms. Abernathy, I simply said, "Yes, I'm Jewel Evans. Here are my documents." I placed the many papers beside her keyboard.

Click ... click ... click ... She continued typing. The printer beside her desk started humming and then spat out several legal-sized forms in triplicate. She took them from the feeder and finally looked over at me. Her hair, the color of my favorite salted caramel ice cream, was expertly framed around her delicate face. She had tiny diamonds in her earlobes, and small hoops in her second and third pierced holes made their way up her petite ears. "Great. I've been expecting you. Mr. Shanahan sent over the necessary forms, so all you need to do is sign this paperwork and your ATM card will be mailed to you within a week."

I smiled. "That's not necessary. I'd like to close the account and take it all now. In cash. Euros, if you have them."

—~—

The Tory Burch shoebox lay open on the bedroom floor next to an envelope of photos that had spilled out. A picture of Mom and Dad, when they were first married and in love, sat atop many other past memories. High school graduation shots and a few from nursing school culmination were among the many assorted memories printed on glossy paper from the local photo center. A favorite caught my eyes. Cate and I were standing side by side on surfboards, albeit on the sandy shore, from our recent Maui vacation. A devilish grin was plastered on Cate's face because we'd just had tequila shots with our instructor, Z, after he'd told us he didn't drink alcohol. Cate had bet him that she could get up on the board on her first try and ride the wave out, but he'd said that after a one-hour lesson, it wouldn't be possible. He took the bet and lost. Little had he known that Cate had been surfing waves for years and was an intermediate surfer. Since I had never been on a surfboard before, Cate had taken her lesson at my novice level, just as besties should.

I fit our photo into the 5" x 7" gold-and-silver frame that had once sat among the other background items on the set of *Gone with the Wind*.

I imagined Vivien Leigh's character, Scarlett O'Hara, looking as clever and self-assured as she did in the epic film, shining through the vintage ornament. Now, it featured Cate and me in bikinis and golden tans on the Hawaiian beach. I placed it on the mantel next to the others.

A small newspaper clipping from the obituary section in the *The Seattle Times*, 1999, peeked out at the bottom of the shoebox: *Jean Suzanne Snow, fifty-one, of Seattle, passed away on May 2nd. Private family service to be held. In lieu of flowers, please donate to the American Liver Foundation. Jean is predeceased in death by Bruce Richard Snow, also of Seattle.*

The yellowed edges of the paper showed its age. I placed the clipping back in the box and covered it with the photos and trinkets, which filled it to the brim. An intricate wind-up music box remained on the floor. I turned the tiny handle, too small for my index finger and thumb. "You are my sunshine … my only sunshine. You make me happy when skies are gray." The movements played through the metal cylinder, and I could almost hear the lyrics filling the quiet space in my bedroom. My mom's once sweet voice sang the song when I was young, although in happier times when Dad was alive. I remembered being about eight or nine when we had walked into an antique store and found the gadget in a basket of grab bag items. It had cost seventy-five cents, but Mom had said no because we were only in the store to look. I wouldn't leave until it was mine. Little did she know that I'd shoved it deep in my pocket, next to a stick of warm Juicy Fruit. After Dad died, my mom's voice had stopped singing. I'd lie awake in bed, lost in the void of loneliness, but at least I had the melody from my treasure. I returned the music player to the shoebox.

The popcorn ceiling, closing in on me for years, now appeared lower and suffocating. The room was smaller, the air acrid, and the constant muffled noise from the neighbors, Beth and Bryson, next door punctuated my existence.

I am alone or am I lonely?

There's no one in my life to share my bed or hang his clothes in the closet that's large enough for two. Friday night dinners on the couch with Sam and the remote control were a distant memory, just as the hope of cohabiting and creating a family with him—or anyone for that matter—were.

Cate had tried to communicate, but her intermittent, one-line texts of "Hey. How are you?" or, "Let's catch up soon," when we never did, presented a lackluster attempt at friendship, so I ignored them.

She'd moved on and had her new life with Dave. I was a memory of what used to be, someone she'd deferred to when she had nothing better to do. It's hard to rationalize that the former life between two people had ever existed when she had the time of her life with that person, but then it was over and a new norm took shape for both parties. Were Cate and I best friends, as I believed? Were we there for each other through the many good and bad times, listening to each other's thoughts as we moved through life together? Or had I imagined the whole thing? I glanced at the framed photos atop the fireplace mantel and sighed. Without saying the words, Cate had told me that she'd moved on, and that I'd been replaced. The new Maui photo played homage to our many years of friendship, commemorated within five and seven inches.

My constant friend for the past year had been weConnect. Ever devoted, although sometimes disappointing, it had always provided comfort with messages from guys who showed interest in what I was doing and who I was. Of course, they were really interested in Estelle, and before her, Chelsea, Amanda, and Raquel, my loyal puppets.

The many messages from eager suitors awaited my response.

Drew, forty-seven, managed a country club, frequented Las Vegas to play in poker tournaments, stated he was looking for a running partner through the weConnect app, and wanted to play twenty questions instead of the usual, boring commentary. He wrote, "Ask me an off-the-wall question, and I'll do the same for you. Let's get to know one another." I'll bite.

"Drew: If you were an animal, which one would you be?"

"Hello, Estelle. Wow. Okay, I would be a yellow Labrador retriever. Loyal, playful, enthusiastic, low maintenance, predictable. What about you?"

"Predictable's no fun. I'd be a red fox. Sly, pretty, dangerous, and hard to catch."

We texted back and forth for what seemed like an hour but then ran out of lively banter. When Drew told me that he had six children from three marriages, but was really on weConnect to find a new wife, I bid him farewell and good luck. Then a message from Benji, the noodler, appeared at the top of my list.

"Hello, Estelle, or whoever you are. Online again, I see." A quick look at his profile showed he still had the one photo and nothing was written in his narrative.

"Right back at ya. Where are the other photos I requested? Can't wait to see what you really look like."

"I'll see who you are very soon."

"???"

"I have your IP address and location from this app, and you're within a ten-block radius. You aren't Anne, a model from Ireland. I reverse searched your photo. I'll find you, Estelle."

Find me?! Sweat beaded on my forehead and soon started trickling its way past my temples and down my back. My chest tightened, and the room began condensing me into a small, former version of myself—a scared little girl, alone and orphaned, without friends or family. I was an imposture. They knew. They'll see who I am and who I'm not.

I panicked, then unmatched Benji, and deleted the weConnect app from my phone and computer, which gave me a newfound strength. Relief washed over me like the night tides on a deserted beach. Okay, noodler, you've won. You reached your bare hand into the water hole and tried to pull me out. But you'll never know who I really am. Located my IP address? How sophisticated were these people? I thought they were having fun on a dating app, just like me. Why not just unmatch us rather than resort to such lengths? Online dating had reached a whole new level.

Using weConnect for the past year had given me solace. I had been sheltered behind a mask, not having to step out into the real world to face scrutiny and rejection—or worse, abandonment. And for that, it had been worth every moment of swiping. My online personas had been anyone I chose. Their careers and interests, back stories and future pursuits, had all been up to me. I'd never hurt anyone while being Estelle, Amanda, Chelsea or Raquel, my catfishes. But in a way, they'd been as real as Max, Liam, and Benji, all of whom had never materialized to anything beyond a few keystrokes. Somewhere in cyberland, they're all out for a fun night on the town. Estelle was hooked up with Liam; Raquel and Max were on their third date, and Amanda and Chelsea were having a threesome with Benji.

My neighbors were up, hitting their walls and causing the sounds to filter through to mine. The pounding didn't subside, and I was about to retaliate and bang my fists on the adjoining wall, but I realized the sound was coming from my living room. Someone was outside my door, knocking loudly and not about to give up until I answered. Benji said he'd find me.

I remained still and waited for silence.

20

Catch Me If You Can

"How I wish … how I wish you were here. We're just two lost souls swimming in a fishbowl, year after year." Sam's voice echoes Pink Floyd's David Gilmour as he sang along with one of his favorite bands. "Running over the same old ground … and how we found the same old fears. Wish you were here." His open window shared the music playing from his apartment to everyone within earshot. A few knocks on his door interrupted the guitar riff, making him turn down the volume. "Hang on!" he bellowed.

Sam opened his door to a woman in her '70s. She stood before him in a long, draping, knitted shawl and chocolate-brown espadrilles, their straps snaking up her legs in crisscross style. The stranger's hair was loosely swept up in an old-fashioned chignon, a hybrid of aging gray-and-blonde highlights. "I'm looking for Jewel Evans. My niece." She leaned to the right, attempting to see around Sam as though her niece were hiding behind him, lost within the space of his small apartment. "211?"

"*I'm* 211," Sam responded, holding his ground and pointing to the numbers attached to the front of his door. "Jewel's 209. But I don't think she's home. Haven't seen her for a while."

"Yes, I know that hers is 209. I dropped by last week, passing through on my way to visit my stepson in San Diego, but she didn't answer the door after I pounded on it for quite some time. I figured she'd be here, at your place. You are Sam … her boyfriend?"

He eyed the woman, slightly suspicious that she was telling the truth. "We're just friends … hmmm, I didn't know she has an aunt. What did you say your name is again?"

"I didn't. Carol. I'm Jewel's Aunt Carol from Florida." She smiled, but her eyes didn't match her upturned lips. "She doesn't know I'm here. I tried calling, but her phone doesn't seem to be working." She turned and looked farther down the hallway. "When was the last time you saw her?" Walking a few steps, Aunt Carol stopped in front of Jewel's door and knocked. And knocked.

"About two weeks or more. I'm not her keeper, you know." Sam leaned back against his doorframe, his arms crossed in defiance. "We don't keep tabs on each other."

"Apparently not." Aunt Carol let out an audible exhale, loud enough for Sam to take notice. "Well, do you think you can help an old woman out? What's the number to the Super?" She almost stomped her foot. "You know … the owner, the caretaker of this joint. Anyone to give me some answers as to why I can't reach my niece. Maybe she's taken ill."

"I have a key to Jewel's apartment—if this helps." Sam surreptitiously retrieved the spare key and stood a few feet from #209, dangling it in the air with blatant opposition that Aunt Carol narrowed her eyes at him. "But I'll have to go in with you." Sam turned the key in the lock and entered the dark, quiet space with the visitor close at his heels. A flip of a light switch brought the room to life.

The apartment looked almost showroom quality. Throw pillows were arranged on either end of the sofa, the floors were spotless, the kitchen sink was sparkling clean, and the only personal items in view were picture frames on the fireplace mantel. The countertops were bare save for a MacBook and iPhone, arranged side by side as though waiting for recognition.

Sam walked to the phone and picked it up. "That's weird. Jewel never goes anywhere without this." He pressed the side button, waiting for the iPhone to come to life while he walked toward her bedroom.

"Carol, can you come here?" he called a few moments later.

Aunt Carol walked quickly but with trepidation toward her niece's bedroom. Sam stood before an open, completely stripped closet—absent of Jewel's clothes, shoes, and purses. "She's gone. She wouldn't have moved without telling me." The bed was meticulously made, which was rarely the case as Jewel wasn't a neatnik, and her favorite faux fur blanket was folded in a large square on the foot. The en suite bathroom was barren—not a toothbrush, shampoo bottle, or comb remained. Sam turned around in astonishment, looking at the floor and scratching his head. "I don't get it."

"Neither do I," Aunt Carol's voice interrupted his reverie. "Who is this person?" She held a framed photo of Jewel and Cate, a close-up selfie taken within the past year.

"It's Cate … why?" Sam took the photo from Carol's grasp and looked at it, remembering the moment they'd taken the picture. It was on a Friday night about a year ago at Jewel's apartment. The girls had been watching a movie on the couch, and he'd come over with two salads and crab cake appetizers. He hadn't known that Cate was visiting and had felt bad that he didn't have enough food for three. They'd shared the food he brought and then ordered a large pepperoni pizza for delivery. The girls were taking selfies, and Sam had tried to squeeze himself into the many photos, but Jewel and Cate had purposely snapped a bunch alone, pushing him out of their girl circle. "She's her best friend."

"Well then, who is the other girl? That isn't Jewel." Aunt Carol took the frame again and then walked back to the living room. She'd taken all six photos from the mantel and had lain them on the coffee table, side by side.

Sam followed her and looked at the many pictures of Jewel and Cate: on the beach, at a restaurant, in a convertible, standing on a surfboard, on a couch curled up in a blanket, shopping for dresses, and the selfie that had been placed next to the others.

Aunt Carol took off the decorative monocle that rested on her décolletage and doubled as a vintage pendant. She peered at the photos through it, moving from one happy scene to the next. "This person is not my niece. She is not Jewel. " Handing the monocle to Sam, she backed away and said, "Jewel has blue eyes, like her father. This woman has hazel. Jewel also has a port-wine stain, about the size of a silver dollar, on her chest. She was always proud of it because it looked like a butterfly. When she was young, she'd drawn the chain in with a pen, making it look like a butterfly necklace. I haven't seen Jewel since she was seventeen, but I know this isn't her." Aunt Carol waited several moments for Sam to respond while she started opening and closing drawers and cupboards, looking for a sign as to who the woman was, masquerading as her niece. "This place is spotless."

Sam hovered over the line of photos, comparing the images with Aunt Carol's handy magnifying necklace.

210

"Are you sure? I mean, then, who is she?" Sam picked up the iPhone that had already powered up. He pressed the home button, and the message of "set up new iPhone" appeared. "It's been wiped." He turned on her computer, and watched it boot up as though it had just been purchased and used for the first time. "This one too. There's no content."

He then made a call on his phone and told the person on the other end to come immediately. "I'm at Jewel's."

Fifteen minutes later, Cate walked through the open door marked 209, looking from Sam to the woman sitting on the couch and then a quick glance around. "Why's it so clean? Where's Jewel? And who are you?"

After getting Cate up to speed, Aunt Carol's incoming text sent her into near hysterics. "Look at this. I called my husband when you first went into the bedroom, Sam. He just sent these from my photo albums at home. They were taken in Jewel's last year of high school. Look, I'm right." She shoved her smartphone's screen in their faces and started to cry. "Where is she? What's going on?"

Cate and Sam scrutinized the many photos of Jewel as a senior at Amarillo High School. The girl's dark blue eyes that shone with kindness and warmth were captured in every photo, just as the birthmark on her chest, three inches below her clavicle. Her blonde hair was shoulder-length, and her frame was petite. Although the photos were taken when she'd been a teenager, it was undeniable that the girl who they were looking at was not the same Jewel Evans, neighbor and friend to Sam and Cate. This girl's cheekbones were more pronounced, and her forehead was slightly bigger than Jewel's. The resemblance was eerily similar, but side by side, their differences removed any doubt.

"Yeah, I see it," Cate said, resigning herself to the obvious fact. "These are two different people, but … why? Where's the real Jewel Evans?"

"Parker. Her last name is Parker. Evans was her married name." Aunt Carol rose from the couch and moved unsteadily toward the door. "I don't know, but I'm going to find out. After her parents died—my sister and her husband—we lost communication. I haven't done a good job as her only living relative. Here's my info. Please keep in touch." She handed Sam a scrap of paper with her phone number and email. "I'm calling the police, just so you know." Aunt Carol looked as if she'd aged ten years within the hour. Without another word, she walked out.

"So now what?" Cate stood like a fish out of water, wringing her hands, waiting for direction. "I don't feel welcome here. We're in some stranger's home."

"No, we're in Jewel's home, but we've got to do some digging." Sam pulled out every drawer and looked behind the couch, moving furniture to find clues as to his neighbor of four years. The refrigerator had been cleaned out, as were the cupboards. Any obvious signs that someone had lived there were gone.

"Sam, come here! Quick!" Cate yelled from the bedroom. She stood with her mouth agape, a shoebox's contents spread out on the duvet. A collection of photos and trinkets was strewn about, showcasing the life of Jane Doe. A gold necklace with a colorful butterfly pendant, which casted a prism of light on the walls, dangled from Cate's fingers. "Look at this stuff. I found this box at the top of her closet. Photos of us, her life with Robert … oh, and look at this." She held the necklace higher so he could see. "Is she collecting them, 'cause I also gave her a similar one for her birthday? Sam, are we wrong, here? Maybe we've got it all wrong."

Sam unfolded a piece of newsprint from the emptied box. "I don't think so."

He held an obituary from 1999's *The Seattle Times*. "Jean Suzanne Snow. Cate, give me your phone."

Sam spent a few minutes reading and scrolling on Cate's phone. "An online memorial from Redmond High School in Washington published this: "With deep regret, we share the news of this sad loss to our community. Senior Melissa Snow's mother, Jean, passed away on May 2nd.' Handing the phone back to Cate, Sam looked at her quizzically. "Who is Melissa Snow?"

Cate read the published article, scrolled a bit more, and then gasped, choking on her words. "She died. Sam … this girl, Melissa, is dead. A fire … a few months later … September, 1999. Look at the next article. What. The. Hell?" Cate handed the phone back to Sam, letting him verify her findings.

"A house fire took the life of local girl Melissa Snow, formerly of Redmond, on September 5th while on vacation in Amarillo, Texas. Melissa had recently moved to Los Angeles to pursue a career in nursing, preparing to begin her studies at UCLA. She is predeceased by her mother, Jean Snow, and father, Bruce Snow, both from Seattle. Diana and Tom Parker of Amarillo, Texas, also perished in the blaze. At the time of publication, memorial service details are still unavaila ..."

"Geez Christmas!" Cate exclaimed as she interrupted Sam. "This just gets better and better. Since I've known her, Jewel's been careful with her money and taking extra shifts at the hospital but twenty years ago found it necessary to give away almost a million dollars to an Ima Jones and her four children from Texas. Check this out. It's a transfer of funds document. Where did she get that kind of money and why did she give it away? Now she's a Robin Hood too?" Cate handed Sam a folded piece of blue paper.

Sam glanced at the document and collapsed on the bed. "We need a drink. Come over to my place. This place is cleaned out of everything. Not even a god-dammed bottle of wine left." Before they left the apartment, Sam took with him the shoebox containing the mementos.

Sam free poured at least three shots of reposado in a small whiskey glass and handed it to Cate. She eyed the tequila with disdain and asked, "That's all I get?" But then she threw it back like it was the '80s, and everyone had a Sex on the Beach shooter. "Another, please—and keep 'em coming. I feel like I'm on a bad episode of *Unsolved Mysteries*. So what do you make of all this?"

Sam also shot back a healthy pour of tequila and then scattered the contents of the girl's Tory Burch shoebox on his brown couch. "We need to look at this with fresh eyes." He picked up a photo and started waving it in the air like a fan. "This girl, someone we've known for a while, is she Jewel, is she Melissa, or someone else entirely? I have a theory."

Cate sat on the floor, looking at photos of her best friend's past twenty years. "Let's hear it, Sherlock."

"They're both her. They're both Jewel. I don't know who this Melissa person is, but Jewel must've had plastic surgery or something. And she had that birthmark removed with a laser. I think she's on vacation, probably traipsing through France right now. She always wanted to see Paris." He continued his conjectures even though Cate was laughing and shaking her head at the absurdity. Then he poured another shot of tequila and settled into the couch.

Cate pointed at the many photos of a pretty blonde, "*You* don't want *this* girl to be Melissa any more than I do." She sat on the floor next to Sam's feet and picked up a gold specked vintage frame that had a photo of Cate and Jewel in it. It was from their recent trip to Maui. They were standing on surf boards, smiling and enjoying their lives together. "Do you think it's weird that she only kept photos of the two of us on the mantel? I mean, I'm flattered, but what about her parents? Why didn't she put their photos up?" Cate rose and started to walk around Sam's apartment. She stopped in front of his fireplace and picked up one of his photos. "Just like this." She grabbed a few of his framed pictures and took them back to where he was sitting on the floor. "Tell me about these people."

Sam took the frames from Cate. He fondly looked at a group shot of five cheerful people at a fancy dinner. "This is my family. My sisters, Theresa and Laura, my mom, Melinda, and my dad, Max. We were celebrating my mom's sixtieth birthday that night. And this one—" he held up a framed photo of three guys—"is my most prized. They're my best friends in the world." The selfie showed a good-looking man, in his late thirties, with two other guys surrounding him and smiling at the camera. Sam's arm was around the guy's shoulder, and the other man in the photo was flanking the other side of a handsome dark blond man. He pointed to the guy obviously holding the phone. "Benji ... and this crazy one is Liam. We grew up in Missouri together. We're gonna meet up this fall somewhere to surf. Liam is an ocean swimmer and will only go places where he can be in the warm water. He has this thing that he won't go to the same place twice, so he can visit the entire world. Liam's one of the top realtors in St. Louis and makes a fortune. I was engaged to his younger sister when I was twenty-five, but she died a year later of leukemia. She was the love of my life. I'll never let myself get close to someone like that again. She's really the reason I don't take dating seriously."

Cate put her hand on Sam's arm, trying to comfort him, but he stiffened and tapped his finger on the other man in the photo. He cleared his throat. "This guy, Benji, just had twins a few months ago, a boy and a girl. Really adorable kids. He works for a local TV station in Kansas City, and is very philanthropic. After many years, he still helps out at food banks and shelters. Super person. A real inspiration to know." Sam touched the photo and smiled to himself. "I miss these guys."

"See, that's exactly what I'm sayin'. That's normal behavior. This girl, whoever she is, doesn't have any photos of her friends or family. I don't even know her childhood friends' names or anything about her parents because she never wanted to discuss personal stuff. It's like she reinvented herself." Cate took another shot of tequila, but this time more slowly. "I think I need to eat something. Feeling kind of nauseas. Dave's home so I should get out of here soon. He will *not* believe this."

She gathered most of the photos and trinkets and returned them to the box. A little silver music box caught her eye. "You make me happy when skies are gray ..." played from the metal box when Cate cranked its tiny handle. Cate felt her heart soften and started to sob. "Sam, this is really painful. She is my best friend. I don't know what to think anymore." Tears rolled down her cheeks and her body shook with every inhale.

Sam stopped cold. "I found more."

He'd been on his iPhone, barely paying attention to Cate's ramblings. He waited a few moments, continuing to read what he'd found as Cate tried to get a hold of herself. "Ready for this? You really should pour another drink." Sam cleared his throat. "'Assisted Suicide, Autopsy Results Claim for Local Redmond Woman. Jean Snow, her was death reported on May 2nd by daughter, Melissa Snow, had suffered from End-Stage Liver Disease, according to her attending physician, Dr. Lara White, from Seattle's Memorial Hospital. Jean Snow had been prescribed the opioid, morphine, and her postmortem confirmed that lethal amounts contributed to her death. No charges will be made in this crime as the accused is deceased.' It's dated September 16, 1999." Sam paused to catch his breath, running his hands through his sweaty hair.

"Cate, it says here that this Melissa girl is a murderer, either intentionally poisoned her dying mother or somehow assisted in her death. Who does something like that? There's also suspicion that she started the fire that killed the Parker family in Texas but then died along with them. None of this makes sense. Why didn't Jewel tell us about this? Those were her parents! What's the connection to Melissa anyway? Was this some kind of sick pact?" Sam slammed his fist on the coffee table, making Cate jump. "Goddammit, who IS this girl? Who's been living door next to me?"

Cate shrieked, "Next door? What about *my* best friend? How do you think *I* feel?" Cate had already made her way to the door and had

215

her hand on the doorknob when she turned back around and laughed uncontrollably, like someone teetering on sanity. Her hair had fallen out of her ponytail and was loose and messy, adding to her maniacal appearance. "My best friend's a murderer. Twice. And maybe, she killed others for all we know, just like a serial killer. What if she's been killing her sick patients at the hospital? She's Lizzie Borden! Somehow my shoplifting doesn't seem so bad now." Cate returned to the kitchen and picked up the bottle, tipping it to her lips and drinking like it was an Orange Fanta. "Sam, I can't take this anymore. I want to know the truth as much as you do, but right now my head is pounding, and I have an Uber waiting outside." With that, she finally left, slamming the door behind her.

Sam's stomach growled, reminding him that he'd missed dinner. Maybe he would've eaten takeout salads with Jewel tonight or watched a movie at her apartment; their evenings together weren't anything if not habitual. Instead, the crazy turn of events had taken centerstage and propelled him to find answers as he played CSI Santa Monica.

Sam clutched several photos in his hands. One was of a toddler taking a tentative step, and another was of the same little girl sitting on an older man's lap with a 1st Birthday hat on her head. A third photo was of a family of three, the mother and father beaming as they hugged their little blonde-haired girl in a horse drawn carriage in Central Park. It had been taken at least thirty-five years ago, according to the date stamped on the back of the paper photo. He then dropped the fourth like it had just burned him. Two girls, around eighteen years old, stood side by side in a kitchen. They were wearing matching aprons and looked identical, if it weren't for the slight variance in their facial expressions and features. Even their hair was cut the same: straight, shoulder-length blonde with a part down the middle. Her look-alike wore a pretty, colorful butterfly necklace.

Sam quickly retrieved the key to Jewel's apartment and reentered. The light had been left on, and he half expected to see Jewel on the couch or running up to him from the kitchen. Muffled sounds emanated from her bedroom, but the noise was from the family who lived on the other side. A glint of silver caught his eye on the mantel. A single key. Sam tried it in the lock to the door, turning it effortlessly.

It felt eerie. Everything had changed. She was gone. He knew it. Jewel, or whoever she was, would not be returning. The few years of hanging out watching TV, drinking margaritas, laughing, and sharing thoughts, were over. Sam looked around at the intimate features of her apartment. Jewel's refuge for as long as he'd known her was now reduced to a pile of esoteric rubble. Even her bed spoke volumes: stiff, private, reserved, confined. Ubiquitous, but somehow, she was a ghost, an apparition.

He remembered the night he'd fallen asleep on her sofa. He'd wanted to sleep in her bed, making her feel safe and protected as a boyfriend should, but they hadn't progressed past friendship status. Jewel was too good for him. He'd always known that. She'd once made a reference to them dating, and he'd laughed, which probably seemed cruel, but she deserved more than he could ever provide. His heart would never be up for grabs. Even the kiss in Las Vegas had crossed the line, giving her false hope. He wasn't an animal, just a vital, single man. And as satisfying as it could have been to check that proverbial box and sleep with a beautiful woman, that's all it would have been because he would have never followed through.

Sam knew she was multilayered and had a veneer so thick that he'd never break through. He realized that a few months after they'd first met. Jewel had never spoken of her childhood, her parents, or her friends. He'd offer stories about his life with his twin sisters and the scare they had with his mom's first bout of breast cancer. He had told Jewel about the time his dad lost his job, and Sam had helped them financially so that they wouldn't lose their house. When he'd shared the details of his mom's eventual death, she cried silently, letting the tears fall down her face while she let Sam tell his story. Jewel was a great listener. She'd comment and offer support, but never countered with her own history. He used to think it was because she didn't want to steal the moment and make it about her, or that nurses instinctually remained at arm's length from someone in emotional distress. But it was soon evident those topics were off limits at all times, so he'd kept it light and easy, which was safer for both of them. In a way, they were very similar; he wanted to date and have fun with women as long as it didn't become complicated, and Jewel was careful to remain at a distance, never allowing anyone to penetrate her bubble. The Jewel he thought that he knew wasn't the Jewel they'd discovered today, and given the past few hours, he probably had dodged a really large bullet.

Sam was relieved that he hadn't met a woman like Jewel on weConnect—one who was hiding behind a false existence, a fake identity. Sam didn't have any qualms about his own catfishing and hiding behind his personas of Max, Liam, and Benji, because he was merely using his dad's name and best friends' names and photos to test the waters on a dating app before he took the plunge. It was all innocent, and no one was the wiser because Liam and Benji lived in Missouri, so no one would see their photos on weConnect and figure it out. Even after communicating with many single gals on the site, such as the hotties Amanda and Estelle, he believed that he was better off being set up by friends or meeting organically. You just never knew who you were texting with online or if you'd ever meet in real life.

"Who are you, Jewel Evans? And where are you now?" Sam said out loud, as though the abandoned room would answer.

The sound of heavy feet entering the bedroom made Sam jump.

Two city policemen stood before him, observing his distress at being caught resting on someone else's bed, like Goldilocks being found by the three bears.

"And just who are *you*, sir? ID and proof of residence. We have a report of a missing person."

21

Dust to Dust

The dungarees that were too small for my growing ten-year-old frame weren't appropriate for the funeral. Mom told me to put on the pink-and-white dress that hung in my closet, even though it wasn't yet springtime. A fresh coat of frost covered the morning grass, which was unusual for the Seattle area, but since the groundhog saw his shadow last month, our chilly weather persisted.

"Mom, I don't have shoes or a jacket for this dress."

"Do you think *I* care? Your father just died. That's all I care about anymore … now do as you're told!" She grabbed me by my hair and spun me around, giving me a kick in the rear end so that I'd leave her bedroom. I vaulted forward and fell on my knees, knocking my head on the linoleum floor. There wasn't any point crying because she already said she didn't care, so I sucked it up. "Let's go."

Mom wore a mismatched brown-and-black pantsuit and cream-colored sandals. Her eye makeup was haphazardly applied to her already aging face of forty-three, and two hair rollers remained in the back of her nest-like hair. Rather than speak, I hesitantly pointed toward her head, thinking that she'd understand. She bent down and slapped me across the face. Hard. Tears welled up in my eyes, making it difficult to see the sidewalk as I walked to the awaiting taxi. Mom sat beside me in the back of the cab, her breath sour from nonstop drinking. When we arrived at the church, she got out and left me sitting in the car with the driver who wanted to be paid for the fare.

Then I was suddenly eighteen. My long, flaxen hair was pulled up in a high bun, held by my favorite neon-green scrunchy. I hadn't showered for days and was wearing the same pink sweats outfit because all my clothes were dirty, either in the clothes hamper or on the floor. My high school counselor had called several times, wondering why I had been absent all week. Rather than tell the truth, I said that I was sick.

Mom was still on the sofa where she'd been for two weeks. She refused to go to the hospital, where they'd told her that she was in the final stages of liver failure. "Hospice. You need to check into hospice, Mrs. Snow." The hospital finally gave up trying to convince her, and her doctor prescribed a large dose of morphine pills to ease her pain.

I was a crappy nurse. Mom was too weak to walk to the toilet, so I let her pee on the giant blue pads that I had bought at the pet store. I placed them under her lifeless body and then changed them a few times a day. I had to hold my breath every time I went near her because the stench of urine was overwhelming. I'd given up trying to make her eat. She didn't have an appetite for food and just wanted her vodka. I let her drink whatever she wanted, since I understood—but didn't quite believe—that the end of her life was days away, so it didn't really matter.

The beige chair, which had a huge divot on the seat from a broken spring, had been my bed for the past two weeks, since Mom would scream for me in the middle of the night, sometimes needing something and other times just wanting to scream. When her legs cramped, I'd massage them for her, but I always did it wrong. "Too hard! You're hurting me!" She'd always try to smack me, but I knew to stay an arm's length away. "You aren't good for nothin'. Big disappointment." I wanted to believe it was the disease talking or the numerous morphine pills she needed every six hours, but deep down, I knew she didn't love me and wished it was me, and not my dad, who'd died many years ago.

A few years after he passed away, we were watching a TV sitcom. My mom was in her usual chair, and I was on the couch. The iconic *Family Ties* show was on, and she seemed to be enjoying herself, a vodka and tonic in one hand and a cigarette in the other. I took the opportunity to ask her why she hated me. She mumbled something that sounded like I was my dad's favorite because he always wanted to be alone with me. *I* was the special one. "Alex P. Keaton, mind your own business!" she shouted and laughed, the smoke shooting out of her nostrils.

Mom looked much older than her fifty-one years, a decrepit woman who was a ball of anger, regret, loss, and depression. I couldn't help her because she didn't want to be saved. She just wanted to die.

"You aren't a jewel; you're a rock. An average grey rock on the road. You'll never amount to much. What a waste," she'd tell me several times a day. I tried to block the words out, but they were like daggers in my heart.

The sun shone brightly through the jaundiced, sheer curtains, but it felt like winter in the living room and not the beautiful day of May 2nd, a promise of summer. Mom had lain awake all night, her screams becoming less audible as delirium came upon her like a creeping malaise. She hadn't peed for twelve hours, and her breathing sounded like suffocation. She wanted the pills every two hours, trying to ease the pain that had settled in her distended abdomen. "Do s-s-something right, Melissa, for once in your life. I n-n-need to be with him again." She tried to reach for the pill bottle but was too weak to lift her arm. "I ... want them a-a-a-all. Help me ... dammit."

One by one, I placed the morphine pills in her mouth, allowing her to swallow them down with vodka, the only liquid that made her feel good. There were fourteen in total, enough to hasten her death and return her to Dad. She didn't argue as I held her hand. Her eyes were fluttering and trying to see, but she was too weak to keep them open. She'd been ready to go for a long time, but I wasn't ready to say goodbye to my mom. As much as she was disappointed in me, her only child, I couldn't let her die in so much pain, so I did what I was told and as I'd always done.

I sat and waited. Waited for life to end. Waited for life to begin. "'Lissa ... sorry ... sorry, my Mel ... issa, my ... sparkling ... jewel." And then, with those broken words, she was gone.

I had just killed my mother.

22

Kindling

"No way! Your name's Jewel? It's so nice to meet you." I stretched out my hand to shake my new roommate's hand, but she lunged at me, giving me a bear hug reserved for close relatives. She smelled like flowers, a white jasmine and pikake combination, her shoulder-length blonde hair wrapped around my face as she held me close for a moment. I didn't want to let her go.

"When I was young, my mom used to talk about a book titled *Sparkling Jewel*. My name's Melissa," I said.

"Melissa. I was hoping for someone like you. We are going to have the best summer together." Jewel beamed at me.

My roommate and I had entered the same nursing program at the UCLA campus. I had submitted my application late in May but was promptly accepted based on the many endorsement letters from my school's faculty. Since I'd never been to Los Angeles before, I opted to be placed with a female roommate in off-campus shared-living condos, which bordered the shops and restaurants of Westwood. This designation would determine who I was paired with as the new students arrived from all over the country and the world. Some had moved in at the end of June and others right before classes were to begin following Labor Day. I couldn't leave the confines of Seattle quickly enough and had moved to Los Angeles the day after I threw my graduation hat in the air. I was going to start a new life, a new Melissa.

We stood in our condo's foyer, looking down the hallway to the place that would be our home for the summer during our four-year nursing program, if we so chose. But I could tell immediately that Jewel and I would be great friends. She had a genuine sweetness, always caring how I felt and doing everything she could to make me feel comfortable in our new situation. She was going to be the perfect nurse.

"Melissa, I brought this for you ... well, from my mom, actually." Without even knowing who would be her new roommate, Jewel handed me a shiny, cream-colored bag that looked like it came from a boutique. There were three designer T-shirts, a yellow blouse, two skirts, a pair of white shorts, and burnt-orange colored pajamas. "It's our state color. Texas Orange."

No one had ever given me a gift before, let alone an entire wardrobe. "Jewel, I can't accept these. It's too much. Plus, I didn't get anything for you," I told her.

"You'd hurt my feelings if you don't take them. You see, it's my mom. She always buys in twos. It's a habit she's always had. When I was young, she'd buy two of every dress, every hat ... I loved dressing up and would always soil or rip my clothes, so she made sure there was always a backup. Plus, you'll look so good in this top."

She held a T-shirt for me to see, the combination of yellow-and-cobalt-blue flowers swirled on the front with the word "beautiful."

"Just like you, Melissa. Beautiful."

"Me?" I was aghast, my knee-jerk reaction was noted by Jewel, as she shook her head and came close to me, taking my hair in her hands and smiling.

"You are the prettiest girl I've ever seen. Look at your perfect hair! And your smile can stop a train!" Jewel held the shirt up to me, nodding her head. "Crazy beautiful."

We had a fairytale summer. Neither of us could cook very well, but we spent our days shopping for groceries, and in the evenings, we tried out new recipes, rivaling dishes from any eatery. "Our housekeeper, Ima, is amazing in the kitchen. Over the years, I had to be careful or I'd weigh two-hundred pounds. Do you know what jerk is, Melissa?" she'd asked me. All I could think of were the stupid guys from my high school.

"Yes, I've met plenty of them."

Jewel loved my sense of humor, and we could spend hours laughing about our pasts. She never faulted me for my upbringing—being raised without a dad and an alcoholic mom who was abusive and emotionally absent. Jewel came from a life of privilege with plenty of money, so they'd never have to worry about their next meal or the monthly rent. Without words, she showed me that the past did not define someone, especially when it was beyond their control. What a person chose to do with their present and future self was more important, or defining.

"God love ya—" she paused to laugh—"I'm going to try and make jerk chicken tomorrow. It's a deliciously spicy, marinated chicken dish from Ima's home of Jamaica. I promise you'll love it, if it turns out."

We never met anyone else those few months and spent every moment together, watching TV, playing board games, hiking, and sharing intimate anecdotes from our lives.

"If I had a sister, I'd want her to be you," she told me one day in early August. "We kind of look alike anyway. I bet if you cut your hair, we'd be twins." I stood still while my long hair fell in golden swirls at my feet. Jewel wielded the scissors like an expert. "I cut all my Barbies' hair. It was either nursing or hairdressing."

I looked in the bathroom mirror, with the reflection of my twin beside me, wearing the same Def Leppard T-shirt. We looked strikingly similar. She'd cut my hair to match her shoulder-length tresses, parted down the middle the same as she'd always worn her hairstyle. From that day on, we dressed in the same clothes, sometimes confusing the cashier at the grocery store and having fun with anyone we could trick. Jewel was lively, free, happy, and generous. She was everything I'd always wanted to be but never could because of my circumstances.

"I'd like you to come home with me, over Labor Day Weekend. My parents want to meet you. Plus, as soon as we get back, school starts, and we'll be too busy for anything. What do ya think? My mom says she'll get your flight, so don't even mention the money. It's our gift to you."

Jewel and I flew together to Amarillo, Texas, arriving at the small international airport. Her parents met us at the gate. Of course this was in the innocent time period before the September 11th terrorist attacks had changed everything related to air travel. It was easy to tell who her parents were—a beautiful couple holding hands and exuberantly awaiting the arrival of their only child. "Jewel!" They rushed toward her, embracing their daughter just as she had embraced me when we first met. The pang of jealousy I should've felt at that moment for not having devoted parents in my life wasn't there. I genuinely loved her so much that I was grateful to know someone who was the epitome of all things kind and loving.

224

"And you must be Melissa. We've heard so much about you. So glad you could come." They gave me heartfelt hugs, apropos of families who reconnect in an airport.

"Mr. and Mrs. Parker, thank you so much for having me, and for the ticket."

"Please, call us Diana and Tom."

Their white colonial house was just as Jewel had described. Its grandeur was surrounded by acres of ranchland and gardens that grew every vegetable imaginable. Fruit trees occupied the backyard, yielding peaches, plums, pomegranates, figs, and citrus.

"Our farm is like a grocery store. We have everything. Our neighbor's cattle farm gives us beef, and there's a dairy farm that way. That ranch over there has chickens, and they sell their eggs." Diana pointed toward the left as we drove up the mile-long driveway. It was hard to know which place she meant, since their property seemed to go on as far as the eye could see.

"It's idyllic," I murmured, but more to myself.

"It certainly is," Tom responded. "But the only downside is being so far from town. The hour-plus drive detours us from shopping as much as we'd like, so we've become quite self-sustaining."

As we pulled up to their large house, the front door opened. "My sweet girl!" an older woman gushed. Her Jamaican accent was undeniable. Ima was semi-retired and lived in a small house in Amarillo, having worked her entire life with the family and raised Jewel from infancy even though she had reared four children of her own. She buried my bestie in her bosom, and Jewel almost disappeared within her embrace. "And who is this? Did you duplicate yourself in California?" Ima radiated pride and accomplishment. She was as gracious as the Parker family.

Their energy was infectious, slowly filling the empty space within my soul. I felt a part of something wonderful, bigger and brighter than I had ever imagined. They treated me like family, just as Jewel had the moment we'd met. She showed me all the special places where she used to play and told more stories of her childhood. I knew her life more intimately than my own, but that was by choice because I didn't want to remember mine—the fear, sadness, grief, and loneliness. I preferred her memories: riding on Baby on the Texas plains, playing dress-up with childhood friends, a doting and loving father, and the special mother/daughter relationship. They were all Jewel's stories, yet they infiltrated my dreams when I was most vulnerable, making them real and making them my own.

Jewel had had a fairytale childhood, one with healthy, normal parents who had protected their child at all cost. She'd shown me every day since we'd met, and just by being herself, how warm and honest a person becomes by virtue of the proper upbringing. She told me how kind and caring I was, but I knew I couldn't compare to her. I had to constantly work on being a better person because I felt slighted for the life to which I was born, looking for someone to blame. That, and watching my mother die by my hands, had prompted a life in nursing. I was going to help and heal others. I'd never let another person die in my presence without them knowing that there was someone to watch over them as they passed to the other side.

Jewel called me to her bedroom on that Friday night. I hurried in to see her sitting on the floor with a large, flat box that she had pulled from underneath her twin-sized bed. The open lid revealed little painted canvases. "These are the paintings I told you about—the ones that my Aunt Carol encouraged me to create, although I wasn't supposed to use *real* paint!" Jewel doubled over with giggles, retrieving an 8" x 8" frame of a colored mishmash of what appeared to be flowers and trees. "I didn't understand what a metaphor was."

She had told me about her mom's sister, Aunt Carol, and the influence she'd had on her. Her aunt always encouraged her to start the day with a "blank canvas" and create any kind of situation she wished.

"What do you make of this?" Jewel laughed, her eyes glistening from the happy tears streaming down her face. "An artist, I am not!"

We joked at her attempt at acrylic painting as an adolescent.

"Your Aunt Carol sounds amazing. I'd love to meet her someday." I truly meant it as I beamed at Jewel for her honest view of the world.

Without preamble, Jewel looked me in the eyes and said, "Always remember that you have a blank canvas. Every morning. You, too, can create your own special day, a new life ... from whatever circumstances befall you." She leaned forward and brushed the hair out of my eyes. "You are an extraordinary person, Melissa Snow, and don't let your past dictate your future. You're better than all of this." She moved her hand in the air, creating an imaginary circle.

We awoke in the morning to sounds of birds singing and horses neighing, and I was thinking about my blank canvas. It was going to be a magical day, a day I would never forget.

"Do you like barbecue, Melissa?" Diana asked, as she stood in the kitchen, cooking a breakfast of poached eggs, baking powder biscuits, and turkey bacon. They'd planned a small gathering for the evening and their weekly Saturday night dinner. A few of their neighbors wanted to see Jewel and wish her well in her new life in California. Tom had just fabricated an outdoor kitchen that was attached to the back patio. He swelled with pride while showing his friends his newly created masterpiece. A pizza oven covered with small Italian tiles sat adjacent to the double stainless steel barbecue. We ate Texas steaks and drank homemade distilled alcohol, something I'd never tried before. My mom's dependence on drinking hadn't impacted my ability to process spirits, although I'd never drunk to excess.

Diana and Tom sat outside with us, long after the neighbors went home. They continued to fill their glasses of the home brew while Tom shared his recipes of the plum flavored moonshine. "From those trees, right there." He pointed toward the orchard, as he had four times in the conversation.

"Yes, Dad, you've already told us—several times," Jewel patiently addressed her father. "That's enough hooch for the night. I think we should take Mom upstairs. She's sleeping on the chair."

We helped her parents to their bedrooms on the second level and then made our way to ours. Jewel came into my bedroom to say goodnight and we stood side by side, wearing matching pajamas.

"Look at us," she said to me, "we're quite the pair. I want you to know how much you mean to me, Mel. I love you more than a sister. You are my soul mate, and I'm so grateful that you are in my life."

We hugged like true, lifelong friends, who never had any unpleasantries or arguments. We'd never fought and had worked out every issue better than most married couples. We were going to be in each other's lives forever.

"I have something for you." She handed me a small, handcrafted, blue box. The tiniest white bow adorned the lid, making it look like it was a large gift for a Barbie. A delicate pendant lay inside, sitting atop a fluffy cotton square. It was a colorful ceramic butterfly on a gold chain, matching the one that Jewel always wore and resembling the shape of the port-wine stain she'd had on her chest since birth. I felt honored to receive such a special gift and immediately put it on.

"Now we look alike more than ever."

—~—

The fire marshal said the blaze had originated outside, in the rear of the house. The barbecue had been left on during the night, and the combination of gas, distilled alcohol, and embers from our firepit had caused a mini explosion and inferno, engulfing the wooden structure. I awoke to the sounds of Jewel screaming at me from the hallway, warning me to get out of the house, but I couldn't see her. Smoke filled the bedroom, and brilliant orange flames lapped at the window from the outside. I fumbled my way around the room, forgetting where the door to the hallway was located. Just as I was about to give up and succumb to smoke inhalation, I found the exit and stairway leading down to the front door. The entire house was ablaze. Every labored step I took, was with the intention of reuniting with Jewel and her family outside.

The night was dark and silent, save for the crackling and popping of wood as the inferno burned red with intensity and intention. There were no sounds of movement, no screams or cries for help, and no sirens. We were too far away from neighbors and an hour's drive from the fire department. As the burning structure collapsed within itself, I knew that the Parker family did not make it out alive.

For what seemed like days, but must have been two hours, I sat next to the big oak tree in shock and waited for help, although the thought of living without Jewel in my life was too much to bear. The night was still dark, and even though the fire had reduced the big, white house to a quarter of its size, it continued to burn. Finally, sirens from two firetrucks and an ambulance made their way down the long driveway, piercing the undisturbed silence as the emergency vehicles' red lights twirled through the stillness. Water shot out from the firemen's hoses as they tried to extinguish the flames, although there wasn't much of anything left to burn other than the wooden frame. The fire had taken everything: the house, my new family, my sister, my soul mate.

"There's a survivor!" The paramedic ran to me, suddenly aware of my presence on the ground. I was a blackened mess, my once-blonde hair full of soot and my face caked with char. He wrapped a red blanket around my shaking body, just as a neighbor's vehicle drove up.

An older man hurried from the car and flung his arms around me. "Oh my God! Where are they? Where are your parents?" he cried.

I couldn't speak. My parents? They died. They're all dead. It's just me.

"Where's Tom and Diana? Jewel, did they make it out?" The older man looked at me with tears in his eyes, choking on his words and the lingering smoke. His aged hand tried to wipe the black dust that had accumulated around my eyes. He hugged me again, pulling me into the fabric of his plaid lumberjack shirt.

The fire was almost out and billowing smoke remained, invading all available cracks and crevices. Nothing beyond the house's frame was discernible, as the black fumes competed with the void of nighttime. The yard was resplendent with burning embers and emergency lights, casting an eerie glow on the front lawn as first responders continued to circle the perimeter with their long hoses, soaking the furniture and the Parker family's personal items.

A defeated firefighter appeared before us, interrupting our reunion of sorts. He held a blackened hat under one arm and an official looking clipboard in his other hand. "I'm so sorry, miss. We were too late to save the house. What is your name?"

"My name? Jewel. Jewel Parker."

23

We'll Always Have Paris

Part Un

"A margarita, *s'il vous plaît.*"

The dimly lit Lulu White Drinking Club was alive with chatter and Louis Armstrong music.

"Do you know what it means to miss New Orleans … and miss it each night and day …"

The great American trumpeter and vocalist's song, a perfect rendition played by a local jazz orchestra, permeated the French bar on Rue Frochot in Paris's Saint Georges neighborhood. The small speakeasy was filled to capacity, yet no one seemed to mind sharing the close proximity with strangers. The big band of a saxophone, trumpet, trombone, small piano, bass, guitar, and drum setup occupied much of the space and crowded the patrons who were enjoying their deliciously exotic cocktails.

The thirty-something bartender with auburn hair winked at me. "American. *J'aime les femmes américaines.*" He gave me the twice-over, winked again, and said, "I'll make you a Lulu White. It's tequila, gin, *génépi, absentroux,* and *cardamome noire. C'est notre* cocktail signature. First one's on me." He chuckled, turned, and then began mixing my drink.

The bar was busy, but the atmosphere was laid back and relaxed. I sat on a tall, dark grey upholstered chair with a few young women on my right, enthusiastically chatting in French about their workday. Their attire was impeccable, right down to the Chanel handbags that dangled from their arms and delicate fishnet stockings adorning their legs. Everyone seemed happy. This was where I wanted to be.

A simple, yet elegant, glass was placed in front of me by a waitress. "Lulu White." She moved on, distributing a few more drinks she had on her tray. A small sip brought the warm licorice essence to my tongue, as the other distinct flavors of tequila and gin danced together in my mouth. Lulu White went straight to my head.

"*Je m'appelle* Luc." My bartender appeared before me, a grin from cheek to cheek and twinkling eyes. He looked from me to the drink and then back to me. "Do you like?"

"Pardon me? Oh, of course. Yes, thanks. It's delicious, just as you said." I took another sip as he watched me, his feet planted firmly on the floor without intention of leaving. The cleverly crafted cocktail went down way too easily. "Ah, nice to meet you, Luc. I'm … Sutton. From New York."

I ordered another and then another. Luc came over to my table. "Take it slow, please. They are good, yes, but very strong. Like me." His sexy French accent was enough to overtake the looks I'd never found attractive in men: longer hair, crooked nose, misaligned teeth. Luc flexed his left arm and pointed to his bulging bicep with his right index finger. "Strong."

We laughed. American men would never do such a thing, especially not in public. They assumed there was no need to point out the obvious and draw attention to their ability to lift a barbell. His innocent Parisian charm was as intoxicating as the combination of flavors he created. The jazz band played "Carnival Time," a favorite of the crowd, as the patrons responded to the lively music, moving to the beat.

Three pretty dark-haired women entered the bar and made their way over to Luc, giving him the customary cheek kisses. They wore tailored dresses and strappy heels. Their makeup was expertly applied, and a hint of expensive perfume wafted over my head.

"*Je reviens tout de suite.* Ladies, meet Sutton, from New York City." Luc told us he had something to do behind the bar and passed his friends on to me, like an offering of a new appetizer that had just been created. They turned to me in unison at Luc's introduction.

"Hallo. My name is Claire." The petite Audrey Tautou look-alike smiled at me without prejudice and seemed genuinely interested in who I was and why I was here.

"Bonjour," Claire's replica responded, her eyes moved up and down my body, judging my attire and probably sizing me up to determine where I would fit within the Parisian echelon.

"Hallo. *Je m'appelle* Cici," the third woman acknowledged me. "It's fine to meet you, Sutton."

After several minutes of broken English and French, we settled into another round of cocktails.

"Try this one, Sutton. *C'est parfait pour toi.* Perfect." Claire number one handed me her peach colored drink with white froth on top. "Try," she demanded. The cocktail in the champagne flute was very sweet and tasted like a hangover.

Claire number two finished her drink and exhaled, looking pleased with herself. "I practice my English. Tell me who is Sutton?"

"So, the company I work for sent me to Paris as a liaison to our investors. We're going to roll out another branch of manufacturing in Japan, but we'll test the efficacy of our product in several European countries first. My husband was going to join me in Holland in a few weeks. Our kids are in boarding school in Maine, so we have time to explore. We've been talking about buying an apartment somewhere central, like Amsterdam or Madrid, so we can visit often. Bradley and I aren't fans of hotel living. I suppose I'll have to learn to speak Dutch or Spanish, though." I shared the details of my life with the strangers, the story weaving itself into a pretty Lifetime Original movie. "I just arrived in Paris yesterday, but it feels like I've been here all my life— probably the many dreams of walking on your cobblestone streets and eating the beautiful pastries."

It was 4:00 a.m., and we were the only ones left at Lulu White. Luc placed our check on the table. "Please, two rounds are my compliments. *L'addition.* Merci."

The women reached for their purses, but I placed my hand on Cici's arm. "It was truly a wonderful night! Thank you, but it's my treat. I have an expense account." I pulled several bills from my purse and placed three hundred euros in denominations of fifty on the tray. "Keep the change. Merci, Luc. Ladies."

24

We'll Always Have Paris

Part Deux

An older, seasoned artist sat on a wooden chair and concentrated her brush on the fine wisps of the white clouds that made up the half-painted canvas. Her easel was situated away from the many people walking along the Seine River, off the well-traveled path of bicycles and baby strollers. She incorporated into her painting a colorful scene of a mother and her two children enjoying a picnic on a red-and-blue gingham blanket. I lingered for a moment to watch the painter accentuate the green tones of the grass surrounding the picnic blanket; the oil paints were dolloped on the palette she held in her left hand.

"*Très beau.*" My compliment prompted an appreciative smile from the painter, as did my attempt at speaking her language.

"Merci beaucoup." She turned back to her work, an expertly depicted artist's rendering and typical of most paintings for sale along the Seine River.

I walked across Le Pont des Arts, a wooden pedestrian bridge that crossed the river. The numerous love locks were still attached to the metal fence, even years after the Parisian government had banned and removed them. The locks caught the sun's rays, creating a blinding wall of light. A couple knelt before the fence and whispered to each other as the woman held a silver padlock in her hand—its attached yellow ribbon blew in the gentle breeze. She kissed the key and tossed it into the river.

I perused the hundreds of locks in front of me, many adorned with notes and handwritten messages.

"2018. Giselle & Paul Forever."
"Abel. Be Mine Always. 09/02/19."
"Sweet Cynthia. Marry Me."
"Philip loves Kenna."

A name I had tried to forget—one that was buried in the recesses of my memories—caught my eye. I held my breath and reached for the gold lock with a baby-pink colored ribbon. Delicately written in black pen were the tiny words, "Melissa. Return to us. Forever in our hearts. Mom & Dad."

It was as though it was a message from beyond the grave—taunting and reminding me that I was estranged and without family. Tears pooled in my eyes and started flowing down my cheeks. If only I had parents who missed me and wanted me to return to them. Mine couldn't die quickly enough, leaving me alone to face the world as an orphan. This chance message was meant for a different Melissa—one whose parents counted the days until a reunion.

My name wasn't even Jewel—I didn't grow up in Texas, have loving parents, or even an Aunt Carol. Those weren't my memories, but the ones I borrowed to replace the childhood I had lived. I barely made it back to my hotel room before I collapsed on the bed, shaking and hyperventilating from the past thirty-nine years.

—~—

Room service was once again left outside my door. The quaint hotel on Rue Jean Rey Entrée Au, a stone's throw from the Eiffel Tower, was situated near every sight a tourist planned to visit. But all I wanted was to stay in my room. The croissants and cold cut meats were now a staple breakfast along with a cafetière of coffee and side of cream. I brought the food tray in and settled back on to the dark green, velour settee that was situated by the bay window.

The month of July in Paris brought everyone outside, making me feel even more isolated than I had in California. Tourists and locals scurried outside on the busy sidewalks as they visited shops, brasseries, pâtisseries, and the many museums nearby. All day long, the open window in my room let in the aromas of French baking, coffee, and the occasional smoke trail from a cigarette, but also conversations from passersby.

234

"*Attends-moi s'il te plaît!*" a younger sounding female voice yelled from below, demanding someone to wait for her.

"*Esmée, viens!*" an older woman responded, wanting the little girl to go with her.

I couldn't help looking outside, curious as to whom the voices belonged to. A girl around eight years old with light brown hair and a fuchsia dress skipped lackadaisically below the window as her mother waited impatiently ahead, stamping her foot. Her arms were full of shopping bags and she looked ready to explode, if it weren't for the many people nearby. The woman was a duplicate of the younger girl, the same hair color and angular face.

"*Esmée, mon petit bijou,*" the mother said.

The little girl ran toward her mother, laughing.

The woman, who had still been full of adoration and love even in annoyance, had called her daughter a little gem, just as my mom had called me her sparkling jewel years earlier. But Mom had seldom adored me and had made it clear she didn't love me, especially at the end of her life.

—~—

A month had passed since I'd left Los Angeles, but it felt like a lifetime ago. I'd settled into the French way of living, although many très chic Parisians would beg to differ. My wardrobe was still very much American—not tailored or purchased from a boutique on Avenue des Champs-Elysées. The pied-à-terre I had rented was fully furnished with a single bed, a small loveseat sofa, and a kitchen table. My bedroom, which was practically in the kitchen, offered little space for anything other than my suitcases that contained every personal article lucky enough to accompany me across the Atlantic Ocean.

Every night was spent scoping out new bars and nightclubs, while I immersed myself in the language and tried to leave the past behind. I laid some euros on the tray to cover the cost of the many margaritas I drank at the cocktail bar named Candelaria, the Mexican taqueria in the historic center of Le Marais. As I exited the trendy bar, hidden behind the secret door at the back of the room, I stumbled forward, my pointy boots catching on the uneven flooring. Or maybe it was from Juan the heavy-handed bartender who thought he was doing me a favor by triple pouring the tequila?

235

"Whoa! Careful. Looks like you've had one too many. It's easy to get pissed at this place," an older British man tried to admonish me as he grabbed my arm to stop me from falling on my face.

"*Merci, mais je vais bien,*" I told him in French that I was fine, hoping I'd nailed the correct translation. The man walked away and returned to his table with tacos and enchiladas aplenty.

The moon was elegantly full at midnight as I walked along Village St-Paul and among the many antique shops. A display of collectible music boxes—just like the ones I first eyed when I was little—was visible through the bay window of a little store.

Wherever you go, there you are.

Even Cate and Sam were ever present—I had seen their faces on the many tourists and locals who had crossed my path or shared the metro. Those strangers didn't judge me for leaving—for disappearing—but offered a silent understanding of the life I had chosen and the one I left behind. Surely, the shoebox's contents would clear up any questions that Cate and Sam would've had. Cate would be the more understanding friend, since she'd also had a tough upbringing and was always in pursuit of love, but she'd move on and find a new bestie, just as people do.

Sam would miss our Friday night dinners, but knowing that I'd seen the weConnect app on his computer, it wouldn't be long before he'd replace me for the movie nights he enjoyed so much. That time would give him a better chance to find a relationship so he could say "I do" to some lucky lady. Sam would also be pleased that I'd decided to live without restrictions and regret.

"*S'il vous plaît, Monsieur,*" a disheveled man, who was sitting on the sidewalk below a shop aptly named Antiques, begged a younger guy who walked past to drop some spare change. The expertly dressed passerby was oblivious to the vagrant's black top hat that lay at his side, and he continued on, probably en route to a fancy dinner. I reached into my purse and pulled out a few bills and then placed them into his open hat, next to three lonely coins.

I dropped the pretense of trying to remember the right nouns and verbs in French. "Down on your luck, sir? Maybe this will help. *Aidera?*" I couldn't remember the word for assist. "*Bonne chance.*"

The man looked up at me and smiled. He had perfect teeth— clean, white, and evenly spaced—showing evidence of many timely visits to the dentist. His attire reflected an expertly tailored suit that had once been dry cleaned and pressed but now was soiled and torn.

"Merci. Thank you, miss." He reached into the hat and touched the bills. "Now I can eat supper." His French was easily replaced by English and a slight familiar accent.

"Are you American?" I asked.

"I am. Been here for many years though. I lost my way. Happens from time to time." The man gripped the euros in his hands and looked up at me as though I were a life preserver. "You've lost your way too." His statement hit me squarely between the eyes.

The night was closing in, in a choking sort of way, and the moon was so low that I could almost touch it. "No. I live over there." I pointed west toward a residential neighborhood, trying my best to avoid his gaze.

"You look just like I did before this happened." The man used his open palm and swept it from his head to his feet, just like Vanna White when she shows the contestants on *Wheel of Fortune* which prize they are vying for. His toes poked out of his shoes, the knees of his jeans were ripped, and his jacket was so stained that it was hard to tell if the fabric was grey or brown. The man's stench of living on the street or under a bridge, wafted toward me, making my eyes water. He could have been thirty or sixty years old. It was hard to tell.

"Before what happened?" I asked, although it was obvious. The large, almost empty bottle of Jack Daniels was nestled between his legs.

"Life. Drinking, drugs, needles, the whole shebang. Was on Wall Street, making a boatload of money. I never saw it coming. Now it's got me and won't let go. Like sticking your bare hand inside a catfish hole, while the fish sinks its sharp teeth into your flesh. Most days I can't tell if I'm the catfish or the noodler."

I sat down on the sidewalk next to the dirty, down-and-out man and exhaled. "I know just what you mean."

Epilogue

Three Years Later

The toddler swung on the grayed, knotted ropes of the pirate playground, dragging his little feet in the sand. "Wee, yay ... wee." His young mother sat on a bench a few meters away, sipping her coffee and chatting on a mobile phone. The boy let go of the rope and fell backward, banging his head on the ground. His cries brought his mother running to help him up, but the toddler was inconsolable.

A woman nearby walked over to see if she could be of assistance. Her long, golden hair reached the small of her back, but the ends were dyed a bright pink and orange ombré combination, featuring blue tips, which gave her an edgy, youthful look. She wore no makeup, and her clothes were black and sleek, complementing her glittery purple Dr. Marten high tops. Her confident stride toward the mother exuded an air of competence and knowledge. She was the epitome of cool.

The boy continued to cry.

"Do you mind if I take a look?" the woman asked the mother who held her small son tightly, trying to comfort him.

The mother narrowed her eyes at the woman, suspicious that a complete stranger would offer help. "Why? Are you a doctor?" she asked with a German accent.

The woman slowly shook her head. "A nurse ... I used to be a nurse. Let's just make sure he isn't bleeding or has a nasty bump that we have to worry about, okay?" Her speech sounded like she could be from Britain, but perhaps after many years of travel, she'd lost her place of origin. She lay her hand on the boy's head and started moving her fingers through his curly, brown hair, feeling his tiny scalp.

The little boy's cries subsided as he looked up at the woman and took the ends of her hair in his chubby hands. "*Rosa und orange. Blau!*" He giggled, forgetting about his pain.

"I think he is okay, but just watch to make sure he isn't dizzy or talking funny, like slurring his words or having trouble speaking the right ones. If so, you should take him immediately to the hospital. He has no problem with the colors of my hair." The woman laughed and wiped away the boy's tears with the back of her hand. She turned to the mother. "He is precious. You are so fortunate. Is he your only child?"

"*Ja.* Yes, but we are expecting one more." The mother gently rubbed her growing belly and then kissed the top of her son's head. She smiled with relief. "*Danke.* You are so kind."

The woman stood and walked away, heading out of Parc de Monterey and toward the Upper Town—Ville-Haute of Luxembourg. Tourists strolled along the Adolphe Bridge, taking selfies with their phones and of the Pétrusse river below. After the brisk thirty-minute walk to the Grund district, on the banks of the Alzette, the woman became tired and parched. She asked a passerby to recommend a lively place for a snack and drink, and the man told her to try Liquid Cafe, which was a few minutes on foot. The woman thanked the man in his native tongue, French. "Merci beaucoup." She walked toward the street he indicated, Rue Münster.

The quaint, English-looking pub was packed with people enjoying lunch or playing board games. Everyone was chatting loudly, unconcerned about disturbing their neighbors at nearby tables. The woman took a seat at the counter and smiled at the cute bartender. He passed a menu toward her and asked, "What'll ya have?"

She glanced at the menu before responding, "I'd like the soup du jour and a bottle of sparkling water, please."

"Water? Sure, but we serve the finest craft beers and our Moscow Mules are legendary."

"Thanks, but I don't drink alcohol."

He looked at the woman's hands, perhaps searching for a wedding ring. "I'll put that soup in for ya." The bartender, who didn't have an accent or distinguishable characteristics, could've been from Canada or the United States. He was quite handsome, in his early forties, and had a happy, carefree attitude. "Are you single?"

240

The woman nodded her head. "It's difficult to meet a nice and normal guy these days." She looked the bartender in the eyes, holding his obvious stare.

He chuckled. "That goes both ways. Have you tried online dating? It's really caught on here in Luxembourg."

The woman let out a long sigh. "Apps really aren't for me. Plus, I don't own a phone."

The bartender opened a bottle of Perrier and poured a glass half full. He placed it before her and said, "No phone, eh? That's interesting. So, young lady, tell me your story."

"Story?" She laughed, shaking her head as she looked around at the many bottles of liquor. She turned back to the good-looking bartender who was sneaking a peak at her as he pretended to dry a wine glass. "I don't have a story. I'm just Maeve. Maeve, from Wales."

Made in the USA
Middletown, DE
29 June 2021

43267916R00146